D0466073

Knight Life

Knight Life

PETER DAVID

ACE BOOKS, NEW YORK

This is a work of fiction. Names, characters, places, and incidents are either the product of the author's imagination or are used fictitiously, and any resemblance to actual persons, living or dead, business establishments, events, or locales is entirely coincidental.

KNIGHT LIFE

An Ace Book
Published by The Berkley Publishing Group,
a division of Penguin Putnam Inc.,
375 Hudson Street,
New York, New York 10014.

Copyright © 2002 by Second Age, Inc.
Jacket art by Tristan Elwell.
Jacket design by Rita Frangie.
Text design by Kristin del Rosario.

All rights reserved.
This book, or parts thereof, may not be reproduced
in any form without permission.

ISBN 0-441-00936-0

PRINTED IN THE UNITED STATES OF AMERICA

YE OLDE FOREWORD

†

FOR YEARS NOW, *Knight Life* has proven to be the most elusive of all my published novels. Folks who came across my work by way of comics, or *Star Trek* novels, or *Howling Mad*, have been unable to turn up the original edition in used book stores and have inquired as to when—if ever—it might be brought back into print. So I shall tell you right now, you should all be thankful to editor Ginjer Buchanan (who shepherded the book through the first time) for pioneering a deal that has not only returned my little tale of Arthur's to print, but has ensured a sequel, tentatively titled *Dead of Knight*.

However . . .

A few years back, during one of the several times that *Knight Life* was optioned for the movies (and never made, as I'm sure you've surmised), I wrote a screenplay version of the book. And as I did, I was struck by all the things in the novel that I did—well, not *wrong*—but not as right as I could have. The story was told, yes, but I took shortcuts in getting there, and there were some problems to be solved in the narrative, which I hadn't solved properly because I lacked the tools as a writer to do so. There were carryovers from the bland journalistic writing style I used at the time and story elements that were put in to serve my convenience rather than the story. It was as good a tale as I could have told then—but I felt I could do better. Crafting the screenplay forced me to think more visually, and ultimately I was happier with the screenplay in many ways than I was with the published manuscript. I wished there was some way that I could go back in time and "fix" the original book; improve upon it.

So part of the deal I cut with Ginjer was that I would return to the original manuscript and fix all the stuff that was fixable. It's ironic in a way: At conventions, one of the standard questions I get is, "Are you writing any new novels?" To which I used to respond, in my smart-ass fashion, "No, I've decided to write only old novels." Well, I can't say that anymore, because that's fundamentally what I've done here, not only incorporating aspects from my script version, but also trying to bring the story more in line with the way my writing style has developed over the years.

There will be some long-time fans of my work who will be irked with this decision, because they will feel they are being "forced" to buy a book they already have. For that matter, they might read it and say that they don't perceive any differences between this and the previous version. To those folks, I will say that the changes that have been made are more than cosmetic. The original novel had just over 65,000 words; this incarnation has 95,000—nearly half again as long.

There will be newcomers to my work who will be irked that they still don't have the original. To those folks, I will say that you may very well have found the original annoyingly dated, in little ways (having an office filled with clattering typewriters and computerization regarded as something new) and in big ways (having Republicans as a non-force in New York mayoral politics.)

And to all of you, what it really comes down to is: If you're buying a book with my name on it, I feel I owe it to you to have it be the best book that I can make it. The original edition was as good as I could make it at the time. Now, I think I can do better, and hopefully, I have.

And before we go any further, there's some final business to attend to.

The author would like to cite the following books and/or authors:

Le Morte d'Arthur by Sir Thomas Mallory

The Once and Future King and *The Book of Merlin* by T. H. White

The Last Enchantment and other assorted titles by Mary Stewart

Tales of King Arthur by John Steinbeck

Arthur Rex by Thomas Berger

All of the above have been carefully read, or purchased, or checked out from the local library and never returned by the author of this work. In the preparation of this manuscript the author has at the very least skimmed the flap copy, sell copy, and table of contents of all of the above, plus many other titles too numerous or obscure to mention.

The author thanks all of the above for their contributions, however small, to this work. But don't expect royalties.

CHAPTRE
THE FIRST

⸸

THE APARTMENT WAS dark, illuminated only by the dim flickering of the twelve-inch, black-and-white Sony that sat atop a scratched coffee table. The Sony itself was showing its age rather severely, having been purchased second hand from a going-out-of-business motel some years earlier. There was a bent antenna on top of it, and a thick film of dust across the screen, which whimsically had the words "Life sucks" etched in it.

The apartment had clearly been allowed to go to seed. The wallpaper was yellowed and peeling, with squares and circles imprinted where various paintings or pictures had once hung. The floor was bare, the boards warped and uneven. Off to one side was a small kitchen that had a gas stove last cleaned sometime around the Hoover administration, and a refrigerator stocked with two cracked eggs, half a stale loaf of Wonder Bread, and a flat bottle of club soda. And three six-packs of beer.

The apartment's sole occupant was also visible in the cathode's unflattering glow. Then again, the only thing that could have been flattering to the occupant at that moment was utter darkness.

An old sitcom was playing on the screen. She had seen it before. She had seen all of them before. It did not matter to her. Nothing much mattered anymore.

She smiled slightly at the antics of the castaways on the screen. Somehow Gilligan was always able to make her smile slightly. A buffoon, a simple jester.

Simple.

She remembered when her life was simple.

She took a sip of the beer, finishing the contents of the can and tossing it off into the darkness. She thought there might be a trash can there to receive it, but if there was, she missed it entirely, for she heard the can clattering around in the corner before rattling to the floor. Or perhaps it had indeed found its target, but there was already such a stack of cans built up that the newest one had simply fallen off. Either way, she didn't much care.

Morgan Le Fey hauled her corpulent body protestingly to its feet. She was clad in a faded housecoat that had once been purple, and her swollen feet were crammed into large fuzzy slippers. Her tresses, once a pure raven-color, were shot through with gray. The formerly fine lines of her face, her sleek jaw and high cheekbones, were now sliding off into her collarbone. She had given up counting her chins, as another one seemed to spring into existence every decade, like clockwork.

As she waddled into the kitchen, her housecoat tugged at the protesting buttons, threatening to pull them all off their thin moorings. She made her way across the kitchen, kicked aside a stray beer can, and pulled open the refrigerator door. She saw something out the corner of her eye, scampering away across the kitchen floor. *Good luck finding something around here of use*, she thought mirthlessly, as she looked into the fridge. She squinted slightly, because the refrigerator bulb was nearly blinding in contrast to the dimness of the rest of the place. She reached in and snapped another can of beer out of a half-consumed six-pack and lurched back across the kitchen, the slippers slapping against the bottom of her feet.

As she sank back into the easy chair, resting her hands in the customary places on the arms, she watched the final credits run on this latest rerun of the adventures of the castaways. Even more than Gilligan, she empathized with the concept of castaways as a whole. She was a castaway too. Drifting, floating, on an island of isolation. Abandoned by happenstance, cast off by fate. Alone, forgotten . . .

And prone to indulging in lengthy exhibitions of self-pity. Don't forget that, she added mentally.

She popped the top on her can and started to guzzle beer. The cold beverage slid down her throat, bathing her in a familiar warmth and haze. She patted the can lovingly. Her one friend. Her familiar.

She held up the can in a salute. "To mighty Morgan," she croaked, her voice cracking from disuse. "Here's to eternal life, and to the thrice-damned gods who showed me how to have it." Morgan choked then, and for the first time in a long time she really thought about what she had become. With a heartrending sob she drew back her arm and hurled the half-empty can square into the TV, which sat two yards away. Except the can was not propelled by a normal arm making a normal throw. Instead, in that throw, was centuries of ennui, of frustration and anger, heaving it in an eldritch fit of pique. Against such a display, the ancient television had no chance. The screen exploded in a shower of glass and sparks, flying out like a swarm of liberated sprites. There was a sizzling sound, and acrid smoke rose from the back of the set.

Her face sank into her hands, and Morgan Le Fey wept loudly. Her sides heaved in and out, her breath rasped in her chest. The rolls of fat that made up her body shook with the rage and frustration she released. She cried and cursed all the fates that had brought her to this point in her life, and it was then that she resolved to put a stop to it. It was not the first occasion she had done so, but every time she had decided to terminate her wretched life, she had always thought better of it. Her loathing had always turned outward. "I still hate," she had always managed to say, and make it sound as if she meant it. But this time, though—this time, something had broken within her. She had no idea what had done it, what single thing had set it off. It probably wasn't any one thing, she realized. It was probably the collective weight of it all, crunching down upon her until—all at once—it had proven unendurable.

"Existence for the sake of existence alone is no existence at all," she declared out loud. "I am a mushroom. A fungus. I have lived for far too long, and it's time I rested."

She waited a moment to see if some other aspect of her mind would tell her that she was wrong, but none did. Knowing beyond question that she was doing the right thing, she stood again, but this time with far greater assurance, for her movements now had a purpose to them other than simple self-perpetuation. She lumbered into the kitchen, fumbled through a drawer crammed with plastic spoons from Carvel's ice cream stores and equally harmless knives from Kentucky Fried Chicken. Finally she extracted a steak knife. She blanched at the rust, then realized that rust was hardly a concern.

She sat back down in front of the TV, the knife now cradled serenely in the crook of her arm. The TV screen had miraculously mended itself. There was a crisscross of hairline fractures across it, but these too would fade in time. Not that this was any concern to Morgan either.

"One last time, old enemy," she said. Her thin, arched eyebrows reached just to the top of her forehead, even though her eyes were little-more than slits beneath painted green lids. She fumbled in the drawer next to her for the remote control, and she started to flick the switch. Time had lost all meaning to her, and she could not recall how long it had been since she had looked in on Him. Five days? Five months? Years? She was not certain.

Once these long-distance viewings had exacted a great toll from her, physically and spiritually. She had had to use specially prepared mirrors, or magic crystals. With the advent of the diodes and catheters, however, had come a revolution in the art of magic. A one-time ensorcellment of the wires and tubes, and she could look in on Him whenever she wished. That was why she had never opted for solid-state components—she didn't trust her ability to control something as arcane as microcircuitry.

She clicked her remote to Channel 1, and the smiling face of the news anchor disappeared. In its place was the exterior of a cave. Erosion and overgrowth had altered the exterior somewhat over time, but not enough to throw her. She knew the cave on sight. And she would take the knowledge to her grave, providing that someone ever found her bloated body and tossed it into the ground for her. Yes . . . yes, they probably would, once her decaying corpse smelled so bad that no one in the neighborhood could take it anymore. She took some tiny measure of comfort in that, that in her death she would at least be able to provide inconvenience for somebody.

She held the knife to her wrist. She should really do this in a bathtub, she remembered reading now. But she hated the water. Besides, she wanted to be here, in front of the entombed resting-place of her greatest magical opponent.

She stared at the cave entrance on her TV screen. "You'd really enjoy this moment, wouldn't you, you cursed old coot? Morgan Le Fey, driven to this, by you. You knew this would happen someday. This is your doing, you reaching out from beyond the grave." She pressed the blade against the skin of her right wrist. "Damn you, Merlin," she said softly. "You've finally won."

She set her teeth against the anticipated pain of the knife digging into her flesh . . . and then she stopped.

She leaned forward, the knife, still against the inside of her wrist, forgotten now. She squinted, rubbed her eyes, and focused again.

Against the mouth of the cave rested a huge stone, covered with moss and vegetation. This stone was far more than just a dead weight. It was held in place through the magic of a woman's wiles, and there is no stronger bond than that. And though the woman, Nineve, was long gone, the magic should have held for all eternity.

The operative word here being "should."

For Morgan now saw that the rock had moved. It had rolled ever so slightly to one side, creating an opening. An opening far too small for a man to squeeze through. But still . . . it hadn't been there before.

Quickly and deftly she manipulated the remote control. Responding to it, the TV screen zoomed in tight on the hole. Yes, definitely new. She had never seen it before, and she could see where the overgrown leaves had been ripped away when the stone was moved. . . .

"Moved!" she whispered. "But who moved it?"

It was more than she dared hope. The camera panned down away from the hole, which was several feet above the ground. There were footprints. She had no clue when they'd been left there. Once she would have known immediately, for in olden times she had looked in on this spot every day. She would have spotted any change, no matter how minor, within twenty-four hours . . . less, considering she used to check two, even three times a day if she was bored. But with passing years had come passing interest, and the occasional look-see had seemed to suffice. Seemed to, but clearly did not.

"Yessss," she hissed, "footprints." But more than that, she realized, barefoot. And something else: They were small. A child's. Heading one way, away from the cave. "A child," she breathed. "Of course. Of course!"

The knife clattered to the floor as Morgan Le Fey, half sister of King Arthur Pendragon, incestuous lover of her brother, mother of the bastard Modred, tilted her head back and laughed. At first it was hardly a laugh, but more like a high-pitched cackling imitation, similar to the sound a parrot would make. With each passing moment, however, it grew. Fuller. Richer. Although the abused body of Morgan still showed its deficiencies, years were already dropping from the voice.

If anyone had once dared tell her that she would be happy over the escape of her deadliest enemy, she would have erased that unfortunate person from the face of the earth. The suggestion was positively ludicrous. But her life had become no less ludicrous, and knowledge of the departure of the cave's occupant from his place of imprisonment had fallen into her lap like a gift from a benevolent—if somewhat twisted—god.

For Morgan Le Fey had come to realize that she thrived on conflict and hatred. It was as mother's milk to her. And without that, her spirit had shriveled away to a small, ugly thing lost somewhere in an unkempt form. Now, though, her spirit soared. She spread her arms and a wind arose around her, blowing wide the swinging windows of her apartment. It was the first time in several years that clean air—or at least what passed for clean air in her neck of the woods—had been allowed in, and it swept through as if entering a vacuum. Fresh air filling her nostrils, Morgan became aware of the filth in which she had resided for some time. Her nose wrinkled, and she shook her head.

She went to the window and stepped up onto the sill, reveling in the force of the wind she had summoned. Above her, clouds congealed, tore apart, and reknit, blackness swarming over them. Far below, pedestrians ran about, pulling their coats tight around them against the unexpected turn of bad weather. A few glanced up at Morgan in the window but went on about their business, jamming their hands down atop their heads to prevent their hats or wigs from blowing away.

Morgan drank it in, thriving on the chaos of the storm.

She screamed over the thunder, "Merlin! Merlin, demon's son! The mighty had fallen, mage! You had fallen. I had fallen. All was gone, and you were in your hell and I was in mine." She inhaled deeply, feeling the refreshing, chilled sting of cold air in her lungs. She reveled in the tactile sensation of her housecoat blowing all around her, the wind enveloping her flimsy garment.

"You're back now!" she crowed. "But so am I! I have waited these long centuries for you, Merlin. Guarding against the day that you might return, and yet now I glory in it. For I am alive today, Merlin! Do you hear me, old man? Morgan Le Fey lives! And while I live, I hate! Sweet hate I have nurtured all these long decades and centuries. And it's all for you, Merlin! All for you and your damned Arthur!

"Wherever you are, Merlin, quake in fear. I am coming for you. Thank you for saving my life, Merlin! *And I shall return the favor a thousandfold. I, Morgan Le Fey! I can live again! I can breathe again! I can have my hatred! I can have my revenge! And I can get the hell out of New Jersey!*"

"HARRY, WHAT'S GOING on?"

Harry peered through the curtains at the window of the apartment across the way. "It's that fat nut again. God, what a slob. I don't know how people let themselves go like that."

His wife, Beverly, eyed his beer belly but wisely refrained from comment.

"She's shouting about some damned thing or other," he muttered as he came to sit next to her on the couch. "Usually she's just regular drunk. I don't know what she's on tonight, but it must be a beaut."

"Bet she's from New York," mumbled his wife.

"What?" he asked.

She repeated it, adding, "It wouldn't surprise me in the least."

"No?" His eyebrows puckered across his open and unimpressive face, thick with lines that had come from worrying that Beverly would learn he was having it off with Mrs. Findelman down the street.

"No," affirmed Beverly. "Because New Yorkers are all crazy. They know it. The government knows it. The whole country knows it. In New York everyone acts like that," and she chucked a thumb across the street in Morgan's direction. "You never know what's going to happen."

"Yeah," said Harry, who didn't mind an element of danger in his life (hence Mrs. Findelman.) "That's why I like it."

"Well, I hate it," Beverly said firmly, as if she'd just turned down the option to buy Manhattan. "All the crazy people there—they all deserve each other. Why, I hear tell it's not safe to walk the streets at night there. You never know what weird thing you'll run into next."

CHAPTRE
THE SECOND

†

GWEN WAS NOT having a good day.
For what seemed the twentieth time during the relatively brief phone conversation, she ran her fingers through her strawberry blonde hair, and when she spoke that Southern twang that she had tried so hard to lose came faintly through. She was wearing the powder blue dress that was her best outfit, her interviewing outfit. The coat she had draped over it was somewhat threadbare, but she couldn't afford to buy another, so she always made sure to remove it before any job interviewers actually saw the shabby state it was in.

She was standing at a payphone stall on the corner of Sixtieth Street and Central Park West, trying to hear and make herself be heard over the roaring of the trucks and incessant police car sirens that were fairly typical for the streets of New York. At least it wasn't raining on her, although the way things were going, she half-expected the cloudless sky to suddenly darken and a downpour to descend upon her. In fact, it would probably center upon her, leaving everyone else unscathed, including the bulky and annoying woman who was standing directly behind her waiting to use the phone. Because of course, God forbid, the woman should think about walking half a block to find a different phone.

"Helloooo? Is anybody there?" she said in desperation, trying not to let the scowl of the woman behind her get to her. She knew she was on hold; she knew no one was listening. She shouted into the emptiness of the phone wires for the same reason that people push elevator buttons repeatedly: In the vain hope that existence will be acknowledged.

Miraculously, in this case it seemed to work. The aggravating hold music—a medley of Andrew Lloyd Webber tunes—abruptly cut off and she heard a voice. Unfortunately, it was not the voice she was hoping for. "Lyons and Herzog," it said briskly.

"Oh, God, I'm back at the switchboard," she moaned.

"Lyons and Herzog," repeated the voice, sounding slightly irritated.

"Yeah, I know, I know," said Gwen urgently. "Look, I'm trying to get through to Mr. Herzog's office. I'm calling in regards to the job interview for a secretary. I'm running late. The subway broke down, and I was stuck, and I'm trying to—"

"Hold, please."

"No! Not again! Not ag—!"

The song "Memories" floated through the phone at her. And then, before she could cry out against the injustice of it all, the money fell through and the music was replaced by a recorded voice saying, "Five . . . cents . . . please for another minute."

Knowing full well that it was a lost cause before she even opened her mouth, she turned to the woman behind her and said, "Do you have a nickel I could borrow? Just one? Please? My life is hanging on this."

The woman stared at her in stony silence.

Gwen didn't even bother to ask again. Instead, with a sigh laced with tragedy, she hung up the receiver and stepped away from the phone stall. She bowed slightly in mock "chivalry" as she gestured for the woman to step in and take the phone. The woman stepped in, reached into her pockets, and came out with a fistful of coins that she piled in a small, silver heap atop the payphone.

"I can see why you couldn't spare one," Gwen said humorlessly. "You had so many, you didn't know which one to choose."

The woman ignored her, and Gwen turned away and stomped off down the street.

Shortly she managed to find a well-dressed fellow, sitting on a park bench, speaking on a cell phone, and convinced him to let her make use of it for just five minutes. He watched her in amusement as she dialed. "You should get one of your own, you know," he suggested.

"Had one. Didn't keep the payments up on the service." She shrugged. "No money. Hopefully, though, this call will help change that."

"Good luck," he said.

She pushed "Send" and a moment later, the same receptionist said, "Lyons and Herzog."

"Yes, Mr. Herzog please. I've been trying to get throu—"

"Hold, please."

She moaned again, prepared for another lengthy runaround, but then to her surprise she heard a female voice say, "Mr. Herzog's office."

"Ohhhh, thank God," said Gwen. She gave an eager thumbs up to the man from whom she'd borrowed the phone. "I need to speak to Mr. Herzog."

"May I tell him what this is in regards to?"

"The secretary job. You see, I'm running late and I—"

"The secretary job," said the woman on the other end. She sounded faintly amused.

Gwen didn't like the sound of that tone. "Yeaaaaahhh," she said slowly.

"You mean the one I was hired to fill five minutes ago?"

With a heavy sigh, Gwen said quietly, "Yes. That one."

"It's filled."

"I kind of figured that."

"If you'd like, we can keep your resume on file. Your name——?"

"Mud," said Gwen, and she ended the call and handed the phone back to the well-dressed man.

"Bad news?" he asked sympathetically.

"No. No, just typical news."

"Well, good luck to you. I have to get back to work," he said. And he patted her on the shoulder in an avuncular manner before heading off.

Gwen sat there for a moment, stewing, and then with an effort, brushed it off. Dwelling on what hadn't worked wasn't going to do her any good. She had to look forward and just hope. With that in mind, she pulled out the want ads from her bag. The page was covered with so many circles and "X's" that it looked like a tic-tac-toe tournament gone amuck. She started going over them, making reminders to herself of where she stood on them.

"Filled . . . filled . . . on vacation . . . filled . . . wanted 85 words per minute . . . wanted steno . . . wanted to squeeze my ass . . ." That last one—she considered the possibility of going to work there and then filing the inevitable sexual harassment case. But somehow it just didn't seem worth the effort.

She continued to study the ads, and it was some time before she actually fully noticed the steady clanking that was approaching her. She was so focused on the ads, in fact, that she might never have noticed the clanking at all if it hadn't been for the shadow that was abruptly cast over her, at which point the clanking stopped. Slowly she turned and looked up.

"Ohhh, you've gotta be kidding me," she said.

There, glinting in the sun, was a knight clad in full armor.

He was covered in armor from head to toe, the plates smooth and curving over his chest, arms, and legs. The armor was excellently made, for hardly a gap had been permitted, and even those were protected, either by small stretches of chain mail or by small upturns in the plates. A full helmet covered his head, and there was a visor with a short blunt point in front of his face. He had a purple plume tapering off the top of his helmet, and the visor was down, obscuring his features. A scabbard hung at his side—it was ornately decorated with dark stones and intertwined lines of design. It was hard to get a feeling for just how tall the actual man was, but he certainly seemed bulky enough. The helmet was tilted slightly, indicating that he was standing slightly askew as he regarded her. At least she assumed it was a he.

Passersby were looking at the two of them in open amusement, and it was starting to annoy Gwen. Why were they looking strangely at *her*? It wasn't as if they were together or she knew the guy. She felt oddly resentful. "Whatever it is," Gwen said impatiently, "I don't want any, okay?"

He didn't say anything, but instead simply leaned in closer as if to see her better. Gwen was feeling rather unsettled by that point. Immediately she started rummaging in her shoulder bag. "Look . . . I don't know who you are, or what your deal is, or what kind of weirdness this is. But I am so not in the mood, it's not funny. I'm warning you," and she pulled out a small aerosol can. "I've got mace."

He straightened up at that, and for a moment she thought he was intimidated. There were slots in the visor, after all, and the mace would pass through those with no problem. But the knight was reaching around back of his armor, and in silent response to her threat, he produced a two-foot-long club with a flanged metal head on it. A mace.

"So have I," said the knight.

Because of the way his voice echoed from within the helmet, it was impossible to make out his tone of voice—whether he was being amused or polite or threatening. And Gwen quickly decided that, no matter what the case was, she had had enough. She got to her feet just as the knight said, "I'm not going to hurt you."

"You got that right," she shot back and, thrusting the newspaper and mace spray back into her bag, turned and headed at a brisk trot down the street.

"Wait!" the knight's voice echoed after her, but Gwen wasn't stopping to hear it. Instead she picked up her pace, covering distance in a fraction of the time that it took the slow-moving knight to follow her. She looked around desperately, trying to spot a cop, but naturally there were none around. They only existed, she felt, to blast sirens while she was on the phone, but otherwise they obviously saw no reason to remain in her presence.

She heard him calling again "Wait!" from behind her, but she had no intention of slowing down. A subway station was just up ahead of her, and she could feel the rumbling beneath her feet that told her a train was coming in. She had her pass; if she hurried, she could run ahead, get into the subway and be long gone by the time the metal-clad maniac got anywhere near the tracks. Snagging the railing, she bolted down the steep stairs that led to the platform below and, sure enough, there was the train. She dashed through the turnstiles and ran sideways into the nearest car, dodging between the closing doors. Moments later the train was whisking her away. She didn't know or care where the subway was going, as long as it was someplace where jobs were plentiful and nuts in armor were scarce.

The knight, in the meantime, had not yet realized that she was gone. He had arrived at the top of the steps and was, for a moment, daunted, having some doubts about the angle of the stairs and the flexibility of his armored legs. But then, deciding that he had no choice, he started to make his way down the steps to the platform. Unfortunately, he only managed to get down a couple of steps and then he overbalanced himself and toppled forward like a great metal tree. He tried to halt his descent, but he failed utterly, and a moment later he was tumbling down the stairs, sounding like a thousand tin cans falling from heaven all at once. Bam, bam, bam, down he went, hitting one stair and another and rolling off each one before finally grinding mercifully to a halt at the bottom.

He lay there for a time, moaning. People stepped over him and around him. No one asked him what was wrong or if he needed help. A train came and went and people emerged from it and went up the steps, none of them affording the fallen knight more than a second glance.

Finally he managed to bring himself to a seated position and slowly he raised the visor. Without the resonance provided by the helmet, his voice sounded surprisingly amiable.

"This," said Arthur, King of the Britons, "is not going to work."

ARTHUR'S COURT WAS a fashionable men's clothing store situated near Central Park. And for Sidney Krellman, the manager, each day was nice and simple. He woke up in the morning. Got dressed (nattily, of course). He went into work and acted politely to most clientele, (enthusiastically to a select handful). At the end of the day he and an assistant would check over the day's receipts, shutter and close up the store, and leave at 7:45 sharp.

Sidney's appearance was fastidious, and he was extremely proud of it. His jackets always hung just right, his ties expertly knotted, and his pencil-thin mustache—

the only highlight of a narrow, bland face—was precisely and meticulously trimmed. His sartorial and tonsorial appearance helped to make up for the fact that, otherwise, he was a billiard ball sort of fellow, with a combover that gave him some comfort, but otherwise served no function. He felt it incumbent upon himself to put the "right" kind of clientele at their immediate ease, while sending an unspoken message to the "wrong" sort that he was simply not going to tolerate their presence. That just wasn't the way things were done at Arthur's Court.

Sidney Krellman expected nothing different on this particular November day. It did not occur to him that it was exactly one year before the next mayoral elections in New York City. Sidney didn't care for politics, or elections, or mayors, or much else aside from his daily routine, and he disliked intensely anything that caused a deviation from it.

That being the case, Sidney was going to dislike, with blinding intensity, what was about to happen. It would disrupt his store-closing routine, throw the end of his day into turmoil, and generally wrinkle the fabric of his well-ordered life.

At 7:30 precisely, Sidney was issuing instructions to Quigley, his young, gawky assistant manager, about opening the store the following morning (Sidney anticipated being late, having a dental appointment scheduled for the next morning. A small hole in a lower bicuspid demanded, simply demanded attention, and there was nothing else to do but attend to it). Sidney was waving one finger in the air, as was his habit, when there was a rap at the glass front door.

The rap derailed Sidney's train of thought, and he turned with an annoyed glance to the door. He froze in mid-sentence, finger still pointed skyward, as if offering directions to a wayward duck. Quigley continued to stare at his superior, waiting for him to continue. When no further instructions were forthcoming, it dawned on

Quigley to follow his boss's gaze toward the front door.

A knight occupied the full space of the door. His own reflection on the glass door bounced back onto the gleaming armor, so that in essence he was standing there with his own armored form ricocheting through tricks of light.

The knight stood there for a moment, as if contemplating the two men within the store.

Sidney and Quigley exchanged quizzical glances, making sure that the other was seeing what each thought they were seeing, lest either one of them speak prematurely and be thought insane by the other. During this time, the knight grew a bit impatient and, raising his gauntleted hand, knocked once more, this time with a bit more force.

It was the wrong move. The metal-gloved hand went right through the glass. The glass hung there for a moment in midair, as if startled at this rather unexpected turn of events, and then with a resounding crash, shattered into hundreds of pieces.

Sidney Krellman's jaw moved up and down and side to side slightly, but that was it. Quigley was not even able to handle quite that much.

The knight looked down at the destruction that he had inadvertently caused. Then the metal-shod hands reached up and lifted the visor of the helmet. A gentle, bearded face smiled regretfully at Sidney Krellman.

"I'm terribly sorry," he said in a polished British accent. "I seem to have damaged your establishment."

Sidney Krellman found it odd that, despite the fact that this man was fully armored, the thing he found to be far more impressive was his voice. It was low and carefully modulated. It seemed to have an age and wisdom to it that contradicted the relative youthfulness of the face. It was a compelling voice, that of a great orator, or perhaps commander of men. The lines of the face that peered out from the helmet were clean and straight. The forehead sloped slightly, and eyebrows that were a bit thick projected over eyes that were almost black. His lips were thin, and, what Sidney could see of his beard, was very dark, but with a few strands of conspicuous gray.

Sidney Krellman shook off the daze that had come over him and gave a small bow. "Quite all right," he replied in a voice pitched two octaves above his usual tone. He quickly corrected his tone and continued, "It could happen to anyone."

The front of the armor rose slightly, bouncing as if from a sharp intake and exhale of air. The knight had laughed. "Anyone who was clad in such a foolish getup. Do you mind if I come inside?"

"Not at all. Not at all." Sidney backed up slowly, his eyes glancing at the scabbard that hung at the knight's side. It had not yet registered on him that there was no sword in it. Then again, in all fairness to Sidney, it might have been that he was distracted by the mace that was hanging from the back of the armor on a small hook.

The knight stepped through the bashed-in door, clanking across the spotless green carpet of the men's clothing store. Glass crunched under each armored foot. "I suppose you're wondering," said the knight, "why I'm wearing this ridiculous armor."

Sidney tried to come up with an answer that seemed safe, since he was still convinced that at any moment this armored maniac might swing his mace and bash in Sidney's skull. Sensing his boss's hesitation, Quigley brightly stepped in with the first thing that came to mind. "Armor?" he said cheerfully. "What armor?" Sidney moaned softly.

The knight laughed softly. "Italian from the look of it," he replied, inspecting one armored hand. "Wouldn't you say?"

"Oh absolutely," agreed Quigley. "You can always tell Italian armor. It has, uh . . . very narrow, pointy shoes."

"Really?" said Arthur, apparently with genuine interest. "I'd place this armor at about, oh, fourteenth century." He tapped the chestplate and smiled at the sound. "I daresay none of your suits would wear for quite so long. Nevertheless I still find it clumsy. In my day we wore leathers. That's when men fought men, not metal shells fought metal shells, lurching their way across the battlefield like overstuffed turtles. I think that was the beginning, you know. The beginning of isolating yourself from your opponent. Now . . . now it's simply the press of a button and," and he mimed an explosion. "No more opponent. Not a way for real men to fight at all. No style, no grace. Taking the fine art of soldiering and turning it into nothing more than mass butchery. Tragic. Just tragic." His thoughts seemed to have wandered, and he pulled them back to the questions at hand. "Tell me, young man, what's your name, please?"

"Quigley," said Quigley, and chucking a thumb at his supervisor he said, "And this is—"

"The manager," said Sidney quickly.

"Ah. Well, Quigley—" The knight leaned against the counter, draping one arm against the cash register—"My name is Arthur, and I—"

"Arthur," said Quigley brightly. "Just like the name of the store, named after King Arthur."

"Just like, yes. So . . . you seem to be an expert. Tell me, what think you of chain mail?"

"I tried that once," said Quigley. "Sent five dollars to five friends. I should have gotten $10,037 back, but I never saw a dime."

Arthur cocked an eyebrow, said nothing for a moment, then continued, "As I was saying, this whole armor thing is something of a practical joke, played by someone whom I thought a bit too old for this sort of thing. I really wasn't anticipating wandering about New York City dressed for the Crusades. I had more imagined, well, something along those lines." He inclined his head toward a three-piece suit that stood handsomely displayed on a mannequin. "Might I try that on?"

"Um . . . I don't think," said Sidney cautiously, "that

it will, um, quite fit over your, um, current vestments."

"I quite agree." He raised his arms, looking decidedly unthreatening. "If you would be so kind as to help me off with these . . ."

Sidney Krellman glanced at Quigley and inclined his head. Quigley shrugged, walked over to the knight, and began to pull at the thick leather straps that held the armor on.

"Do you have experience in this sort of thing?" asked Arthur as he pulled his helmet off.

"Well, I took shop once," offered Quigley.

"Metal shop?"

"No. But I made a baseball bat with a lathe."

"Ah. Well . . . I suppose you'll do."

Passersby were glancing in the windows of the store as they went about their business. Some looked at the destroyed door while others focused their interest on the man in armor who stood in the middle of the store, arms extended out to the sides, while the young assistant manager worked busily removing the heavy plating. Quigley's glasses kept sliding to the end of his nose, and his longish hair was constantly falling into his eyes, but piece by piece he got the job done. He staggered and grunted under the weight of each component of the armor and muttered at one point, "How do you wear all this stuff?"

"With as much dignity as I can muster," replied Arthur patiently. "I can readily assure you of that."

By this point Sidney Krellman had long since dispensed with the notion of contacting the police. The last thing he wanted to do was draw the attention of the storeowners to this bizarre turn of events. The shattered door he would be able to chalk up to vandals. Quigley he would be able to swear to secrecy. Then Sidney looked up and saw the pedestrians looking in through the window, and with a frown he walked over and pulled closed the folding shutters that ran along the inside of the windows. This was enough to discourage most of the idly curious.

Sidney turned and was astounded to see the knight now clad in a simple tunic and a longsleeved and -legged white undergarment, the assorted pieces of armor scattered about the store. In the armor he'd seemed immense, even threatening. Here he was under five-and-a-half-feet tall. For a moment Sidney entertained the thought of throwing the unarmed and largely unclothed man out of the store. As if Arthur sensed what was on Sidney's mind, he turned his gaze on the clothing-store manager, and Sidney felt something within him wilt. It wasn't just that he was suddenly concerned about the man's physical prowess. He had a feeling that Arthur might very likely be able to wipe the floor with him. But it was more than that. There was a quiet, confident sense of command about him, one that made the notion of laying hands upon him simply unthinkable. Sidney dropped his gaze to the floor, the brief fire of rebellion easily extinguished, and said, "So why don't we try that suit you had your eye on?"

Some minutes later Arthur was clad in an outfit more in keeping with the period, and from the look of him, one would have suspected that he was born to wear three-piece suits. The dark blue pinstripe fit him as if it had been tailored for him, except for being slightly tight across his broad shoulders. His hair, which was a shade lighter than his beard, hung in the back to just below the jacket collar. He had picked a cream-colored shirt and a dark red tie to complete the ensemble. Although they did not carry a wide selection, the store also provided a variety of shoes, and a pair of black Oxfords now adorned his feet. He admired himself in the mirror, turning first right and then left, and decided finally, "They are cut quite nicely. Not at all what I'm accustomed to wearing, but—"

"Clothes make the man," burbled Quigley, "although in this case I'd say it's more the man making the clothes."

Sidney cleared his throat loudly, but the moment Arthur's gaze shifted to him, Sidney felt an abrupt weakening of nerve. He pursed his lips, clearly intended to keep his concerns to himself, but Arthur caught the gesture and scowled darkly. It was enough to cause Sidney to tremble slightly from the look. "Come now, sir. If you have something to say, say it. Screw your courage to the sticking point."

"Nothing," said Sidney quickly. "I was just . . . well . . ." He thought for something to say that wasn't inflammatory. He didn't want to bring up the issue of money. That could cause a ruckus, and again, he knew the mind-set of the owners. "Arthur's Court" was a gentlemen's establishment, and the owners would frown mightily upon news stories relating to the armored man who had shown up out of nowhere in the store. Undoubtedly the papers would make great hay of it, having fun with the entire connection between a "knight" and a place called "Arthur's Court" in obvious reference to the legendary king of the Britons. A gentlemen's establishment did not have its name bandied about in garish tabloids. And if it did, the owners would have something very profound to say to the manager. The manager, for his part, did not want to hear it. So if it meant swallowing the expense of a suit, then Sidney would open wide. So often people had to worry about spending money to obtain publicity; well, Sidney was willing to spend it in order to avoid publicity. "It's just that it's getting late, and I have things I have to do, including get home . . ."

"Oh, but I haven't settled with you yet."

Sidney's voice was a mouselike squeak. "Par-par-pardon?"

"Why, yes," Arthur said mildly. He held out either side of the jacket carefully. "I assume this suit costs money, and your door that I accidentally destroyed also would amount to a sum."

"Oh, no. No, that won't be necessary. Obviously this was an emergency situation, and as such, I hardly think it fair to take advantage of—"

Arthur waved a hand in peremptory dismissal. "I

wouldn't hear of it." He began to pat the pockets of the
suit, as if looking for a wallet. This, thought Sidney Krellman, was rapidly degenerating into the ridiculous. How
could this lunatic possibly think that he could check the
pockets of a brand new suit and find a wallet in it? Then
again, what other behavior could one possibly expect from
a lunatic? But then Arthur's probing hand stopped at a
vest pocket and a slow smile spread across his pleasant
features. From the inside pocket he produced a small wallet, and from that he extracted a familiar platinum card.
"Do you take American Express?" he asked.

Sidney snatched it away, scowling, and studied it. His
eyebrows knit and he stared, squinting, at the card. Quigley looked over his shoulder. The date of issue was the
current month. They stared at the name, and Quigley
looked up. "Well, Mr. Penn . . ."

Arthur looked at him in befuddlement. "Who's 'Mr.
Penn' . . . ?"

"According to this card, you are." He held it up and
Arthur leaned forward, looking at the name in the embossed letters.

"Ah. So I am." He sounded a bit sheepish about it.
"Arthur Penn. Yes, that would be me."

For a moment Sidney wondered if the card was stolen,
and then decided that it would be far better if such concerns were American Express's rather than his. He quickly
processed the card for the cost of the suit, not even bothering to add in the cost of the door (still preferring to
stick to his story about vandals). He handed it back to
Arthur, who was watching with amusement Quigley's attempts to stuff the pieces of armor into a variety of different boxes and bags.

"Don't bother, please," he said, laying a hand on Quigley's shoulder. "I assure you that if I never see the wretched
stuff again, it will not trouble me at all." A stiff wind was
blowing through the destroyed door, and Arthur felt the

chill even through the buttoned suit jacket. "You know, I think I might have need of an overcoat."

Sidney dashed around to a rack of coats, picked a long tan one out, ran back and gave it to Arthur. "This is perfect. It'll be just what you need."

He regarded the coat with scrutiny. "You don't have anything in purple, do you?"

"Not unless you're a pimp," Quigley said helpfully. Then he shut up as Sidney glared at him.

"No need for concern, then. This will do just fine." He slid it on, signed "Arthur Penn" on the charge receipt, took back the card, and then frowned. "I should pay for this coat as well . . . and certainly breaking the door was . . ."

"Please," Sidney said, and his voice began to tremble, "please. Please go. I can't take this much longer."

"All right," said Arthur, a trifle befuddled. "But let me at least pay for—"

"It's my gift to you!"

Arthur stepped back, eyes wide. "If you put it that way, all right. I shall remember you for this kindness."

"No! Don't remember me. Forget you ever saw me!" His fists were clenching and unclenching.

Quigley took Arthur by the elbow. "I think you'd better go, sir. He gets like this when things go a little . . . wrong."

"Well," said Arthur, buttoning his coat. "That's the true mark of a man. To be able to take minor variances in routine in stride. He could stand a bit of work on that score."

"Yes, sir."

"You be certain to tell him that."

"I will, sir," Quigley assured him, bobbing his head obediently.

"When he stops crying, that is."

"Yes, sir."

He walked over to Sidney, who cringed slightly back

from him, and extended a hand. Sidney looked at it as if it was the hand of a leper.

"In my time . . . that is to say, in the old days," Arthur said softly, "we preferred hands in order to show that we carried no weapons. It was considered a very suspicious sign when one person would refuse to present his hand to the other for inspection."

Sidney immediately grabbed Arthur's hand. Arthur shook it firmly . . .

. . . and for no reason that Sidney could readily discern, he felt . . . at peace. As if merely clasping the man's hand was more than enough to assure him that everything— the world, his life, everything—was going to be just fine.

"Take heart," Arthur told him. "I've returned . . . and everything is going to be all right."

"That's . . ." Sidney drew an unsteady breath. "That's . . . good to hear."

"Yes. I imagine it would be." He released his hand, patted Sidney on the shoulder, and said, "Good evening to you, then."

"Good evening, sir."

Arthur turned and walked out of the store, stepping delicately over the broken glass. Sidney watched him go and then, after a long pause, turned to Quigley and said, "We're going to get this cleaned up, report a break in, and when all that is attended to . . . then we're going to go out and get drunk. How does that sound to you, Quigley?"

"Like a plan," Quigley said with certainty, and he went to get a broom. He noticed the mace lying on the floor, picked it up, and put it behind the counter. Wouldn't hurt to keep it around; there were all sorts of weirdos walking the streets these days.

CHAPTRE
THE THIRD

                                            ✝

ARTHUR SHOOK HIS head in wonderment, tilting back leisurely on his heels so that his gaze could follow to the tops of buildings that caressed the skies. He felt mixed emotions: On the one hand, they seemed heartless and cold. There was no style or design to them, really. There were some minor variations, but for the most part it was just tall building after tall building. Not even a decent gargoyle in sight. On the other hand, the sheer height and immensity of them were enough to take his breath away. It led him to conclude that modern man was incapable of doing anything with genuine flair, but was able to turn out rubbish in staggeringly impressive fashion.

It was a cloudless night, with more than a considerable nip in the air. Arthur hardly noticed, so captivated was he by the sheer enormity of the city around him. And the thing he found more staggering than anything else was that the evening's pedestrians seemed to be utterly oblivious to the wonderment all about them. No one looked up to admire the architecture or whistle at a building height that, in Arthur's time, would have been considered a fantasy. If Arthur were able to go back to his own time, he could have assembled a hundred architects of the period—all great and learned men—presented them with drawings of what he was beholding, and been assured by every single one of them that it was simply physically impossible. That any building that tall would topple over, a victim of its own pretensions. They would have dismissed the drawings as a pleasant fantasy, nothing more.

"How things change," he murmured. "Now these buildings are the reality, and it is I who have become the fantasy."

He jammed his hands deep into his coat pockets. He had kept only one piece of his previous ensemble with him: The scabbard. He felt the comforting shape of the empty scabbard through the cloth. Only the tip was visible, peeping out every so often from the long coat, and Arthur was certain that no one could possibly spot—

There was a gentle tap on his shoulder, and he turned to look up—gods above, why was everyone so bloody tall?—into the face of a middle-aged, uniformed man, whom Arthur promptly and correctly took to be a police officer. He was sizing up Arthur with a gaze perfected over years of staying alive when, in his uniform, he was a walking target. He said, "Excuse me. Might I ask you what you're wearing under that coat?"

Arthur smiled politely. "Certainly. It's a scabbard."

"Ah." The cop smiled thinly. "Are you aware of the laws, buddy, against carrying a concealed weapon?"

Arthur's voice abruptly turned chilly as the evening air. He was, after all, still a king, and there were certain tones of voice that he simply was not going to tolerate. He had suffered enough ignominy this evening, and this latest assault on his self-esteem was simply unwarranted. "I am aware of a great many things—" and he glanced at the officer's name badge, "Officer Owens, the main of which is that I do not appreciate your tone of voice, nor shall I endure being addressed in that manner."

The police officer set his jaw. "You know what they call me back at the precinct house, buddy? Iron-Spine Owens. Because I never backed down from anyone in my life, and I—"

Arthur wasn't hearing it. "And do you know what they do *not* call me?" His voice never rose in volume, but it did in intensity. "They do not call me buddy, pal, friend, chum, or old sock. They treat me with the respect that I am due, and you will extend the same courtesy. Is that clear?" Without waiting for Owens to reply, he repeated, *"Is that clear?"*

Owens locked gazes with Arthur for a moment, but only for a moment, and then he dropped his stare and—sounding for all the world like a recalcitrant child—he said softly, "Sorry, sir. But—"

Arthur, with no letup, continued, "For your further information and, if you insist, for your peace of mind, the scabbard is empty. There is no sword in it, and therefore no need to concern oneself with concealed weapons. And I might add that if mankind had not worked so hard to perfect weaponry that any fool could hide in a pocket and use to launch a cowardly assault from yards away, with no more skill or finesse than a diseased crow, then we wouldn't have a need for quite so many laws about concealed weapons." He shook his head. "Most insane bloody process I've ever seen. Create the weapons, then legislate against them. It doesn't stop in New York, you know. It pervades society. Create nuclear weapons, and then try to stop them from being used. The moment they used the first one they should have stopped when they saw what they had on their hands. I certainly would have."

"Well, sir," said Owens contritely, "it's a shame you weren't around then."

"Oh, I was. But hardly in a position to do anything." He sighed. "Hopefully I shall remedy that now."

Owens looked at him with unrestrained curiosity. "Pardon my asking sir, but . . . are you a politician or something?"

Arthur reflected a moment and then said, "I'd have to say I fall under the category of 'or something.' Why, do I come across to you as such?"

"Well, sort of. Except you sure have the rest of them out-classed. You got a way with a phrase. Let me tell you, if you ever run for public office, you'll have my vote."

"Really?" Arthur was most intrigued. Considering that, only moments before, the man had been harassing him, he had done a considerable turnaround in an extremely brief time. "On what basis?"

"Basis?" Iron-Spine Owens laughed out loud, coarsely. "You don't need a 'basis' to vote for people anymore. You vote for the guy who looks good or sounds good. It's not about messages. It's about sound bytes and guys who seem normal, likable. Most of the time it's just a matter of voting for the guy who's the least idiotic. Anyone who enters politics has to be an idiot anyway. Just look less like an idiot than the other guy and you'll win whatever office you're running for."

"That is . . . very interesting. Well . . . good evening to you, then."

Owens touched the brim of his cap with his finger. "Evening to you, too, sir. Oh, sir . . . you weren't thinking of heading into the park, were you?"

Arthur looked across Fifty-ninth Street to the edge of Central Park. There were a few stray couples walking arm-in-arm along the sidewalk running around the park, but no one was actually entering it.

"That had, in fact, been my intention, yes. Why? Is there some reason I should not?"

Owens rubbed his chin thoughtfully. "Well . . . most of the time it's safe enough. Sure safer than it used to be. Nevertheless, I'd advise against it. Unless you have a way of occupying that scabbard of yours with a sword."

"But if I were to carry a sword, you would then feel compelled to arrest me for it."

"First rule of being a New York cop is knowing when to look the other way."

"I'll remember that," said Arthur. "Good evening to you, sir." He watched the police officer walk off and then turned and headed into the park.

IRON-SPINE OWENS SPUN on his heel and went on his way whistling an aimless tune, his hands resting in a relaxed manner behind him. It was not until he was eight blocks away that he suddenly realized he had just totally violated the "Iron-Spine" character—the ultimate "tough cop"—he had created for himself and maintained all these years. With just a few choice words this lone, bearded man had taken Owens firmly in hand, and in moments had him rolling over and playing dead. And Owens hadn't minded!

He considered for a moment running back after the man, challenging him, rousting him, maybe even finding something to arrest him for. Just to gain back something indefinable that he'd lost. But when he even considered the notion, he was sufficiently dissuaded from it just by imagining the scowl of disapproval the man would give him. Owens whistled softly in awe. "I don't know just what that man has going for him," he said, waiting for the light to change at the corner of Fifty-first Street and Fifth Avenue, "but whatever it is, I wish I could bottle it and sell it. I'd sure as hell make me a fortune." A woman with a dachshund on a leash looked curiously at the police officer mumbling to himself, and walked quickly away, shaking her head.

ARTHUR WALKED BRISKLY through the park, the soles of his shoes slapping with satisfying regularity against the blacktop. A cyclist sped by him in the opposite direction and didn't even afford him a glance.

Although Officer Owens was dwelling upon the encounter with Arthur, Arthur was giving the exchange no thought whatsoever. Instead his energies were focused on the young woman he'd encountered earlier; the one who looked lost somehow. The one who'd threatened him with a mace, although she didn't seem to be carrying one. The one over whom he'd made a total jackass of himself by tumbling down the stairs of the subway in full armor. The one who reminded him so much of . . .

. . . of her.

Gwynyfar . . . how are they spelling it now? Guinevere, yes. His queen.

He tried to shake the notion out of his mind in the way that a cat would thoroughly vibrate his body to toss off every last drop of water. First and foremost, it couldn't be . . . her. She was gone, long gone. Second, she didn't look all that much like her . . . well, maybe a little bit.

All right, a lot.

But then again, he hadn't seen her for centuries. All he had in his mind's eye was an idealized vision of a woman with beauty that was not so much surface as it was depth. His beloved Guinevere had never, upon first glance, appeared a great beauty. Instead her beauty had come from a deep, inner greatness of spirit that became more and more visible the longer people spent time with her. Individuals who met her and initially thought her little more than plainly pretty, came away believing that Helen of Troy would throw herself to her death upon meeting Arthur's queen, convinced that the legendary Helen's beauty had met not only its match, but its superior.

Still, this poor, befuddled, even frightened New York woman . . . she had some of that same old Guinevere magic about her. Then again, Arthur had to admit to himself, he might wind up feeling that way about any woman he encountered just because he missed his beloved Jenny so much. He resolved to dwell upon it no more; it was simply not worth the mental aggravation. Jenny was just gone, that was all, long gone. And no amount of fanciful reimagining of her was going to change that simple fact. Instead he returned his attention to his environment.

Arthur's pores opened, his senses expanding to drink in the greenery around him. This was something to which he had an easier time relating. This wood-and-leaf forest was something that came far more naturally to him than the brick, steel, and concrete forest that loomed all around, hemming in the park at all sides. This brought back pleasant memories of home . . .

Home? What was home to him now? He had no friends, no loved ones. No family. Only descendants, and even they were completely screwed up. Held in high esteem by the modern British, Arthur had in his day actually fought against the ancestors of the modern-day Englishman. But a lot could be forgiven and forgotten in over a dozen centuries, he decided.

Camelot long gone, lost in the mist of time and memories. Guinevere gone, Lancelot gone, all . . . all gone. But he had survived, only he . . .

Or . . . was he falsely assuming? Were they genuinely gone? None of the others had been locked away in an enchanted cave all this time, of course, as he had been . . . or had they?

But no, that was impossible. Only Arthur and Merlin had survived, and Merlin would certainly have told Arthur if any of his latter-day companions were still with them.

Wouldn't he?

It was hard to be certain with Merlin. He was, after all, a wizard, and wizards were renowned for keeping key points of information to themselves. They were not the most trustworthy of individuals . . . and the fact that Arthur was depending so heavily on such a being made him exceedingly uncomfortable.

So lost in thought was Arthur as he made his way through the park that he failed to notice the two men lurking in the bushes.

But they most certainly noticed him.

THEY WERE EXACTLY the reason that most people didn't walk around in Central Park at night. Calling them "men" might have been a bit too generous a term. With their wild manes of black hair and their equally scraggly beards, they were of an indeterminate age. They each gave off a fairly pungent odor but, because they had hung with each other for as long as they had—since the 1960s, when they'd first met at an antiwar rally, gotten stoned, and fried just enough brain cells to remain in a permanent haze—neither of them came close to noticing it. Both of them bone skinny, they acquired their wardrobe through the simple expedient of crawling into the narrow chutes of the Goodwill boxes and scavenging clothes from them. Their fingernails were permanently dirty, although, curiously, their teeth were in perfect condition (since they were both big believers in flossing.) One had blue eyes, the other brown, which was pretty much the only way anyone could possibly have distinguished them. Indeed, on some days it was the only way they had of telling each other apart.

Much of what was real and what was not floated in and out for them, and there had only been a handful of things that they agreed upon that absolutely, truly existed. Artificial stimulants headed the list, followed by money. Then came superheroes—after all, in the whole world there had to be at least one, somewhere. And the fourth was rock and roll, which they were convinced would never die. Their own names long forgotten, they had adopted sobriquets that were in keeping with that philosophy.

The blue eyed, taller one, Buddy, stood slowly, disentangling his beard from the snarl of the branches. "There he goes," he murmured. "You see him?"

Elvis nodded and chewed on the remains of a stale pretzel. He stood as well, coming just to Buddy's shoulder. He wiped his large nose expansively with his shirtsleeve but said nothing. Talking had never been his strong suit. Nor was he very sharp on conscious thought.

Their most recent foray into clothes shopping, this time into a Salvation Army drop-off box (or, as they referred to it, their Uncle Sal) had garnered them dark sweatshirts and tattered jeans with holes in the knees. Buddy was also wearing battered basketball Nikes and a thin windbreaker. In his social strata this alone was enough to qualify him for the best-dressed list.

Buddy said, "Look at him. Like he's got the whole world for his oyster. He must have enough on him to keep us goin' for a few days, at least. Geez, he must be from out of town. C'mon."

He and his partner, or what there was of him, stepped out of the bushes. Buddy looked down and scowled. "Who told you not to wear shoes, you idiot. Geez, aren't your feet cold?"

Elvis looked at him blankly. "Feet?"

The two ill-equipped, ill-advised, and generally just plain ill muggers found themselves quickly at a disadvantage. Their intended victim was walking quite quickly, and they felt compelled to remain in the background. The general intention was not to be spotted by the victim until it was too late.

Their own paranoia made this problematic. They insisted on taking refuge behind trees and shrubbery every time they thought, even for a moment, that they might be detected. These brilliant attempts at camouflage consisted of noisily rustling bushes or tripping over projecting roots. Colorful profanity and frantic shushing usually accompanied such endeavors. At one point Elvis and Buddy were almost within striking distance, but out of nowhere a police car materialized. It prompted them to dive headlong into the bushes to avoid detection. When the police car drove on past, they emerged cut and bleeding, and Elvis wiped at his nose and asked if they could go home now.

"That's it," growled Buddy. "We're endin' this right now."

They scuttled ahead but found, much to their chagrin, that they had lost their quarry at the fork in the road. Trusting to his luck, which had not served in good stead for over a decade, Buddy pulled his partner to the right and walked as quickly as he could.

ARTHUR SMILED, ENJOYING the game. There was no way of his stalkers knowing that the man they were pursuing was possessed of a warrior's sixth sense, which warned him that a couple of badly intentioned but inept thugs were following him. But he made no effort to discourage them. They seemed harmless enough, and in a perverse sort of way he was very curious as to how they would react to the events that would shortly transpire.

At one point he felt he was losing them, so he waited and watched from the shadows, and when he saw them coming, stepped back out onto the path. If they had guessed wrong, he'd been prepared to clear his throat loudly to guide them on their way. He began to walk, paused momentarily, and cast a glance over his left shoulder. There was the expected crash and curses as the two leaped into the bushes once again. Arthur laughed to himself. He hadn't had this much fun in centuries.

The road angled down, and within a few more moments Arthur stood at the edge of Central Park Lake. His nostrils flared. He could smell the magic in the air, like a faint aroma that lingered long after a great feast had been cleared away. It was a pleasant scent, a familiar one. After all, he had lived with it for more years than any man could rightly expect to live. Magic had cured him when he'd been struck down through the duplicity of his bastard son, Modred, and magic had kept him alive. It was as mother's milk to him . . . except he distrusted it. But sometimes one has to learn to live with that which one distrusts.

He looked out across the lake and waited. It would be here, he knew. It had to be. All he had to do was wait. The stillness of the night air hung over him. Faintly he heard an ambulance siren, or perhaps a police car. Closer, he felt the small animal life all around him. The creatures of the woods had tensed as well. They, too, sensed it.

Arthur let his breath out slowly, and mist filled the air in front of him. It was chilly, rapidly approaching thirty-two degrees—the point at which water freezes.

Which did nothing to explain why the middle of Central Park Lake was beginning to boil.

Arthur stared in rapt attention as the water in the center of the lake bubbled, swirled, and undulated, as if a volcano were about to leap forth, spewing lava into the park. Then, somehow, the water folded in on itself, creating a small whirlpool. The air seemed to hum, as if energy was building up towards a powerful release. Now there were no nearby sounds of forest animals scavenging for the last scraps of food, or faraway sounds of ambulance sirens. It seemed New York City had shut down, leaving only the noises of the churning water.

It was then that it emerged from the center of the lake. Arthur's eyes widened, and for one moment he was no longer Arthur Rex. He was Arthur the wondering boy, dazzled and stunned by the wonders that were his to witness. Arthur, he who had once been called Wart, whose entire world had been small and isolated, and suddenly discovered—through the tutelage of a great mage named Merlin—all the infinite possibilities that were his to explore. All the powers and spectacle that a world of nature and magic had to offer, if only he knew where and how to look.

He was looking now.

At first only its tip was visible, but then it rose, straight, proud, all that was noble and great and wondrous. The tip of the blade pointed toward the moon, as if it would cleave it in two. The blade itself gleamed, a beacon in the night. There was no light source for the sword to be reflecting from, for the moon had darted behind a cloud in fear. The sword was glowing from the intensity of its strength and power and knowledge that it was justice incarnate, and that after a slumber of uncounted years its time had again come.

After the blade broke the surface, the hilt was visible, and holding the sword was a single strong, yet feminine hand, wearing several rings that bore jewels sparkling with the blue-green color of the ocean. It was a moment frozen out of time—another time—as the man at the lake's edge watched the entire scene, unmoving but not unmoved.

Slowly the hand began to glide toward him, cutting through the water and yet amazingly not leaving a wake behind it, bringing its proud burden straight and true. As it neared Arthur, the water receded as more and more of the graceful arm was revealed. Within moments the Lady of the Lake stood mere feet away from Arthur, the water reaching the hem of her garment.

She looked like hell.

Weeds and slime had ruined her beautiful white dress. Her hair, also filled with slime, hung limply. In her jeweled crown a dead fish had somehow managed to lodge itself to stare glassy-eyed at the world. She pulled another dead fish, plus an orange rind, out of the cleavage of her dress while Arthur, onshore, glanced away in mild embarrassment. She glared at him for a moment and then, in an attempt to restore some measure of dignity, took a majestic step forward. But she missed her footing, slipped, and fell flat into the mud.

Arthur reached down to help her but she waved him off, pulling herself to her feet. Using the sword to balance by thrusting it into the silt, she lifted one foot and pulled an empty cigarette pack off the bottom of her shoe. While one hand made vague attempts to wipe off the sludge, with the other she gave the still-gleaming sword to the man on shore.

"Thank you, lady," he said, and bowed to her.

She pulled a crushed beer can from the hem of her dress and said two words in a musical voice that would have shamed the Siryns of myth.

"Never . . . again."

And with that the Lady of the Lake turned and trudged slowly back as the roiling waters reached out to receive her.

Carefully Arthur examined his sword. They were two old friends, reunited at last. It gleamed in his hand, happy to see him. In many respects, he had felt naked without it. Now he felt ready to take on the world. Suddenly all the doubts, the confusions about the woman he had met, the wistful missing of those centuries agone . . . all of them fell away as the only thing that remained pure and unsullied from that majestic time sang gently to him as he whipped it through the air.

He stepped over to a large, dead tree and swung at a low branch. The branch was as thick as the arms of two men, but the glowing sword passed through it without so much as slowing down, giving off a low hum like a swarm of powerful bees. Apparently startled that it could so easily be severed, the branch hung there for a moment before thudding to the ground.

Arthur heard the rustling behind him and he spun. Automatically he grabbed the hilt with both hands, holding the sword Excalibur in such a manner as to be both offensive and defensive. His eyes glittered in the dimness. "Who?" he called out. "Who is there?"

But he knew the answer even before they stumbled forward. In the wonderment of it all he had completely forgotten about his two would-be assailants. He was fortunate, he realized, that they were as incompetent as they were. Had they been even mildly formidable, he would have left himself foolishly vulnerable. As it was, they stumbled out with eyes like saucers. One of them, taller with blue eyes, came right to Arthur's feet and then, to the returned king's surprise, the scruffy skulker dropped to one knee. His companion looked down at him curiously. Without returning the glance the taller one reached to his partner's pants leg and pulled him down also. His knees crunched slightly as he hit the ground.

Arthur lowered Excalibur, holding the pommel with one hand and letting the blade rest in his palm. "May I help you?"

"I'm . . ." He could barely speak, his voice barely above a hoarse whisper. "I'm Buddy . . . this is Elvis . . . and . . . and we swear . . ." he said fervently.

This came as no surprise to Arthur, but he waited with polite curiosity to see if that was the end of the pronouncement. It wasn't.

"We swear our undying allegiance to the man with the Day-Glo sword and the submersible girlfriend."

King Arthur gave a little nod of his head. "Thank you. That's very kind." There was a long pause, and then Arthur said, "Is that it?"

Buddy looked up at him as if Arthur were a drooling idiot. "We're waiting for you to knight us."

Arthur suppressed a cough. "When hell freezes over," he said.

Buddy gave this some thought. Finally he nodded. "All right," he said agreeably. "We'll wait. Won't we?" He nudged Elvis in the ribs.

Elvis stared at him forlornly. "My feet are cold," he sniffled.

They left the park together, their feet crunching on the gravel of the path.

It's not the Round Table, thought Arthur, *but it's a start*.

CHAPTRE
THE FOURTH

†

GWEN STEPPED OUT of the shower, now refreshed and prepared to face the new day that was shining so nauseatingly through the bathroom window. It was the bathroom's only source of illumination, the fluorescents having burnt out some time ago. There had been no money to buy new ones.

She ran the towel over her slim body, rubbing it briskly across her back. Here in the womb-like security of the bathroom, the day didn't seem quite so bad. She had just done the shower breast examination that she always dreaded, and was pleased to have found no lump in evidence. So she had her health, knock wood. And even better, she had a job interview this morning. And she could only think that it was going to go better than the disaster of the previous week. As if ignominiously losing out on the job wasn't bad enough, to be pursued by some lunatic dressed as a knight? What the hell had been up with *that*?

And yet . . . there had been something about that moment that had seemed . . . right.

She shook it off. This was absolutely no time to allow

herself to fall prey to yet another bout of romantic non-sense. She instead had to keep focus on what was important, and give no consideration at all to daydreaming.

She wrapped the light blue terry cloth towel around her body, and another towel around her strawberry blonde hair. She kept it short and manageable enough that drying it took only a few minutes. She was not one for wasting a lot of time on external frivolities. Gwen wrinkled her nose at herself in the mirror. She hated her face because it was perfect. The nose was just right. The eyes were just the right space apart, the eyebrows just the right thickness. Her cheekbones were not too high or defined. Her skin displayed no mars or blemishes. She was, on the whole, very attractive, as far as most people were concerned. But she did not agree. She longed for some distinguishing feature to give her face the character she felt it lacked. All the truly elegant women, she believed, had some feature you could hang a description on. A majestic profile caused by highly arched eyebrows, or a nose that was a tad too long—that was what she wanted.

She had even gone to a plastic surgeon once. He had laughed at her. Laughed! He told her that his patients would kill for looks like hers. He'd advised against unnecessary surgery and told her to go home for a week or so and think it over. She had never gotten the nerve to go back.

Gwen padded quietly into the living room, which doubled as an office. She found him—her boyfriend—as she knew she would. He was slumped over his computer, his head resting comfortably on the keyboard. She scowled as she saw row after row of gibberish letters scrolling across the screen. God only knew how long it had been doing that. She slid the keyboard out from under his face, and his head thumped to the tabletop. She ran her fingers through his greasy black hair and whispered, "Hon? Honey, go to bed. You really should go to bed."

He grunted as he stood, balancing himself against the

table. His eyes did not open as she took him firmly by the shoulder and steered him toward the bed. He passed an open window and snarled, and she noticed with distress that he was developing a most unhealthy pallor. It was beginning to feel like she was living with a vampire . . . which made sense. He never went outdoors, at least in daylight, and he was sucking her dry . . .

Stop thinking like that. You can't lose faith in him. Not you. You're all he has.

"Hon, have you considered trying to get outside a bit more?" she said carefully.

She was treading on tricky ground—the last time she'd broached such a subject, he had construed it as a criticism of him, and worse, an implication that he should get a job. *"How can I get a job?"* he'd screamed at the time. *"I have my work!"* He had then gone into a silent tantrum that lasted three days. It had been three very peaceful days for her.

This time he barely uttered a reply before collapsing onto the couch. It wasn't the bed, but she decided to leave him there. It wasn't worth the aggravation somehow, and besides, she had to get to the interview. She had to get the job. She just had to. If for no other reason than the fact that, within two days, the employment agencies would no longer be able to get in touch with her. The phone company would be disconnecting the phone.

She let the towel drop to the ground as she looked at the small assortment of clothes that hung in her closet. She heard a stirring in the living room and for one moment fantasized that he was waking up. That he would come into the room, see her standing there as she was, naked, her hair wet, and her body slim and supple. That he would take her in his arms and make wild, intense love to her. Despite the fact that she had to get to the job, she would welcome that kind of spontaneous, wildly romantic lovemaking in her life. It would be a nice change of pace.

He snorted and turned over on the couch.

She hoped against hope there would be further noise, but there wasn't. So she allowed herself the luxury of sitting down on the threadbare bedspread and sobbing for five minutes. Then she dressed quickly and quietly, went back into the bathroom, washed the tears from her face as best she could and let herself out of the apartment. The soft click of the door roused the man sleeping on the couch only briefly.

GWEN LOOKED UP at the small office building on Twenty-eighth and Broadway. The words "Camelot Building" were stenciled in fading gilt letters on the glass above the entrance. An ironic name, she thought, for Camelot was a place of pageantry and legend. This somewhat rundown building was hardly that. It was, in every way, unremarkable. Then again, she thought, so was she. She immediately chided herself for taking such a defeatist view. It was exactly the kind of thing her therapist had warned her against, back when she could afford a therapist. She took a deep breath to steady herself, tried for the hundredth time to get herself pumped up for the meeting while simultaneously not magnifying its importance out of all proportion, and then entered the main lobby.

The guard at the front desk had to be at least sixty and didn't seem especially capable of guarding anyone from anything unless it was a threat that was moving very, very slowly. He glanced up at her. "Can I help you, miss?"

She had been looking at the directory on the wall, and turned to him now. "Yes. I'm trying to find the offices of a Mr. Arthur Penn."

He looked blank for a moment, and she felt her hopes sink. She wasn't even going to get out of the starting gate on this one. This whole thing had been some sort of confusion or wild goose chase. She was beginning to wonder if she was her own worst enemy, her inability to get a decent job sabotaged by her own ineptness. But then his face cleared and he said, "Right. New fella. Thirteenth floor."

She looked at him askance. "I thought buildings didn't have thirteenth floors."

The guard shrugged. "Fellow who built this place wasn't a superstitious sort."

"Oh, really?"

"Yeah. And he was a lucky fella too. He was fortunate enough to see his work completed." He coughed. "Day after, he got hit by a truck. You can go on up."

"Gee, thanks." How comforting to know that, just when she thought she couldn't feel worse . . . she could.

He chucked a thumb toward a far door and said, "Main elevator's out. Better use the freight 'round back."

She headed down the hallway, departing the tiled floor and entering a back hall with cement flooring and a strip of green carpeting down the center that had enough holes in it to sink the *Titanic*. The corridor light was dodgy at best, flickering slightly and making her worry that within moments she was going to be plunged into darkness. But the lightbulb managed to keep its diminishing life sustained for a short time longer, and she made it to the freight elevator. She'd hoped there would be an elevator operator, but it was self-service. The elevator car itself was a rickety affair that moved up the shaft with a maximum of screeching and clanking. She felt out of place, neatly pressed and dressed, wearing high-heel shoes and trapped in a huge elevator with metal walls and floor. A dying bulb lit the elevator, and she felt as if she were being carted up to her execution. Then this bulb, unlike its brothers in the hallway, gave out, and it became so dark in the elevator that she literally could not see her hand in front of her.

"How nice. A little preview of death," she muttered, as much to keep up her flagging spirits as anything else.

She had never been so grateful for anything as when the doors opened on the thirteenth floor. She stepped out and the elevator bounced up and down like a yo-yo. As the doors closed behind her with a thud like a guillotine blade descending, she walked out into the main corridor. What she saw astounded her.

The offices of Arthur Penn were beautifully put together, but far from modern. All the furniture was antique; solid, dependable pieces everywhere she looked. The walls were paneled in knotty pine. The carpeting was deep plush in royal blue. Her breath was taken by the extreme contrast between this office and the rest of the building. It was almost as if one of them—the building or the offices—was in the wrong place. She started to wander about until a firm voice called her up short, saying, "Can I help you?"

She looked around and saw a fierce-looking receptionist seated at a desk, and she wondered how she had missed the woman the first time. She had the demeanor of a pitbull and, unlike the guard downstairs, seemed perfectly capable of wrestling intruders to the floor and tearing out their throats with her teeth. And enjoying it.

"Oh, yes, I'm sorry. I have an appointment. An appointment with Mr. Penn."

The receptionist glanced down at a calendar on the edge of her uncluttered desk and asked, "You're Gwen?"

Gwen nodded.

The receptionist seemed slightly mollified by the fact that this person was supposed to be here, but still looked like she regretted not having an opportunity to give someone the heave-ho. She said, "Very well. Take a seat, please. Mr. Penn will be with you shortly."

Gwen nodded her thanks, sat in an ornately carved chair and looked down at a coffee table next to her, on which several recent news magazines rested. She started to reach for one but then paused and asked, "Would you like me to fill out a form or something?"

"No. That won't be necessary." The receptionist didn't even bother to glance at her. Instead she had returned to

staring resolutely ahead, like a griffin or some other mythical creature waiting for some intruder to try and breach
the doors.

*Why the hell had she thought of such a thing? Mythical
beasts? Why had her mind wandered in that direction, of all
things?*

Still feeling confused as to her status, Gwen asked, "But
how will the people in personnel know anything about
me?"

The receptionist slowly swiveled her head back toward
Gwen and focused on her, like an irritated snake studying
an especially annoying bird. "We don't have a personnel
department," she said deliberately, as if addressing an imbecile. "Mr. Penn himself will see you and decide either
yes or no. All right?"

"Yes. All right," said Gwen, feeling completely cowed.

"Any more questions?" she asked in the tone of someone who didn't want to hear any.

"No, ma'am."

The receptionist went back to watching. What appeared to be an unspeakably long time passed, and finally
Gwen ventured in a small voice, "Nice weather we're
having, isn't it?"

She'd barely gotten the words out when thunder rumbled from outside and rain smacked in huge droplets
against the single office window. Gwen glanced heaven-
ward.

"He will see you now," said the receptionist abruptly.
She was still looking away. What the hell was she watching for?

"Who will?" said Gwen, but quickly recovered. She
stood and said, "Well, thank you. Thank you very much."
She smoothed her denim skirt. "You've been very kind."

"No, I haven't," was the tart response. "I've treated you
like garbage."

"I beg your—"

Now the receptionist had once again focused her attention on Gwen. She spoke briskly and incisively, dissecting Gwen as if her words were scalpels. "You let people walk over you, dear, you'll never get anywhere." She stabbed a finger at Gwen. "Your personal relationships have the success rate of buggy-whip manufacturers, right?"

Gwen drew herself up to her full height. "Now I don't think that's any of your—"

"You don't think? Hmph. I bet." The woman chucked a thumb at a closed office door, and it was only then that Gwen noticed what incredible green eyes she had. "Go in. He's expecting you. And for pity's sake, don't let yourself be used as a doormat. You've got too pretty a face to let it be filled with shoe prints." And with that she went back to watching the front entrance.

Silently Gwen walked past her, completely confused. She went right up to the door, then swung about on her heel to face the receptionist.

There was no one there.

Gwen's eyebrows knit in confusion. She walked back to the desk, looked around. Nothing. Under the desk was nothing. But the receptionist hadn't gone out the door— it had creaked horrendously when Gwen had entered; she would have heard an exit. Out of curiosity she rested a hand on the cushion of the seat behind the desk. It was cool, as if no one had been sitting there all day.

"Ooookaydokay," she said finally, went quickly to the office door that the receptionist had indicated, and swung it open.

She was a little surprised to see a bearded man deep in discussion with a boy who looked to be about eight years old. They were speaking in low, intense tones, and it was quite clear to Gwen that there was none of the typical adult condescension in the man as he argued with the boy. Not the slightest. Apparently this Arthur Penn, if that was who this in fact happened to be, treated everyone as an equal.

Either that or he had a thing for little boys. This naturally set off alarm bells in Gwen's head, but she didn't want to rush to judgment. Still, she promised herself that she'd keep a wary eye on him, and if there was even the slightest sign of any impropriety, not only would she be out of there but she'd make personally sure that the police were brought in.

The most curious thing she heard was the scolding tone of the young boy. "The main thing you have to do differently this time around is think things through! That was always your greatest failing, thinking."

"I've had plenty of time to dwell on mistakes . . ."

"Plenty of time may not be enough time. You have to promise me that you're not going to be impetuous. That you'll make calm, considered decisions, rather than impulsive notions from your gut."

"Such decisions come from my heart, Merlin, wherein all true knowledge lies—"

"Oh, bollux! The heart is nothing but a glorified water pump, with about as much knowledge as a sofa cushion . . . or for that matter, your gut. The only thing of use to you is your brain, Arthur, your brain!"

"Honestly, Merlin, sometimes you treat me as if I'm a child."

Suddenly the young boy was glancing in her direction. "Arthur, we have a guest."

"I am perfectly capable of making decisions and watching out for . . . pardon?"

"A guest." The boy was skinny, his hands too large for his arms, his feet too large for his legs. His silken brown hair was longish in the back, and his ears virtually stuck out at right angles to his head. He was nattily attired in dark blue slacks, shirt, striped tie, and a blazer with a little sword emblem on the pocket. Bizarrely, the man's clothing was identical, but the boy looked better in it. Penn turned, and the moment he saw Gwen, he appeared startled, as if he recognized her from somewhere. She couldn't imagine from where that might be; he was a total stranger to her. But he quickly covered whatever might be going through his mind and instead gave a broad smile. The kid he'd addressed as Merlin, on the other hand, frowned deeply.

Gwen found herself staring into Arthur's eyes. She had never seen such dark eyes, she thought. Dark as a bottomless pit, which she would willingly plunge into . . .

She tore her gaze from him, swung it over to the boy he'd called Merlin, and stifled a gasp. It was like looking at two different people in the same body. The lines of the boy's face were youthful enough, but his eyes were like an old man's, smoldering with wisdom of ages and resentment when he looked at her. He seemed to have what could only be called an "old soul." There was a wisdom, a depth in those eyes that was not only beyond what she saw in children, it was beyond what she saw in most adults. He frightened her terribly, and she stared down at her shoes.

Penn appeared oblivious to her thoughts. "How unforgivably rude of me," he said. "You're the young woman who was sent over by the employment office."

"That's right," she said quietly.

Penn regarded her for a time and then said, "Is there something particularly intriguing about your feet, my dear?"

She looked up, her cheeks coloring. "I'm sorry. I just—" She laughed, somewhat uncertain. "Your, uh . . . your receptionist rattled me slightly."

"Ah, Miss Basil. Yes, she'll do that. What is your name, child?"

The boy had asked the question, and the phrasing was, at the very least, extraordinary. She gaped openly at him. "My what?"

"Nom de guerre. Moniker. Name."

"Oh, name!"

Merlin let out a sigh, clearly not one to suffer fools

gladly. In the meantime she managed to stammer out, "G-G-Gwendolyn."

"I'm sure you won't mind if we simply call you Gwendolyn and leave the guh-guh-guh that preceded it to more formal occasions," Penn said, deadpan.

Then she saw him smile again and managed a nod, saying wryly, "That'd be fine."

She realized that Arthur was staring at her, but he did not look away, continuing to gaze at her in a manner that was wonderfully open, and unembarrassed. "Forgive me for staring so," he said, "but you remind me a great deal of someone I once knew—"

"Arthur," said the boy warningly, "what were we just discussing?"

"Merlin, please," sighed Arthur in obvious irritation. "My apologies, Gwendolyn. I am Arthur Pendr—Arthur Penn. My associate"—he chuckled slightly on the word—"is Merlin."

"Last name?" asked Gwen.

"Last one I intend to use," snapped Merlin.

"As you know," continued Arthur, "I am in the market to hire a personal assistant. This may not seem necessary now, but I assure you in the months to come this office will become quite busy. I would like to know all about your background, everything you've done in the past several years. We have several people to see, so I'll tell you right now that it may be a week or two before we can let you and your agency know for certain. Stop glowering, Merlin. You'll get crows' feet. Remember the last time that happened, you couldn't walk properly for days."

Gwen laughed, but Arthur stared at her with an upraised eyebrow and said, "Was something funny?"

"No. Not at all. I understand. Find out about me, more people to see, a week or two for response. Got it."

"Right. After all, any decisions we make along these lines must be thoughtful and considered," he said, tossing Merlin a glance. If he was waiting for the boy to nod in approval, he was going to be disappointed. The boy simply sat there like a disapproving statue. Clearing his throat, Arthur said, "Fine then. Let's begin."

Arthur pulled around a comfortable chair for Gwen and seated himself across from her. He leaned back, steepled his long fingers, and said, "So, miss . . . I'm sorry, Gwen, I didn't catch your last name."

"Queen," she said. "Gwen D. Queen. The *D* is from my mother's maiden name, DeVere. So it's Gwen DeVere. But that's probably more than you needed to kn—"

"You start on Monday," said Arthur.

Merlin, seated on the desktop, moaned.

WHEN GWEN DEVERE Queen returned home, the apartment seemed a little less gloomy, and as she marched in the door she called out, "Lance, I got it!" She stood in the doorway, dripping little puddles at her feet, uncaring of the fact that it had been pouring outside. She had a job, she had a feeling of self-worth for the first time in ages, and she had some celebrating to do.

There was no response. She sighed, the wind slightly taken out of her sails. She should have known. Lance only went out when it was a downpour such as this. He got inspiration from foul weather, he said. He had once filled a cup with rainwater, held it in front of her and informed her that an entire allegory of mankind could be found in that glass of precipitation. When she'd said she only saw rainwater, he'd emptied the contents on her head.

Friends told her that she should have walked out right then. But they didn't understand him the way that she did, didn't understand his temperament. Didn't understand that she had really brought it on herself, why . . . it wasn't his fault at all. It was hers, purely hers, and she had to be willing to take responsibility for her screwups, just as her parents had always taught her.

Still . . . she couldn't help but think briefly about what

the phantom receptionist had said. About standing up for herself, not letting people walk all over her.

Well, what did the receptionist know? She was a stranger. She was nothing to Gwen. With that certainty tucked in her mind, she went into the bathroom, her feet squishing in her shoes. She slid out of her clothes, relieved as one always is when divesting oneself of sopping garments. A few minutes later, wrapped in a towel, she went to the window and looked out at the street. It was covered with garbage, and derelicts were huddling in doorways for shelter. There was a constant tension in the neighborhood; a tension that she supposed was natural in the city. But it wasn't natural to her, and she wasn't going to live with it if she could help it. Perhaps, once she'd been working steadily for a while, they could afford to move out to a nicer area. Maybe someplace out in Brooklyn, or maybe even the Island.

If only Lance would get a job. But his writing always came first.

She glanced over at his work area, for it could hardly be called a desk, and then her heart leapt with joy. There, piled in the printer, was a stack of paper. He'd been working, writing and producing for the first time in ages. She remembered when, not too long ago, he'd looked at her with full sincerity and said fervently, "You are my muse." Well, here was proof of his sentiments, of the difference she made in his life. It was a sizable sheaf of paper; he must have been writing like a fireballer. She crossed quickly to the printer, lifted up the paper and began to page through it.

Page after page after page, the same thing: "All work and no play makes Jack a dull boy."

She cursed the day that she'd suggested they rent *The Shining*.

If only Lance would get a job. If only she could leave him. But he was all she had, and vice versa.

She flopped down onto the bed, reached over and

snapped on the small, black-and-white TV, purchased second hand at Goodwill. The picture was fuzzy, but discernible. She recognized the old movie as soon as it came on—Danny Kaye in *The Court Jester*.

Knights and knighthood. Those were the days. Chivalry. Women were demigods back then, she thought, and men their protectors. Now it's everyone for themselves. She reached over to the bureau, opened her purse and dug through it. Eight dollars and change. What the hell. She reached over to phone for a pizza, figuring it would arrive two hours later, cold and soggy. But it wouldn't really be dinnertime for two hours yet, anyway, and she could heat it up. And maybe the pizza guy would come riding up on a silver charger, balancing the pie on a gleaming shield. . . .

CHAPTRE
THE FIFTH

✝

Late into the night the offices in the Camelot Building's thirteenth floor blazed with light.

"*You're out of your mind.* You know that, don't you? Ten centuries to contemplate, and you're no smarter now, Wart, than you were then."

Arthur had removed his coat and tie and was sitting in shirtsleeves, watching Merlin stalk the room like a cat tracking a mouse. From his reclining position on the couch he called, "Now Merlin, I think you're exaggerating a bit."

The lad turned on him. "You think?" he said in a voice ringing with authority despite its boyishness. "Now you think! I read you the riot act, telling you that you should think, and the first major decision you have to make is done without thinking! It's a little late to start forcing the old gray cells to snap to attention, now, is it not?"

Arthur's voice was sharp as he said, "I caution you, Merlin. You will not address me in that manner. I am still your—"

Merlin turned, placing his hands defiantly on his narrow hips. "My what? Finish the sentence. My king? Well huzzah, Your Majesty," and he genuflected mockingly. "You rule a kingdom of one . . . unless you planned to return and lay claim as king of all the Britons. I can just see it!" He rubbed his hands together, relishing a good laugh, as Arthur shifted uncomfortably on the couch. "I wonder how they would react, those ineffectual, impotent figureheads who do nothing for the populace except provide them with tidbits to gossip about in taverns at tea time. There you'll be, presenting yourself as the once and future king. What the bloody hell do you think will happen? Do you think the queen is liable to step down and say, 'Good of you to show, old sod. We've spent centuries keeping your place warm. Have the throne.' Perhaps they'll revoke Magna Carta for you. That would be a sweet thing. Disband the House of Commons, House of Lords, put you in charge of the entire affair? Eh?" He slammed a small fist on a table, jiggling an ashtray. "What are the imperial thoughts, Arthur? Tell me, oh king of nothing!"

They glared at each other for a long moment. Then, finally, Arthur's eyes softened slightly and he said, "All right. They can keep the House of Commons. How does that strike you?"

Merlin laughed lightly. "Ah, Arthur, you madman. I should let you go in and try it. Either they'd lock you up, or maybe, by God, maybe they would make you king."

Arthur sighed and shook his head. "Aging backwards hasn't improved your disposition, Merlin, although your sense of humor remains as curious as ever. Depositing me in the middle of the city, wearing that . . . that clanking contraption."

"At least I provided you with the modern magic of plastic to obtain new garments. I'm not entirely without pity."

Arthur loosened his tie, amused at the curious piece of cloth that hung around his neck. In some ways it seemed like a sword, pointing straight down toward his privates.

What sort of message was that supposed to be sending? "If I can't understand the simplest thing about this world, such as its clothing accessories," he mused out loud, "how can I possibly contribute in any significant, meaningful way? Damn it all, Merlin, what am I doing here?"

"Ten centuries in a cave wasn't sufficient?" replied Merlin.

Arthur stood, smiling, and started to pace the office. His hands were folded behind his back. "Perhaps the time is not right for us."

"What would you wish then? A return to the cave?"

"It has crossed my mind."

"Well uncross it. Not the right time for you? Don't be absurd. Look around you. Go into a bookstore, what do you see? Dozens of books on you. Fact, fiction, and everything in between. There have been countless movies about you." Now he was ticking off items on his fingers. "There are TV programs. Broadway shows. Buildings and businesses named after you and Camelot. People dress as knights and stage mock jousts and battles. Home entertainment games with medieval settings, knights battling monsters, that sort of thing."

"So knighthood has become a valuable entertainment tool. So what?"

"Life reflects in its art, Wart. And also remember—the fondest, most mythic times this country remembers, in its political history, is a presidency which has come to be known as Camelot."

"Camelot," echoed Arthur.

Merlin nodded. "I know it sounds a bit bizarre. But don't you see, Arthur," and the king stopped his pacing, "the time is ripe for your return. More than ripe—the seeds are bursting forth from their fruits. They need you, Arthur, to show them the way."

Arthur half smiled. "You're sounding messianic this evening, Merlin."

"Hardly. Merely stating the facts."

"But, what am I supposed to do? You say they want me. But they don't want a king . . ."

"They want a leader, and you're certainly that."

"But who would I lead? Shall I start a cult following?"

Merlin shook his head mournfully. "Arthur, Arthur, you have to learn to think on a larger scale, the way you used to. Realize, then, that if you are to do any good, you must rule again. And you must rule, or lead, in a country that has clout."

"And I must go about it in a civilized manner," said Arthur sternly. "That means no military junta in a banana republic." He abruptly snapped his fingers. "But now, Merlin, let us say I could master the electoral system of this country and become their . . . not prime minister— president! That's it."

Merlin gave an approving nod. "Very good, Wart."

Arthur sat on the edge of the Chesterfield couch, leaning forward excitedly. "I haven't been idle all this time, you know. The animals in the cave with me, they brought me information from the outside world. I kept abreast of matters, for I knew that when I returned I would do no one any good as a clanking anachronism. And yet, for all my careful preparations, I was never altogether certain what I was preparing for. But I know now." He bounced excitedly to his feet and went to a window, looking out over the city. "Merlin, by all the gods that's it! I shall become president of the Soviet Union of America."

Merlin moaned and flopped onto a chair. "Arthur . . . first rule of acquiring information: Vermin don't know their arse from their elbow. You'll need to put in a bit more study time."

"Do you really think so?" inquired Arthur.

"I know so. And you must remember this, too, Arthur: History has a habit of repeating itself. You mustn't allow yourself to be drawn into the same elements that caused the destruction of Camelot."

"Damnit, Merlin," Arthur said, knowing full well what

Merlin was referring to. "It was just a name. She's nothing like Jenny was . . ."

"Don't lie to me!" thundered Merlin, or at least that was his intention. Unfortunately for him, due to the sheer boyishness of his voice, it came out sounding far more like a petulant rant. He winced at the sound of it. "I hate this," he said through gritted teeth. "I hate aging backward."

"You never told me how you wound up in that state of being," said Arthur.

"Possibly because it was never any of your business. Do you know the old saying, Arthur, which goes, 'If I knew then what I know now . . .'? Yes? Well, once upon a time it seemed like a good idea to me that I could know now what I know then, and have the youth and strength to do something with that knowledge. Unfortunately I didn't consider the long-term consequences."

"But how did it come about?"

"Promises were made," he said impatiently. "Favors called in. Bribes exchanged. It was all very long ago, and of no relevance. Furthermore, Wart, I think you're trying to change the subject."

"Am I succeeding?"

Merlin was clearly not amused. "I want honesty from you, Arthur. Without it we've no chance. None."

"Honesty." He leaned forward, interlacing his fingers between his knees. "All right. When I was first clanking about in the streets of the city . . . I saw her. I was staggering around, endeavoring to get my bearings, and suddenly I saw her. When I looked upon her, it was as if I 'recognized' her somehow. I saw her sitting there, and she looked up at me, and suddenly . . ." He shivered slightly at the recollection. "I saw *her.* My Gwynyfar, Guinevere, Jenny . . . so many names, all of them barely able to encompass the one woman. She was smiling at me from ten centuries ago, dressed in ermine, long candles flickering in our bedchamber. And Camelot was so damned cold, Merlin, you remember. On chill nights the wind would cut like the sharpest of blades, but when she was with me, there was warmth in the room, and a peace and happiness such as I never knew . . ."

"Until she betrayed you for Lancelot."

"You're so quick to remind me of that."

"Possibly because you're so quick to forget."

"But it could be fate, Merlin!" Arthur said with growing urgency. "Don't you see that? For me to stumble across her, so soon after you magically freed me from the cave, and now she shows up here again. Does that not sound like the hand of fate to you?"

"Possibly. But need I remind you, Arthur, that the Lady Fate has never exactly been an ally of Camelot? You have been well and truly buggered on a number of occasions by fate, and if you think that returning you to your lady love is some sort of positive inducement, then you, highness, are being even more self-delusional than usual. Except it's not her. It's not Gwynyfar."

"But how can you be so certain?"

Merlin sighed and shook his head. "Arthur . . . mariners of old would report that they had seen mermaids capering about in the waters they sailed. Now I have seen many wondrous things, Arthur, and know even more than I have seen, and in all of that I have never come across a genuine child of the sea. Do you know what those old sailors actually saw in their travels? Manatees."

"What?" Arthur's brows knit in puzzlement. "What are—?"

"Great, lumpy cows of the ocean, with as much resemblance to a woman as any other cow might have. But because these men had been at sea for so long, just about anything looked good to them and reminded them of women. Do you see what I'm saying here, Arthur?"

"You're saying," Arthur sighed, "that when I saw Gwen she reminded me of Gwynyfar because I had been away from her for so long, so anything would remind me of her."

"That's exactly right, Arthur. You were a stranger in a strange land. It is natural that you would have sought out something that reminded you of days of yore."

Arthur was silent for a time, and then he rose and walked to the window. He looked out at the glittering skyline before him. "Perhaps you are right," he said finally. "Perhaps it is madness to think that she could be Jenny, somehow miraculously returned to me. Still . . . it was nice to hope for a time. That is what Camelot was built on, Merlin, was it not? Hope?"

"No," Merlin said flatly. "It was built on belief. A belief that it, and you, could make a difference. And that is the same foundation upon which you will build your political career. But if you do not believe, then you're going to have nothing."

"Political career," snorted Arthur. "Merlin . . . if there is one thing that has been driven home to me in all of this, it's the vast scope of the world nowadays. I never realized what a small pond was dwelt in by me, the large fish. Who am I now? I am nothing to them. Nothing."

"You've forgotten, haven't you," said Merlin sadly.

"Forgotten?"

"What it was like for the young King Arthur. To all of those knights, you were nothing as well. A snot-nosed boy awarded the throne of Britain through a sorcerer's parlor trick. Have you forgotten the looks upon the faces of the warlords and warrior kings when they were asked to swear allegiance to you? Half of them revolted at the outset. You had to put down the rebellion. You, barely into your teens. And look what happened!"

"I know what happened, since you are so quick to remind me. My wife and best friend betrayed me . . ."

"Yes, yes, yes," came the impatient response. "But until that happened, you had built something truly great. Yes, your destiny was unfortunate. However, you can make up for it now. And with the world such a vast and yet easily accessible place, you can do even more good now than you did back then. My magiks have given you a second chance, Arthur. All you need to do is be careful not to fritter it away obsessing over 'lookalikes' of Gwynyfar . . ."

"It's not that she's a lookalike. It's that she evokes the spirit of . . ." But then he shook his head quickly. "No. No, you're right, Merlin. I shall simply concentrate on what needs to be done."

"Excellent. And my first piece of advice to that end is call the Queen woman, tell her there's been a mistake, offer her a nice severance package and be done with it."

He shook his head. "I cannot. I gave my word."

"And you gave your word to me, as I recall," said Merlin. "Your dying words, whispered on your funeral bier. You said, 'If I only had one more chance . . . I know I could do it right.' Well, you've got your chance, Arthur. You're lucky. Beyond lucky. Most men in this world don't have the opportunity to do even once what you're going to be doing twice. May I strongly suggest, Wart, that you do everything you can not to screw it up this time?"

"I shall take your kind advice to heart, mage," said Arthur, and he bowed once and deeply.

But even as he did so, the lovely young woman from centuries agone moved through his mind's eye, smiling at him, beckoning to him.

He spent the rest of the evening trying to convince himself that he had made a mistake and that he should contact Gwen immediately and inform her that the position was not available. He was not, however, able to do so, and couldn't decide—for the life of him—if that was a good thing or a bad thing.

CHAPTRE
THE SIXTH

†

TWO WOMEN IN Arthur's life were involved in very different pursuits one evening . . .

THE V HAD burnt out in the "Vacancy" sign that hung outside the beat-up roadside motel situated just off of the interstate. The signs posted nearby had promised waterbeds and triple-X-rated films in the room. Just the sort of thing the average passing traveler would be looking for. As it so happened, Morgan was passing, and a traveler, but she was certainly far from average.

When she'd checked in, the desk clerk had gaped at her openly. Part of her was tempted to put him in her place, but another part was flattered by the attention, and it was this aspect of her that saved the clerk's life. It had, after all, been a very long time since any man—even a bald, potbellied specimen such as the desk clerk—had looked at her appreciatively, or even at all. Being subjected to scrutiny by even as pathetic a specimen as this was still appreciated. As for the desk clerk, he was able to go home that evening, unaware of the fact that he should be relieved that he was alive or that his brain hadn't been melted under a sorcerous curse. Instead he had a normal-functioning brain, which was carrying secret fantasies acted out with the stunning woman who had checked in at the scummy little motel he managed.

The clerk had no idea that, weeks earlier, Morgan Le Fey would hardly have turned any heads. Indeed, she might have turned a few stomachs. But the excess weight she'd been carting with her all this time had slid away like melting butter. All the extra chins had vanished into memory, leaving her with the one jutting chin that stuck out so proudly. The raven hair was black through and through—no gray at the roots—and her feet, once swollen and cracked, were now slim and strong.

In the dingy hotel room, she stripped to the buff and examined herself in the full-length mirror that hung on the inside of the bathroom door (unaware that a young blonde woman, with whom her path would eventually cross, had subjected herself to similar scrutiny not too long ago.) She couldn't help but wonder who the genius was who thought that mounting a mirror inside the bathroom—and, as a consequence, directly opposite the toilet—could remotely be considered a good or flattering idea. It meant that when she was relieving herself, the only view she was afforded was herself, sitting on the toilet, leaving her to grumble to herself, "Well, *that* looks about as dignified as I always thought it did." But at that particular moment, she wasn't dwelling on it. Instead she was busy admiring the contours of her muscular body. She thought of the lethargic lump she had let herself become and was filled with silent rage.

But that loathsome creature was long gone. And Morgan Le Fey was back in business.

The naked sorceress rolled back the threadbare rug, bracing it with her foot against the wall. Then she padded back to the bare area and removed a piece of chalk from the pocket of her long black coat. She knelt down, then, and, brushing strands of hair from her face, carefully traced a circle, with a five-point star enclosed within. She then reached into her beat up duffel bag and extracted five black candles, fondling the length of them almost sexually. She placed one at each point where the star touched the circle. She stepped back, admired her handiwork, and smiled.

Then she rolled the television set near to the circle and sat down facing it. The floor chilled her bare rump but she ignored it, as she composed herself and then snapped her fingers. The five candles around her promptly lit. It was a minor exhibition of her power, but it pleased her nonetheless. Again she snapped her fingers, and the television flared to life.

The sight on the screen afforded her momentary amusement. It was a couple madly rutting, panting like twin locomotives. But then it reminded her of just how long it had been since she herself had indulged in such carnal pleasures, and it caused her to frown in irritation and wave a hand as if brushing a flea away. The picture vanished from the screen, replaced by blankness.

Morgan concentrated, reaching out with her mind and tracing the waves of magic, charting the ley lines that filled the air around her. She'd been doing this regularly, going from town to town, city to city, setting herself up at different intersection points of the earth's ley lines, trying to discover a mystical trace of Merlin. It had proven to be frustrating. Merlin had covered his tracks too well. If she'd begun the trace from the moment when he'd escaped from his centuries-long confinement, she could have picked up on it in no time. But this was no longer possible. Just as a fox can cover his trail and scent given time, so had Merlin been able to erase any sign of his person.

However, if Merlin had been practicing magic lately, he would most certainly have been tapping into the ley lines that encompassed the earth. Any adept was able to detect the pale ribbonlike trails that filled the air. But not any adept would have been able to do what Morgan was attempting: To track back along ley lines as if they were mystic telephone wires, tracing along and discovering where a particular caller—Merlin, in this instance—had most recently made use of them. Had Merlin been using his sorcerous powers, Morgan should have been able to retrace him down those mystical bands as if she were tracing a telephone call. But she had found nothing, which meant either that he had been using no magic lately, or—more disturbing—that he'd discovered a means by which to cover any track of magic use. If it were the latter, Morgan would certainly have her work cut out for her. She should have felt some degree of frustration over that possibility, but instead she merely warmed to the task. The more difficult Merlin made it for her going in, the sweeter her triumph coming out.

She found a faint whiff of magic along one stream and immediately ran it back to its source. The TV screen flickered and then the image of a young girl appeared. She was a teenager, naked as was Morgan, seated in what appeared to be the middle of her high school's athletic field. She was chanting quietly to herself and burning a photograph of a handsome young man. The candle was white.

Morgan pursed her lips. Amateurs dabbling in love spells. This was the sort of tripe she'd been unearthing in her searches these past weeks. Still . . . there was no reason she couldn't have a bit of fun at that.

She sent an eldritch wave back along the ley line, and many miles away, the girl's candle suddenly flared. The girl fell back, gasping in surprise, and Morgan's image appeared in the flickering flame of the candle.

"I am Hecate, goddess of witches," murmured Morgan, delighting in the way the would-be witch's eyes went wide. "Hear me, novice. I have seen your future, and it does not include this boy. He is using you, toying with your affections, but he does not and never will love you.

He will bring you hurt and pain and misery, and he will do it to others of your spiritual sisters as well, unless you stop him. Have you the heart to do so, my child . . . ?"

The girl's mouth moved, but no words came out. She managed a terrified nod.

"Now listen carefully. Here is what you must do," said Morgan, and she quickly outlined a spell that would cause eruptions and boils all over the boy's skin, scarring him for life. The girl nodded eagerly, clearly taken by the notion of having that kind of power over someone that was destined to cause her so much grief.

"And never forget what you have learned here this night. Now go, my child . . . go, and do as you are bidden." Then she laughed in a satisfyingly demented manner and broke the connection. She wondered in an offhand manner if the girl's original spell would have worked, or whether the boy really did love the girl after all, or would ever have. Ah well. No use concerning herself about it any further. On to more important matters: Where the devil was Merlin? Where—

The screen suddenly went black, and Morgan jumped slightly, startled. At the same time she knew instinctively what had caused it. And so she waited, and eventually it came.

Within moments the image of an office with antique furniture appeared on the screen, and there, seated in a large easy chair, was a boy who looked far too old for his skin. His feet dangled several inches above the ground; his hands were interlaced behind his head. He had a smile on his lips that was not mirrored in his eyes. He looked straight at her as he said, "Hello, Morgan. You're looking well-preserved these days."

She inclined her head in acknowledgment. "Thank you, Merlin. You're too kind."

"I know." He studied her for a moment. "You're not surprised to see me?"

In truth she was very disconcerted. It had not occurred

to her that Merlin's power would be so great that he would detect her attempts to find him; that he would turn the tables back on her, apparently without effort. He did not seem to have undertaken any conjuration. He had simply commandeered her equipment. Could his power really have grown so? Was everything so effortless for him now? If it were true, he would be far more than formidable. He would be invincible.

All of this passed through her mind in a moment, and then she said, "No. I'm not at all surprised. Your overwhelming ego would only allow you to perform some such stunt as this."

"Ah, how well you know me," sighed Merlin, sounding almost pleased by it.

"I knew Merlin the man, not Merlin the tot," she said airily. "I had thought the legends exaggerated. I see now they were not. You do indeed age backward."

He nodded. "Just so. And, intriguingly enough, I become more powerful as well. It's quite a combination, Morgan: the energy and drive of youth combined with the wisdom and skill of an older man. An unbeatable combination, wouldn't you say?"

She leaned back, uncaring of her nudity. Her long hair hung discreetly over her breasts. "You would certainly say so, Merlin. Then again, there's always the chance that you will wind up being tripped up by your staggering sense of overconfidence. I will admit I'm impressed. Magic wards were placed all around the cave in which you were imprisoned long centuries ago. How did you get through them? Even at the height of your power—"

"Remember what I taught you, Morgan. Wards are nothing more than mystic prison bars. These were small enough to contain any man. However, sliding between the ward bars in a child's body was quite simple, really."

"So you simply allowed time to take its course. Since you're long lived, it took centuries for you to reach this point . . . but ultimately, reach it you did."

"Quite true." Merlin slid forward, alighting on his feet, and came "closer" to the screen. "And I'm sure you realize that I subsequently arranged for Arthur's release."

"Time off for good behavior, no doubt."

This time Merlin did not even try to smile. "Now listen carefully, Morgan. I did not have to contact you this way. I can assure you that mystically you would never have found us. However, before too long Arthur is going to be in the newspapers. Rather than give you the satisfaction of locating us, I decided to expend the smallest aspect of my power to issue you a warning."

She raised an arched eyebrow. "Warning, is it?"

"It is. Arthur will be running for mayor of New York City. As I said, you would undoubtedly read of this in the newspapers, for Arthur is destined to be quite a controversial candidate. I would not wish you to think for even a moment that we were living in fear of your discovering us. So I give you our city of operations ahead of time, secure in the knowledge that there is not a damned thing you can do to deter us."

She frowned. "Arthur? Mayor? I would think that president would be more appropriate."

Merlin shook his head and his image flickered on the screen. "You and Arthur, half brother and half sister, thinking alike. That was Arthur's first inclination. But he has too much he has yet to learn, including," he said ruefully, "the name of this country. But that is neither here nor there. A complete unknown cannot come sweeping into the greatest office in the land from nowhere. He has to establish a political track record. New York is a highly visible city. And they could really use him. So," he concluded, "mayor of New York it is. It's inevitable, so don't even think about averting it. You do not have anyone to aid you any more, Morgan. Modred is long-gone bones. You command no legions of hell—human, mystic, or otherwise. It is just you, rusty in the use of your powers, versus me at the height of mine. You might say I've been working out."

"Are you trying to scare me, Merlin?"

Instead of replying, Merlin merely smiled. Suddenly Morgan heard a low humming, as if power was building up from somewhere. She realized immediately that the television was the source of it, and an instant after that realization, sparks began to fly from the set. She dove for cover as heavy crackling and smoke followed the sparks. An instant later the TV screen blew outward, spraying glass all over the motel room. It flew with enough velocity to embed itself in the wall, in the carpet, and if Morgan had presented a target, in Morgan herself. She, however, had moved quickly enough to knock over and hide behind a coffee table, and so was spared the inconvenience of having her skin ripped to shreds.

And Merlin's fading voice floating from the still-sparking speaker. "Trying? No. I believe I've succeeded. Stay out of my way, Morgan, or prepare to suffer dearly." And then there was silence.

She waited until she was certain that the violence was over. Slowly she raised her head, picking a few shards of glass out of her hair. She looked around. Gray smoke was rising from the now silent television. There was faint crackling in the air, and her nose wrinkled at the acrid odor. She stood fully and then slowly, daintily, picked her way across the floor. She stood in front of the television and, somewhat unnecessarily, turned it off. Then she padded across to the telephone, picked it up, and waited impatiently for an outside line.

When it came she dialed a long-distance number quickly, efficiently. Her face was grim, but her spirits were soaring. She felt the blood pulsing in her veins for the first time in centuries. There was almost a sexual thrill, matching wits and powers with Merlin. She had been little better than dead all these decades.

The phone on the other end was picked up and a slightly whiny male voice said, "Yeah?"

Her eyes sparkled as she said, "He's contacted me. They're in New York."

"They're in New York?!" The voice was incredulous. "But *I'm* in New York! How could I not have known?"

"Because you're a great bloody twit. I'm on my way up there now." She paused, frowning. "We have only one thing going for us. Merlin is not as all-knowing as he believes himself to be. He thinks you do not exist, Mod-red. He thinks I am on my own. It may prove to be his fatal mistake."

"Fatal?" There was an audible gulp. "You mean like dead?"

She sighed, and hung up without another word. Then she leaned back on the bed, brushed away pieces of glass, and closed her eyes.

"Great bloody twit," she muttered. "This is going to be tougher than I thought."

"YOU'RE LATE."

Gwen stopped in the doorway, openly surprised. Lance was seated at the kitchen table, his chair tilted back against the wall. He looked impatient, even huffy. And she realized with a shock that it had been ages since she'd really taken a look at him, so rarely had he been both around and conscious these days.

He pushed his thick glasses back up on the bridge of his nose. The unhealthy pallor he'd acquired had not improved. In addition his lips were dry and cracked. The blue check shirt he'd worn for four days straight was taking on a life of its own. His jeans were threadbare at the knees, and his socks were standing over in the corner, retaining the shape of his feet as if from memory.

Not too long ago, such appearance on his part seemed almost romantic to her. Now it just seemed . . . creepy somehow. But then she promptly scolded herself. She was not about to lose faith in him. He was a creative type, and much smarter than she was, and besides, she had known going into the relationship that writers were creative types. That they had to be indulged, not pressured, their imaginations permitted to run wild without having to worry about trivial matters like hygiene and . . . and . . .

God, was that smell him?

"Lance," she managed to get out. She glanced at her watch. "Am I really that late? It's only a little after six."

He tapped a bony forefinger on the tabletop. "I expect dinner by six P.M. sharp."

She looked askance at him as she removed her coat and hung it on a hook near the door. "Since when, Lance?"

"Since when what?"

"Since when do you expect your dinner at six P.M. sharp," she said patiently. "You're usually not home then. And even if you are, you might be asleep, like as not."

"Are you criticizing me?" He'd spoken in a tone that was guaranteed to make her back down, to force her into a sniveling apology. But as she crossed the room and sat down across from him, his face registered with a distant sort of surprise that such an apology was not to be forthcoming.

"I am not criticizing you," she said slowly, thoughtfully. She took his hand and held it gently, affectionately, trying not to flinch from how clammy it felt. "If you have a regular schedule you'd like to maintain, I'll be more than happy to aid in maintaining it. But don't try to change things on me and then get mad because I can't read your mind."

His eyes narrowed. He had tilted the chair forward, and now tilted it back, interlacing his fingers in a gesture he imagined made him look very authoritative. "I think you should give up your job."

Her eyes widened. "Stop working for Art? Are you nuts?" Her voice went up an octave. "He's the best thing that's ever happened to me! The past weeks I've been working for him have been—"

His body stiffened, suddenly not listening to anything else she was saying. "Wait a minute. Best thing? What about me? I thought I was the best thing that's ever happened to you."

Gwen huffed in irritation. It was so annoying. She'd come home in such a good mood, and suddenly she felt as if she was being sandbagged by Lance. When he'd acted this way in the past, she'd always chalked it up to his being in one of his moods. Suddenly, though, that explanation felt . . . inadequate. "Well, of course you are, Lance. I'm talking about two different things."

"Two different best things."

She shifted uncomfortably in the seat. "Kind of. Ow." That last came from the fact that he was squeezing her hand more tightly than she liked.

"Best thing means best thing," he informed her. "It doesn't mean anything else." Releasing her hand in what amounted to disgust, he stood up, swaying slightly, and it was only then that Gwen realized he had a few drinks in him. The alcohol was easily discernible in the air now. "I should know. I'm a writer."

Her impatience with him flaring, she shot back, "So you say," and immediately wished she could have bitten her tongue off. She stood quickly and started to head for the bedroom when Lance's hand clamped on her shoulder. She turned and faced him, and his eyes were smoldering.

"What do you mean by that?" He spoke in a voice that was low and ugly. "What do you mean?"

"Nothing, Lance. I—"

"*What do you mean?*"

She pulled back ineffectually. With an angry snarl he shoved her away and drew himself up to his full height. "You seem to forget our college days, Gwen. You looked up to me then, remember?"

"I still look up to you, Lance." Gwen backed up slowly

until she bumped into a wall and could go no farther. The entire thing seemed surreal, like it was happening to someone else. She'd always known Lance had a temper, always. But it had never bubbled over into anger in this manner.

"Remember those days, huh?" he asked. "I was somebody then. All the English teachers knew me. They said they wished I'd never leave."

They said they thought you'd never leave, Gwen wanted to scream at him. *You flunked bonehead English, twice. Creative writing teachers said you were incomprehensible. I was the only one who believed in you. I still do. It's . . . it's become so ingrained a habit that I can't stop believing in you, even though every ounce of my common sense tells me I should.* She thought all of this, but didn't say it. Instead she told him, "I remember, Lance. I remember. But I can't quit my job. We need the money. And Arthur's going to be the next mayor. You'll see."

Lance guffawed and waved his hands about as he spoke. He bumped the single bulb that hung overhead in the kitchen, and it sent wildly distorted shadows twisting on the wall. "Mayor, is he? Has he been out canvassing for votes? Has he even got the signatures of people who say they want him to run for mayor? Gwen, the man is a loser. You always hook yourself up with losers. You have a streak of self-abuse that . . ."

His voice trailed off as he realized the double-edged sword of the words he had just spoken. She was looking at him in an assessing manner. With a snarl he stormed over to the front door of the apartment, yanked it open, and barreled out into the hallway, down the stairs to the next landing, and eventually out the door of the building.

In the past Gwen would have chased him down the stairs, begged him to come back, apologized for not having faith. She sensed greatness in him, she was sure of it, and was positive that she was destined to bring it out in him. But this time she went to the window and simply watched him go. He stopped at street level and looked up at the window. She looked down at him, her face carefully neutral, although from that distance he couldn't see the single tear trickling down her cheek. And Gwen, for the life of her, couldn't decide whether she was crying for him, or for herself, especially because she knew to some degree that Lance had been right in his assessment of her judgment of men. She didn't know what was worse, though: the thought of how it applied to her and Lance, or the thought of how it might apply to her and Arthur.

With a roar Lance pushed his way into the crowd that had just come out of the subway and vanished from Gwen's sight . . . had she been looking, of course. Instead she was looking elsewhere, looking inward—at the shape and course of her own life.

She thought of her parents, strict and demanding, for whom nothing she had done was ever good enough. She remembered how she had come home one day all excited from school, at the cusp of adolescence, waving the scores she had received in a series of evaluation tests. It indicated that she was quite bright, good enough to go to advanced schools.

But her parents had looked down their noses at such endeavors, not wanting their daughter to mix with "those smart-ass know-it-alls."

On some level, Gwen had spent the rest of her life trying to please *somebody* . . . although the last person who factored into that equation was she herself. She knew that . . . and she also knew that over the past several years she'd been living in limbo. Waiting for Lance to complete his book and sell it (he'd made it sound so easy!) Waiting for her life to take some direction. A lady in waiting.

She pulled herself up with a smile. That's what she liked about Arthur Penn, she decided. He didn't make her feel like a lady in waiting. He made her feel like her surname. Like a queen.

CHAPTRE
THE SEVENTH

$$\dagger$$

Ⅰ N HIS OFFICE at the Camelot Building, Arthur gaped at Merlin, utterly thunderstruck. Had Merlin not been so troubled by Arthur's displaying a naïveté that was astounding in a man nearly a millennium old, he would have found it amusing.

"Is it possible," Arthur inquired, his face a mask of perplexity, "that there might be some people who won't vote for me?"

Merlin stared at him. The legendary king looked so modern in the dress pants and shirt, and yet he was so innocent of the world around him. *What in the name of all the gods have I thrust the king into*, he wondered. *Maybe I should let him go back to the cave at that. Maybe he really has no place here at all, and I'm subjecting him to the worst sort of cruelty by putting him through this.* But then the boy wizard put the thought from his mind and concentrated on the issue at hand. Second-guessing would only lead to disaster. His direction had been chosen, and he had to have the resolve to stick to it. "Yes." He laughed tersely. "There is an outside chance."

"But . . . who would not vote for me?" asked Arthur, clearly still unable to wrap himself around the concept.

"Well," Merlin said reasonably, sitting by the window and glancing out at the crummy view, "People who would want to examine your record of past achievements, for one."

"But my achievements are legend—oh, I see." He slumped against his desk, his hands in his pockets. "I see the problem."

"Yes." Merlin looked away from the window, trying to figure out the best way to put the difficulty across to his liege. "Understand, Arthur, in this form my power is a force to be reckoned with. I can conjure up credit cards. I can create things like Social Security numbers, driver's licenses—although for pity's sake take a few lessons first— and I can put records of your birth in Bethlehem . . ."

"How very messianic."

". . . Pennsylvania," Merlin continued. "I can conjure up a history of military service for you. I can, essentially, create an identity for you, Arthur Penn. And these days, such stunts are easier than they ever could have been."

"How so?"

"Computers, Arthur," said Merlin with a smile. "Everything's on computers now. Everything."

"Yes. Computers. That would be . . . one of those things," Arthur said uncertainly, indicating the PC situated in the corner of his office. "They're rather complicated. Are you quite positive they're not simply a passing fad?"

"No, from everything I've heard, they're definitely here to stay," Merlin told him wryly. "I should know. I had a hand in them."

"You did?"

"Even from my cave, even in my exile, I was able to keep my hand in. See this?" and he pointed to the letters on the front of the computer. "IBM: Invented By Merlin."

Arthur looked at him askance. "You're joking."

"I'm a wizard, Arthur. Allow me my mysterious ambiguities." Merlin walked over to the machine and touched it, smiling in satisfaction as the screen flared to life. "Cyberspace isn't really all that different from magic, when you get down to it. A mysterious realm where things unseen dwell, where people can send and receive information, and even cast destructive spells upon one another—they call them 'viruses.' You are speaking, Arthur, to the foremost master of computer stunts in the world. I can use these devices—aided by a few sorcerous tricks I know—to shape the reality of information. However, I cannot alter by sheer force of will the entire public consciousness. I can't make people like you. That will be your task."

"And if I'm not up to it?" inquired Arthur, looking uncertain.

"Then," Merlin informed him archly, "you are not the young man I trained, and will be a disappointment to me. Oh . . . and the world will likely be doomed by the end of the first decade of the twenty-first century."

"Ah." Clearly not knowing what to say to that, Arthur replied, "Well . . . I'd best get to it, then."

"I could not have given more sound advice myself," Merlin said.

HAROLD AND ALICE, a young, well-dressed couple, were walking briskly down Fifth Avenue near the park, Alice's heels clacking merrily on the cobblestones, when the mugger leaped from behind a tree.

Instinctively Harold pushed Alice behind him. His desperate gaze revealed, naturally, that there was not a policeman in sight, so he pulled together the shards of his shattered nerve and held up his fists. At that instant the young man, a longtime advocate of gun control, suddenly changed his opinion on the subject and wished that he had a firearm in his hand, the bigger, the better.

The mugger stared at them for a moment, puzzled, and then slapped his forehead with the palm of his hand in self-reproachment. "Right! Money! You think I want money! Buddy!"

"I'm . . . I'm not your buddy," said Harold, peering over the tops of his fists and wishing his voice hadn't cracked when he said it.

"No, my name's Buddy," said the mugger.

Alice, sounding almost afraid of the answer she'd receive, said, "You . . . you don't want our money?"

"Nah! I mean, in the vast, general socioeconomic strata of the world, yeah, sure I want money. I mean, it makes the world go around." He paused. "Or maybe that's gravity or something."

There was dead silence. And then Harold said slowly, "Yes. Well. We have to be going."

"Fine. Well, you have a nice day," said Buddy.

"You bet. Same to you."

"Real soon."

The couple was slowly backing down the street. Buddy stood there, waving the filthy fingers of a filthy hand, his beat-up army poncho blowing in the breeze. They turned quickly then, but had only taken several steps when a voice screamed out from behind them, "Hey!"

"This is it, Harold," muttered Alice. "We're going to die now."

Buddy came barreling around them and faced them for a moment, his shaggy head shifting its gaze from one of them to the other. Then he thrust a clipboard forward. "I'm getting signatures for an election."

Harold looked at him incredulously. "What . . ." He cleared his throat, "What are you running for?"

"Who, me? Oh, geez, no. It's for mayor. I'm helping the guy with the Day-Glo sword and the submersible girlfriend become mayor of the city."

"Which . . . which city?"

Buddy paused a moment and frowned. "Holy geez, I never asked. You think it's this one?"

"With my luck," muttered Alice.

"Look, we don't want any trouble," Harold began again. He noted the fact that people were walking right past without offering any aid to them, even though Harold and Alice were obviously in distress. Indeed, they seemed to pick up their pace. Harold suddenly hated New York even more than he usually did. "If all you want is for me to sign this, I'll be happy to—"

"Harold!"

He fired her a look that told her, without a word being spoken, to shut her mouth.

"Hey, man, you're great." Buddy thrust the clipboard forward once again, and this time Harold took it, holding it gingerly between his fingers.

"Um," Harold said, and patted down his pockets. "I, uh, I don't seem to have a pen."

"Not to worry," said Buddy. He patted all the pockets in his limply hanging poncho and then in his tattered pants. With a frown he checked the hair behind his ears and then his beard. It was from that unchecked growth of facial hair that he finally extracted a Bic pen and extended it to the couple.

"I'm going to be sick," said Alice between clenched teeth. "I swear, God as my witness, I'm going to be sick."

Not settling for looks this time, Harold muttered, "Shut up, Alice," as he took the pen and signed the petition. "Maybe you would have preferred it if he had assaulted your virtue."

Buddy and Alice exchanged glances. Neither seemed particularly enthused with the idea.

"Harold!" she said after a moment. "You're putting our address!"

"Yeah. So?"

"So . . ." Her eyes narrowed as she inclined her head toward Buddy and, speaking in an urgently low voice in hopes that Buddy couldn't hear her, she said, "What if he tries to—you know—come to the house?"

And then she jumped slightly as the obviously sharp-eared Buddy said, "Oh, I'd never do that." Then he gave the matter some thought. "Unless you invited me."

Harold tried to smile pleasantly. What he achieved was the look of a man passing a kidney stone, but he continued valiantly, "What a . . . what a marvelous idea. We have to do that, real soon."

"When?"

"What?" Harold felt as if the ground was shifting beneath his feet.

"When do you want me to come over?" Buddy looked eagerly from one of them to the other.

"I'm . . . I'm not sure. It's going to be pretty hectic for us, too hectic to make social plans."

"Oh." Buddy looked crestfallen, but he brightened up. "Well, I'll give you a call, okay?" He smiled ingratiatingly.

"Okay," said Harold gamely. "You bet."

Harold quickly handed back the signed petition, and then they walked at double-time down the street. Buddy watched them go, and when they were almost out of earshot he screamed, "Are we talking dinner or just coffee and cake here?"

He shrugged when he got no response, and looked down proudly at his first signature. Only a few thousand more and he could knock off for the day. Then he reached into his beard and moaned. "Crud! The sons of bitches took my pen." He shook his head in disillusionment. "You just can't trust anyone these days. There's freaks everywhere."

PROFESSOR BERTRAM SOTHERBY, noted geologist, was emerging from the depths of the New York University subway stop on the BMT when a shadowy figure materialized in front of him. In one hand was a switchblade. In the other was a clipboard.

"Hello," growled Elvis. "I'd like your support for Arthur Penn, who would like to run as an independent for mayor of New York City. Sign this or I'll cut your fucking heart out."

Elvis collected 117 signatures. Before lunch. Without breaking a sweat.

U P IN DUFFY Square, in the heart of the Broadway theater district, Arthur Penn stood on a street corner near a Howard Johnson's, feeling extremely forlorn. About a block away, Gwen was likewise working on canvassing passersby.

A likely looking pair of elderly women approached him, and he started to say, in a very chatty and personable manner, "Hello, my name is Arthur Penn, and I would like your support in my candidacy for mayor . . ." which was more or less the phrasing that Merlin had told him to use. But the two women picked up their pace and stared straight ahead. His voice trailed off as Arthur realized with a shock that they were not only ignoring him, but they were pointedly ignoring him. Then he thought that perhaps he was judging them too harshly, that maybe they simply had not heard him. The elderly were notorious for being hard of hearing. Yes, that may very well be it.

So the next time a youngish, businessman-looking sort approached him, he began his approach again of "Hello, my name is . . ." But again he got no further than stating his *raison d'être* before this chap, too, was out of earshot.

No. It was not possible. People of any age could never be so unspeakably rude as to ignore someone who was pointblank addressing them. Could they?

Arthur checked his appearance in the reflection in the display window of the Howard Johnson's. No, his suit was well cut and smart, his grooming immaculate. He presented, to anyone who bothered to look, the perfect image of an educated and intelligent individual, not a threat or someone to be overlooked. It started to sink in to him that everything Merlin had said to him very early this morning, before he'd gone out canvassing, had been absolutely correct.

He exchanged a look down the block with Gwen, who was clearly feeling equally frustrated. She shrugged and gestured vaguely at the people bustling around them. For the first time he turned and saw, really saw, the raw, almost manic energy of the area around him. It was a nippy day, but the sun was shining brightly. It was twelve thirty, the height of the lunch hour. Furthermore, it was a Wednesday, which meant many people were out looking to pick up matinee show tickets. Arthur was not prepared for it, for the pulse of the humanity around him. Every blessed one of the passing people was in a hurry, as if they had an inner spring mechanism unwinding at an incredible rate.

It had not dawned on him at first that it had any direct bearing on him, but now he realized the error, the short-sightedness of his thinking. He couldn't expect people to stop in their tracks for him. He had to attempt to adapt himself to their speed. He had to be flexible, after all. The wise man—the civilized man—knew when to be firm and when to adapt. So he began to speak, faster and faster, and soon the words were tumbling one over the other, like cars piling high on a crashing locomotive.

"Hellomynameisarthurpennandiwouldlikeyour . . ." One syllable after another, indecipherable and incomprehensible, and the only result it had was to prompt people to move even faster than before—a feat he would not have previously thought possible. Some of them would cast glances at him that ranged from pitying to contemptuous to outright bewilderment.

Abruptly he stopped talking. His lips thinned and his brow clouded. He looked across the street and noticed that there was a traffic island, a solitary oasis in the sea of cars that stretched as far as he could see in either direction. On the island there was a mob of people, all milling around in loosely formed lines. Reaching out, Arthur stopped the first passerby, a delivery boy carrying some-body's called-in lunch. There was a spreading wet spot on the bag, which indicated that whatever was inside was leaking, which meant that the boy was in a hurry. Arthur almost let him pass on that basis, but then realized that everyone in the damned city seemed to have a reason for hurrying, and he might as well stop the first person that seemed worthwhile. So he did, snagging the confused boy by the arm. Before the delivery boy could ask what was going on, Arthur was pointing to the crowd across the way and asking, "What is the purpose of that gathering?"

The delivery boy rallied. "Look, asshole, I'm runnin' late and I can't—uuuhhnnnff!" That final, startled gasp came as a result of Arthur grabbing a handful of the boy's windbreaker. Despite the fact that he and the teenager were the same height, Arthur effortlessly lifted him into the air. The boy's eyes bugged out, not from lack of breath so much as from pure astonishment. The lunch he was carrying was sitting inside a cardboard cover from a Ham-mermill paper box, and Arthur caught it as it slipped from his fingers. His gaze, however, did not waver from the startled young delivery chap. And at first, when he spoke, it was with a voice like thunder, for the one-time king of the Britons was not accustomed to being ignored, and couldn't say he liked it much. What he could say was, "I will be ignored no longer!"

He saw out the corner of his eye Gwen's reaction to what he was doing, and then he noticed the lack of color in the boy's face, and immediately his anger lessened as he mentally chided himself, *Is this what it has come to then, Pendragon? Threatening hapless errand boys?* Arthur felt something he had not experienced in years: shame. Cer-tainly it was a feeling he'd known from his youth, with even distressing regularity, as Merlin would teach young Wart lessons about all manner of things. And more often than not, those lessons were very deep and very profound and very painful. They were, he thought at the time, the worst time of his entire life. How he missed them.

He lowered the boy gently to the ground. "Art well, lad?"

"My . . ." He gulped once, afraid to say the wrong thing and set his captor off again. "My name's not Art. But I'm okay, yeah."

And now Gwen was at his side. "Arthur," she said (initially having addressed him as "Mr. Penn" until he had insisted on the use of his first name) "are you all right?"

Arthur let out a sigh, but his anger was still quite evident. "I have been at this for much of the day, and the paltry few signatures that I have accrued—*blast their eyes!*" He smashed a fist against a nearby wall. The wall did not show any signs of yielding. Arthur's fist, on the other hand, had newly acquired bruises that would be there for days.

"That's not going to help," she said urgently, taking his fist in her hands and examining it for signs of damage. The delivery boy had, by this point, scampered. But Arthur wasn't paying attention to that; he was too busy ranting. "That I should have to endure this just so that I can offer them my aid. The leadership I should be given by right I have to scrabble for . . ."

"By right?" She laughed reflexively, but then saw the hurt in his eyes and said, a bit more gently this time, "Arthur . . . in this life, nothing's given to you. Even the stuff you think you have a right to, sooner or later you wind up fighting for it."

"I suppose," he sighed.

"What was up with the boy just then?"

"Up? Oh . . . I was just trying to determine the purpose of yon gath—of that gathering over there."

"That's the TKTS line," said Gwen, pronouncing each

letter individually. "People stand there on line and can buy tickets for half price to—"

Arthur had been doing a slow burn all day, and even as he was inwardly surprised at the vehemence of his reaction, he nevertheless exploded. "*That* they have time for? By Vortigern, they make time to await tickets for entertainment purposes and yet cannot spare half a minute on topics that could alter the face of this city . . . of this nation! *Gods!*"

"Arthur!" said Gwen, but he was no longer paying attention to her. Without heeding the traffic around him, he stormed across the street. Cars screeching to a halt mere inches from him did not even catch his notice. Horns blasting didn't faze him. He reached the TKTS mob and elbowed his way through, earning shouts and curses from his would-be constituency. In an abstract way, he knew that he wasn't doing himself any favors by alienating those very people whose vote he was hoping to capture, but at that moment he was more interested in recapturing his own pride.

Arthur found himself at the base of a statue that was labeled Father Patrick Duffy. With quick, sure movements he scaled it, and moments later was shoulder-to-shoulder with the fighting priest from World War I. A few people glanced at him and then turned away. The rest ignored him completely.

At that point, he was almost accustomed to being ignored, which was a fine state of affairs for someone who—a mere millennia or so ago—had entire regiments of knights snapping to attention at his every passing comment. With one arm still wrapped around the statue, he reached across his body to his left hip. He felt it there: the pommel, and then the hilt of Excalibur. He had flatly refused to go out onto the street without the comfortable weight of the enchanted sword by his side. So Merlin had added a further enchantment, rendering the blade invisible as long as it remained in the scabbard.

Now, though, was not the time to keep his weapon concealed. Arthur pulled on the sword and it slid from the scabbard with ease. Excalibur sparkled in the sun, and Arthur thrilled to the weight, to the joy of it. No one was paying any attention to him, with the exception of Gwen, and she was momentarily distracted since she was busy trying to cross the street without being run over.

"My arm is whole again," he whispered reverently. Then he swung the sword back, brought it around, and smacked the flat of the blade against the statue. The resulting clang was on par with a Chinese gong, and although it nearly deafened Arthur himself, it also served to get the attention of everyone within a block's radius.

"All right," he shouted. With practiced smoothness he had already returned Excalibur to its sheath, returning it to invisibility as well. "I have had enough. Enough of this street corner posturing and mindless games. By the gods you will attend my words. Rip your minds for a few minutes from mindless frivolities and ant-like natterings! I am running for mayor of this city!" He saw their reactions and added, "Yes, that's what this is all about. I see it in your faces. This is why I want a moment of your precious time."

"Screw you," called someone. And someone else shouted, "Who told you to get up there and be insulting?"

Arthur laughed. "I? When I am treated as if I was a nonentity, to be snubbed and ignored at their discretion? I merely call a halt to the insults that have been dealt me this day." He held up a clipboard, and the sheets of paper affixed to it rustled noisily in the breeze. "Do you see these?" Without pausing for a response he continued, "These are petitions. In this free society not just anyone can declare himself a candidate for office. I have to obtain ten thousand signatures, which actually means that I have to have twice that number, since it is generally assumed that half of you will be bloody liars. So I'm going to want every one of you to affix your signature to this most noble document. Is that clear?"

And suddenly a strong, clear female voice—Gwen's voice—called, "Why should we vote for you?"

Arthur was caught completely off guard. Gwen was now standing a few feet away, and he stared at her in utter befuddlement. Why in the world would she be challenging him? "What?" was all he managed to get out. There was a ripple of laughter from the crowd at his bewilderment. He was garnering attention, but he couldn't exactly say he liked the way it was happening. He was going from being ignored to being considered a joke. That was hardly an improvement.

"You haven't even told us your name!" It was Gwen again, and there was something in her voice other than mockery, if mockery had ever been her intent. It was . . . it was prompting. She was . . . prompting him . . .

Of course. Oh, of course.

"I am Arthur. Arthur Penn." He could have kicked himself for the brainless oversight. Quickly, though, he rallied, and continued, "If you wish to make your mark on history, no matter what else you fail to accomplish, know this: Sign your name here, and someday you will be able to balance your grandchildren on your knees and say, 'Yes, I mattered. I accomplished something, because I helped Arthur Penn become Mayor of New York.' "

"Why should we vote for you, Arthur Penn?" said Gwen, and now he fully understood. She was serving as a sort of patsy in the crowd, one who would put forward questions that would allow him to grab people's attention, speak of things that might be of interest to them.

Except that it couldn't all remain in Gwen's control, for now someone else shouted, "Yeah, you get up there, call us ants and stuff. Who are you, hot shit?"

"Why should we vote for you?" Gwen said again, with even more urgency in her voice, trying to get a usable answer out of him.

"Because . . ." he began, wishing frantically that Merlin had tutored him better. But then Merlin had not been aware that Arthur was going to take his first shot at addressing crowds at a completely impromptu political rally.

𝕬T THAT MOMENT Merlin was not too far away. At Bryant Park, behind the Forty-second Street Library, the wizard was watching an old drunk, watching as he rocked slowly back and forth against the cold, his coat pulled tightly around him.

Merlin shook his head. "Pitiful. Simply pitiful." Hands buried deep in his New York Mets sweat jacket, Merlin walked over to the derelict and dropped down onto the cold stone step beside him. He wrinkled his nose at the stench. At first the drunk didn't even notice him, but was content to rub the bottle with his cracked and blistered hands. Eventually, however, he became aware of a presence next to him, and he turned bleary eyes on Merlin. It took him several moments to focus, and when he did, he snorted.

He was a black man of indeterminate age. His wool cap obscured much of his head, although a few tufts of curly white hair stuck out. Much of his face was likewise hidden behind the turned up collar of his coat. His eyes were bloodshot.

"Youakid." Three words into one.

After a moment of meeting his gaze, Merlin turned and looked straight ahead. "Looks can be deceiving," he observed.

"You got money on you?"

"No."

"Parents care where y'are?"

Again he shook his head, although feeling somewhat amused at the question. "No," he said again.

The black man snorted. "You a kid, all right. Ain't no doubt."

Merlin winced. "Why must you talk like that? You're perfectly capable of proper grammar if you so desire."

This time the drunk looked at him more carefully. "You're a smartass kid, besides," he finally concluded.

"Probably." His bottom becoming chilled by the cold stone, Merlin shifted his position and sat on his gloved hands. "My name is Merlin. The wizard."

At this, the drunk snorted. "Believe it or not, kiddo . . . I knew Merlin. I worked with Merlin. And you're no Merlin. Although I'll say this for you . . . you've got enough sass to be him, sure as anything." The drunk proffered his almost empty bottle, wrapped in a brown paper bag. "You want some lifeblood, little wizard? Not much left, I'm sorry to say."

"It's full," said Merlin quietly.

The drunk laughed, a wheezy, phlegm-filled laugh that became a hacking cough within moments. When the fit subsided he told Merlin, "If there's something I always know, little wizard, it's how much I got in this here—"

He hesitated, because suddenly the bottle felt heavy. He slid the bag down and saw the top of the liquid sloshing about less than an inch from the mouth of the bottle. Then, ever so slowly, he refocused his eyes, as if seeing the mage for the first time.

"You little shite," he said slowly. "Where the hell have you been?"

At this Merlin truly did laugh, out loud. He stepped down two steps so that he was on eye level with the drunk. His thick brown hair blew in the wind. "Enjoy it, Percival. Or do you prefer 'Parsifal,' as in the old times?"

The drunk's eyes narrowed. "Percival is fine," he said slowly.

"Either way," continued Merlin, "it's the last drink you're going to be having for a time—ever, with any luck. We're going to sober you up and put you back in harness."

"After all this time . . . now you come to me? Talk about putting me in harness like I'm some kind of beast of burden? A horse?"

"No. If you were a horse, we'd simply shoot you and put you out of your misery."

"What the hell happened to you?" Percival was looking at him wonderingly. "I mean, I know what happened to me . . . but what happened to you?"

He wiped at his nose with the sleeve of his sweat jacket. "You will not find this simple to comprehend, Percival, but I live backward in time. In another fifteen centuries—by my reckoning, not yours—I shall be an old man. The price of immortality. It's difficult to maintain the form of an old man for an excessively long time, which is what would have been required had I aged as other men—had I been spawned as other men, Mary Stewart notwithstanding. But to age backward, to be forever becoming younger—I can maintain this body for decades, centuries to come. When I said fifteen centuries by my reckoning, I meant backward to the fifth century. Forward into the twenty-fifth century I shall be much as you see me now . . . if not a tad younger." He saw the blank look in Percival's face, and didn't wonder at the puzzlement there. There was really no point in dwelling on it to excess. He held out a hand. "Come with me, Percival. Let's go somewhere and talk. We can use you."

"Now you can use me. Now." Percival shook his head. "After all this . . . after I gave away my life. You never told me, never warned me . . . gods, you are evil, Merlin. You must know that."

"Yes. I know that. Now tell me something I do not know . . . such as, for instance, how long we're going to have to sit here while you wallow in your misery." When Percival didn't respond immediately, he said, "Percival, look around you. Look at this place. The leaves have disappeared from the trees. Winter is hard upon us. All that's left for you to do is huddle and shiver on cold, uncaring stone stairs. And when the winds blow hard, the best you can hope for is to find shelter in some pile of garbage. Human refuse blending in with the rest of the trash." He leaned forward, his small fists clenched and his voice pleading. "Whatever resentment you may have for me, Percival . . . you were great once."

"None of them made mention of my skin color . . . did you notice that?" Percival spoke as if he was talking from very far away. "None of those who wrote about the Grail quest. None of them mentioned I was a moor. As if . . . as if it was some sort of dirty secret that the court of Camelot numbered a dark skinned man among its membership."

Merlin sniffed disdainfully. "Is that what you're stewing about?"

"I'm not stewing . . ."

"Your story transcends race, Percival. The Grail—"

Percival spoke with sudden urgency, the first time in years he had felt such a drive. He gripped at Merlin's outer garment and said in a voice low and filled with tragedy, "In my hand, Merlin . . . it was in my hand . . . the water from it passed through my lips, and now . . . now . . ." Tears started to fill his eyes. *"Now I am this? This was my reward?"*

"No. This is." And Merlin hauled back a hand and slapped the startled Grail knight across the face. His brow was dark, his voice impatient and with an undertone of threat. "Now stop feeling sorry for yourself just because you consider to be a curse what others would consider a blessing."

Percival said, in a low and resigned voice, rubbing his cheek, "It's my life, little wizard. Why not let me live it?"

"Because it's not a life. And it's not living. I need someone with your skills, Percival. You were among the best. I know what you were, Percival. Before the Grail." He rose and extended a hand. "Come," said Merlin. "We'll talk."

The silence seemed to extend forever. Finally:

"Okay."

They left the park together.

"**A**RE YOU DEMOCRAT or GOP?" Gwen called.

Arthur felt terribly exposed and vulnerable, up high on the statue in Duffy Square. "I'm an Independent," he called. "I subscribe to no party line save for the dictates of my conscience."

Several people nodded in approval, but others smirked or snorted or said things like, "Great, someone else to waste a vote on."

And suddenly yet another voice, depressingly familiar, called out, "Oh, Jesus, Mary, and Joseph, not *you* again."

Arthur turned, knowing whom he was going to see before he even saw him. "Officer . . . Owens, wasn't it?"

"Yeah," said the self-proclaimed Iron-Spine Owens. He was shaking his head, looking amazed that he had run into this same nutcase again. "You just can't keep out of trouble, can you."

"I'm afraid I have a history of being rather in the middle of it," Arthur said, although he didn't sound especially apologetic about it.

"And what do you think you're doing here?"

Gwen looked worried, her gaze darting from Arthur to the policeman and back. But Arthur didn't lose his equanimity for a moment. "Why . . . I'm simply taking your advice, officer. About politicking. I'm endeavoring to run for mayor of this city. Will I be able to still count on your vote?"

A small crowd was gathering. Apparently, Arthur reasoned, this was the way to garner attention: be challenged by a police officer. People were always willing to stop whatever they were doing if it meant getting to see someone being dragged off by a uniformed law enforcer. That was when he suddenly recalled a headline he had read the other day. He read so many newspapers and continued to do so, aided by a memory retention potion that Merlin had cooked up for him. He'd have been lost without it, since there was so much to remember. "I read recently one of your number was slain," Arthur said to Owens, genuine sympathy in his voice. "My deepest condolences. The loss of a fellow blue knight is always difficult."

Owens shrugged stoically. "Unfortunately, cops are targets. It comes with the shield," and he tapped his badge.

This . . . *this* was what was considered a shield for knights of this day and age? Arthur looked at it, not with derision, but with sadness. Was this the best that they had to offer their defenders? "A shield should provide protection," Arthur noted.

"Go talk to the judges," Owens said with a long-suffering air. "Guys know you can kill a cop and walk." Then he eyed Arthur curiously. "Okay, Mr. Politician . . . where do you stand on capital punishment? There are some people who are making noises we should get rid of it again. What do you think?"

Arthur looked to Gwen. Her eyes were wide, and she shrugged in a "You're on your own" manner.

"Execution of the guilty," Arthur sighed. "There was a time," he said, "not so long ago at that, when disputes were settled man to man, on the field of honor. Frequently it resulted in death. The matter was ended . . . but the cost was wasted life. Life . . . is too precious to waste." He paused, gathering his thoughts on the matter. "I do favor allowing the death penalty in instances of murder. However, I do not feel that it should be up to the state to decree whether a man live or die."

This got genuine puzzled looks from the rapidly growing crowd. It was Gwen who said, "Well, then, who?"

"The injured party," Arthur said matter-of-factly.

"You mean the dead guy?" said a bewildered Owens.

"Hardly," he said. "The problem with the criminal justice system is that it gives to lawyers and judges power that should belong to others who matter far more. I'm not advocating a return to trial by combat. But when it comes to actually deciding upon death, the determination should be made by those whose lives are to be permanently affected, namely the survivors of the victim."

A sharp wind came up and he clutched more tightly onto the statue for fear of being blown off. Then the wind switched about, carrying his words out to the entire crowd—a crowd that had grown considerably beyond merely those people waiting for tickets. And his voice rang out, strong and clear. "If a woman has her husband taken from her, it should be up to her to decide whether the man who did the deed should live to see another sun or not, for it is the woman, not the judge and not the state, who must come home to an empty bed."

The crowd was buzzing, thrilled by the novelty of the notion. In a world of politics where one answer sounded much like another—canned, rehearsed, and remarkably the same—the bizarre uniqueness of the idea was attractive to them.

Owens said, "Aren't you just passing the buck?"

"Is advocating a true trial for the people passing the buck?" asked Arthur. "On the contrary, it's the perfect solution. No one will be able to feel that a proper sentence has not been meted out, for it will be the sentence of the people whose lives had been hurt the most by the criminal's actions." Raising a fist proudly, he unashamedly mixed up quotes as he declared, "Trial by jury of the people, by the people, and for the people!"

Traffic didn't move for an hour.

And across the street, standing just inside the door of an adult movie theater . . . a man was watching. A man with a fox-like face, ferret eyes, narrow beard and black hair that came to a widow's peak. A man who drew his coat around himself as the chill wind cut through him and watched as a TV news van, which literally happened to be passing by, slowed and a news crew hopped out to see what the commotion was all about.

"This . . . could be a problem," he muttered, before he mingled with the crowd and hurried away.

CHAPTRE
THE EIGHTH

✝

IT WAS SOMETIME later when the ferret-eyed, bearded man from the crowd entered the Eighth Avenue Health Club and made his way down to the racquetball courts. He slid through empty seats mounted on tiers, moving down as close as he was allowed to the actual court. A large piece of Plexiglas separated him from the two men aggressively battling it out for final points on the court. One man was tall, lean, a sharp and accurate player. The other man was much shorter, heavyset, with a beer belly he liked to smack affectionately and refer to as his "old hanger-on." His legs were spindly and looked as if every sudden shift in direction might cause them to break like twigs. His thin blond hair was tied off in a sweat-soaked bandanna, and his LaCoste shirt was plastered to his chest. The first man was, by contrast, calm and self-possessed. His opponent was on the ropes, and he had barely broken a sweat.

The bearded spectator rolled his eyes as the heavyset man lunged at the ball and missed it by the width of several states. He thought to himself, as the two players shook hands, *See if you can pick the likely candidate for mayor*, and groaned silently.

The beer-bellied man turned and spotted him. "Moe! Hey Moe!" he called in that annoying "Three Stooges" imitation which he apparently never tired of. He waved a beefy hand. "Come to see your next mayor in action?"

Moe managed a grimace and a nod. "You bet, Bernie. You bet."

The exceptionally jovial (exceptionally, considering he'd just been slaughtered at racquetball) Bernard Keating dragged his opponent by the shoulder. "Moe, you gotta meet one of the top eleven players I ever met. This is Ronnie Cordoba. Ronnie, this is Moe Dreskin, one of the top three P.R. hacks I ever met. Ronnie, Moe. Moe, Ronnie."

Moe reluctantly extended his hand and felt several fingers crack in Ronnie's grip. He grimaced again, and gingerly unwrapped the remnants of his hand. "Bernie, we have to talk."

"So we'll talk. We're talking."

"I think he means just the two of you," said Ron. "I'll be shuffling off to the locker room."

Bet he tosses a salute, thought Moe.

Ronnie smiled a perfect smile and tossed a salute before turning his broad back and trotting away, arms held perfectly for jogging.

"So what's to talk?" said Bernie. "Newspapers already start giving their endorsements for me?" He grinned broadly, displaying teeth yellow from cigar smoke. "I mean, come on. I'm the best DA this city ever had, so they know I'm tough on crime, plus I've lived here my whole life—I'm not some carpetbagger—plus the outgoing mayor gave me his personal endorsement. I got it sewn up, even before the primaries. They know that. I know that. We all know that."

Moe said, "Bernie, sit down."

Bernie looked at him oddly and stroked the faint stubble on his cheeks. "What do you mean, sit down?"

Moe sat and patted one of the solid wood foldout chairs next to him. Bernard Keating sat down. He drummed his fingers on his knee impatiently.

"Bernie," said Moe slowly, "I agree with you that you have the Republican nomination sewn up. You've got your years as the DA, that's true. Plus you've got your high profile participation in well-covered charity stunts and your seat in the Macy's Thanksgiving Day parade, and all of that. You've got great TV presence, an aggressive stand that lots of New Yorkers find easy to handle—"

"Moe," said Bernie cannily, "you didn't want to talk to me to tell me all these wonderful things about me."

"This is true," said Moe, lowering his gaze. "What I'm saying is that you may have your work cut out for you after the primaries."

"After?" He eyed Moe suspiciously. "You trying to tell me you think the Democrats really have a prayer? This guy, Kent Taylor . . . he's really going to be a problem?"

Kent Taylor was Moe's personal nightmare, because Taylor was everything that Moe was not. The broadshoulder, handsome actor had played the mayor of Chicago in a popular drama called *City Hall*, which had run for six years on NBC. He was telegenic, he had a good smile, he was slim and well-muscled, and most of all, he was already fixed in many people's heads as the ideal mayor just because they'd watched him playing one on television.

"No, I don't think so, Bernie," Moe assured him.

"But the polls have him—"

"I don't care where the polls have him now, Bernie," Moe said patiently. "Ultimately, Taylor's an empty suit. He can deliver scripted lines like no one else, but don't worry. Once he has to start improvising, thinking on his feet, the voters are going to see there's no 'there' there."

"Not necessarily. We've had presidents who got elected who were empty suits, and the voters didn't notice."

"That's because their opponents didn't have me making sure that people did notice."

Bernie's eyes narrowed and glinted with anticipation. "You talking dirty tricks, Moe?"

"Don't ask, don't tell, Bernie."

"So what's the problem?"

"There's an Independent candidate—"

Keating laughed hoarsely and shook his head. "You're kidding me, right? An Independent candidate? Some schmuck who puts up his own soapbox and starts pontificating to the public? Bullshit! I do not for one minute—"

"Bernie," and Moe's tone as always was unpleasant, "you pay me quite handsomely for giving my advice, and I am telling you now," he waved a thin finger threateningly, "that if you do not listen to what I'm telling you, you will have thrown your money away."

Bernie leaned back in the chair. He stroked his chin some more and then said, "All right, Moe. So who is this *wunderkind* you're so concerned about, if it's not Kent Taylor."

Moe cleared his throat, covering a sigh of relief. He had finally gotten Bernie to listen to him. That was three-quarters of the battle right there. "His name is Arthur Penn," he said.

Bernie rolled the name around in his mouth and finally shook his head. "Never heard of him."

"Neither has anybody else. But you're going to."

"What. Why do you say that?"

"He's got . . . something. Charisma. Charm. He's . . . he's real."

"Real. What do you mean, real?"

"He's a leader, Bernie. A true leader. I don't think you really understand just how hungry people are for one."

"What, you're saying I'm not a leader?" Bernie was laughing slightly, as if the idea was absurd.

But Moe wasn't laughing. "Never confuse someone who leads with someone who's a leader." Before Keating could seek clarification, Moe continued, "He was over by TKTS today. He climbed up on a statue and started speech making. Impromptu, off the cuff. The crowd clustered to him like nothing I've ever seen. Bernie, it was frightening. They weren't just standing there. They were actually listening, hanging on his every word. Anyone who came within earshot of his voice was mesmerized instantly. People asked him questions, and he started giving these Loony Toon answers, and the crowd ate it up."

"Loony Toon answers? What answers? What sort of questions?"

"Well, the death penalty. He said that the decision whether to execute a criminal should be left to the survivors, since they were the ones most affected by the crime."

Bernie's eyes widened so that they threatened to explode from his head. "What is he, nuts?" He started pacing angrily back and forth, up and down the narrow stairway that led up the aisle between seats. "Allowing the people to pass sentence. That's crazy! Sentences are passed in accordance with the laws of this state. Certain crimes demand certain sentences. The angered or bereaved victim can't begin to grasp the subtleties, the complexities of passing a—"

"Bernie," said Moe impatiently. "I know that. You know that. For all I know, even Arthur Penn knows that. But the people don't."

"But the people don't run the courts!"

"True enough. But they run the polling booths. And if they find this Penn's sideways view of the world attractive, they might say so come Election Day. New York is a city of nonconformists," he pointed out. "Our television ratings never match. Our buildings don't vaguely resemble each other in style. New Yorkers are rude in situations where others are polite, and polite in situations where Gandhi would bite your head off. They might just buy and slice this crock of baloney."

Bernie had barely listened. He was too busy shaking his head, saying, "The laws dictate the punishment that should fit the crime. Can't he see that? It's impossible."

"People don't care, Bernie. Don't you get that? They don't care about practicality, or what's reasonable, or even what makes sense. They care about what sounds good and what looks good, and right now he sounds and looks pretty good."

Bernie scratched his head. "So how do you figure we deal with this nutcase?"

"Frankly, I'm not sure yet. I think we can only take a wait-and-see attitude for now." Moe interlaced his fingers and crossed his legs almost daintily. "I mean, we shouldn't start attacking his positions yet. All that will do is give him publicity. Hell, maybe that's what he's hoping for."

"Too bad," muttered Bernie. "I'd like to take this guy apart in public."

"You may yet get your chance, if he sticks around. Which, I have a sick feeling, he's going to do." His nose wrinkled slightly. "Go hit the showers, Bernie. With the sweat you worked up, you're starting to smell like New Jersey."

M OE PUSHED OPEN the door to his Park Avenue office and stopped dead in his tracks. His secretary had said nothing about anyone with an appointment waiting for him, and yet there she was. And from the back, at least, she was a knockout (she had her back to him, gazing out the window at his impressive view). She was clad in a black leather jumpsuit that had revealing openings up the legs, and the back of the suit was cut all the way down to the dimples just above her buttocks. She had thick black hair cascading around her shoulders, and even from behind he could tell that she practically radiated sex.

Gods, let the face match the rest of it . . . and you know what? Even if it doesn't, that's why we have bedroom lights that shut off and eyes that close, he thought as he adjusted the knot in his tie and said—with as much suavity as he could muster under the circumstances, "Well, hello . . . did we have an appointment?"

She turned to face him and, sure enough, the face matched the body. "Or," he continued smoothly, "we could discuss your personal situation over dinner . . . at my place, perhaps . . . ?"

Then she spoke, and the voice cut right through him as she said, "I think, little dear, that sex with my half-brother is about as far as I wish to push the notion of incest."

His voice jumped an octave. "M-mother! My . . . my God," and he stepped back, stumbling into a chair he kept for clients and sitting down in it hard. "You're . . . that is . . . you're . . ."

"Younger?"

He bobbed his head. "I . . . didn't recognize you . . ."

"I surmised as much." She turned and looked around, pretending to be impressed. "You've been doing well for yourself, Modred."

"It's . . . it's Moe Dreskin now, Mother." He tried to sound cheery about it. "Who would believe a PR man named 'Dread?' "

She leveled her gaze upon him. "Who would believe the bastard son of King Arthur as a PR man named Dreskin? A PR man, Modred? Centuries you had lain out before you, like jewels in the sand . . . and you did nothing to exploit your longevity? Your thirst for power?"

"*Your* thirst for power, Mother. Me, I've learned the lessons of history. And the lessons say that the person at the top, sooner or later, falls off the top. I far prefer being in the background, making a healthy living manipulating those who are stupid enough to make themselves targets."

"Indeed," was all she said . . . but with that one word, her dripping contempt for her son spoke volumes.

He felt a bit weak in the knees, but he didn't like the

way his mother seemed to loom over him, and so he forced himself to walk past her. He leaned on his desk in what he hoped appeared to be a nonchalant fashion and said, "Last time I saw you, Mother, you looked like hell."

"Flatterer."

"So . . . have you been working out? What?"

She stared at him in open disbelief. "You can't truly be that obtuse. It's exactly what I told you, Modred. Arthur's returned. Providence set Merlin free from his imprisonment, and he in turn released Arthur from his. And they're here in New York."

"Yes, I know. Running for mayor."

He took grim satisfaction in the surprised look on her face. "How did you know that?" she demanded. "I hadn't told you that."

"I make it my business to know these things," he said airily. The truth was that he had stumbled upon Arthur's little pep rally purely by accident, but he wasn't about to admit that.

"Good. Now," she said briskly, "I am going to be endeavoring to attend to him, quickly and cleanly and—ideally—in the messiest fashion possible."

" 'Messiest?' "

She smiled nastily. "I still have resources, Modred. Creatures that are beholden to me, beasts of the night that I command. However, I wished to alert you personally, face-to-face, that I may have need of your aid as well."

He had known this was coming sooner or later, the moment he'd spoken to her on the phone. He had practiced the speech a hundred times in his head, and even so it was a physical effort for him to get it out. "It is . . . kind of you to think of me, Mother, but you don't seem to understand my situation."

"Situation," she repeated tonelessly.

"Yes. Situation." He was feeling more confident with each moment. "The simple truth, Mother, is that it was a thousand years ago. I had my revenge. I killed him. The fact that he returned doesn't change the fact that I avenged myself upon him. I did what I set out to do. I feel no need to do it again."

"You don't."

"No. I don't." Even though it didn't need it, Moe turned to a mirror hanging on the wall and adjusted his tie once more. It gave his hands something to do. "Revenge burns brightly for you, Mother dear, but for me it's the faintest of embers. And I don't see any need to stir them up. So if you'd be so kind as to leave me out of—"

Suddenly his image in the mirror changed. He was aging rapidly, horrifically, his skin wrinkling, teeth rotting away, eyes receding into their sockets, his hair whitening and falling out in clumps. And as he stood there, transfixed, staring in horror at himself, he heard his mother say with icy calm, "I would hate to think, my love, what it would be like for you if the friendly confines of my sorcery were to be removed. The years can be . . . merciless."

Modred let out a pitiable shriek and fell back, his hands going to his face. And then he discovered that, to his touch, his skin felt perfectly normal. Very slowly, as if afraid his face might fall off if he let go of it, he lowered his hands. It was everything he could do to look in the mirror, but when he did, he was rewarded with a reflection of his normal face.

He let out an unsteady breath, and then he turned and faced Morgan, managing a stiff bow. "Your servant . . . as ever, Mother."

"Good," she said calmly. "Cheer up, 'Moe Dreskin.' If my little catspaw does as he is supposed to, you won't even factor into this business. And if he doesn't, well then, my love . . ." and she rubbed her hands together, "It will be just like old times."

"Oh . . . joy," he said.

CHAPTRE
THE NINTH

✟

ARTHUR LOVED THE crackling of the torches that lined the wall of his castle. He loved the solid feeling of flagging beneath his feet, the cool touch of the stone wall against his hand. He loved the tapestries that hung upon those same stone walls, and the rich assortment of leather-bound books that lined the shelves. But most of all . . . he loved having the telephone in the castle. Oh, would that they had had such a glorious device back in the olden days. What a difference in his life it would have made.

The telephone rang, summoning him now, and of course there was only one person it could possibly be. Arthur grabbed up the telephone before the first ring had ended. "Hello, yes? Merlin!"

Merlin's voice was overwhelmed by traffic noises in the background. "Calm down, Arthur. You're not getting a call from the Messiah, after all."

"Merlin, where the devil have you been?" The excitement in his voice was not very king-like, but he didn't care a bit. "I haven't seen you in over a week. I have so much to tell you! Where are you? What are you doing? What are you up to?"

"Arthur, please! I don't understand," came Merlin's confused voice. "What's been happening? I mean, you've just been out getting signatures, haven't you? What could be so exciting about that? It's—"

"Oh, no, Merlin! It's gone beyond that. Way beyond that."

Merlin sounded extremely wary. "What are you talking about?" he said slowly.

Arthur sat back in his throne. Surrounded by the walls of his castle, he felt power surging through his body and spirit. "I," he said proudly, "have been politicking."

"You've been what!"

"Politicking. Getting people to like me. That was what you said we had to do, after all."

"Yes! We! In tandem, Arthur!" Merlin's voice sounded exceptionally put out, and Arthur wasn't pleased with the tone. "I didn't intend that you should go running about half-cocked!"

"I was not half-cocked, Merlin. I was—"

"Completely cocked?" he said disdainfully, and before Arthur could say anything Merlin continued, "Wart, who told you that it would be a good idea to start addressing . . . what, a few people?"

"No, crowds."

Merlin moaned. "Crowds. Why were you talking to crowds? You just got up and started spouting off?"

"Not exactly. Gwen fed me questions that—"

"Ohhh, Gwen. Of course, Gwen," Merlin moaned even louder this time. "I mean, naturally, if something related to you is going to become a complete and utter balls-up, then of course Gwen would have to be intimately involved with it."

Arthur frowned. "I don't think I like the tone of your voice, Merlin."

"Tone of my—"

"One would almost think that you were jealous that I was receiving aid from someone other than you."

"Then one would be an idiot," Merlin shot back tartly. "Arthur, what in the name of the gods have you been saying to the people? How did this start?"

"It began the first day I was out," said Arthur cheerily, as if relating the details of a thrilling game of cricket, and proceeded to describe in detail what had happened at the rally.

"I wish I was there to see your brilliance," Merlin said dryly.

"Oh, don't worry. You'll be able to. We videotaped the news broadcast that carried it. Remarkable things, these machines that enable you to tape—"

"News broadcast?!"

"Yes, they happened by. Asked me questions. I told them about my campaign. Excellent publicity, correct?"

"Are you out of your mind?"

Even though Merlin was speaking over the phone, Arthur bristled at the tone. "Merlin . . . do I need to remind you who, exactly, is the king?"

"Only if I'm entitled to remind you who is the wizard, the demon spawn, the one who sees the far destinies, the planner, the seer, the soothsayer, the—"

"All right, Merlin, I get the picture."

"No, that was merely the frame, Arthur. The picture is what we're now endeavoring to sketch in. We were to rehearse everything you were going to be saying. Have you forgotten all of that?"

"No," said Arthur. "No, I haven't." And his voice took on an edge hard as steel as he said, "But before you start throwing all your titles, or nicknames, or sobriquets at me, I think it would be good if I reminded you just who is going to be the next mayor of this state."

"City, you great barbarian oaf! Not state! You—"

Arthur slammed the phone down. He stared at the receiver for a long moment, snapped angrily, "You colossal pointy-hatted complicator of issues! I need have no truck with you! I can function perfectly adequately on my own."

Then he sat there in the dark of the castle, the main room illumined only by firelight, and stared at the phone. It didn't ring. He willed it to do so, commanded it to. It ignored him. Well, why not? Everything else did.

"I know," he said to no one. "I'll get up and walk out, and that will make the bloody thing start ringing." He got up and walked out of the throne room, and sure enough the phone started to ring again. The room remained empty, though, Arthur making no effort to hurry back. The phone rang a dozen times, and when Arthur finally came back in, the hem of his purple velvet dressing gown swished around on the floor, stirring up dust. He made a mental note to get the place swept, then stood there and let it ring another few times before he picked it up. But before he could get a word out Merlin said, sounding very small, "I'm sorry, Arthur."

Arthur hesitated, his eyes wide. His grip on the phone relaxed marginally. "Merlin," he said softly, "I think this is the first time you've ever apologized to me. About anything."

Merlin coughed slightly, sounding a bit more comfortingly surly. "I don't intend to make it a habit. And the only thing I'm apologizing for is the barbarian remark. Everything else stands. You're supposed to follow the script I've laid out."

"I'm not an actor, Merlin. I'm . . . a politician."

"Same difference. Listen, I'll be seeing you in a day or so. And I've got a new member for our group. He's going to be our accountant."

"Good man?"

"One of the best. Utterly dedicated."

Arthur felt a slight lurch inwardly, as if he should know what Merlin was talking about, and was frustrated that he didn't. "Where have you been for the past week or so?"

"Sobering him up and cleaning him off."

Arthur laughed. "What a sense of humor you have, Merlin. What did you do, pick him up off the street?"

"More or less."

Arthur nodded slowly. "Um, Merlin—I'm going to assume you know what you're doing. What's the fellow's name anyway?"

"Ohhh . . . I'd rather it be a surprise."

"Merlin, I can't say I like surprises."

At that, Merlin made a triumphant squawking noise. "Well, what do you know about that? His highness doesn't like surprises. Huzzah, huzzah. You know what, Arthur? Neither do I. Do you see now why I was less than ecstatic upon hearing about your little Times Square debut?"

Arthur's face flushed momentarily, although naturally Merlin couldn't see that. Or . . . who knew . . . maybe he could. He was still unclear on what Merlin's full abilities were, and that was enough to keep him in a perpetual feeling of unease. "It was Duffy Square, but all right, Merlin. Point taken. I shall endeavor not to allow myself to become swept up in the tide of events in the future."

"Thank you. I would appreciate that."

"So who is our accountant?"

Merlin paused a moment—for drama's sake, Arthur would later decide—and then said, "Percival."

It took a moment for the name to register, and when it did, Arthur could scarcely believe it. "Percival . . . *the* . . ."

". . . the Grail knight, yes. Percival. Who were you expecting, Galahad? Great, whining, virgin twit. Never had any patience for him. But Percival, well . . . he was cut from a very different bolt of cloth."

"Percival," Arthur said the name again in wonderment. "Still . . . alive? How is that possible?"

"You're asking that of me? You, of all people, asking me, of all people?"

"But I don't see how—?"

"I'm sure he'll be more than happy to tell you when you see him. He'll help watch your back, Arthur. And he'll keep you honest."

"What do you mean, honest?"

"I mean in the event you are tempted to do the wrong thing, for any reason, Percival will make certain you don't. He did the wrong thing exactly one time in his life, and has been paying for it ever since, so if anyone is sensitive to right and wrong, it is he." He paused. "It is him. Or is it . . . ?" Then he made an annoyed noise and muttered, "Damn language."

"Merlin . . . I have to ask . . . with my return, and yours, and now Percival . . . could Gwen Queen . . ."

"That last is a coincidence, Arthur, nothing more. Gwynyfar is dead, and the sooner you come to accept that, the better off all of us will be. Don't allow whimsies of happenstance to be confused with patterns of fate. Understood?"

"I suppose I'm just being wistful."

"Kings don't get wistful. 'Wist' isn't even a word. You can be prideful, scornful, hateful. You can't be full of something that doesn't even exist. Wist. Stupid concept: He's full of wist. Cannot happen. Do not dwell on it any further."

"Very well, Merlin," Arthur said evenly. "I won't wist time on it."

This time it was Merlin who hung up. Arthur grinned.

I T WAS DEATHLY quiet in Arthur's office at the Camelot Building that evening. Everyone, it seemed, had gone home, and the only noise to be heard was the squeaking of the wheels of the janitor's rolling trash can.

There was a rustling noise at the keyhole, although oddly enough no key was inserted. Then the door swung open and a figure stood in the doorway, glancing this way and that. It was a short but broadly built individual, and

strange, though it was, the flickering light from the outside hallway seemed to bend right around him. That had
to be the case, because the janitor who was heading off
down the hallway would certainly have made some sort
of noise had he actually noticed the individual standing
there. But he didn't notice or say anything, which was
probably just as well since the janitor had a wife and three
kids at home, and if he had spied the person in the doorway, he would have been very dead very quickly.

The dark figure stepped through the doorway, and the
door closed noiselessly, which was also fairly impressive
considering the hinges tended to squeak something fierce.
The dark figure squinted in the dimness. He was more or
less prepared to come back here every evening, for as long
as it took, because it was what *she* wanted and he but lived
to fulfill her desires. He was rather pleased to see, however,
a light flickering toward the back, from the area that he
would presume would be King Arthur's office.

His nostrils flared. Something felt . . . off. Then he realized what it was.

When he had been approaching the front door to the
offices, he had smelled rats along the way. Rats scuttling
in the walls, rats scouting for food behind the closed doors
of the other offices. But in this office, in the place that
was inhabited by Arthur Pendragon, there were no rats.
He couldn't understand why that might be. Not only did
he not smell rats, he didn't smell anything living. Which
made him wonder whether there really was anyone in the
back office, or if someone had just carelessly left the lights
on.

No . . . no, he definitely heard something. Heard it, but
didn't smell it. He pressed the bridge of his nose, blew
out, and tried to figure whether or not his sinuses were
congested. Then, very slowly, one foot gliding in front of
the other and making no sound, he crept toward the back
office. He found the door open, the light dim but more
than sufficient.

A woman was seated behind the desk. She looked as if she was waiting for him, with her fingers interlaced and folded neatly on the desktop. She had green eyes that glinted in the dimness.

"Hello," she said. "I'm Miss Basil."

"Hello," said the dark man uncertainly. Once more his nostrils flared, trying to pull in a whiff of her, endeavoring to seek her essence. Nothing. She might as well not have been there at all.

She smiled. "I know what you're trying to do," she told him, and she didn't rise from behind the desk so much as she seemed to uncoil. "I know who you are. I know what you are. But you do not know me, and you find that disturbing."

"Look, uhm . . . I can come back some other time," said the demon, chucking a thumb in the other direction. But the woman did not turn her gaze from him, and he was transfixed by it for reasons he couldn't understand.

"That would certainly be your intention. Why? To set some sort of trap that would snap upon Arthur? Or just to kill him outright? Yes, yes . . . that's the more likely. I know your type, and I know your master. You serve Morgan. As for me, I serve Merlin . . . for now. I am indentured to him for another decade or so. After that, I am free to kill him, or try to. Or perhaps I won't. I haven't decided yet."

"Who . . . are you?" The demon was beginning to be a bit disconcerted by the fact that he wasn't moving, feeling as if it was coming from outside him rather than within.

"You know. Don't you."

She smiled at him, and it was a terrible thing to see, and then he did know. His legs trembled, but still didn't move. "Ba . . . basiliskos . . . ," he whispered.

"Ah. You know my name of old. 'Little King,' it means, did you know that? Yes, I perceive that you did. You are an ancient Greek demon. So you would appreciate that it only seems appropriate that one king serve the needs of

another, does it not? Now . . . I know what you're thinking," she said as she came around the desk. "You're thinking that I'm supposed to be able to kill with my stare.
I'll tell you a secret: That's exaggeration. What I do . . .
merely seems like killing you. You see, demon . . . I perceive my victims for what they are. They have no secrets
from me. I look into them, through them, and in an instant, know all their most private aspects. Things that
they don't want anyone to know. Things that they themselves do not know about themselves. But I see it all, and
they know I do, and then they see it, too, and they'd rather
die than live with that knowledge. At which point . . . I
attend to it. Would you like a demonstration?"

The demon tried to shake his head, but couldn't. He
tried to run, but couldn't.

She looked at him, looked through him, and her eyes
went from green to jade green and then green flecked with
red. The dark creature sobbed deep in his throat, and his
bowels released, but since he wasn't human what dribbled
down his pants legs was more like a thick black tar, smok-
ing and burning a nasty little hole in the rug. The demon
then knew himself more than any demon could or should,
more than any living thing could or should.

"You want to die now, don't you," asked Miss Basil,
but it wasn't a question.

"Y-yes," stammered the demon.

"All right." And the Basilisk opened wide her elastic
jaw, her great snake form elongating, and she swallowed
him whole. After she had done so, she let out a long,
satisfied sigh, because it had been quite some time since
she'd had Greek food. She sat there all night, savoring the
fullness in her belly, feeling relaxed and languid but nevertheless alert, and when one foolish rat, not heeding the
warnings of others, strayed into the office, her tongue en-
folded him in less than a moment, and then he was gone,
providing a nice dessert.

Miss Basil decided she liked working in politics.

*   *   *

ERCIVAL BORE LITTLE superficial resemblance to
the man Merlin had found behind the library a week
ago. He was now dressed in a straight-arrow, three-piece,
black pinstripe suit. There was no trace of liquor on his
breath, although it had left a haunted look in his eyes.
He was neatly groomed, his fingernails trimmed. His eyes
were bloodshot, but Visine would take that away in time.
A cup of black coffee sat in front of him, the remains of
dinner strewn around the table.

"Why me?"

They were seated in a diner across the street from the
Camelot Building. Merlin sat opposite him. The waitress
kept giving him looks every time she walked by. He ignored them; he was used to it.

"Why you?"

Percival stared at him evenly. "You have to understand,
Merlin: When it first started, when it all first started . . .
I would never have had the nerve to ask you. You were
who you were, and I was . . ."

"We're still who we were, Percival."

He smiled mirthlessly. "Oddly enough, I remember
you as being a lot taller, Merlin."

"Very funny."

"And I'm not who I was. I've seen too much, done too
much. And I want to know . . . why me?"

"In what sense?"

"Why," said Percival patiently, "was I the one chosen
to find the Grail? Did you arrange it? Was it some . . .
some cosmic jest? Why was I blessed? Why was I cursed
to end up feeling an emptiness in my gut that only alcohol
could erase?"

"Don't whine at me, Percival. You were a knight. It's
unseemly." He looked down for a moment, composing his
thoughts. "In the time of Camelot, there came a period of
discontent. The knights became bored with the ideal of

chivalry and civilization. Arthur had achieved a goal, namely, the use of the power of knighthood for something other than hacking enemies into small bits of meat. Men were treating men like human beings, and women like chattel that needed protection, which was a damned sight better than the way both genders were being treated earlier."

Percival nodded. It wasn't as if this was news to him, but obviously the mage felt it important to bask in nostalgia.

Merlin poured himself another cup of coffee. "But, as human beings are wont to do, the knights wound up needing a new goal to stave off the oppression of boredom. So I gave you all one. You were to search for, find, and recover the Holy Grail. The cup from which Jesus Christ drank at the Last Supper . . . and which caught his blood at the crucifixion."

"Why? Why the Grail, though?"

Merlin shrugged. "I don't know. It was the first thing that popped into my mind. It was either that or the Holy Plate. It hardly mattered what I came up with, as long as it was something to keep what I laughingly refer to as the knights' 'minds' occupied . . . no offense."

"None taken," said Percival, although he was feeling pretty damned offended about then. "So you're saying . . . that the entire quest for the Grail was the equivalent of busywork?"

"In essence, yes. I knew the legends of the Grail, but I didn't think it really existed. I thought it *might*, but there also *might* be flying saucers and the Loch Ness monster and honest used-car dealers and whatever other fantasies the human mind is capable of conjuring. What I'm saying is that I thought I was just exploiting a fantasy, a myth. I would have said anything to delay the splintering of the Round Table. I didn't know you'd actually go and find the damned thing! When all the others gave up . . . you found it."

"At the tree at the end of the world," whispered Percival, remembering it all. It was ten centuries agone, but he could still feel the chill wind in his lungs . . . still hear the hiss of the great serpent wrapped around the tree, the sizzling sound of the dripping venom as it thrust at him. "And I brought it back to Arthur, and . . ."

"And you saved his life," Merlin said softly. "For all that has happened since, for all you feel that the poets and scribes didn't give you your due . . . you know what happened. You know that Modred mortally wounded Arthur. That if you had not returned when you did, and he had not drunk from the cup of Christ, he would have died."

"Right . . . right . . . and look how I was repaid," Percival said bitterly. "I did great deeds . . . but one mistake . . . one mistake . . ."

Merlin leaned back in his seat, and there was impatience in his face. "You're whining again. Percival, not only did no one tell you drink from the Grail, but the Lady of the Lake specifically told you *not* to. To simply put it back where it was. But you could not resist, could you? Could you?"

He knew that Merlin was right, and couldn't look him in the eyes. "No," he said so softly that it was barely audible. "But I didn't do it for personal gain. I wasn't wounded. I just . . . wanted to drink from the cup that the Christian Savior drank from. To see if I could connect with one who preached peace, but in whose name so many have died. How could I have known that—"

"You couldn't have, which is why doing something when you don't know the consequences is damned foolishness," said Merlin. "The Grail cures injuries if one is injured. If one is not injured, then the Grail's healing properties retard all of the body's tendencies to break down. Retards it to such a slow pace that the one who drinks from it is functionally immortal."

Percival shook his head. "I didn't know . . . I didn't

know," he whispered. Then he looked to Merlin. "Can you help me? Die, I mean?"

"I can," Merlin said calmly. "Do you wish to die now . . . at the time when Arthur has his greatest need? After centuries of waiting, and not truly knowing what you were waiting for . . . is this the outcome that you've been seeking? Or is the dedication of the Grail knight truly as mythic as the Grail itself was intended to be?"

Percival slammed his open hands on the table, rattling the plates and startling other customers, who looked at him nervously. He drew in a breath, steadying his nerves. "You are a true bastard, magician."

"You couldn't even begin to grasp my parentage, Percival. And you haven't answered my question."

He looked down, frustrated. "I will serve . . . in whatever capacity I am needed."

"Good."

There was silence between them for a time, and then Merlin said, sounding casual, "Tell me . . . after you drank from the Grail . . . what happened to the cup itself?"

"I don't know," said Percival. "For centuries I've wondered that very thing. I will tell you this, though . . . it was . . . so strange. I drank from the cup in a place that was barren, parched. Only a tiny brook ran through it, providing me the liquid with which to fill the holy cup. I drank . . . and there was an explosion of light behind my eyes such as I have never seen before or since. When I awoke, the land around me was lush and plentiful . . . but the Grail was gone. Unfortunately, its effect on the land was not to be as long-lasting as its effect on me, for when I came through those same parts a year or so later, the land was once again barren." Then he noticed grim amusement in Merlin's eyes. "What?"

"Percival, you idiot," sighed Merlin. "The land *was* the Grail. It changed shape."

"What?" he said again.

"You were standing on the Grail. After it had its effect

on you, it transformed itself into the land. The Grail can do that. It has four shapes," and he ticked them off on his fingers, "the cup . . . the land . . . the sword . . . and the belt. Each form has different abilities and different blessings. If you had simply remained where you were, sooner or later the Grail would have shifted back into a more recognizable shape, and would have been in your possession. As it is . . ." And he shook his head.

"As it is, what?"

"As it is, after you departed, sooner or later someone came along and took the Grail. Either it had shifted back into something more recognizable, or the person who took it was so powerful that they were able to perceive it for what it was, even as the land."

"Who? Who did it?" asked Percival anxiously.

"I don't know," Merlin told him regretfully. "As much as I am loath to admit it, Percival, there are some things even my power does not allow. Probably because I had dealings with the dark arts. That was a double-edged sword. It enabled me to withstand the doings of Morgan, to fight fire with fire . . . but employing such arcanna as Satan would find delightful forever binds me from having dealings with the purely divine. I cannot detect the Grail or its whereabouts now, Percival . . . nor am I about to send you out on a quest to find it. We have other, more pressing problems."

"Such as?" Percival said with a growing sense of urgency, feeling the old need to accomplish greatness surging within him. "For what do you require my services?"

"For starters, you have to balance our books. They're a mess."

Percival stared blankly at him. "You're joking."

"No, I'm not. You have considerable accounting skills, do you not?"

"Merlin, I've lived a thousand years. I have skills in many things. Granted, number crunching was my most recent vocation before I got bored with it . . . as I get bored with everything sooner or later. Immortality will do that to you. But why—?"

"Because it wasn't simply a matter of your getting bored with it, was it? You were a good accountant. One of the best," said Merlin evenly. "Worked for a big firm and discovered irregularities—funds disappearing for which you could not account. You discovered a higher-up, a man you respected tremendously, had been jerking the company around. He fed you a sob story that wrenched your heart. Ever sympathetic to the human condition, you agreed to cover for him. And you did, until the auditors found it. But the higher-up managed to pin the whole thing on you. Fired. Disgraced. No one would hire you. Your world in the toilet, you had no goal to achieve. So you sought escape in a bottle—"

"That's enough," Percival warned him.

Merlin bobbed his head in acknowledgment, but then said softly, "We have odd sources of income, Percival. Converting gold and jewelry to money and such. I need someone that I can work with who will make it seem less odd. Someone I can trust. That's you. Are you with me or not?"

Percival let out a long, incredulous sigh, and then shook his head.

"Why couldn't the Christian Savior have drank from a paper cup and crumbled the thing?" he muttered.

"Cheer up, Percival," Merlin said. "I have a new goal for you. The election of Arthur, your former king, to a position that will be his stepping stone to creating a new order of peace and greatness for mankind. And you will serve as something very important, Percival." He stabbed a finger at him. "You're going to set an example for Arthur. So he won't get distracted."

"Distracted? By what?"

"There are," Merlin said with a sigh, "certain aspects of the human condition which are eternally recreated. One such is evil, although if its personification exists reincarnated in this time, I have yet to find it. That worries me. But another aspect has already manifested itself. And poses a threat."

"What would that be?"

With barely a trace of bitterness, Merlin said, "The eternal ability of the human race to make a muddle of the best laid plans. A shapely monkey wrench has entered the works, and Arthur has cheerfully put it into the tool-box." He shook his head in wonderment. "Sometimes I think there's just no understanding that man, no matter how many centuries I know him."

CHAPTRE
THE TENTH

ARTHUR WAS IN tremendous spirits when he came into the office the next morning. "Good morning, Miss Basil!" he said cheerfully to the receptionist. "You're looking like the cat who swallowed the canary this morning!"

She looked up at him with less than a kindly expression. "Guess again. By the way . . . I can't stand it."

"Miss Basil, my sweet, nothing is going to dampen my mood. Not even you." He leaned over her desk and whispered conspiratorially, "But exactly what is it that you can't stand, hmmm?"

"First you have those two drug-addicted freaks out beating the drums for you—"

"Are you referring to Elvis and Buddy, two of my most dedicated helpmates?" he asked archly.

"Right, the freaks. Then you hire that shrinking violet to be your personal assistant, and already she's calling in sick—"

Arthur frowned at that. "Sick, you say? She seemed quite healthy just the other day."

"Well, she called, and she's not coming in." Basil shoved the piece of paper on which she had taken the message over to Arthur. He picked it up, glanced at it, and his frown deepened. "Get Gwen—Miss Queen—on the phone for me, if you please." But then he saw that she seemed distracted. "What's wrong?"

"Someone is heading this way."

"Well, this is a place of business," Arthur said reasonably. "Perhaps it's someone who wants to conduct business with us."

But Basil shook her head. "It's someone who wishes to prevent you from obtaining your goals. I can smell it from here. Someone who inhales lies and exhales insincerity with stunning ease."

The door was thrust open. A ruggedly handsome man stood in the doorway. He was tilting his chin slightly in one direction, presenting his good side. His graying hair was meticulously coifed, his chin had a perfectly positioned cleft, and in Arthur's opinion the man looked better in a suit than just about any other man on the planet. Several print and TV reporters were right behind him as if they'd been born there.

He looked Arthur up and down and then held out a hand. As he did so, still cameras flashed and TV cameras recorded. "Kent Taylor!" he said with impressive exuberance, "actor and politician!"

"Well, that explains the lying and insincerity," muttered Basil. "Damn this eternal accuracy of mine."

For a moment Arthur had thought that the newcomer thought that he, Arthur, was named Kent Taylor, but quickly realized that he was introducing himself. "Arthur Penn," he said, gripping the hand firmly.

Taylor looked a bit surprised. "Solid grip you have there, Art."

"Arthur," Arthur corrected him gently.

"Not going to go all formal on me, I hope," Taylor said. He sounded to Arthur like someone who was constantly addressing a back row in a theater that wasn't there. "Maybe you'd prefer, 'Your highness.' "

"It's not necessary," Arthur assured him, and then added softly after a moment, "anymore."

But Taylor didn't hear him, or if he did, he wasn't paying attention. He turned to the cameras and said, "Gentlemen, ladies, I'd like to confer with Mr. Penn alone, if that's all right. So take five, everyone, okay?" There were a few half-hearted attempts at shouted questions, but a fearsome look from Miss Basil silenced them, and they allowed themselves to be herded out the door. "Sorry about the press boys," he said when the door to the hall was closed. "They follow me wherever I go. Wish I could do something about it, but . . . I'm me," he shrugged, as if caught up in something that was far greater than he could hope to control. Then he added, "I hope I haven't been overly presumptuous."

"It's a little late to start worrying about that," Basil said, making no attempt to hide her irritation.

"Don't concern yourself about it," said Arthur, "or about Miss Basil here. Why don't we talk in my inner office? Miss Basil, do try to get in touch with Gwen for me, would you?" Basil scowled, and Arthur had a feeling that the chances were fifty–fifty at most that he would be picking up the phone and finding Gwen on the other end anytime soon.

He led Kent Taylor to the back office and left the door open. He went around the desk to his chair and sat, tilting back in a relaxed fashion and gesturing for Taylor to sit. Taylor remained standing, hands folded behind his back, looking around the office at pictures and objects of art— the wall-mounted swords and armored helmet. "So," said Taylor after a few moments of silence, "you've seen me on *City Hall*, I take it."

Arthur gave him a politely blank look. "Should I have?"

Kent Taylor laughed and pointed an approving finger at Arthur. "Good for you. Television's a useless waste of mental processes. And our show was no great shakes. But, to be honest, I couldn't be where I am without it."

"You couldn't be in my office?"

Taylor laughed uproariously this time, as if Arthur had said the funniest thing in the world. "I like the way you play dumb, Arthur!"

"Thank you. The effect does not come without practice," replied Arthur, wondering whether or not he'd made a serious blunder letting this man into his office.

Taylor leaned forward, resting his hands on Arthur's desk. "Art, let's be honest, shall we?"

"That is the only way I can be."

"Well, that's going to make you unique in politics. But then, I guess I shouldn't be surprised, huh? The news coverage on you so far makes you come across as a little, well . . . hey, you got money?"

"Some. Why?" asked Arthur, momentarily nonplussed.

"Well, then the word's 'eccentric.' If you got money, you're eccentric. Otherwise, you're just plain crazy." Taylor laughed and Arthur joined in uncomfortably. When his self-induced humor had subsided, Taylor continued, "I think what you're doing here is great. The whole thing with an independent party, a little guy trying to go up against the big guys. I think that's all great, really great."

"Yes, so you've said. Great."

Taylor gave no indication that he heard the sarcasm in Arthur's voice. "I've just about got the Democratic nomination for mayor all sewn up. It's a done deal and, frankly, it's time we got this city back into Democratic hands. You with me so far?"

"I believe even one such as I, with my limited cranial capacity, could be following you, yes."

"Now I'm in a pretty good situation here." He smiled, clearly pleased with himself, and it rapidly became evident to Arthur that he was stating, not his own opinions, but those of others. "Thanks to *City Hall*, my demographics, my Q rating, all of it is sky high."

"And . . . that's good?" For Arthur it was clearly a question, but Taylor apparently didn't hear the curious upturn in his voice at the end of the sentence.

"That's exactly right that it's good," Taylor said forcefully. "You know what they call me already? 'The Acting Mayor.' You can't buy that kind of publicity. However, my people assure me that if it comes down to Bernie Keating and me, it's going to be a tight race, nevertheless. He's very, very popular, and you didn't hear that from me."

"I didn't?"

"No."

"But you just said it."

Taylor smiled thinly. "Forget that I did."

"I doubt that I can," said Arthur in his most reasonable tone. "And let us say, by some miracle, I was able to do so . . . why, then, that begs the question of why you told me in the first place."

Taylor looked at him very oddly. "Is English a second language to you there, Art?"

"No," said Arthur pointedly, "but oftentimes I get the feeling that it's a second language for Americans."

Taylor blinked a few times, clearly not getting it, and Arthur could almost see the mental process at work that prompted him instead to shift gears. "Here's the point," he said, apparently deciding that not getting to it was proving counterproductive. "The news media seems to like you. You're getting news coverage; small, but in hip venues."

"That's nice to hear."

"And in my experience, this kind of thing can snowball if it's not monitored. You can't possibly get enough votes to win, Arthur. You must know that."

"Do I?" said Arthur, his eyebrow raised.

"You're trying to build an independent party, and I can totally respect that. But in the final analysis, a vote for you is the same as a vote for your opponent. Because there's simply no way that you're going to pull in enough votes with your fringe ideas and amateurish notions—no offense meant—to do anything other than draw votes away from me. You'll be hurting the best man for the job while having no chance of your own to get in."

"Is that a fact?" Arthur said. Behind his desk, he might as well have been made of ice for all the emotion he was showing.

"Yes, I'm afraid it is. On the other hand, another fact is that—if the nice media people want to keep talking to you, and you endorsed the Democratic Party and the ideas of—"

"I would endorse any idea that overlaps with mine, but otherwise I would only support my own concepts, Mr. Taylor," Arthur said evenly, rising from behind the desk. "And although you claimed to mean no offense, I nevertheless *do* take offense at such comments as 'fringe ideas' and 'amateurish notions.' First and foremost, sir, I treasure honesty. Honesty in those who work under me, honesty in those whom I encounter. I do not suffer fools gladly, and the deceitful I treasure even less. I find you patronizing and annoying, and utterly lacking in respect."

It was that last comment that seemed to generate the most amusement for Taylor. "Art . . ." He stopped when he saw Arthur's clouding face and amended, "Mr. Penn . . . again, no offense intended, but if what you're looking for is respect, you're running for mayor of the wrong town. This isn't Paducah. This is New York City, the home of cynicism and dissing. If you think for even one moment that you're going to be accorded the kind of respect you seem to believe is your due, then you're going to be bitterly disappointed."

At that moment the door to Arthur's office opened and Merlin walked in, side-by-side with a beefy black man, who took one look at the standing Arthur and promptly went to one knee with bowed head. "Highness," he said.

Taylor's jaw dropped as he looked from the black man

to Arthur and then back. Then he made a tactical mistake: He laughed. "This is a joke, right?" he demanded of the kneeling man. "Is this a joke? I mean, no African-American I know bends a knee to anyone. The subservient thing went out a hundred years ago—*aggghhhh!*"

That last comment came as a result of Taylor suddenly finding himself being grabbed by the right ear and dragged to the ground alongside the kneeling man, who was glaring fiercely into Taylor's face. "You will show courtesy and respect due to my lord," he said tightly.

"Yes, I . . . I love God! I go to services every Sunday! The archdeacon endorses me! Not the face, not the face!" Taylor was babbling.

"Percival, let him up," Arthur said gently. "And you too, get up. It's unseemly. As Mr. Taylor pointed out, after all, this is New York. Not . . . somewhere else."

"Are you certain, highness?" Percival did not look pleased at the order.

Arthur smiled. "Yes, I'm afraid I am. And I think 'Mr. Penn' will do. Now release him."

Percival did as he was instructed. Taylor backed up, his gaze darting frantically among them. Then he pointed a trembling finger at Arthur. "You're . . . you're crazy!"

"I thought I was eccentric," Arthur said mildly.

"I'm . . . I'm going to tell everyone that—"

"That a black man abused you?" It was Merlin who had spoken, and he sounded quite amused by the notion. "By all means, do. And by the time we're finished responding, the entire black community of New York will decide that you're a racist for accusing Arthur's 'African-American' right-hand man of being some sort of thug. By the way, Mr. Taylor, you have no African-Americans, Latinos, or Asians on your staff. Why is that?"

Taylor looked like he'd been pole-axed. "Who is *this*?"

"My manager," Arthur said without hesitation. "Was there anything else, Mr. Acting Mayor?"

Straightening his tie, endeavoring to regain his composure, Taylor said calmly, "No. No, I don't think so. It's been a . . . unique pleasure, Mr. Penn."

"Yes, it has. Oh, and Mr. Taylor," Arthur said almost as an afterthought as Taylor was about to leave. "Don't forget: Vote early, vote often."

Taylor didn't deign to reply as he walked out the door. As soon as he was gone, Arthur turned his attention back to Percival. Although inwardly he was amused, he couldn't let it show. "Percival, that was inappropriate."

"I'm sorry, highness," Percival said, bowing his head slightly. And then, to his surprise as much as anyone's, he laughed softly. "It caught me off guard a little, I have to admit. After all these years, I didn't expect that I was going to . . . well . . . switch into the mode of the dutiful knight. Some habits, it appears, are harder to break than others."

"Understood. But it is a different time and place. We should take care to act in accordance with the local mores. I value your good right arm and your dedication, Percival. Plus Merlin tells me you're a gifted accountant."

"A thousand years is enough to pick up a variety of skills, highness," Percival said modestly.

Arthur's voice took on a more serious tone. "And Percival, I can only imagine what it was like for you, all these years. I was in isolation . . . but, I suspect, of the two of us, it was harder for you."

"Why, highness?" asked Percival, unable to keep a hint of bitterness from his voice. He was standing now, but unmoving, like a storm hovering just off the coast of a town. "Just because any relationship I undertook was doomed from the start? Because after the first couple of times watching a woman I loved age away from me, I swore never to let myself love again? Because I never sired a child . . . and even if I had, I would have had to endure the same wretched loneliness of immortality? Because I had to watch mankind, capable of achieving greatness, spend its existence engaging in pointless war and violence,

over and over, as if we're all condemned to repeat a cycle
of insane self-destruction? Because there's no greater loneliness than being alone in a crowd? Because of all that,
highness?"

Arthur found that there was nothing to say to that, and
so, very wisely, he said nothing. He simple clapped Percival once on the shoulder and then called, "Miss Basil!
I'm waiting for you to get Gwen on the phone!"

Basil appeared at the door. She didn't walk over to it
and stand in it; she just seemed to appear there. "I tried,"
she said tersely. "She said she couldn't come in. That she
didn't know when she'd be in. And if you wanted to fire
her over it, she'd understand."

Arthur was now utterly perplexed, but the lines of his
face quickly settled into a certainty of his next action.
"Get me her address. I'm going over there."

"No. You're not," said Merlin.

"Yes, I am, and what business is it of yours?" Arthur
turned to face him, his arms folded across his chest.

"Arthur," Merlin said with as much patience as he
could muster, "Don't you go after her."

"She's in trouble, Merlin. I can sense it."

"This is the 21st century, Arthur. If a woman's in trouble, she has options other than waiting for a hero to come
rescue her."

"That's true, highness," Percival said.

"See?" Merlin pointed at Percival, clearly grateful for
the backup.

Continuing to think out loud, Percival said, "Of course
. . . there *are* women who are trapped in abusive relationships and are unable to do anything about it, for any number of deep-seated psychological reasons, ranging from a
misplaced belief that they can change the man to self-
esteem problems that compel them to believe that they
deserve—"

"All right, that's more than sufficient help, Percival,"
Merlin said.

Arthur had heard enough. "Miss Basil, Gwen's address. Now. *I saw that!*"

"Saw what?" Basil said quickly.

"You looked to Merlin for confirmation as to whether you should do what I say. Merlin is not in charge here. I am. You will do as I say, and you will do it now. Is that clear?"

Basil started to reply, then saw the look in Arthur's face and clearly thought better of it. "I'll be right back with it," she said, and turned on her heel.

"Arthur," Merlin began.

"Don't say it, Merlin."

"I will say it, Arthur. If Gwen is having a problem, give her time. She's going to have to deal with it herself."

Arthur looked at him uncertainly. "My every instinct—"

"Your instincts," Merlin said, not ungently, "have been known to cross you up every now and again. Arthur, I've never known a man of a more decisive, unyielding nature than you—except where it came to women. They are your fatal flaw. Especially this—" Then his eyes widened and he stopped talking.

Too late.

"What . . . do you mean?" Arthur said slowly. He was walking slowly toward Merlin, regarding him as if truly seeing him for the first time.

"Nothing. I was going to say, 'Especially this time.' "

"No . . . no, you weren't," Arthur said, looming over Merlin, who was, surprisingly, backing up. "You were going to say, 'Especially this one,' weren't you?"

"I was simply trying to say—"

"Merlin, from the moment I laid eyes upon her, I knew, I sensed in my soul, that there was something about her. Perhaps it's ridiculous to believe in reincarnation, but is it any more unlikely than believing in an ageless wizard, a king kept alive by sorcery, or the powers of the Holy Grail granting immortality?"

"It's not her! I swear to you, Arthur, if it was Gwen's soul, brought back to you in a brand new package, I would know! I would know, and I would tell you!"

"Would you? Look at me, Merlin," and his gaze seemed to bore straight into the wizard. "Would you? Or would you try to do exactly what you've done? Discourage me from having anything to do with her. Tell me not to hire her, tell me to keep away from her, denigrate her."

"She's a harmless, normal, nonreincarnated woman!" Merlin said desperately.

"Then she poses no threat, and you won't care that I'm going over."

"*No!*"

Suddenly Arthur turned to Percival and said, "Percival, my understanding is that drinking from the cup of Christ, in addition to giving an uninjured person immortality, also gives one substantial protection from magiks . . . especially magiks that have base in darkness. True?"

"So I am told, highn—Mr. Penn," said Percival.

"Good. Break Merlin's neck for me, would you?"

Both Percival and Merlin gaped at Arthur. "What?"

"I am your liege, lord," Arthur said sharply, although he never raised his voice, "your king, to whom you swore undying fealty and obedience. You are alive, as am I. That oath is still in force. Do as I command."

Without hesitation, Percival took two quick steps forward, lifted Merlin off his feet and slammed him back against the wall, placing his hands in such a way as to snap the young mage's neck like a twig.

And in a voice filled with fury and fear, Merlin screeched, "*Yes! Yes, damn you! It's her! But you don't need her, Arthur! She's going to bugger the whole works, just like she did last time! She's the eternal screwup!*"

"I don't care if she's the eternal bloody flame," Arthur snapped. "We belong together!"

"You belong in an asylum!" Merlin's legs pumped furiously. "Tell him to put me down!"

"Release him, Percival, but not gently."

Percival obediently drew back his arm and flung the boy wizard the length of the office. Merlin slammed into the large sofa and rebounded onto the floor. He lay there, moaning.

Without another word Arthur turned and stormed out of the office, pausing only to snatch the address of Gwen's apartment off Miss Basil's desk. Basil, for her part, had come to the door of the office when she heard the commotion and was staring at Merlin, who was staggering to his feet and rubbing his throat. He glared at Percival who returned the look impassively. "I scrape you up off the gutter . . . and this is how you repay me?" he croaked.

"I repaid you by doing what you wanted me to do: serve Arthur Pendragon," Percival pointed out calmly. "I can't help it if he gives me orders that run contrary to your interests."

"Should I try to stop him, Merlin?" inquired Basil.

Merlin shook his head and winced at the pain that the gesture inflicted.

"Uh, Merlin . . . I know I'm not your favorite person just now, but if it's okay, I'd like to offer a piece of advice."

Slowly Merlin turned his head to Percival. "And what . . . might that be?"

"If Arthur convinces Gwen to come back with him, I wouldn't get in his way if I were you."

"Point . . . taken, Percival."

At that moment Buddy and Elvis burst in, stumbling over each other in their excitement. "We got it," crowed Buddy. "We have got freakin' it!"

"What?" asked Merlin impatiently.

"Signatures, kiddo!" They waved sheaves of paper in their filthy hands. "We got enough! All you need and lots more. Arthur, the guy with the Day-Glo sword, is now officially a candidate for mayor of New York!"

They stood there, arms spread wide, as if accepting thunderous applause. There was dead silence.

"Well," grumbled Elvis, "don't thank us all at once, y'know."

CHAPTRE
THE ELEVENTH

✝

GWEN HAD MANAGED to stop crying, but her face
was still tear-streaked as she fumbled in her purse
for her apartment keys. She breathed silent invocations,
thinking, *Please, please, please let him still be asleep.*

She fished out her keys, unlocked the door, and stepped
inside the dimly lit apartment. She glanced around at the
empty living room and sighed with relief. She didn't
know where he was, and she didn't care. At least he wasn't
at home. After getting the call from Miss Basil, wanting
to know where she was, she had to get out for just a few
minutes. She'd felt as if the walls were closing in on her,
and she knew that if she stayed there a moment longer,
she would just start screaming and never stop. That would
certainly wake Lance, and he wouldn't be happy about
that at all. But if he woke up and discovered that she'd
gone out, that would also infuriate him.

Lance stepped out of the bedroom, his hands on his
hips. "So. You came back, did you?"

Gwen moaned and moved away from the door. She
pulled the sunglasses off and tossed them carelessly on the

floor, as she staggered over to a chair and sagged into it. "I just went down to the corner for some beer," she said.

"So where is it?"

"They were out," she replied tiredly, too mentally exhausted and aching to come up with anything even approaching a decent lie.

Lance walked over to her, laughing loudly, and took her chin in his hand, turning her head one way and then the other. "Quite a shiner you got."

"I know. It's the birthday present you forgot to give me last month, right?"

"Now, now," he said and swaggered away. "There's no need to get bitter. After all, you brought it on yourself."

"Me!" She lurched to her feet, feeling the familiar sting of tears at her eyes and fighting them off. "You're the one who came home drunk last night. Boozing and . . . and sleeping with whores. God knows what germs you picked up."

"Whores!" His voice went up an octave. "How can you say that? How can you say I was getting laid by strange women?"

"You reeked of cheap perfume."

He snorted. "I can't help it if women cling all over me."

"Lance, your pants were on backward! Why did you come home to me with your pants on backward?"

"It was a joke, for chrissakes."

"No, Lance." She shook her head furiously, thinking about the job that she had probably lost, and thinking also of the man for whom she worked . . . the man whom she felt as if she'd known all her life. "This whole relationship is a joke. And I'm the punch line. Especially when you came home the way you did last night, and you wanted to make love to me all reeking and disgusting. And when I refused you did this to me." She pointed at her eye. "You did this. Not me. You!"

"Yeah?" He got louder, angrier, and he advanced on

her, his fist clenching and unclenching. "And I can do it again. And again. I'm tired of your superior attitude. I thought you understood me. But you're just ignorant, like all the rest. Ignorant! But I'm gonna teach you!"

"Teach me? Teach me what!" she said defiantly. "Hit me again and swell both my eyes shut, so you can teach me not to look at you! Because you're disgusting! Look at what you've become!" It all spilled out of her, everything she'd been bottling up. "When I met you, you were bigger than the whole world. You were young and confident and full of fire! And I keep praying that the Lance that I fell in love with will return somehow. But he's not coming back! All you're doing is dragging me down with you! I can live on love. But I can't live on pointless hope anymore! I can't!"

He shoved her hard, and she hit the floor. "Big man!" she spat out. "Show who's tougher! We're the two biggest losers in the world. And the really sick thing is, I don't deserve better than you!"

"I'm going to show you what you deserve," Lance shot back. He swung his fist back. Gwen shrieked, throwing up her hands to defend herself.

Suddenly the front door was smashed open, wood splintering everywhere. Arthur stood in the door frame, and there was cold fury in his eyes.

Lance took one look at the intruder, grabbed a steak knife off a nearby table and charged. Arthur effortlessly sidestepped, grabbed the knife hand at the wrist, and drove a knee into Lance's gut. Lance gasped, unable to draw a breath, and Arthur tossed him like a sack of bones across the apartment, sending him crashing to the floor.

He turned and looked at Gwen with infinite sadness, as if seeing something that he had fully expected. "What happened to you?" he asked.

Operating on reflex—a reflex that told her to cover for Lance whenever possible—Gwen stammered out, "I . . . I . . . punched myself in the eye."

"You hit your*self*?"

"Yes."

"In the eye?"

"That's right."

He shook his head sadly. "Why in God's name would you do that?"

"I was aiming at my nose and I missed."

Arthur's attention swiveled back to Lance, who was going for the fallen steak knife again. Gwen's eyes widened in shock as Arthur, still nattily attired in a royal-blue, three-piece suit, reached to his left hip under his coat. For a moment she thought he was about to draw a gun. Instead there was the smooth sound of metal on metal as a gleaming sword was drawn from its sheath, seeming to appear in his hand like magic. In the dimness of the apartment the sword glowed with a life all its own. Lance scuttled back, crablike, toward the wall, never taking his terrified eyes from the darkly furious face of the man standing over him. Arthur knocked a lamp out of the way with a sweep of the sword, advancing on Lance until the frightened man could back up no farther. He pulled his knees up to his chin like a frightened child.

"You . . . you wouldn't kill an unarmed man?" he managed to say.

"Not a man," Arthur said. "No. But you . . . you little pissant . . ."

He drew back his sword, ready to strike. Gwen cried out, "No!!"

Arthur looked to her and said, his contempt for Lance clear in his voice, "You would spare this . . . this thing?"

"Please," she whispered, her eyes fixed upon the gleaming blade. "The moment I saw that sword, my whole life . . . made sense . . . if you kill him, you're a murderer, and nothing will make sense anymore . . . I can't go back to that . . . I can't . . . don't make me."

Arthur took two steps back and sheathed the sword. Lance let out a long, unsteady breath, but it caught in his throat as Arthur said, "If you ever raise a hand to this woman . . . or any other woman . . . I shall cut it off. Then I will make you eat it. Do we understand each other?" Lance managed a nod, but not much more than that.

Arthur turned to face Gwen, who was still looking at him in wonderment. "Why?" he asked.

She couldn't look at him, but she wrapped her arms around his neck. "Why what?" she whispered.

"Why did you stay here?"

"I had nowhere else to go."

He basked in the warmth of her body, held close to him. "Now you do."

He walked with her to the door. He looked back at Lance who still cowered in the corner, then smiled again and said, "Have a nice day," and left with Gwen on his arm.

They went down to the street, and Arthur called "Taxi!" to the first unoccupied cab he saw. The cab swung over to the curb, and they popped into the back. As Arthur pulled the door shut behind them, Gwen said, "I couldn't believe it. I just couldn't believe when you whipped out your sword—"

"Hey!" said the cabbie angrily. "I know this is New York, but let's keep the filthy talk to a minimum, okay?"

"Yes, sir," said Arthur meekly. He glanced over at Gwen and winked, and she smiled. It was her first real smile in weeks.

"So you two lovebirds want to tell me where you're going?"

"Yes," said Arthur. "Central Park."

"Sounds good." The car eased its way into the busy lunch hour traffic.

"Central Park?" said Gwen. "What's there?"

"My home away from home."

"Oh." She paused. "Thank you. About not hurting Lance."

Arthur turned and looked at her with surprise. "His name is Lance?"

"Yes. Why?"

"No reason," he said grimly. "Just . . . sick coincidence, I suppose. As for Lance, the only reason I didn't hurt him was because you asked me not to. But he hurt you."

"I suppose in a way he was right. I had only myself to blame. Because I let him get away with it. But never again."

"That's the way I like my queen to talk."

She took a deep breath, and then said, "The sword . . . it was Excalibur, wasn't it."

The surprise was evident in his face. He seemed both astonished and relieved that she was one step ahead of what he was going to say.

She looked up at him dreamily. "I'm really your queen? You're really—"

"Yes. I am."

"And I'm really—"

"I think so."

"How can we know for certain?"

Arthur smiled. "We'll think of something."

YE OLDE SOUND BITE

✦

"Firefighters responded quickly to the blaze and were able to extinguish it within a matter of minutes. No one was hurt. And now Louise Simonson brings us up to date on the doings of New York's most offbeat candidate for mayor. Louise?"

"Thank you, Walter. Well, it was certainly the most unorthodox beginning to a mayoral campaign in recent times. He calls himself Arthur Penn, he is a self-described "Independent" candidate, and his ideas are, well, novel. First drawing attention to himself by climbing atop a statue in Duffy Square and putting forth intriguing and—some say— lunatic ideas about capital punishment, it was today announced that he has gained the requisite signatures to officially enter the race for mayor. The campaign managers of front-runners Kent Taylor and Bernard Keating had no comment other than to say that they welcomed all comers . . . even, according to DA Keating, the 'clearly nutso' ones."

CHAPTRE
THE TWELFTH

†

B ERNARD B. KEATING was accustomed to coming
out of court rooms and being surrounded by the
press. He smiled now into the cameras as they crowded
around him on the steps of the big marble building he'd
just left. Bernard struck a dramatic pose, one hand jaun-
tily on his ample hip, his head cocked to one side, a smile
plastered across his face. Moe floated unobtrusively in the
background.

Bernard waited for questions about his plans for his
campaign, his opinions on the current hot issues, his plans
for the city if elected. And it was a tribute to Bernard B.
Keating's skill as a politician that he did not turn and
slug the questioner when the first question out of a reporter's mouth was, "What do you think of Arthur Penn's
chances in the upcoming mayoral race?"

"He's made quite a splash with his soapbox speeches,
Bernie," shouted the reporter from Channel 4 news. "And
some of the proposals he's made are real unorthodox. Do
you have any comment on—"

Bernard waved off the question and managed to keep

his smile glued on his mouth. "Now boys, I have all of Mr. Penn's proposals under consideration, and before I make further comment I'm getting the opinion of my advisors on the matter." Switching into his stump speech, he suddenly said, "This city needs me and, more important, I need this city. And I'm hoping that you guys are going to put me where I can do the most good . . . and no, not on unemployment." He felt briefly buoyed by the laughter that line got. "We've got too many whining creeps on the city's doles already. We don't need welfare cases cluttering up houses. We don't need homeless people to trip over in the streets. Now I've got as much humanity as the next guy . . . unless the next guy is a sucker. Bottom line is this: New York for New Yorkers."

"But Arthur Penn . . ." another reporter began.

And Keating promptly cut him off. "That's all, that's all." And he brushed by the reporters with uncharacteristic abruptness.

Moe followed on his heels, not thrilled by the turn of events, and when Bernie hopped into his waiting limo, Moe was even less thrilled that Bernie waved for him to get in as well. Bernie slid over to accommodate Moe and tossed one last wave to the reporters as the limo pulled away.

Once they were under way his friendly facade melted away like butter in a hot skillet. "What the hell was that all about?" he demanded.

"I'm not sure what you mean exactly," said Moe slowly.

"Then I'll explain it, exactly." Bernie lit up one of his dread cigars, and opened the window a crack to allow the smoke to trail out behind them. "You were telling me a couple of weeks ago that there was barely any interest in this Arthur Penn, that he was going to go away."

"I never said that, Bernie," said Moe reasonably. "I said I hoped he'd go away. There's a big difference."

"Wonderful. So how come all I get are questions about

Penn? Now what, I wonder, put the press on to this guy. Huh?"

"Well, uh," Moe tugged uncomfortably on his collar, "I suppose in a small way it's my fault."

"Your fault. How is it your fault?"

"I called one of my contacts with the *Daily News*. I asked him to check through Penn's background to find what he could dig up, dirtwise. He owed me a big favor, and he's one of the best muckrakers in the business. Frankly, I'm surprised the *National Enquirer* hasn't snatched him up yet."

"The point, Moe. Get to the point."

"The point is that he did the investigation. Real deep. Real thorough." Moe turned a dead glance on Bernie. "Know what he found? Nothing."

"Oh, come on," Bernie said incredulously. "Your man just didn't do his job, is all. Everybody's got something in their past that can be used against them as a weapon."

"This guy is squeaky clean, I'm telling you. My friend checked with everyone from the FBI and the IRS to the Department of Motor Vehicles. Not only does Arthur Penn not have any sort of negative record anywhere—not even so much as a parking ticket or late credit card payment—but he has a distinguished service record in the army. Everything about this guy checks out perfectly."

Bernie took a long, thoughtful drag on his cigar, ignoring Moe's wincing as the fumes filled the car. "Maybe too perfect, you think?"

"It has crossed my mind, yes."

"You gonna keep digging on him?"

"I'm not exactly sure where to dig at this point. It backfired the first time around, because my reporter friend became so fascinated by Penn that he wound up doing a big spread on him. A lot of people have started getting turned on to Penn. If I get more people looking into his background, with my luck *60 Minutes* will come in and canonize him."

"So what do we do now?"

Moe interlaced his fingers. "We start analyzing his proposals, and elaborate for the edification of all and sundry exactly why they are stupid and unworkable."

"Sounds good."

"And in the meantime we can pray that our luck holds out."

"Our luck?" Bernie shook his head. "I don't see—"

Moe fixed him with a look. "Penn could be making a lot more hay of this attention than he is. Instead he's playing it close to the chest. He surfaces for a few hours in random parts of the city, pontificates, then vanishes again. It's like he's making it up as he goes along."

"Not exactly the way to make friends and influence people."

"My feelings exactly. Let's hope that we keep it up. The main thing we have going for us is this Penn's utter lack of experience."

"Yeah." Bernie laughed with a cheerfulness he did not feel. "Can you imagine a guy who makes speeches and then vanishes? Never accessible to the press? What's he trying to do, run a campaign through word of mouth?"

"So it would seem. There's one thing that bothers me though."

"Yeah? What's that?"

Moe paused thoughtfully. "What if it works?"

ARTHUR STOOD OUTSIDE the door to his offices, wrestling with a crisis of conscience. There was a part of him that wanted to take Gwen and hop on the nearest bus out of town. Or plane. Or boat! That would be excellent. A nice long cruise over the ocean, far away from Merlin and his machinations.

He looked at his reflection in the opaque glass. Who was he? he wondered. What had he become? For as long as he could remember—and he could remember quite a

ways back—every action in his life had been made because
he'd *had* to do it. Not because he wanted to, but because
he had to. His was the eternal sense of obligation, and it
had begun to take a toll on him after all these years.

"Why me?" he said to no one in particular. "Why can't
I have a normal life? Why must I always be a tool of some
'greater destiny'?"

"Because that's the way it is."

Arthur looked down. Merlin was standing at his side,
looking straight ahead. No matter how many times Arthur saw him, he didn't think he would ever get used to
seeing his mentor clad like a street urchin.

"You've been dressing down lately, Merlin," he observed.

The young wizard shrugged. "I've always worn what's
most comfortable. In this age it's jeans, sneakers, and
T-shirt. Where the devil have you been the past week?"

"You know perfectly well where I've been, Merlin.
There is no way you could not know." He paused and
then said, almost tentatively, "No hard feelings about . . .
you know."

"Telling Percival to kill me? Oh hell no, why should I
carry a grudge about a little thing like that? It's not as if
my life is worth anything to anyone."

"Good. I'm glad you feel that way."

Merlin snorted in contempt. "Are we going into the
office? Or are you trying to figure out whether you should
simply run off with your precious Gwen? Oh, don't look
so surprised, Arthur. There's no way that woman can bugger matters that I haven't already anticipated and—
frankly—dreaded."

"Then you're living your life in fear, Merlin, which is
a sad way to be. Pardon me if I don't choose to do the
same."

Merlin said nothing, merely glowered, and Arthur
opened the door, feeling for some reason that he had
achieved a minor victory. What that victory was, he

wasn't quite sure. But it was something. He swung open the door and was slammed with a blast of noise that was like a living thing.

Phones were ringing, people shouting to each other. As he stepped into the waiting area, he saw to his shock that the entire interior of the office had been redone. The partitions between the small offices had been torn down, and now all the square footage stretched out like a small football field. Desks were sticking out in every possible direction; there were about a dozen in all. Each one had a phone, and there was a young man or woman on each phone. Arthur's eyes widened as he recognized a girl from the crowd who had been wearing an NYU sweatshirt . . . his first speaking engagement, of sorts. She was the first to glance up and see him, and she immediately put her phone down, leaped to her feet, and started applauding. Others looked around to see the source of her enthusiasm, and when Arthur was spotted, everyone else in the crammed offices immediately followed suit.

Arthur was dumbfounded, astounded, and flattered by the abrupt and spontaneous show of affection. He nodded in acknowledgment, put up his hands and said, "Thank you! Thank you all. You're too kind, really." He leaned down to Merlin and whispered, "Merlin, who are all these people?"

"Volunteers, mostly," said Merlin pleasantly as he guided Arthur into his private office. "Some paid office workers. Word of you is getting around, Arthur. We're going to have to start putting together a solid itinerary for you. Perhaps even explore a series of commercials."

"The packaging of the candidate, Merlin?"

Buddy and Elvis bowed deeply as Arthur passed. "We saw the news thingy about you, Milord," said Buddy. "You looked really sharp."

"Thank you, gentlemen," Arthur said briskly. "Now . . . back to what you were doing."

"We weren't doing anything," Elvis said.

Arthur glanced at Merlin, who shrugged, and looked back to them. "Yes," he said encouragingly. "But you were not doing it so well."

Buddy and Elvis smiled at one another, quite pleased to receive such a heady compliment.

Arthur and Merlin entered the office and Merlin sighed as he closed the door behind them. "I remember a time when you wouldn't have wasted a second with such fools as those two."

"I remember a time when you didn't get your clothes from the youth department at Sears," Arthur rejoindered. "Times change, Merlin."

Arthur was in his office until eight o'clock that evening, going over plans and itineraries for the next several months. He noticed and appreciated the fact that Merlin was deliberately hanging in the background, letting him run the show without unasked-for advice. And he found his blood really pumping for the first time. The excitement was beginning to build as a plan was formulated. Arthur was fond of strategies, of form and substance. There was no time for the earlier, self-centered fears and frustrations of someone wishing that they were something they could never be.

Nevertheless he was glad when the day was over, for he had other things to do . . . and other people to do them with.

THE CAB DROPPED him off in Central Park, and he made his way across, lost in thought. This night there were no interruptions from would-be muggers or helpful policemen. In the distance on one of the streets that cut through the park, Arthur heard the nostalgic sound of horse's hooves clip-clopping on the road. By the rattle of metal he could tell that it was a horse-drawn carriage. He drew a mental picture for himself, however, seated proudly on a great mount, his sword flashing, the sunlight glinting off the shield he held and the armor he wore. It was an image to do him proud.

But it was just that—an image. A part of himself he could never recapture.

The castle loomed before him, and yet so lost in thought was he that he almost walked right into it. Everyone knew the castle in the middle of Central Park. A complex weather station was situated inside. Whenever early-rising New Yorkers' ears were tuned to their radios, the statement that it was such-and-such degrees in Central Park came from the readings taken there, at Belvedere Castle. Yet a weather station was no longer the only thing occupying the castle.

Arthur walked slowly around the other side, looking for a certain portion of the wall that he knew he would find. And sure enough there it was, as it had been the other nights—a small cylindrical hole in the wall toward one stone corner. He withdrew Excalibur, reveling as always in the heady sound of steel being drawn from its sheath. Then he took Excalibur and, holding the hilt in one hand and letting the blade rest gently in the other, he slid the point into the hole.

With a low moan and the protest of creaking, the section of the wall swiveled back on invisible hinges. Before him was a stairway, the top of which was level with the ground in front of him, the bottom of which disappeared down into the blackness that was the castle—or at least an aspect of the castle. Arthur was never thrilled about the prospect of going somewhere he could not see, but he knew he was going to have to live with it. He entered the doorway, and the moment he set foot on the second step, the door swung noiselessly shut behind him. He was surrounded by blackness, illuminated only by the glow from Excalibur, which accompanied him like a friendly sprite. "My old friend," he whispered.

He walked for a time, impressed as always by the total silence of the supernatural darkness. Then, several steps before the bottom, Excalibur cast its glow upon a heavy oaken door. He walked the remaining steps down to it and pushed. It yielded without protest, and he stepped into his castle.

He passed through the main entrance hall, with its suits of armor standing at attention like legions waiting for his orders. He entered his throne room and looked around in satisfaction. Everything was exactly as he'd left it, and yet he could sense, somehow hanging in the air beyond his eye but not beyond his heart, the presence of the Woman. He smiled, the mere image of Gwen in his mind's eye enough to bring an adrenaline rush that made him feel centuries younger.

There was a painting hanging behind his throne. In it was a representation of Arthur at the Round Table. Seated around it was an assortment of knights clearly engaged in some deeply intense discussion. None of them really looked like the knights Arthur remembered—the depiction of him was recognizable only because of the larger chair. But that was all right, since the artist had doubtless created it centuries after the table and its members were part of the legends rather than living, breathing men.

"It's very nice. I've been admiring it for some time now."

Arthur turned and a grin split his face. Gwen was standing in one of the side entrances. She was wearing a simple blue tunic that hung to her knees, and gray leggings. The bruises from earlier had completely disappeared. She ran her fingers through her strawberry blonde hair and said, a bit shyly, "Hi."

"Hi, yourself. Good to see you up and around. I admit, I was feeling just a little nervous."

"And I was feeling a little guilty."

"In heaven's name, why?" He walked over to her and took each of her hands in his. It was cold in the castle, yet she felt warm.

"Because I haven't been much of a guest. Most of the

time I've just been sleeping and sleeping and sleeping."

"Why do you think that is?"

"Because," and she let out an unsteady sigh. "For the first time in ages, I feel . . . safe."

"Then I take your slumber as a compliment, and not any sort of commentary on my ability to be a host." He laughed and draped an arm around her shoulder as they walked toward the dining room.

"I'm still having trouble . . . believing this place," she said slowly. "It's like I'm in a dream. You live here all the time, when you're not at the office? And . . . and how . . . ?"

"It's Merlin's doing," Arthur told her. "He designed it to be a sort of . . . home away from home. Oh, I have an apartment in the Bronx, for appearance's sake. But this is where I prefer to spend my time."

"Why the Bronx? Why not Manhattan?"

"A reasonably priced Manhattan apartment?" He snorted. "Some things are beyond even Merlin's magic. Is your bed comfortable?"

"It's unbelievably comfortable. And it's so quiet here, but not, you know, quiet in a spooky way. Quiet in a friendly way. You can just lie back and listen to nothing, and enjoy it."

She turned then and faced him. Arthur was amused to recall that once upon a time his Guinevere had had to almost crane her neck to look at his eyes. Now they were practically on eye-to-eye level. Arthur mused that if he disappeared into a cavern for another millennium, he would be a midget when he came out.

"Arthur, where are we?" she asked intently.

"Why, we're right outside the dining room." With a sweep of his arm he indicated the table, which was already set. As always there was enough food there to feed a regiment—where it came from, Arthur never knew. It was just there when he needed it. With the bounty available,

KNIGHT LIFE 159

sustenance for his "castlemate" had been no problem at all.

She shook her head. "No, that's not what I'm saying. I once took a tour of Belvedere Castle, and I know for sure that there was nothing like this. Yet you say that we're in that castle. I find it so hard to believe, and yet—"

"Gwen," he said firmly. "I never lie. Not to you. Not to anyone. To lie is to diminish one's own feeling of self-worth."

"I know, but then . . . how?"

"You saw how when I first brought you down here a week ago."

"Yes, I saw the mechanics of it. But I didn't understand. I mean," she stepped away and shook her head in puzzlement, "I saw what you did with the sword, and the door swung open and the darkness. But none of it really made all that much sense or registered. I think part of me believed that I was actually dreaming."

"In the middle of the day?"

"Why not?" she said reasonably. "After all, many of my daylight hours have been nightmares anyway. Arthur, I don't understand how any of this works."

"I told you. Magic."

"But, that's no answer. It doesn't explain anything."

Nodding slowly, Arthur crossed to his throne, pulling at his beard as he searched for a way to explain it to Gwen. He went up the two steps to the throne and paused there a moment. Then he said. "Gwen, how do you turn on a light?"

"What, you mean like when you enter a room?" He nodded. She looked at him suspiciously. "Is this a trick question? Like 'How many Jewish American princesses does it take to screw in a lightbulb'?"

"What?" he asked in utter confusion.

"No, I guess not. Uh, okay." She leaned against the stone wall thoughtfully. "To turn on a light, you just flick the wall switch."

"Right. And what happens?"

"The light comes on."

"Yes, but why?" He leaned forward and regarded her with infinite patience. "Why does it come on?"

Now Gwen was confused. "Because you turned on the light switch. Arthur, if this is your idea of an explanation, it really sucks."

"Gwen," he said patiently, "what is it that makes the light go on when you turn on the switch?"

"Electricity, I guess. It makes the bulb come on."

"How?"

She stamped a shapely foot in irritation. "Who cares? I'm not an electrician, for heaven's sake. You turn the switch, and it activates some doohickey, and the doohickey feeds electricity into the whatchamacallit, and the light comes on. It doesn't matter to me so long as it works."

"Precisely."

"Precisely what?"

Arthur sat in his throne, looking bizarrely incongruous in his three-piece suit. "When Merlin arranged this little sanctum for me, he said it would be someplace to which I can return at night and feel that I belong, after spending a day feeling like a living anachronism. And he was right, that is how I do feel, despite my best efforts to acclimate to this odd little civilization of yours. Merlin was quite pleased when he put this together. He even tried to explain it to me—something about transdimensional bridges and relative dimensions in space and other nonsense. And I said to him about New Camelot exactly what you say to me about electric lights—who cares as long as it works?"

"But Arthur, you don't understand!"

He frowned thoughtfully. "Odd, that's just what Merlin said."

"Electricity and lights—that's all science. This is . . ." She waved her hands around helplessly. "This is magic!"

"The only difference between science and magic, Gwen, is that scientists doubt everything and magicians doubt nothing. That's why magicians get so much more done. And if scientists acknowledged that magic existed and put their considerable talents to discovering what made it tick, a great deal more could be accomplished in this world. But scientists have decided that magic does not and cannot exist, so naturally they don't go out of their way to try and find the reasons for it." He shook his head. "Very shortsighted on their part."

Gwen put her hand to her head and sat down in a comfortable armchair. "Arthur, you don't seem to realize that I'm a rational human being. I don't believe in magic. I don't believe in things just appearing because you need them."

"Oh no?"

"No."

"That chair you're sitting in? It wasn't there a moment ago."

She sprang from the chair as if propelled by springs. Her hands fluttered to her mouth, and her voice was a combination of surprise and hysterical laughter. "This is crazy!"

"Why?"

"Because I was always taught to be a very rational person!"

"Faugh!" Arthur said dismissively. "Rationality always gets in the way of common sense. Common sense tells you that no other explanation is possible for what you see. But when you try to rationalize the unexplainable, you run into problems." And as she delicately tapped the arms of the chair, Arthur added in a softer voice, "Like us."

She looked over to him and saw the way he was looking at her. She felt her cheeks color and looked down. She couldn't remember the last time she'd blushed.

"Arthur." She looked up at him tentatively. "Ar-

thur . . . are you really him? I mean, the original King
Arthur?"

"Yes."

"But . . . but it's so difficult to believe."

"Ah-ah," and he put up a finger. "You're rationalizing
again. Didn't I tell you how that gets in the way?"

"But if I believe what you're saying," she said, walking
slowly around the perimeter of the room, "then I would
also have to accept the part about my being a reincarnation
of your Queen Guin . . ." Her voice trailed off and her
eyes widened in surprise. "You know, Arthur, my name—
Gwen Queen—that sounds a lot like Queen Guinevere,
doesn't it?"

"By Jove, you're right!" He sagged back in the throne.
"Fancy that."

They smiled at one another, and then Arthur stepped
off his throne and walked slowly toward Gwen. She stood
there, her arms hanging loosely at her sides. He came very
close to her, then paused and ran his hand gently across
her face. She closed her eyes and sighed, and a little tremble rushed through her.

"Arthur . . . we were married once, weren't we?"

He shook his head. "No. We were married always."

"But I hardly know you."

"You've always known me," he said softly. "We have
always been. We shall always be. Not time, not distance,
not lifetimes can do more than momentarily interrupt the
coexistence we are meant to share."

He felt the softness of her hair, and she said, "Arthur?"

"Yes?"

"Have you really been locked in a cave for eleven hundred years?"

"Thereabouts, yes."

She whistled. "You must be the horniest bastard on the
face of the earth."

The expression on his face did not change, but he said,
"Gwen, would you mind waiting here a moment?"

"Uh . . . sure."

Arthur stepped back and went into another room. She pricked up her ears and heard the sound of pages turning. She heard him mumble "Horn . . . horned . . . hornet," like someone skimming through a dictionary to find a word he did not comprehend. She stifled a desperate urge to giggle. There was a momentary pause in the page turning, and then she heard the book close. She fought to keep a straight face but felt the sides of her mouth turning up involuntarily.

Arthur came back into the room and faced her, looking deadly serious. "Gwen," he said with great solemnity.

"Yes, Arthur?"

"You're right."

They both dissolved into laughter.

THEY SAT OPPOSITE each other at the dinner table, with the easy comfort in each other's presence that it takes most couples years to achieve, if they ever do.

"I don't know," Gwen said, picking delicately at the drumstick she was holding in her small hands. "It's like, my whole life, I've felt that . . . that I don't deserve happiness."

"Guilt from another lifetime, perhaps?"

She moaned. "Oh, great. Other people, they get to blame it on their parents. My parents weren't wonderful. I just figured I could pin it on them, which is sort of a grand tradition of modern man. But no, no, not me. I have to carry mistakes from a couple of centuries ago."

"Mistake or not," Arthur said calmly, with the air of a man who had long since resigned himself to things that once had pierced his heart, "my queen, Gwynyfar, and my best friend, Lancelot, did the only thing they could. Love is something so powerful that not even Excalibur could cleave it. My kingdom rose and fell on emotion. It could have been no other way." In an offhand way he added,

"And it was ten centuries, by the way. Not a couple."

"And where have you been . . . all that time? You and Merlin?"

"Merlin had been imprisoned in a cave by a temptress, Ninivae. And I . . ." He paused. "Are you sure you want to hear this on a full stomach?"

She lay down the drumstick and interlaced her fingers. "I can take it if you can."

"Very well. I . . . after my final battle with my bastard son, Modred, left me with my skull split like an overripe melon . . . I was brought to an island called Avalon. It was a place of healing. And when they had done all they could do for me in Avalon, my semiconscious body was also placed in a cave, a different cave from Merlin's. It was one I think he prepared far in advance, as if knowing I would need it some time. That wouldn't surprise me in the least; there's very little that Merlin doesn't anticipate, I think. It was ensorcelled, temporally sealed so that I would not age while I resided within. Once I recovered, I stayed there, waiting . . . until such time that I was needed."

"I need you," Gwen said, and then quickly corrected herself, "I mean . . . we all do."

"Of course," he said. Then he stared at her for a long moment and said, "Gwen . . . Jenny . . . that's what I used to call you at . . . certain times . . . Jenny . . . I know this is a good deal for you to comprehend. You've borne up extremely well under it, considering the—well, the oddity of the circumstances. Yes, I was your husband . . . but I recognize that it was many lifetimes ago, and the lifetime of another woman. Her spirit may live on within you, but you are your own woman with your own concerns and desires. I will not do anything to make you uncomfortable. I have treated your departure from your previous domestic situation, and your stay here, as if you were recovering from a devastating battle. You may stay here as long as you wish, and you may depart this place when you wish. And you may regard me . . . in whatever capacity you desire. All matters, all choices are in your hands."

"I . . . haven't felt so in control for a long time . . . if ever," Gwen said softly.

"To be honest," he said with grim amusement, "I don't know that we ever have a right to feel that way. We are creatures of destiny in many regards, you and I. Sometimes we think we are in control of ourselves when, in fact, we are driven in manners we cannot possibly foresee or even comprehend."

"When do we know that our will is our own?"

"We don't," he admitted. "We simply make the choices we make, and hope for the best."

He rose and came around the table to her, then took her hand in his and kissed her knuckles gently.

"Good night . . . Gwen Queen," he said softly.

ARTHUR LAY IN bed that night, alone, as he had been all the previous nights. He slid his hand slowly across the empty side of the bed and sighed deep in his chest, deep in his soul.

He heard a footfall at his door and sat bolt upright, his hand already reaching for Excalibur. The door swung open and Gwen was there. Candlelight from the hallway illuminated her from the back, showing the silhouette of her body through her white shift.

His breath caught as she said in a low voice, "I don't think you'll be needing a weapon, Arthur. I'm unarmed."

She glided across the floor to him and sat down slowly in the empty part of the bed. Arthur touched her arm and felt an inner trembling. "Gwen, you don't have to. Not if you're not ready."

She laughed lightly. "According to you, I've been waiting for you for centuries . . . lived many past lives, but you were always my Mister Right. When has any girl had to wait as long for her perfect man as me?" She stroked his beard and asked, "Arthur? Am I . . . do I look as pretty to you as when you first knew me? Back in . . . in your days?"

His voice choking with emotion, he said, "You are as I have always loved you."

He took her to him as Excalibur glowed in the dimness.

THE SWORD WASN'T the only thing giving off a pale light in a darkened room.

Some miles away, Merlin sat in his own sanctum, illuminated by the glow of the computer monitor. On the monitor were the images of Arthur and Gwen, doing the kind of thing that disgusted Merlin since it invariably led to trouble.

"I know where it's going now," he muttered. "Straight down the damned privy is where it's going. I wonder . . . I wonder if I have a spell that can somehow turn back time so he never meets the girl in the first place." He ran the query through Spellcheck but couldn't find anything. In the meantime the gasping and moaning on the screen became a distraction, and he punched up solitaire. As he proceeded to win hand after hand, he sighed. "Kings. Can't live with them, can't live without them."

Ye Olde Sound Bite

"And over to Louise Simonson on the campaign watch. Louise?"

"Thanks, Walter. Well, it has now been close to two months since Independent candidate Arthur Penn first clung batlike to the statue of Father Duffy and began espousing his views. In that time interest has mounted as word spread throughout the city, and it has become quite a cachet to have been present at one of Penn's 'guerrilla stump speeches,' as they've come to be known. However, campaigns cannot be won solely through word of mouth, and so it was that the press was cordially invited one day to the cramped, busy offices of Arthur Penn at the Camelot Building, to officially meet the Independent candidate for mayor of New York City. The results were, shall we say, unique."

CHAPTRE
THE THIRTEENTH

✠

THEY'D RENTED A small presentation room in a nearby hotel. Chairs and a podium were set up. Wine and cheese were served, and the reporters milled around, trying to pump the Penn-for-Mayor volunteers for information. The workers merely smiled, having been primed not to say a word until after Arthur had had an opportunity to address the press. Eventually the reporters started interviewing each other. One of them bumped into a small boy nattily dressed in white ducks and a blue blazer with a little anchor on the pocket.

"Hey, kid," he said heartily. "You should be in school."

"You should be in traction," retorted Merlin, pushing his way past the reporter to the cheese balls. He glanced in Miss Basil's direction and was pleased to see that she was off in her own little world, as it were, scanning the crowd, serving in her customary guardian capacity. Anything of a sinister bent that tried to obtain entrance would find a very hostile reception.

Abruptly he bumped directly into Gwen. She was looking down at him expectantly. "Well? What is it?" he said impatiently.

"You could compliment me," she told him.

"Nice shoes. I didn't know they still made that style."

"I mean on this," she said, indicating the press conference. "I did help arrange it, after all."

"Miss Queen," he said with obvious annoyance, "if infinite monkeys typing for an eternity could produce the works of Shakespeare, I think even you should be capable of putting together a simple press conference. But if this desperately minor exercise of talent requires a pat on the back, then it shall be as you wish." He reached up and chucked her on the shoulder, a painfully fake smile on his lips. "Well done, you."

"Do you think you could at least try to like me?" she asked.

He pondered the question a moment. "Yes. I could try," he decided, and then moved around her for the cheeseballs. She rolled her eyes.

There was a rapping at the podium. Percival was standing up front, and in a strong, proud voice, he said, "Gentlemen and ladies of the press, I would appreciate it if you could take your seats. I thank you all for coming, and I assure you that it will be well worth your while."

Chairs were shuffled while the TV camera crews stood to the sides of the podium, checking the lighting and their range. Percival paused a moment and then said, "As you know, Mr. Arthur Penn has been creating quite a stir throughout the city over the past months. His style has been referred to in the press as guerrilla politics. The truth of the matter, gentlemen, is that Mr. Penn has been so busy meeting the people, it rather slipped his mind that he should really be getting to work on the business of being elected mayor of this great city." There was a small ripple of laughter, and Percival continued, "And make no mistake, my friends, I guarantee that you will be looking at the next mayor of New York when I say that I would like to introduce Mr. Arthur Penn."

Percival stepped away from the podium as the once and future king made his way from the back of the room.

As if reading their minds, Arthur called out, "You gentlemen and ladies are the veterans. The ones who have been in the trenches. The ones who have been doing this for far longer than I have." As he worked his way through the crowd, it seemed as if he was genuinely looking at, shaking hands with, and greeting every single member of the press corp. "I'm sure you've met many a politician in your collective lives. You've seen all the types—the charismatic ones, the old-boy ones, the intellectual ones, the forthright, the sneaky, the slick, the snake-oil salesmen, and every permutation of human being in between." Heads nodded all around, silent acknowledgments of what he was saying. He continued, "And I would wager that they all had one thing in common: They all regarded the press as a necessary evil. Something that had to be lived with, tolerated, used, and maneuvered. But I want you to know that I appreciate your role as chroniclers . . . as molders and shapers of recorded history. You have a sacred duty to be as truthful and accurate as possible . . . and I, certainly, will do no less during our association."

Merlin noticed the almost patronizing looks the reporters were giving Arthur and each other. They weren't swallowing a word of it. Gods, what a cynical bunch.

Suddenly, Merlin heard a clip-clopping noise. It sounded vaguely like the beat of horses's hooves. Arthur heard it, too, stopped walking, and turned around. Buddy was standing directly behind him, holding two half coconut shells, which he'd been banging together to simulate a horse's canter.

"What are you doing?" Arthur asked patiently.

"I saw it in an old movie," Buddy said. "On the Comedy Channel."

"Well, stop it. It's annoying."

Buddy shoved the coconut shells into his jacket pockets, and without any further interruptions, Arthur made it up to the podium, slapped Percival affectionately on the shoulder, and faced the press. He blinked repeatedly as flashbulbs went off, looked around at the crowd facing him, and then saw Gwen standing in the back. He smiled to her, and she smiled back, almost schoolgirlishly, as he said, "As you will be able to tell from the press kits you should all have, I am Arthur Penn. We've paid outrageous sums for the production of my biography and to have a photographer take a black-and-white photo of me that makes me look as attractive to female voters as possible. So I would greatly appreciate any attention you might pay them." There were appreciative laughs, and he continued, "I've taken this opportunity to meet with you because I value your function very highly. I am hoping that you will be able to pass my message on to the wide voting public, since I have researched the matter very carefully. For me to speak personally with all of my potential voters would take at least five years, and I'm afraid that I have not been allotted that much time."

He paused a moment and smiled. "My friends, quite simply, I wish to be the next mayor of New York City. I will now take questions."

There was a moment of surprise, and then hands were raised. Arthur picked one at random. It was a slim, waspish man from one of the New York tabloids. "Mr. Penn—"

"Call me Arthur, please."

The reporter blinked. "All right . . . will we still call you Arthur if you're elected mayor?"

"I should think 'your highness' would suffice."

In the back Gwen stifled a giggle and turned away.

The reporter smiled and said, "Arthur . . . that was a very short opening statement."

"I was always taught to regard brevity as a virtue."

"Mister . . . Arthur, I'd be very interested in your background."

"So would I. Feel free to read through the papers before you to see what sort of records my staff has fabricated." He pointed to another reporter. "Yes?"

"Sir," said the reporter, "according to this, your primary career has been investing. Investing in stocks, in dot-coms . . . in all manner of things. You have no experience in politics at all."

"You say that as if it's a bad thing," Arthur smiled.

"Yes, sir, it's just that . . . do you have any track record in leadership at all?"

Arthur chuckled softly. "Not that I'd care to share."

There were befuddled looks among the journalists. "You . . . could tell us . . . but you won't? Were you a Don or something?"

"No, no, I've always been an Arthur," he said, which generated a laugh. It was obvious to Merlin that Arthur had no clue why what he'd said was funny, but his polite smile made it look as if he had been going for a joke. But Percival, standing just to his left, very softly murmured something in his ear in such a way that no one save Merlin noticed. Imperceptibly, comprehension dawned on Arthur's face and he added, "I assure you, my activities have stayed solidly on the side of the law."

"Then why won't you say?" asked another reporter.

To Merlin's surprise, Gwen came forward. She stood to one side of the podium. "Modesty forbids Mr. Penn from doing so. I'm Gwen Queen, Mr. Penn's press aide." (*Since when?* Merlin wondered.) "He could cite you chapter and verse of all his accomplishments, but the problem is that he would be accused of stretching the truth. And we've all seen just how destructive such accusations can be. Although, guys, y'know," she said conversationally, "I have to admit, I never understood why you guys make such a big deal about that. Any political campaign, for mayor, governor, even president . . . all it is, really, is one big,

long job interview. That's all it is. Except instead of
having one potential boss, a politician has millions. And
how many people out there have 'beefed up' their resumes,
made themselves sound better than they are, in order to
make themselves more impressive? Including most of you
guys." There was some appreciative, acknowledging
laughter from the reporters. "See? That doesn't mean that
you're a bad guy, or a nasty guy, or a guy who's not
trustworthy. It just means that you're human and that
you really, really want the job because you know that—
once you've got it—you can be terrific in it." Abruptly
Gwen seemed to really fully understand that all eyes were
upon her and she looked embarrassed to have that much
attention. "I'm . . . I'm sorry, I'll shut up now."

"No, Gwen, that was very well said," Arthur told her
approvingly.

Merlin rolled his eyes. Still he had to admit that Gwen
had deftly deflected, and dealt with, a question that could
have provided a sticking point. Because Arthur, despite
Merlin's best advice to the contrary, was resolved to be
utterly candid and not lie.

Throughout the rest of the press conference, impres-
sively, Arthur stuck to that vow. He answered every question, and if it was about a potentially touchy subject, he
deadpanned the absolute truth and usually got an amused
reaction from his audience. Remarkable.

One reporter said, "Arthur, I'd just like to toss out a
few hot topics, and find out how you stand on them."

"Let's find out together," said Arthur.

"Prayer in school, for example."

Arthur shrugged. "You mean before a difficult examination?"

"No," said the reporter, unsure whether Arthur was
joking or not—a state most reporters would find themselves in during the months to come. "I mean organized
prayer."

"Oh, of course! Organized prayer in the morning, that

sort of thing. Well, I've never been one to stand in the way of how someone wishes to worship. However, I recall reading something in the Declara—no, the Constitution, isn't it? About separation of church and state. It would seem to me that prayer and church are usually equated, aren't they?" The reporter nodded, and Arthur smiled. "Well, schools aren't churches. However," and he smiled that charming, impossible to hate smile, "the ultimate, sacred temple that all of us have is our own body. That place of worship is open twenty-four hours a day, seven days a week. Prayer can be held there, in private, in a sincere fashion, without violating any constitution, now, can't it."

"But it's not that simple," said the reporter.

"Then it should be. What else would you like to know about?"

"Your stand on abortion?"

Arthur shuddered. "Terrible mess. None of my bloody business, though, what a woman does with her body."

"Are you in favor, then, of state money and government money going to fund abortions?"

"I imagine it's better than feeding the poor little buggers, isn't it, once they're born into unwanted and miserable situations?"

The reporters looked around at each other. One of them whistled silently.

"Are you concerned, sir, that some pro-lifers may find your attitude, well . . . callous? That you're sentencing unborn children to death?"

Arthur regarded him oddly. "I have seen more death, son, than you could possibly imagine. Not to become maudlin, but I value life no less than does anyone else. But life is difficult enough when you come into it wrapped in the arms of a mother who wants you. Coming into it unwanted is more than any helpless infant should have to bear." His eyes misted over. "I was . . . walking a hill once, when I was a young man. And I tripped over

something. I got up, dusted myself off, and chided myself
for my clumsiness, for I had walked that path a hundred
times. Then I saw that I had tripped over the body of an
infant. It was still covered in the blood in which it had
been birthed, and there were footprints on either side of
it. The mother had . . ." He took a breath. "The mother
had given birth, there in the road, and simply left the
child behind. And there it had died, cold, unwanted . . .
alone. Alone." He was silent for a moment. No one dared
say anything. Then, more softly, he said, "It used to happen routinely, long ago. Unwanted children left exposed
upon a hillside. Or women bleeding from their bellies,
thanks to the tender mercies of charlatans pretending to
be doctors. At a time such as that people prayed for the
knowledge to prevent such monstrosities and outrages.
Now we have it, it would be equally as monstrous not to
use it. Yes, money to help those unfortunate women,
when needed. But most of the time, I don't believe it
should be."

This garnered confused looks. "Why?" asked one reporter, speaking pretty much for all of them.

"Why, the man should pay for it. That's certainly a law
I'd like to see. If, thanks to available choices today, the
woman decides to have an abortion, the man should bear
that cost."

"Why shouldn't the woman share the cost?"

"Because the man can't share the physical pain and haz-
ards of the abortion, so at the very least he should be
responsible for the entire cost of the procedure. At the
very least, I'd wager men would give at least a modicum
of thought to putting a woman at risk of pregnancy."

"You are aware," said one reporter with a half-smile,
"that some of your attitudes may be regarded as controversial."

"Yes. I suppose so. Common sense usually is. That's a
bit of an oxymoron, isn't it? 'Common sense.' Seems rather

uncommon, really." He pointed to another reporter. "Yes?"

"Gun control?"

"Ah. Yes, I've been thinking about that one. Seems to me it's based on the entire 'militia' business. Fine. Anyone who owns a gun should have to belong to a militia. Otherwise I don't see any reason for them to have one."

"Self-protection."

"Get a sword. Broadsword, preferably. Builds the upper torso nicely, and children can't lift them because they're too heavy."

More puzzled looks. "Sir, many people feel that they should have guns to protect themselves against a potential government gone bad."

"Yes, I've heard that. People don't trust the government. It's odd, though. If they don't trust the government, how is it they know that they can speak against it with impunity? They must trust it on *some* level. Besides, the entire matter is nonsense, if you ask me, which, I suppose, you have. If the government goes bad, handguns won't save you. Better to work together to support a good government than arm oneself against a bad one."

"Sir, there are many facts which gun advocates can present—"

"First thing you'll have to learn about me," said Arthur reasonably, leaning over the podium. "I never want to get bogged down with facts. Facts get in the way of decisions. Give me a basic summary of the situation and I will generally decide," and he tapped his chest, "based on what I feel here. I would wager that others will bog themselves down with umpteen reports and countless charts and the like, and it will all still boil down to the basic feeling of what's right and what's wrong." He smiled. "After all, it beats trial by combat. Next question?"

"Mr. Penn," one reporter said, "I'd like to go back to the abortion question for a moment. Just out of curiosity . . .

have *you* ever gotten a woman pregnant and, if so, did you pay for the abortion?"

Dead silence.

Arthur sighed deeply, but he never lowered his gaze. "Yes . . . when I was a very young man, a long time ago . . . I impregnated a young woman. I could cite you chapter and verse how I was seduced into it, and how it was her doing, not mine, and it would be true to a point . . . but only to a point. Ultimately, one takes responsibility for one's actions. Abortion was not an option, nor was marriage. Had it been, I would have pursued either. As it was, well . . ." He let out a long, unsteady breath. "To forestall any further questions . . . I have not seen the young woman in many, many years, and the offspring died. But I can tell you in all honesty—which is the only way I know how to deal with matters—that not a day goes by where I don't think of him, and dwell upon the many ways in which I wish things could have gone differently. Then again . . . what else can anyone, particularly someone who calls himself a potential leader, do, other than try to impart his own mistakes to others so that they will learn from his errors and not commit the same ones. Next question."

ARTHUR, GWEN, MERLIN, Percival, Buddy, and Elvis sat draped around various parts of the meeting room. Merlin sat upright and cross-legged while the others were fairly at ease. Buddy was stirring a Bloody Mary with his finger. The others were drinking soda or iced tea.

The reporters had left some time ago to file their stories, and everyone in the room seemed concerned about what would be said. Everyone except Merlin and Arthur.

"I did my best," said Arthur reasonably. "If they don't like what I had to say, what am I supposed to do? Be sorry that I said it?" He shook his head. "No, they're going to have to warm to me or not, based on who I am."

Gwen smiled. "If they knew who you were, they'd vote for you in an instant."

"Would they?" asked Arthur, scratching his beard thoughtfully. "Do you think so? My earlier endeavors hardly ended in glowing triumph, now did they?"

"Oh, people remember what they want to remember," said Gwen. She stood and walked over to Arthur's side, sitting on the arm of his chair. "After all is said and done, most people remember Camelot as a time of achievement and pride. I mean, the happiest times this country remembers were with Kennedys' whole Camelot thing."

"Ah!" declared Arthur. "Merlin said that to me once. Didn't you, Merlin? You see—the two of you do see eye-to-eye every now and again."

Merlin made a face. Then he said, "Arthur, I think it best that you spend the night—the next few nights, in fact—in your Bronx place."

"Oh, Merlin, is that really necessary?" said Arthur unhappily. "It's so bloody small. The castle is really so much better."

"Arthur, try to be reasonable. It wouldn't be good form for the press to discover that the Independent mayoral candidate makes his home in a pile of transdimensional rocks in Central Park."

Elvis perked up slightly and said, "Sounds okeedokee to me."

"Proof enough," said Merlin tartly. "Arthur, it's been set up for you, and I suggest that you try to make use of it. If all goes well, the press is going to become intensely interested in such minutiae as how you like to have your English muffins for breakfast. And if you have mysterious comings and goings, it could prompt digging in areas we'd much rather leave undug."

"All right, all right," sighed Arthur. "Gwen, let's go."

"He's going to have a roommate!" yelled Merlin. "That's just ruddy wonderful!"

Arthur's tone was warning. "Merlin . . ."

But a gentle touch rested on his arm. "No, Arthur, Merlin's right," said Gwen reasonably. "Your style is going to be somewhat . . . unorthodox for a number of voters. Perhaps we shouldn't try to drop too much on them right away. I'll find someplace."

"She could bunk in with us," offered Buddy.

Gwen looked at them. "Oh. How . . . nice," she said, with as much enthusiasm as she could muster.

"Yeah! We got a brand new refrigerator box."

She smiled, trying to look genuinely thankful. "I appreciate your concern, but I have a friend I can stay with out in Queens until I find a place of my own." She shook her head in wonderment. "You know, I've never had that. When I went into college I went from living with my parents to living in a dorm. And from there I went to living with Lance."

"Lance?" Percival looked up.

Arthur shook his head. "No relation."

"So I'll finally be out on my own. It's scary." She looked thoughtful. "Poor Lance."

"Why poor Lance?" asked Percival. Arthur leaned forward, curious to hear her response.

"Why, because the more I've thought about it, the more I've come to realize that he needed me a hell of a lot more than I needed him. He was just determined that I not know that. I think my being on my own is going to be a lot harder on Lance than it will be on me."

Arthur's mouth twitched. "My heart bleeds for him."

L ANCE LEANED AGAINST the wall of the building to keep himself from toppling over. He felt the solid brick waver under his fingertips for a moment before righting itself, then he breathed a sigh of relief that it had sorted itself out before falling.

It was a starless night. The full moon was blood red—it would have tinted the clouds, had there been any clouds.

There were only a few cars heading uptown on Eighth Avenue this late at night. Most people drove through that area with their car doors locked tight. Drivers would glance disdainfully at the human refuse that lined the streets. Lance was one of those receiving the disdainful glances.

He sank slowly to the ground and smiled, incredibly happy. Lance had certain images of himself that he felt constrained to live up to. Once that image had been of Suffering Writer. To that end he'd spent long hours churning out reams of garbage, comprehensible only to himself (oh, Gwen had pretended to like them, but he knew better). He had starved himself, refused to go out in the daylight if he could help it. When he did feel the need for sexual release, he'd found hookers with hearts of gold to whom he could vent his creative spleen, not to mention his pent-up urges. For naturally, as with any good tortured writer, he had a woman who did not understand him and wanted him to get a regular nine-to-five job. At least, that was the way he saw it, and how he saw it was really all that mattered.

When Gwen had walked out, it had permitted him to shift over to a new persona—Utterly Dejected Writer at the End of his Rope. He looked at his distorted reflection in a puddle of water and was overjoyed at what he saw. He was strung out. Dead-ended. Down and out. Ruined by the complete collapse of his one true love's confidence in him, he had now attained that point where he could die alone, unloved and misunderstood in a gutter in New York. Then some students or somesuch, cleaning out his papers, would discover the heretofore undiscovered brilliance of Lance Benson and make it public. He'd be published by some university press somewhere and become a runaway hit. He smirked. And he'd be dead. They'd want more of his brilliance, and he'd be dead as a doornail. That would sure show them!

The clack-clack of the heels had been sounding along

the street for some time, but Lance had taken no notice of them. Now, though, he could not help it. The heels had stopped right in front of him—stiletto heels supporting thigh-high black leather boots, which were laced up the front.

Slowly Lance looked up. The woman before him was dressed entirely in black leather. Her clothes looked as if they'd been spray painted on. The only part of her body that was not covered were the fingers, projecting through five holes cut in each glove. She wore a black beret on her head, which blended perfectly with her black hair. Her lipstick and mascara were black as well, floating against the alabaster of her skin.

"Hi," she said. Her voice was low and sultry. "Nice night."

"If you like the night," he said indifferently, and looked down.

"Oh, yes. Yes indeed, I love the night." Her voice dropped to a whisper. "What's your name?"

"Lance."

"Lance." She rolled the name around on her tongue, making it sound like a three-syllable name. "Lance, you look very lonely. Would you like to have a good time?"

He laughed hoarsely. "Yeah, sure. But my idea of a good time and your idea of a good time probably don't jibe."

"Oh, really?"

"Yeah, really." He felt even colder, as if the temperature around him had just dropped by a few degrees with no warning and no reason. "My idea of a good time is sitting here and watching my life pass before my eyes as I prepare to die."

"You're right," said the woman. "You're very right." She shook her head. "That's not my idea of a good time at all. Tell you what—why don't I show you my idea of a good time? If that doesn't do it for you, then we'll bring you back here and you can continue your little headlong drive to self-destruction. How does that strike you?"

Lance shrugged. "Whatever makes you happy. I don't much care." He got to his feet, and the woman took his hand. He hobbled at first, since his right leg had fallen asleep. "So where are we going?"

"My place," she said. She wrapped her fingers in between his, and he shuddered. Her hand was cold, and he told her so. She nodded her head slightly in acknowledgment. "Yes, I know. But don't worry," she said, licking her lips slowly, "I can warm up quite nicely."

Abruptly Lance dug into his pocket. "I don't have any money, really," he said.

That prompted a laugh. "You charming boy! You think I'm a prostitute! How sweet!"

"You're . . . you're not?"

"No, I'm not."

"Then, why are you interested in me?"

"Because, Lance my love . . . I think you have potential. Enormous potential."

"Really?"

"Yes, really. And I'm going to help you fulfill it."

His spirit brightened for the first time since Gwen had left him. "That's . . . that's incredible. I mean, really incredible of you. What's your name?"

"Morgan."

He nodded. "Morgan? Isn't that a man's name?"

She smiled. "Only if you're a man. But I happen to be a woman, my dear Lance. More woman, I would suspect, than you would ever believe you could possibly handle."

"Oh," said Lance uncertainly, and then he smiled with grim determination. "Well, I guess I'll just have to do my best."

"Oh, yes, Lance," said Morgan. "I know you will, I just know it. As will I. Although my best, as it so happens, is also my worst."

YE OLDE SOUND BITE

"Hello. I'm Arthur Penn. I want to be the next mayor of New York City. Vote for me. Thank you."

"PAID FOR BY THE ARTHUR PENN FOR MAYOR COMMITTEE."

CHAPTRE
THE FOURTEENTH

†

"IT WAS JUST on!"

"Damn! I blinked and missed it again!"

Percival, hunched over his ledgers in the offices of Arthur Penn, the checkbook and bank balances spread out nearby, shook his head in grim amusement. The television set was on in the background. Campaign workers sat around stuffing envelopes and sealing them, or canvassing telephone books and comparing names to lists provided by the League of Women Voters, to see if they could encourage those not already registered to do so.

On the portable color Sony, Arthur's commercial had just aired. It had been shot in an empty studio, the only prop on the set being a stool. Arthur was leaning against it, gazing out at the viewer with that easy familiarity of his.

"Hello," he said pleasantly. "I'm Arthur Penn. I want to be the next mayor of New York City. Vote for me. Thank you."

The screen then went to black, and Gwen's voice,

sounding very sultry, said "Paid for by the Arthur Penn for Mayor Committee."

Percival, laughing softly, returned to his work. He remembered when Arthur had first presented the script for the commercial to all and sundry. There had been a long moment of skeptical silence, but Arthur had remained firm, despite the swell of subsequent protest and disbelief. As the primaries approached, Arthur had studied the commercials of other candidates very carefully. His decision was to try and find a different angle. Once he had eliminated the Meet-the-People Approach, the Photographed-in-Front-of-a-Recognizable-Monument approach, the Meet-My-Family-Aren't-We-Wholesome approach, the Hard-Hitting-Tough-Talker approach, and the My-Opponent-Is-a-Cheating-Son-of-a-Bitch approach, that had left him with exactly one option.

"But h—Arthur," Percival said, still working hard to break himself of the habit of calling his liege "highness" no matter how instinctively right it seemed. "All that's going to happen is that people will see your commercial and wonder, 'Yeah, but why should I vote for him?' "

"Precisely!" Arthur had said delightedly. "The beauty of this commercial is that it's only ten seconds long. So we can afford—what is it called, Gwen?"

"Saturation," she said.

"Yes, exactly."

"But Arthur," Gwen cut in, "when I mentioned that as an option, it was just that, an option. I didn't mean you should base the whole of your TV campaign around . . ."

"Whatever you meant or didn't mean, Gwen, I've decided it's the best way to go. This way, we'll get people curious. People like to be tested, to be challenged. Every politician sounds like every other politician. As far as I'm concerned, people are no different now than they were centuries ago. Before you can accomplish anything, you have to get their attention. And frequently the best way to get their attention is to hit them on the nose with a rolled-up newspaper." He grinned. "My entire campaign is directed toward hitting them with that newspaper. To a large extent what I say is irrelevant, as long as it's making people—" he tapped his temple with his forefinger, "—think! No one thinks anymore. Well, my friends, this campaign is not going to lay things out in nice easy packages."

That's for sure, Percival thought. He shook his head. This whole campaign was hardly an easy package. As the treasurer of the Arthur Penn for Mayor Committee, he had his work cut out for him.

Merlin had certainly done his groundwork, paving the way for Arthur's return. That much was certain. The creation of an entire fictional history of Arthur being silent partner in a number of extremely successful businesses, as well as selling the public on the notion that he was an independent thinker (and therefore, likely, a canny investor) had given credence to Arthur's personal fortune. The actual origin of the fortune was unknown to Percival, although he had a suspicion that if someone happened to stumble over the pot at the end of the rainbow, they might now find it empty. Merlin had a knack for making things happen. That same fictional history had supported Arthur's bid for the mayoralty. Coming from outside of politics, he could claim no prior party obligations. Coming (ostensibly) from a background in business, he could claim that he had a businessman's sense of running things, and that was what New York City needed. Someone who knew how to eliminate waste, to maximize profits. In short, to run New York City like the profit-making center it should and could be.

It all sounded great. Percival just hoped that Arthur could pull it off. And he hoped that no one tumbled wise to the whole setup. Percival wasn't sure, but he had a feeling you could go to jail for being the treasurer of an organization backing a candidate for mayor who had supposedly died centuries ago.

                              *   *   *

ℳOE DRESKIN, HIS middle swathed in a white towel, sat back in the steam room of his favorite health club. He could feel his pores opening, his skin breathing in the healthful mists around him. Sweat beaded his forehead, slicked his back and upper arms. His hands rested comfortably on his lap. It was a pleasure to relax, particularly after having had to deal with Keating flipping out on him.

"I'm getting damned sick of that commercial!" Keating had howled. "It's all over the damned place!"

"Of course it is," Moe had said with forced patience. "It's saturation. It doesn't hit people over the head. And it makes them want to find out who the hell this guy is, already. It's much easier to *get* people interested than to *make* them interested."

"I don't want semantics! I shouldn't have to put up with this shit!"

"I'm working on it," Moe said. "Don't sweat it." And naturally, right after saying that, Moe headed off to his health club, where he proceeded to sweat it, hoping to symbolically exorcise the cranky demons of Bernard Keating from his system.

He wasn't concerned about Kent Taylor. He was a pleasant enough actor, but Keating was a pit bull, and he was reasonably sure he could take him. But Arthur . . . Arthur was going to be a problem. Because Keating was right about one thing: That damned, omnipresent commercial made it seem like Arthur Penn was everywhere.

The door to the steam room opened. Moe looked over with half-closed eyes and dimly made out a figure through the steam. "Is that you, Cordoba?" he called out.

There was a pause, and then a voice called back, "No. It's me, Arthur."

Moe shrunk back against the wall as Arthur stepped out of the fog, smiling pleasantly. He wore a towel as

well, except that it was wrapped around him like a toga.
And it was purple.

"You wouldn't by any chance be referring to Ronnie
Cordoba, would you, Moe?" asked Arthur with what
sounded like only mild interest. "The old racquetball
companion of your leash holder, Bernie Keating? You
might be interested to know that, with the primary only
a month away, old Ronnie has joined my team. Seems he
has a flair for public relations and Bernie was attempting
to funnel it into the standard channels. So Ronnie came
over to us. We're a good deal more flexible. And he told
me all about you. You sounded so familiar, just from his
description. So we checked out some old news footage of
Keating, and there you were, standing right behind him.
Isn't this nice, that we should have such a chance to get
back together again."

He sat down next to Moe and patted him on the back.
Moe, paralyzed with fear, nevertheless recoiled from his
touch.

"So," said Arthur, "this is our first opportunity to really
talk. Have a family reunion, so to speak. So tell me—how
are you doing, you little bastard?"

"Mister, um, Mr. Penn, I don't see—"

Arthur raised a preemptory hand. "Don't. Don't even
try to lie to me. It's foolishness." He sighed and shook his
head. "I thought we'd seen the last of each other on the
field of battle, Modred, those many centuries ago. But,
believe it or not . . . I'm willing to give you a chance."

"A . . . a chance to what? Die naked in a sauna?"

When Arthur spoke, it was as if he was talking to Modred from a great distance. "You may not recall, Modred,
but on that last day, when I received the wound that
nearly killed me, you claimed you were willing to make
a peaceful settlement. Suddenly, at the last moment, a
poison adder appeared from nowhere and laid me low. My
men, not seeing the snake, thought you had betrayed me,
so they attacked. And that was the finish of us all." He

leaned toward Moe. "The thing I've always puzzled over, and the thing to which I doubt I'll ever get an answer, is my question of whether you arranged for that poisoned snake yourself, or whether you were actually willing to negotiate for peace. On that basis, Modred, my bastard son, I offer you a place within my organization. Because I want to be able to trust you."

Modred met his gaze levelly. "And because you feel it's best to keep your friends close . . . and enemies closer?"

"As you say," Arthur replied.

Modred stood then, and said very quietly, "I've waited centuries to say this to you." Then he saw something in Arthur's eyes that he clearly didn't like, and he said, "Enjoy your *shvitz*," as he got out of there as quickly as he could.

"I hope it was worth the wait!" Arthur called after him, and then leaned back and laughed softly to himself as he did, indeed, enjoy his *shvitz*, knowing that Modred was sweating a lot more outside the sauna now than Arthur was inside.

CHAPTRE
THE FIFTEENTH

GWEN STOOD IN front of the door to her former apartment, listening carefully for some sound of movement. There was none.

It had been a rainy day, and Gwen pulled her raincoat more tightly around her. She tossed her head, smoothing out the damp strawberry blonde hair, which she had permitted to grow to shoulder length, because that was the way He liked it. She smiled mirthlessly to herself. Lance had always insisted that she keep it short. She wondered what he would say now.

She wondered for the umpteenth time if she should have told Arthur she was coming back to her former home to finally reclaim items she'd abandoned when he'd carried her away. How long had it been? she wondered. She couldn't quite recall, for the past months had been idyllic. Although Arthur had been residing in his more traditional-style apartment, he and Gwen had found an occasional evening to sneak off to the castle and have, as Arthur referred to it, a dalliance.

In addition her self-respect had shot up a hundredfold

when she'd been voted president of Arthur's election committee. Merlin had pitched a holy fit on that score, but it had been fair and square. Everyone who worked with Arthur had come to genuinely like Gwen, and she'd blossomed under the appreciation to become a hard-working, quick thinking, aggressive woman—the woman she'd always had the potential to be, until Lance had smothered it. But he could only smother it for as long as he was an influence on her. And now that influence had been broken.

And yet . . . and yet . . .

She was back. Because she'd left behind books, clothing, and other personal possessions. But mostly because she had left behind a part of herself. And she wanted to reclaim it, clear up the "unfinished business" between herself and Lance, put closure to it all. Last time she'd left, she had been swept up and saved by her shining knight (and what a warm feeling just thinking of that moment gave her). This time she wanted to walk out on her own, head held high. It was what she knew she needed.

So why, with all that, did she feel a mixture of disappointment and relief that Lance might not be home and, thus, her big confrontation would not occur? She didn't know, but rather than stand in the hallway and procrastinate any longer, she reached into her purse and pulled out her keys. It didn't occur to her until that moment that Lance might have changed the lock. Fortunately he hadn't. She opened the door and stepped into the apartment.

A woman was lying on the couch, waiting for her.

Gwen's breath caught in surprise, and she glanced at the door to make sure that she had the right apartment.

"Oh, yes," said the woman. "You have the right place. Come in, Gwen, come in," she said, gesturing in a lazy, "come hither" manner. Gwen walked in slowly, cautiously, the hair on the back of her neck prickling. The apartment was dark, illuminated only by the hazy glow of the television set, which faced the couch. "Who in hell are you?"

The woman chuckled. Eerily, it reminded her slightly of Arthur's laugh. "Oh, not in hell, child. Not yet, not yet. I've been waiting for you for quite a while now. You've certainly taken your time."

The glare from the television played odd light images off the woman's angular face, flickering, giving her a look of nonsubstance. She was wearing a long black gown with a low-cut front that displayed a generous amount of cleavage. Again Gwen said slowly, "I don't know you . . . do I?"

"From another time," said the woman slowly. "Another life. However, I won't take it as a personal affront that you don't recall me. My name is Morgan."

Gwen blinked. "Morgan. Morgan . . . Le Fey?"

Morgan inclined her head graciously.

"Arthur's sister?"

"Half sister, if you please, my child."

"I . . . I thought you were dead. A long time ago." Gwen felt a weakening in her knees, and she rested one hand against the wall to support herself. She saw the look in Morgan's eye when Arthur was mentioned, and for the first time that she could ever recall, she actually feared for her life. She wanted to run screaming from the apartment, but some instinct warned her that backing down from Morgan now would most certainly mean her end.

Morgan shrugged. "That is what was believed. Of me. Of Arthur. Of Merlin. But it's difficult to extinguish pure good . . . or pure evil." She laughed. "Tell me, Gwen . . . do I look evil?"

"I'm not . . . no. That is, I'm not sure." She felt a chill in the air, and it was not a normal one. It felt as if a hundred thousand needles were pushing through her pores.

"Looks can be deceiving," said Morgan pleasantly. She leaned forward and, in a conspiratorial, just-us-girls tone, she whispered, "I'll tell you a secret, my child—good, evil, it's all subjective. No one really knows what good and evil are, except that those in charge invariably judge themselves good, and those who are not, are judged evil by those who have judged themselves good. Do you see? And if I were in charge, I would be able to label as evil the actions of those whom I did not like, and I would be considered good. And who would there be to say me nay?" She gestured for Gwen to come toward her. "I have something to show you."

But Gwen didn't move from the wall. "Why haven't you then? Tried to put yourself in charge, I mean?"

Morgan smiled. "Oh, my darling, if you could only have seen what I've seen all these centuries. When Arthur was first locked away in that cavern, after his near-fatal wound in battle, I could scarcely believe my good fortune. Arthur was gone. Merlin was already long gone. The world was easy pickings for me, or so I thought." She sighed, sounding as if she was discussing the height of tragedy. "The problem was, I had spent much of my life's work on Arthur's destruction. It had become such an obsession for me that, once he was out of the way, I found myself then facing the rest of the world. It was, to put it mildly, daunting."

She sat up, tucking her long legs under her. She patted the couch next to her, but Gwen still kept her distance. Morgan shrugged. "Oh, I had my followers. I had demons upon which I could call for assistance. But many of these were susceptible to cold steel—very susceptible. In any sort of pitched battle my forces would have been slaughtered, and not all my magiks could have prevented it. So I appeared at courts, but my name and image were already well known. Many kings and landowners shunned me, would not even let me into their homes, and those who did, did so only under a feeling of obligation to their departed liege, Arthur. And they kept quite a close eye on me, I can assure you.

"So I became a wanderer. And as I wandered, I plotted how to—as you said—assume the power that I sought. My wanderings led me to some incredible discoveries— the infinite prolongation of life, for one. Astral projection, a feat that had been beyond me during Arthur's lifetime. And the most depressing discovery of all—that time was against me. The world was growing, my pet. Beyond my meager ability to control it."

She got up from the sofa, then, with a little huff of impatience, and walked over to Gwen. She stroked Gwen's cheek gently, and Gwen shivered with horror at the cold-ness of the woman's touch.

"Oh, I kept my hand in, of course. At the time I was very embittered, you see. I had been given a world that was free of Arthur and Merlin, and yet that world had not become the easy pickings I thought it would be. I admit I had considered no further than what would happen once those two blights were gone. Then they were—and I had nothing. So I vented my frustration. I like to think I cut my own swath through history. You could see the hand of Morgan if you knew where to look. A plague here, a disaster there. A normal man who inexplicably began slaughtering helpless innocents. A demon cult arising, performing ritual sacrifices. An honest family man who inexplicably butchers his family, or an occasional genocide when I was feeling ambitious. Overturning society's order when the whim struck me and I could do so. 'Tell them to eat cake, Marie. French peasants love dessert. They'll thank you for suggesting it.'" She laughed at the recol-lection. "Fortunes lost, lives destroyed." She shook her head. "But one can only have random fun for so long before it begins to pall.

"And finally, after uncounted years, my anger began to turn to a sense of helplessness. Inflicting misery on others can only bring happiness for a time. And the unspeakable happened—I started to reminisce for the good old days. The days when my goals were clear-cut. Destroy Arthur.

Destroy Merlin. Thwart their horrendously humanitarian intentions, bollix their plans at every turn. Bring about the downfall of everything my accursed half brother held dear. Those were pleasant times, and I wanted them back.

"So I waited. Oh, I could have set Merlin or Arthur free, I suppose. But that would have destroyed the spontaneity. Besides, knowing those two, they would have gone back into seclusion, contending that they would come out when they were damned ready."

She circled the apartment like a shadow. "Thus did I become a sentinel. Keeping vigil. Waiting for the time when they would leave or escape their imprisonment, and the battle for supremacy could begin anew. But century after century passed, and I began to despair of their ever returning."

She turned away from Gwen and folded her arms. "A year ago, my sweet, you could not have recognized me. I shudder when I think of what I became. But it's all behind me now."

During Morgan's speech, Gwen had stood quietly and just listened. But as she had done so, something akin to anger had begun to build within her. Here this . . . this creature was speaking about disasters and horrors over a period of centuries, and she was doing so with with an air of nostalgia! She took pride in it! She was saddened over the fact that she hadn't done more. And all she wanted to do now was make Arthur's life miserable, and, by extension, Gwen's as well. Emboldened by her anger, and also—admittedly—by the fact that she wasn't dead yet, which led her to believe Morgan wanted something from her, Gwen took a step from the wall, standing on her own two feet, and said brusquely, "What have you done with Lance, you bitch?"

If she was expecting Morgan to show some sign of surprise or respect or something other than smugness, she was disappointed. Morgan just laughed. "Well, now look who is calling the kettle black." She came around and leaned right in Gwen's face, placing one hand against the wall. Gwen didn't back down, but it wasn't easy. "Who was it," continued Morgan, "that skulked around behind the back of her husband the king, carrying on an adulterous affair with her husband's best friend? An affair that led to the cracking of the Round Table, the greatest force for good in the history of mankind?"

Taking a deep breath, Gwen let it out unsteadily. "I . . . wasn't myself," she said.

Morgan seemed amused by that defense. "Indeed. Try being me, why don't you?"

"Where is Lance?" Gwen asked again.

Morgan faced her, a wolfish smile on her face. *My God, she even looks like Arthur,* thought Gwen. With relaxed, swaying steps, Morgan walked over to the TV and gestured to it. "Come here, my sweet. Come and see."

Slowly, haltingly, Gwen approached the television set and looked on the screen. Her hands flew to her mouth to stifle a scream.

Lance was on the TV. He was naked, chained and spread-eagled against what appeared to be the wall of a dungeon. His head lolled against his chest. The image was there for a moment only before the screen abruptly went blank, but it had seared itself into Gwen's mind. She spun on Morgan, her fists clenched. "Why?"

"Because," said Morgan easily, "I want Excalibur."

Gwen stepped back, aghast. "I . . . I don't know what—"

Morgan raised a cautioning finger. "Now, now, love— don't try lying to someone who is infinitely your superior when it comes to lying. You know Excalibur. Where does Arthur keep it?"

"With him. All the time."

"*All* the time?"

Gwen blinked a moment, not understanding, and then she colored. "You mean, like when we're—"

"Thaaaat's right."

"Oh, no. No, I couldn't."

Morgan crossed to her quickly and grabbed her by the wrist. Her pleasant demeanor disappeared as she spat out, "Then your precious Lance dies."

Their gazes locked and then Gwen said as levelly as she could, "So kill him."

Morgan released her in surprise. "What?"

Gwen shrugged, her stomach churning as she said, "Kill the bastard if you want. It doesn't matter to me."

Morgan smiled then, that same wolfish smile. "Very good. Oh, that's very good. I wasn't expecting that." She started to walk toward the door. "Very well, my queen. As you wish. Lance is as good as dead."

She got to the door, opened it, and then Gwen came up behind her and slammed it shut before she could exit. Morgan turned, and the two women faced each other, Gwen glaring, Morgan imperious.

"You kill him," said Gwen slowly, "and Arthur will hunt you down and kill you."

"Are you sure?" said Morgan quietly. "My understanding is that there's no love lost between Arthur and your former beau. Are you willing to gamble Lance's life that that threat will keep me in line—particularly since I believe it to be without substance?"

They stood there for a long moment, neither moving, neither willing to bend an inch in will or spirit. Then Morgan said, "Lance has spoken of you recently. I must say he's taking being chained up very well." Morgan walked back into the room with a jaunty little bounce to her step. "When I told him I'd be seeing you, he asked me to ask you for forgiveness. If you must know, his exact words were, 'Tell her not to worry about me. Whatever happens, I deserve it. But she won't care anyway, because she doesn't love me.' "

"He's right about that," Gwen said, trying to sound harsh. "I . . . I don't love him. Not anymore. Sometimes I wonder if I ever did."

"Well then," Morgan shrugged, "it should be simple for you. If you feel absolutely nothing for him, the choice is as good as made."

"You don't have to love someone not to want to see them killed."

"*I* do," replied Morgan. "And not even then. Perhaps we're more alike than you would think, my little queen. So . . . what will it be?"

Gwen's features crumbled momentarily, but she managed to quickly compose herself. "Look, Morgan," she said, trying to sound reasonable, "even if I waited until after Arthur and I had . . . you know . . . and tried to get away with his sword, it would never work. He's so attuned to it that the moment I'd lay a finger on Excalibur he'd snap awake and want to know what the hell I was doing."

Morgan regarded her, her eyebrows arched, and said, "You may be right, my love. Very well then. I believe we can hit upon a compromise, if you are amenable. Here is what I propose."

ODRED STARED AT Lance in grim amusement. Lance, hanging from the chains, didn't notice him. Both of them sensed Morgan's nearness at the same time and turned to look at her as she swept in.

"Trust me on this," Moe said sarcastically to his mother, while indicating Lance. "Next time, wallpaper instead."

"Wait outside," Morgan told him. "Plans are in motion. I'll fill you in shortly."

Modred nodded and exited the dungeon, while Lance fought to keep his head raised and his vision focused on Morgan.

Morgan smiled at him. Lance pulled against his chains, then, his hands flexing frantically as he said, "Morgan! Oh, please, no, not again!"

She nodded slowly, and reached behind her back as she said, "I just saw a friend of yours."

"Friend?"

"Yes. Barely an hour ago." Her hand made some motion and her black gown dropped to the floor. She stood naked before him. "Your friend was very concerned about you."

"Morgan, please! I'm telling you, I can't . . ."

She pressed her body against his. The smell of her was intoxicating, and he trembled even as, much to his shock, he felt himself becoming aroused.

"Didn't think you could again, eh?" said Morgan, nibbling at the base of his neck. "You might be interested to know, your friend wants me to let you go."

Lance moaned. "No! Please don't! Please don't let me go. Morgan, please . . ."

"Hush, my love." She placed a finger against his lips. "No need to worry. Morgan is going to take care of everything." She ran her fingers along the length of his body, toward his groin. "Everything . . ." she said languorously.

YE OLDE SOUND BITE

"Over the months Arthur's prevailing attitude of 'Don't bother me with countless facts, they only get in the way of making decisions' has become fashionable. Arthur has rapidly become a candidate with broad appeal. His no-nonsense attitude is refreshing, and his self-possession has come across superbly both in person and on camera. Is that how you see it, Amanda?"

"Frankly, Jimmy, I couldn't disagree more. I think Arthur Penn's candidacy is a culmination of everything that's wrong with politics, not only in New York, but in general in our country. Simple, facile statements are being presented as if they were intelligent policy, and the voters are eating it up . . . not because it would be of any long-term benefit, but because it's simplistic enough for them to wrap themselves around. The little man loves Arthur Penn because Penn uses enough one-syllable words."

"So you're saying he doesn't have a hope of getting your vote, Amanda?"

"Oh, hell no, I'm voting for him. He's totally hot."

"I have to agree, Amanda. Frankly, I'm almost tempted to turn gay for him. This has been Punch/Counter-Punch. Back to you, Roger . . ."

Chaptre
the Sixteenth

†

T HE RENOVATED STOREFRONT had a huge banner draped across it, reading ARTHUR PENN FOR MAYOR HEADQUARTERS. It was situated several blocks away from Arthur's main office in the Camelot Building. The move had been made due to space needs, not to mention higher visibility. Arthur and company now had 1,200 square feet, and although at first that seemed like a staggeringly large amount of room, it had filled up pretty quickly.

It was eight in the morning, a faint nip from the night fading in the air, and Arthur sat hunched with Ronnie Cordoba, a list of meetings and appearances between them. All around them, plastered on the walls, were the campaign posters that featured his picture and the tagline, *Arthur Penn: Common Sense*. Arthur was shaking his head in despair. "Are these all really necessary, Ronnie?" he was asking. "Why can't I just continue as I have been?"

"Because you need more concentrated media exposure," Ronnie said. He leaned back in the creaking wooden chair. "Your earlier tactics were fine, Arthur, in terms of basic introduction. But the Democratic and Republican primaries are just around the corner, and the election's only two months after that. We're just kicking into high gear now."

"Just kicking into high gear? Ronnie, look at this schedule." He slapped the piece of paper. "Appearing in front of groups I've never heard of to discuss subjects I know nothing about." His collar was unbuttoned, his tie draped over the chair nearby. They'd been working practically the entire night and the strain was beginning to show.

"It would help if you had a speech writer and standardized talks," said Ronnie reasonably.

Arthur stood and stretched his arms, painfully trying to work the kinks out of his shoulders. "Now, we've been all through this. I don't want to hire somebody to write for me what I'm going to say."

"It enables you to get your message across consistently by repeating it."

"My message is honesty and integrity. If I simply adhere to both, then that assures my message can't go astray."

"But . . . Arthur, everyone else works off prepared text!" complained Ronnie.

"Yes, and they all sound homogenized—that's the word, isn't it? Gwen used it the other day. Every single word of every speech, carefully considered, studied, gone over and weighed, drained of any possible juice, any possible chance of putting a nose out of joint here or costing a vote there. A prepared text is a sign of an unprepared soul."

Ron sighed, knowing better than to argue with Arthur when he was like this, which was pretty much all the time. He leaned back, rubbing the bridge of his nose. "Thanks for the homily, Arthur. I'll treasure it always. By the way, speaking of Gwen, where is she? She's been missing in action. This is the wrong time for her to turn into vapor mist on us."

Arthur shrugged. "She's had something on her mind the past few days. I've tried not to pressure her about it. I've discovered with women that it's not a good idea to try to make them talk when they don't want to. They'll generally come around."

Merlin walked in, dressed casually in jeans and a T-shirt. "Morning all," he said. "Percival's right behind me—he's stopping to get a bagel." He shook his head. "Fascinating thing, a bagel. Not quite a donut, but not quite a muffin. Not quite anything, and yet it's everything. All things to all people. It's the brunch of baked goods."

"Merlin, good God, it's too early to wax philosophical, okay? And what do your folks think about your involvement in politics?" asked Ronnie. "I mean, are they going to make you cut back on your time here when school starts?"

Merlin glanced at Ronnie, then back at Arthur. "Oh. That's right. We haven't told him, have we?"

Ronnie glanced around curiously. "Told me what?"

"About Merlin," said Arthur. "He's lived—"

"Alone," said Merlin quickly. "Alone, for quite some time. Both parents died, very suddenly."

"I'm sorry," Ronnie said, sounding very upset that he'd brought it up. "What happened?"

Arthur's mind raced and, for reasons surpassing understanding, he said, "A tragic . . . pogo stick accident."

This brought a very befuddled stare from Ronnie. "Pogo stick . . . accident?"

Arthur looked to Merlin for help. He had just taken a feeble attempt at an untruth, and it had gone about as well as one could expect from an insufferably honest man. Merlin quickly stepped in. "Yes, it was . . . tragic. They were bouncing on them, and then the things just . . . well, just flew apart. Became embedded in . . ." He managed to put across a shudder. "Well . . . it wasn't a pretty sight."

"I would think not. Merlin, do the authorities know? That you're living on your own, I mean. You're underage; I doubt they'd approve."

"I don't see that it's their business."

"Whether you think it is or not, Merlin, doesn't change the fact that this could hurt us." Ronnie looked to Arthur for support on his position. "Arthur, this is an unsupervised minor who's practically part of the campaign."

"Practically?" sniffed Merlin. "Without me you'd all be peddling nonworking watches on Thirty-fourth and Broadway."

"And if the press pick up on it, there could be lots of difficult questions," Ronnie continued as if Merlin hadn't spoken. "We can't take any sort of risk of endangering a minor or . . ."

"I'd be lost without him," said Arthur simply.

"Besides, don't get yourself in an uproar, Ronnie," said Merlin. "I'm living with someone now. Percival's moved in with me."

"Ah!" Ronnie let out a sigh of relief. "Well, I wish you'd said so in the first place. Would have spared me a few bad minutes there. So where's this place of yours?"

"On the Island."

"Oh," said Ronnie, nodding in understanding. "Long Island? Staten Island?"

"Bermuda, actually."

Arthur prayed that Ronnie wouldn't pursue the line of inquiry, and was silently relieved when Percival walked in carrying a small brown bag. "Morning, everyone." He cocked his head. "Ronnie, you okay? You look pale."

"Me? Naaah," said Ronnie, smiling raggedly. "Merlin, he was just kidding around with me, that's all."

"Oh, I see. You know, Ronnie," Percival said solicitously, "you've been workin' real hard. You should come out to Bermuda. Get some rest."

Ronnie nodded slowly, then leaned over the agenda for

the day. "Ooookay. Arthur, most of this stuff is routine. Grab a couple of hours sleep, first off. Then you've got a women's group in the morning, senior citizens lunch, a citizen's watch group in the early afternoon, and then you're meeting with a group of Jewish community leaders in the late afternoon. Then we've got the fund-raiser tonight—"

"Oh, right!" Arthur said briskly, obviously glad to be reminded. "I'm very upset about that, and I'm not going."

Merlin turned in surprise. "What are you talking about? Our money is starting to run low."

"There are limits as to what I will do, Merlin. Gwen told me about this dinner tonight. She said I'd have to wear a monkey suit. Now if you think for one minute I'm going to dress like an ape simply to get votes, then, my little wizard, you have quite another think coming."

He sat there, arms folded resolutely, eyes smoldering. Ronnie and Percival looked at each other, trying not to snicker. Merlin slowly shook his head. "Someone is going to have to talk to you, long and hard, about slang," he said.

THE BANQUET HALL was filled with men and women dressed formally, seated at large round tables, finishing their Chicken Kiev and assorted vegetables. And although the conversation at the tables was lively, attention kept returning to the long dais at the front of the room, where Arthur, Gwen, Percival, and several known and respected celebrities in New York were seated. It was their first lengthy meeting, and they found themselves, as always, charmed by Arthur's openness and frank manner of discussing issues.

Still, Arthur's attention kept turning to the extremely reserved Gwen sitting next to him. He leaned over at one point, making sure that the microphone wasn't turned on, and whispered, "Do you want to discuss it?"

"What?" She looked at him blankly. She was wearing a scoop-necked blue chiffon dress, and looked ravishing . . . and tragic.

"It. Whatever is on your mind," he said.

She looked down. "Oh."

"Well? What in the name of Uther is bothering you?"

Shifting in her seat, Gwen said, "Nothing."

He fiddled with his butter knife. "The past days it seems, whenever I ask you a question, I just get a one-word answer. Have you noticed?"

"Really?" she said.

Arthur shook his head and dropped the conversation before it had really had a chance to get going.

Merlin was seated at a table close to the front. Arthur had wanted him to be at the dais, but Merlin had demurred, observing that they didn't want or need endless speculation as to who the young boy seated with all the dignitaries was.

Seated in the middle was a former head of the United Nations General Assembly—a distinguished-looking man with graying temples, a bald head gleaming so brightly that some thought he had polished it with a chamois, and an avuncular manner that hid a spine of iron. He stood and rapped his fork briskly on the side of his glass. Slowly, conversation throughout the room quieted, while in the back of the room TV news cameras focused.

"Ladies and gentlemen, I thank you all for coming this evening," he said in a deeply timbered voice that carried a vague, middle-European accent. "I hope that you all enjoyed your dinners—usually these things seem to have meals made from Styrofoam." The guests laughed in agreement. "However, trust our host to be more concerned about the welfare of his patrons than that. As have many of you, I have been fascinated by Mr. Penn's rapid rise to public awareness in the past months. As have you, I have found myself impressed by his straightforward thinking, his unflinching way of addressing any problem. While other politicians seem to delight in straddling both sides of the fence, Arthur Penn is unafraid to speak his mind. To those people who agree with him, he is a sound ally. To those who disagree with him—well they respect him nevertheless and know, at least, that if Arthur Penn tells them something, it comes from the heart, and it's not going to be changed to cater to whims or political expediencies.

"Let me give you a little background on the Independent candidate for mayor of New York City . . ."

As he spoke, the waiters in the room, who had been scattered at random points throughout, slowly began to work their way forward.

Merlin felt a faint warning. He wasn't sure what it was—some bothersome feeling in the back of his head, like an angry gnat, letting him know that something was not quite right. He looked around his table. The eleven other people seated with him seemed harmless enough, attentive enough. He looked at the other tables, but saw no cause there for alarm. So what was it? *Where* was it?

I have not, thought Merlin, *lived this long without learning to trust to my instincts*. He wished he could signal Percival somehow that there was danger present; Arthur would have no greater guardian if there was some sort of strike intended at him.

A movement caught the corner of his eye. One of the waiters had an odd look on his face, a look of great intent. Merlin pursed his lips. He looked around and saw a half-dozen other waiters, all with the same determined expression. No, something was definitely not right. Merlin quietly slid a heavy glass dish off the table. It had been filled with slices of raw vegetables, but was now empty. Fortunately, nearly everyone in this century seemed to be on a diet. He reached into the pocket of his black jacket— his monkey suit jacket, he thought grimly—and pulled out a small flask with blue liquid inside. With one small hand he uncorked it and poured the liquid into the dish.

It spread rapidly, like a thing alive, coating the surface with blue. Moments later he held the dish up to his eye, peering through the blue filter of the liquid.

He gasped as he looked at the waiter nearby.

"And so, ladies and gentlemen, I give to you, Arthur Penn!"

Merlin's head snapped around. Arthur had risen behind the dais and was smiling out at his supporters. He started to stand, to shout out to Arthur exactly what was surrounding them. Then he slowly sat again, unsure of how to warn Arthur without setting off a general panic. Or how not to sound insane. He tried to signal to Percival, but the Grail knight was looking at Arthur, not noticing the frustrated mage at all.

Arthur leaned forward and said, "My friends . . ."

And that was when all hell broke loose.

J UST AS ARTHUR started to speak, there was a low moan from his left. He looked around in time to see Gwen, hand on forehead, eyes closed in a swoon, topple over backward.

"Gwen!" he shouted, and immediately moved to her.

At the end of the table a noted attorney asked loudly, "Is there a doctor here?" prompting a number of people to glance at their watches and wonder if this might not be a good time to leave.

Arthur knelt at Gwen's side, having already dipped a napkin into a glass of ice water. He stroked it across her face, saying urgently, "Gwen? Gwen, what's wrong?" She opened her eyes. He saw no illness in them. Only fear.

"Gwen, what—"

There was a sudden tug at his hip. He looked around to see a waiter behind him. The man's face was narrow, almost satanic, as with a fierce certainty he grabbed the invisible scabbard that hung at Arthur's side and yanked. There was a rip as the scabbard came free and the waiter leaped back, the invisible prize in his hands.

Arthur completely forgot about Gwen as he leaped toward the waiter, who backpedaled furiously. The entire room was now in an uproar. Everyone was demanding from each other what the hell was going on, and no one knew. Men grabbed for their wives, wives grabbed for their evening bags.

The waiter banged into Percival, who was standing behind him like a dark brick wall. Percival, however, not realizing that the waiter was clutching the invisible sword, acted with the instinct that comes naturally to a knight whose primary concern is protecting his liege. He picked the waiter up by either arm, grunted slightly, and threw the waiter off the dais. He crashed into the front table, knocking it flat, sending plates, utensils, and the centerpiece crashing to the floor.

Percival's moment of satisfaction lasted only as long as it took Arthur to whisper to him fiercely, "He's got Excalibur!" Realizing his error, Percival tried to vault the distance to the waiter, but now there was too much commotion, people shouting in confusion, crowds of people stumbling over each other and blocking a clear path.

The waiter darted past Merlin's table. Arthur hesitated for only a moment, glancing at the fallen Gwen, who now seemed unconscious, saw the crowds of people surging around, and said tightly to Percival, "Stay here with Gwen. Make certain she's all right and restore order to this insanity. I'll go after Excalibur."

"But, highness!" protested Percival, slipping momentarily into the old-fashioned form of address after months of remembering to call him "Arthur" or, more comfortably, "Mr. Penn."

"It's *my sword*," Arthur reminded him with burning pride, and moments later the former King of the Britons was hard on the heels of the fleeing waiter.

"Arthur!" shouted Merlin, and he tossed the blue-stained dish. Arthur caught it without breaking stride and

shoved it in his pants pocket, without the faintest idea
why Merlin had blessed him with such an odd gift at this
particular moment. Just before he was out of earshot, Merlin shouted, "Look through it!"

The half-dozen waiters had regrouped, and as one they
ran out the side of the room, through the swinging doors.
Arthur was right after them, and directly behind them
came the TV camera crews, excited by the thought that
what had seemed a standard money-raising dinner had
suddenly blossomed into a potential lead item for the
eleven o'clock news.

The waiters smashed through the kitchen, the holder
of Excalibur in the lead. Cooks were pushed roughly out
of the way and kitchen utensils clattered onto the floor.
Arthur did not even take the time to mutter "Excuse me"
as he shoved past. There was a rolling cart of dishes off to
the right. One of the waiters paused momentarily,
grabbed it, and toppled it. A resounding crash rang
through the kitchen, as miles of dishes spilled out and
shattered in Arthur's path. He vaulted, skidding slightly
when he landed, but he continued the pursuit. The camera
crews, on the other hand, were not as lucky. They slid
headlong into the mess of dirty dishes and leftover food
on the previously spotless floor, and with a multitude of
yells, went down, one atop the other.

One of the fleeing waiters stumbled, banging into a
water pitcher set to one side. The water tumbled off and
it splashed on the waiter's leg. To Arthur's confusion, he
let out a strangled cry and clutched at the leg as if it had
been injured, before limping out the door as fast as he
could after his associates.

Arthur burst out into the open air of the back alley. It
took a moment for his eyes to readjust to the gloom of
the night, and then he saw the bright red jackets of the
waiters only yards away, dashing down the alley toward
the street. Arthur gave chase, shucking his expensive dinner jacket and tossing it aside.

The waiters made it to the sidewalk and then did exactly what Arthur feared they would do—split up. Arthur felt a surge of panic, suddenly regretting that Percival wasn't by his side to aid him in his pursuit. How was he supposed to follow the one with the invisible sword? Which one had it?

He felt a bulge in his pants pocket and remembered the dish Merlin had tossed him. What had Merlin said? Look through it. He pulled out the dish and peered through the blueness, and the moment he did, he made an awful sound deep in his throat. Spotting the waiter bearing Excalibur turned out not to be a problem: through the blue lens the sword became visible, even though it had not been drawn from its scabbard. But what horrified Arthur was the thing holding it.

It was covered completely with brown scales, its torso elongated so that it was hunched over. Its hands ended in three long, tapering claws. Its head was similar to an alligator's, except the snout was not quite as long. It turned its malevolent green eyes on Arthur and snarled a guttural warning through a double row of pointed teeth. However, it did look snappy in its red waiter's jacket and pressed black slacks.

It turned and faced Arthur, drawing Excalibur from the sheath. Arthur saw his sword glowing dimly in the evening light, and rather than fear, he felt rage that this . . . this thing was soiling his beloved sword with its foul hands.

Passersby who saw only an angry waiter, incensed perhaps because he'd been stiffed on a tip, nevertheless drew back in fright when they saw the immense sword he wielded. Arthur approached cautiously, arms spread out, legs flexed, never taking his eyes from his opponent. He growled low in his throat as he inched closer and closer to the demon. Cars slammed to a halt on nearby Forty-seventh Street. Two small children, who lived in an apartment above a deli that had closed for the night, leaned out their window and watched in fascination.

The demon swung Excalibur in an arc and hissed, "Morgan Le Fey sends her regards, King of Nothing!" The demon slashed Excalibur down and Arthur dove to one side, rolling and quickly getting to his feet. The demon closed on him, swinging the blade back and forth. It whizzed through the air like an angry hornet, and Arthur could do nothing except stay the hell out of the way. He stumbled once and the demon almost caught him flat-footed, swinging Excalibur around, and Arthur leaped out of its path. The blade sliced through a parking meter, cutting it neatly in half at the middle of the pole.

Arthur backed up, looking around desperately for something to intervene. He heard a police car's siren, but it was a long way off, and besides, there was a chance that police would not be able to aid him against this nightmare creature.

"Afraid, Arthur?" crowed the demon. "You have a good head on your shoulders. Let's see if you can keep it there."

Arthur retreated farther, thankful at least that the by-standers had had the sense to get away. Then his retreat was momentarily halted as he bumped into a large iron object behind him. His questing fingers immediately informed him he'd run up against a fire hydrant.

The demon was barely a yard away, and this time Arthur didn't flinch. "All right, you bastard," he snarled. "Give it your best shot."

With unearthly glee the demon swung Excalibur back over its head and then brought the blade racing downward. Arthur waited until the last possible instant, waited until the weight of Excalibur would make the sword's trajectory unalterable. And when it was bare inches from the top of his head, Arthur sprang catlike to one side. Excalibur sliced deep into the fire hydrant.

In a rage the demon yanked Excalibur to one side. The blade effortlessly cut through the rest of the hydrant, and in a sudden gush, water blew forth from the broken hydrant. It sprayed upward and sideways. The demon was caught in the face and chest by the full impact of the water. With a howl it went down, clawing at the clean water that, to the demon, was like acid. Excalibur flew from its grasp and clattered to the ground. Arthur watched with grim satisfaction.

Arthur was on the sword in an instant, and within the next was upon the demon. He held the sword at the creature's neck and snarled, "What was the plan? Why did you want Excalibur? Tell me. Tell me or I swear to heaven—"

And to Arthur's momentary astonishment, the creature suddenly flung itself forward, running itself through upon Excalibur. It grinned in what could only be seen as a perverse sort of triumph, as what passed for blood in a demon seeped to the ground.

A hole appeared in the demon's chest. Arthur looked down in surprise as a small creature darted forth from the already disintegrating body. It flittered this way and that, leaving a trail of flame behind it. Arthur stared at it in wonder and muttered, "A fire elemental. Upon my sword, I thought I'd seen the last of—"

The elemental gingerly danced around the water droplets, still spraying from the fountaining hydrant. Then it caught sight of Arthur, and it flared in alarm and anger. Arthur frowned, suddenly aware that this small creature intended no good at all. He yanked Excalibur from the demon's throat and in one smooth movement sliced upward at the fire creature. The little ball of flame avoided him, spun around his head so close that it singed his eyebrows, then headed straight for the building that housed the closed deli.

"No!" shouted Arthur, but it was too late. The elemental hit the building at full speed. There was a loud *fwoosh*, and it was as if the two-story building had been firebombed. The downstairs windows exploded as fire leaped out from them, illuminating the street in a night-

marish glow of orange. Smoke poured out from the shattered windows, both downstairs and upstairs.

As Arthur's gaze took in the second floor, he was horrified to see two children in one of the windows. The air
crackled and became acrid with the biting sting of the
smoke. The children screamed.

The police car was pulling up, and one of the cops was
shouting into the radio, "Forget the disturbance call! Get
a fire truck here!" but how long now before the firefighters
would arrive? Furthermore, Arthur realized—as he looked
around the area in horror—there would be nothing for
them to hook up to. The hydrant had been slashed in half,
thanks to his brilliant tactic.

Without hesitation Arthur stepped into the stream of
water that gushed from the hydrant. The water soaked his
clothes, his body, his hair. He glanced over to where the
demon lay, and was pleased to see nothing but a small
pile of soot where the creature had once been. That was
convenient—he hadn't relished the thought of explaining
the presence of a recently slain corpse to the authorities.
Arthur stepped out of the water then, grabbed up Excalibur's scabbard, and slid the weapon back into his sheath,
buckling the now unseeable blade back onto his belt even
as he raced toward the burning building. He heard the
police officers shouting for him to come back but he didn't
hesitate.

THE PLACE WAS pandemonium. People were surging toward the exits, hearing the police sirens, hearing explosions, trying to determine what the hell was
going on. Percival was on the dais, trying to shout for
order and calm and, unfortunately, being ignored.

Merlin, in the meantime, was watching Gwen, who was
now sitting and looking ragged and not just a little frightened . . . and suspicious . . . and guilty.

Something was wrong, extremely wrong. Although

part of his instinct was to go out and help Arthur, he was now convinced that something was definitely up with Gwen. Although Merlin might have disputes about the way Arthur handled himself in front of voters and reporters, he was absolutely steadfast in his confidence in the king when it came to matters of combat. Arthur in the short term over demons didn't worry him; Gwen, in the long term over anything did, and it was time to sort things out.

Merlin started toward her, questions forming on his lips, when someone blocked the way. The young wizard glanced up. It was another waiter, with a very unpleasant look. Merlin stepped back, but the waiter drew back his fist and sent a roundhouse punch sailing toward Merlin's chin. A ring glowed momentarily on the fist that came toward him, punching through the defensive ward Merlin hurriedly tried to erect. Merlin went down as if he'd been poleaxed, the floor spinning around him. He tried to stagger to his feet even as the waiter/demon grabbed up a chair and brought it slamming down on the magician's head. Stars exploded in Merlin's skull and he fell to the ground, unconscious.

T HE TV CREWS emerged from the building just as the police cars pulled up out front. Seeing the fire, the newsmen automatically trained their minicams on the blaze. It took them a few seconds to realize that there were children trapped inside, and even a few seconds more before they saw that the would-be next mayor of New York was risking his life in a mad dash into the inferno.

Arthur took one glance upward, saw that the children were hysterical, saw that there was no way he was going to be able to talk them into trying to jump down, even though they would likely survive the drop—especially if he used his own body to break the fall. However, he did not relish the idea of entering the building—the intensity of the heat was almost overwhelming.

Then, as he studied the wall, he had an idea. He removed his shoes and began to scale the side of the building.

It was easier than he'd dared hope. The building front was brick, and the windows and doors had been built with so many outcroppings that it had been practically designed for handholds. From the corner of his eye Arthur saw that residents of the building were charging out the front, as were those to either side, and he was thankful for that. There was only so much he could do in terms of getting people to safety, and he had to deal with one crisis at a time.

He went higher, higher. Flame flared out from the window beneath him, licking at his pants cuff, and he had to reach down to pat it out. The wall was heating up under his touch. In moments it would be too hot for him to hold on. Bracing himself, he thrust himself higher, and his desperate reach grabbed the outcropping of a narrow ledge. It was all that he needed to pull himself up and away from the window. He scrabbled apelike (and he thought for a moment of Gwen's reference to a monkey suit—how right she had been) with his hands holding the ledge and his feet braced on the wall directly below.

He heard the sound of the children before he saw them. Hundreds of sparks flew at him and dissipated on the fabric of his wet clothing. He thanked his common sense for the protective move he'd made earlier, or otherwise he'd have had a lot more to worry about than that one singed pants cuff.

EVERYONE FROM MERLIN'S table had already moved away, and so they did not see the incident. Only Percival and Gwen were left at the front table, everyone else having headed outside. But Percival saw, and he leaped over the head table, shouting, "Hey! What the hell do you think you're doing? Put him down, right now!"

He closed in on the demon, but the monster swept its arm around, throwing Percival back like a rag doll. Percival fell over the table, knocking over the centerpiece and catching up the tablecloth. He hit the ground and lay still.

"What are you doing?" shrieked Gwen, running toward him. "You only wanted the sword! Morgan said all you wanted was the sword!"

The waiter grinned at her in an unearthly way. "Morgan lied," it growled. "She does that sometimes."

"Put him down! Now!" She grabbed at the thing, grabbed at its shirt, and a piece of it tore off in her hand as it shoved her back effortlessly, knocking her over several chairs. With a contemptuous sneer, the demon threw Merlin into the middle of a tablecloth, rolled him up in it, and moments later was darting out the kitchen exit with the unprotesting bundle slung over its shoulder. And just like that, Marlin was gone.

$\mathfrak{A}$RTHUR LOOKED UP through the smoke at the crying children. "Hold on," he called. "I'll be right there!" His heart pumping furiously, he pulled himself up so that his face was even with the bottom of the window. He saw the frightened, smoke-smeared faces.

"Come with me!" he shouted.

To his utter astonishment, they backed up, shaking their heads. The little girl said, "Our mommy will be mad! She . . . she said she was just running out for some milk . . . she'd be right back . . . we weren't supposed to go anywhere!"

"We're not allowed to go with strangers!" the boy said, as the room filled with smoke.

"Oh, for God's sake!" bellowed Arthur as he stepped in through the window and approached the children.

They pointed at him and started shouting over and over again, *"Stranger danger, stranger danger!"*

"This is ridiculous," Arthur muttered, as he slung them under his arms, and turned toward the window to get back out.

Then he saw it. Between him and the window, there was a leaking gas line, and flame was leaping right at it.

There was no time. The closest exit was now the door, and Arthur slammed into it at full speed, taking the entire impact with his shoulder. He crashed through the thin door, sending wood flying everywhere, just as the apartment behind him exploded. He fancied that he could hear the screams outside as they saw the window through which he'd entered obliterated by a wall of flame.

The children were no longer screaming in protest. They were clutching on to him for dear life, the only sound coming from them being soft whimpering.

There was fire everywhere. He had stopped breathing, fearing the smoke would collapse a lung. Flame was licking at the banister of the stairs, and the wooden steps were smoldering but had not yet gone up. He ran down them, trying not to fall, overbalanced as he was with the children in tow.

Suddenly, his foot went through one of the steps and his leg went through up to his knee. With a howl of pain and fury, Arthur extracted the leg, which was now cut and bleeding. He fought off the pain; there wasn't time for it now, it would be dealt with later. He stumbled, staggered down the steps, hearing a cracking overhead that told him the roof was in danger of collapsing.

The door was just ahead of him. Unfortunately, so was what appeared to be a wall of flame. The heat almost drove him back, but to go back was to perish. Arthur steeled himself for a moment, holding the children as close to him as he could, and charged. He darted through the flame, almost losing consciousness, and suddenly he was in the open air, stumbling down the front steps of the building. He lost his grip on the children, heard them sobbing as they tumbled away from him, and then he realized that he was on fire. Without hesitation he fell to the ground and rolled, and the quick movement was exactly what was needed to snuff out the flames before they consumed him.

Police officers pushed through the crowds of people starting to encircle them. Now there were more sirens coming—fire engines and ambulances. Two policemen wrestled momentarily with the TV cameramen, who also wanted to push through the crowd to get close-ups. "Move it or lose it!" snapped one of the cops, and the cameramen got the hell out of his way.

Arthur lay in the center of the circle, moaning softly, but sitting up. The children's mother was sobbing, clutching them to her, a bag of groceries lying forgotten on the ground nearby. Everyone was shouting questions at once, and Arthur simply sat there for a moment, dazed, trying to take it all in. Then he fought his way to a standing position.

"Whoa, fella," one of the cops said, "steady . . ."

"Gwen . . ." Arthur said through parched, broken lips. "Have to get . . . to Gwen . . ." But there was a sharp pain in his chest, and he started to cough violently. "Gods, I'm centuries too old for this sort of thing."

From all around him, people who had been guests at the dinner were murmuring in amazement at what they'd seen. It was as if all wanted to reach out, to touch him, to say something to him in low, reverent tones.

As the fire trucks rounded the corner, there were shrieks as the roof of the building collapsed in on itself with a heartrending crash. The firemen were already leaping off, looking at the shattered hydrant in confusion, and seeking out alternate sources of water.

"Arthur!"

He turned and saw Gwen shoving her way through the crowd. But she was having trouble doing so; fortunately enough, Percival was right behind her. Moments later he was in front of her, strong-arming people out of the way so that she could get to Arthur.

Arthur let out a long, unsteady sigh of relief. "Oh, thank the Lord, Gwen. It's good to see you." He winced as he touched his leg. "Help me get back to the hall. People paid good money to hear me babble about some nonsense or other."

An ambulance had pulled up, and paramedics were already leaping out of the back. "Arthur, don't be crazy!" Gwen was saying. She shouted to the paramedics, "Over here!"

"Attend to others! I'm fine!" Arthur snapped.

"Now!" Gwen insisted, and he realized she wasn't taking no for an answer.

Moments later they were seated inside an ambulance. It was not, however, moving, as the paramedics were busy offering aid to others, assessing the situation and seeing who—if anyone—needed immediate conveyance to the hospital. The firemen were busy battling the blaze and, apparently, winning. Gwen sat next to Arthur, as the king drew in oxygen from a tank, while Percival stood just outside the ambulance, ensuring privacy and keeping everyone at bay.

"What happened, Arthur? How did—?"

"That can wait," he said, speaking through the oxygen mask on his face. "Where's Merlin?"

No reply.

Arthur looked up into Gwen's eyes. "Gwen?"

She turned away. With forced calm, Arthur said, "Gwen! Where the hell is Merlin?"

"One of those waiters," she said tonelessly. "Knocked him out. Percival tried to stop him; so did I. He made off with him."

"*What?!*" Arthur was trembling with rage. "Why didn't Percival himself tell me this?"

"Because this is the first moment alone we've had, and

we wanted to wait until we knew you were out of immediate danger. You inhaled smoke, you were bleeding,
you—"

"Damnit, Gwen, they've got Merlin! I cannot believe
Percival allowed them to—"

She tried to restrain him. "Arthur, come on! Percival
was caught off-guard by a demon! He tried! It's not right
to blame him!"

"Yes . . . yes, of course," Arthur managed to calm himself, albeit just barely. And then, suddenly, a thought
lanced through him, like a spear. His hand had been resting on Gwen's shoulder, but now it flexed so hard that
Gwen yelped.

"Arthur! What's—?"

His voice was a sick whisper. "How did you know?"

"W-what? What do you—"

He turned to confront her, and Gwen's body shook
with fear from the look in his eyes. "How did you know
Percival fought a creature from hell, a demonspawn, and
not a human being?"

"You told me."

"No."

"Yes. Just now. You—"

"Don't make it worse!" he shouted at her. "Don't lie to
me!"

Tears streamed down her face as she tried to shrink from
him, but there wasn't room in the ambulance to get away
from him. "Arthur, please don't—"

"How did you know?"

"*Morgan told me!*" she screamed. "She told me they
would be there. She arranged for everything." She was
speaking desperately, words tumbling one over the other.
"But she told me she just wanted the sword. That's all.
She swore no one would be hurt. I thought—"

"And you provided the distraction." His words were
cold, burning with an icy flame that also blazed in his
eyes.

"Yes. Bu—"

He shoved her away roughly, fists clenched as he trembled with repressed fury. "Damn you! How could you betray me again?"

Her body racked with sobs, as she said, "Arthur, please. I had no choice. Lance—"

"Don't talk to me. Don't even look at me." His voice was pure venom. *"You're not fit for human company!"*

He shoved open the door of the ambulance, tossing aside the oxygen mask, and immediately there were cameras going off, mikes in his face, reporters shouting things like, "Mr. Penn, what does it feel like being the man of the hour?" "What were you thinking when you were hanging from the side of that burning building?" "Did you think you were going to die?" "How did you feel about—"

Arthur grabbed the first newsman who came within arm's length and shoved him roughly out of the way. He spun and shouted, "Get away from me! Just . . . leave me . . ." His voice caught as he looked at Gwen's tear-stained face. "Leave me alone."

He limped away into the darkness, illuminated briefly in the flickering of the rapidly dying fire.

I**T WAS LATE** at night in Central Park. Clouds obscured the moon, and there were no sounds other than a young woman pounding on the uncaring stones of Belvedere Castle.

The sides of her hands were abraded from the stone as she continued to smash her hands against the wall in supplication. "Arthur, please let me in," sobbed Gwen. "You've got to let me explain!"

There was a tap on her shoulder and she whirled around. "Oh, Arthur, I—"

"No, my sweet," said Morgan quietly. "It's not Arthur."

When the moonlight hit her, she seemed to drain the brightness from it.

"*You! You . . . bitch!*" She leaped at Morgan, fingernails bared like claws. Morgan caught her flailing wrists and tossed her roughly to the ground. She stood over Gwen and laughed harshly. "What a pathetic little fool you are." She nodded toward the castle. "Arthur's not in there."

"How do you—"

"I know a great deal about a great deal. Arthur's wandering the streets right now," said Morgan easily. "Angry. Confused. Hurt. I could attack him now and probably defeat him utterly. But I think we'll let him stew. You, on the other hand, little queen," she said, smiling menacingly, "you have served your purpose."

In a pure, white-hot fury, Gwen hiked up the hem of her evening dress and swept out with her legs. She knocked Morgan's legs out from under her, sending the sorceress toppling to the ground. Within moments she was upon Morgan, tearing at her hair, her eyes, her face. Morgan shrieked in anger and indignation.

Gwen felt herself abruptly being hauled off of Morgan's writhing body. She flailed at the men who stood on either side of them.

"Whoa! Hey! C'mon, slugger," said Buddy, struggling to hold on to the infuriated Gwen. "This is, whattaya call, undignified."

Gwen stopped, looking from Buddy to Elvis and back again. "What are you guys doing here?" she demanded.

"We live here," said Buddy simply. "Here in the park. That's how we first met the king. And now we see you and this nice lady who you were tryin' to kill. I tell ya, y'meet the best people around here."

Morgan staggered to her feet. "You'll regret that," she said, gingerly touching the scratches where Gwen had raked her face. "You'll regret that most dearly."

"What are you going to do?" demanded Gwen. "Kill me? I feel dead already. You couldn't hurt me any more than I've already hurt myself. Damn you! I should have gone straight to Arthur—"

"Yes. You should have," said Morgan with a twisted smile. "Are you wondering where your precious Lance is? I still have him. And you know why? Because he doesn't want to leave. It seems he's developed a fondness for bondage. Isn't that interesting?"

Buddy raised an eyebrow. "Well, it's certainly got my interest."

"You're lying," snarled Gwen. "You lie about everything."

"Not about this," said Morgan. "I don't need to lie about this. It's too delicious to be otherwise. It was all for nothing, little queen. That's all it ever was. That's all it ever will be."

Elvis took a step forward. There was a switchblade in his hand and a distracted tone in his voice. "You know, I don't like you."

Morgan stared at him for a time, stared at the switchblade, and then she turned in an abrupt swirl of her long black cape. She strode off into the darkness and merged with the shadows.

Buddy shook his head. "She must be zero fun at parties." He turned to Gwen and shook his shaggy head. "You look so sad."

"She's telling the truth," Gwen said slowly. "About Lance. I can feel it. I know it. And I . . . I had it," said Gwen. "I had it all. And I lost it. And I can try to blame Morgan, or Lance, or anybody I want."

Elvis stepped forward. "You can blame me if you'd like."

She smiled unevenly and patted his thick beard, then unconsciously wiped her hand on her dress as she said, "That's sweet. But what I'm trying to say is that there's really nobody to blame but myself. That's the part that's tough to take."

Buddy nodded, not understanding in the least, but determined to be helpful. "Gwen, if you'd like, you can stay with us tonight."

"What, under a tree? Gee, that's nice, but"—she wiped her nose—"I don't think that would be, well, right."

"Oh. You wanna, y'know, get married first?"

Gwen stared at him, and then she frowned. "She walked away. From the knife. And you. That's . . . that's interesting." She was speaking in a distant voice, as if she was in shock. Or as if there was something going through her mind. "Thank you," she said to Elvis abruptly, and then she rose and walked away, leaving the two of them looking extremely puzzled. Then again, since that was the way they usually looked, had anyone else been there, no one would have been inclined to notice.

YE OLDE SOUND BITE

⸸

"Caller, you're on with Marv in the morning."

"Marv, hi, this is Tricia, first time caller from Long Island. And I just want to say that, with the primaries over, we should be happier than ever that someone like Arthur Penn's come along. I mean, the primaries were so predictable. Keating was predictable, Taylor was predictable. Democrats and GOPs with money behind them, and their attack ads and everything. And here's Arthur Penn, and he's not out there trying to beat up on other candidates. It's like he doesn't even notice them, y'know? He's just out there, laying everything on the line, and saving people and (bleep). Oh, jeez, I'm sorry, I can't say (bleep) on radio—aw, (bleep!)"

CHAPTRE
THE SEVENTEENTH

✝

ERNIE KEATING SHOULD have been happy. He was, in fact, anything but.

It was past midnight as he huddled with his staff in a classic smoke-filled room. Bernie sat forward, rubbing his eyes, his vest open to allow for his considerable girth. Moe Dreskin sat to his immediate right. The various officials who ran his campaign were also there, in varying degrees of wakefulness.

Bernie looked around and slammed his open hand on the table, effectively rousing everyone. "What the hell are we going to do about this Arthur Penn character?" he demanded.

Effecting a gangland tone, his treasurer said, "You want we should have him whacked, boss? I'll go round up Rico and the boys and—"

"Shut up, Charlie," said Bernie tiredly. "Now damnit, I'm serious. You know my philosophy about political opponents." He paused expectantly.

Moe filled the void, reluctantly. "Stick it to 'em."

"Stick it to 'em. That's right. Except what the hell are

we supposed to do about this Penn guy?" He got up and started to circle the room. Moving through the smoke as he was, he looked like a steamship penetrating the fog. "He's got no political record to speak of. For most people that would be a detriment, but he makes it work to his advantage. The voters see him as a fresh face in a jaded political arena, and it gives us absolutely zilch to work with. His business practices? Squeaky-clean. Hell, the man's never been investigated. All of his investments are sound and aboveboard. He's hardly been involved in running anything day-to-day, so although there's virtually no one to vouch for him, there's no to say anything bad against him either. And if that's not enough for you," said Bernie with genuine indignation, "the guy has to go and save kids from a flaming building. Kids! Isn't that just friggin' fabulous! With TV news crews there to tape him." A sudden thought struck him. "Hey, maybe he started it. Stan, you're the press liaison. You have the contacts. Anyone checking out that possibility?"

Stan shook his head. "Police looked into it for weeks and still aren't sure what caused it. It seems like some sort of spontaneous combustion. Either way, certainly no sign of any incendiary device."

Marcia, the head of clerical, put in, "That whole thing gets bigger with every retelling. The children were telling reporters that our Mr. Penn, before the fire started, was fighting a man with a sword, and the man supposedly turned into some sort of creature and then crumbled away once Penn defeated him."

Bernie moaned. "Just what we need. Urban legends about this clown. So where does this leave us?"

Moe shook his head. "In a couple of days there's the televised debate. It's going to be you, Kent Taylor, and Penn. Now—"

Bernie hauled his carcass to his feet. "Penn's in the debate? Since when?"

"Since the local TV stations became interested in ratings," said Moe sourly. "Since Penn won that citation from the Fire Department for gallantry. Since *New York* magazine put him on their Most Eligible Bachelor Politician List. Since he did *'Letterman.'* Penn was getting himself a following before, but that whole fire business made him really hot, so to speak. They decided that a debate would not really reflect the voters' interest in the candidates unless Penn was present. Frankly I can't blame them."

"Well, that's just wonderful, Moe," retorted Bernie. "Look, what it boils down to is this—I don't want to lose this race. I really don't. And the key to winning is, I suspect, bringing down Arthur Penn."

"For what it's worth," said Marcia, "I think Penn's worst enemy right now is himself."

"Come again?"

"He was on a local morning show the other day. He was snappish, irritable. Short with the interviewer. It's as if his mind is a million miles away."

"You know," said Stan, "come to think of it, he's been like that ever since the whole fire thing. Maybe it shook him more than he lets on. He could hurt his image if he keeps it up. Because it's starting to look as if he can't stand pressure."

"Yeah, well, it's looking that way to us, but not to the general public. Not yet at any rate. So we're going to have to bring it to their attention." Bernie looked around the table. "We're going to have to start playing hardball, ladies and gentlemen. I hope that we have a clear understanding of this. Because if we don't win . . ." his voice rose dramatically, and then he paused.

"Then we lose?" suggested Marcia helpfully.

Bernie covered his face and said quietly, "Meeting adjourned. Go home. Get some sleep. See you all tomorrow." He glanced at his watch. "Sorry, make that later this morning. Hey, Moe," he said far more halfheartedly than he usually did. "Stay a minute. Rest of you, just remember one thing: We're going to kick Penn's ass."

Moe sat down again opposite Bernie and waited until the room cleared. He looked worn out.

"Penn's going to kick my ass," he said quietly.

Moe leaned back and sighed. "Bernie, you're being too hard on yourself—"

"No, I'm being realistic. I'm going to suck in a televised debate."

"Bernie," laughed Moe, "don't be absurd! You're a lawyer, for Pete's sake."

"Yeah, so was Nixon. Whatever else I may be, Moe, telegenic, I'm not. I'm telling you, under those studio lights, in that face-to-face situation, I'm gonna come across like the guy in grade school who always stole your milk money. And TV cameras love Penn's face. It'll be like JFK and Nixon. Nixon had more substance, but he looked like a criminal."

"He was a criminal," Moe reminded him.

"Yeah, but not until years after that."

"You're going to win, Bernie," Moe said with confidence. "If you hadn't asked me to stay, I would have hung back to talk with you anyway."

There was something in Moe's voice that lent momentary wings to Bernard Keating's heart. "What is it?" His voice dropped to a confidential level. "You got something on Penn? Please, say you've got something on him."

"Oh, I've got something on him, all right," said Moe slowly. "But you're not going to like it."

"How can I not like it?" He frowned. "Is he gay? Don't tell me he's gay. Not that I wouldn't use it," he added quickly, "it's just that I find that whole thing so, I don't know . . . *yuucchh*."

"No. It's nothing like that." Moe took a deep breath. "You're going to have to be prepared to do something a little unorthodox. At the debate this Friday I want you to ask Mr. Penn something—"

"But we're not supposed to be talking directly to each

other. Questions are being posed by moderators, and we're supposed to answer them."

Moe laughed curtly. He leaned back in his chair and said, "You telling me you're reluctant to start breaking rules?"

"Only if it's going to net me something big."

"It should."

"Only should?"

"All right, will, then." Moe took a deep breath and said, "I want you to ask Arthur Penn who he is."

Bernie looked at him blankly. "What?"

Moe repeated it, and Bernie paused a moment, stroking his chin. "Moe, you know what the first rule is that a lawyer learns in the study of cross-examination? Never ask a question to which you do not already know the answer. So am I correct in assuming that the answer is going to be something other than the obvious?"

"Arthur Penn," said Moe, "is not his real name. At least, so he believes."

"What, he changed his name? I'm not following you, Moe."

"Arthur Penn," said Moe, "is short for Arthur Pendragon."

"Pendragon?" He rolled it around in his mouth like marbles. "What the hell kind of name is that?"

"Medieval. Bernie, your opponent believes himself to be the original King Arthur."

The portly man stared at Moe. "Moe, let's cut the crap, okay?"

"I'm not kidding, Bernie. The man believes that he is King Arthur, Lord of the Round Table, ruler of Camelot, King of all the Britons."

Bernie heaved himself to his feet, knocking his chair back. "Moe, this is just too ridiculous! You're telling me that my main obstacle to being mayor of this city is bug-fuck crazy?"

"I'm saying that the man thinks he's the original Arthur, son of Uther, Lord of—"

Bernie put up a beefy hand. "Please, spare me the family tree, okay? You got any proof of this?"

"I've got one Lance Benson. He's ready to swear that Arthur attacked him with a sword while 'rescuing' Benson's girlfriend from the supposedly vile clutches of Benson himself."

Keating's mouth dropped open. "Are you serious?" he whispered. "I want to meet this Benson guy."

"He's tied up at the moment," said Moe dryly. "But I'm sure he'd be happy to come forward when you need him."

Bernie was silent for a long moment, trying to assimilate this new information. "He really, honest to God thinks he's King Arthur?"

"That's right."

"This is too much. But wait—" He turned on Moe. "How do I know that, if I ask him point blank, he won't just lie about it?"

"Not Arthur," said Moe with absolute certainty. "He prides himself on telling the truth. It would be totally against his dementia to lie about who he thinks he is."

"Too much. Just too much." He stabbed a finger at Moe. "You're asking for one hell of a leap of faith here, Moe. If I come out looking like an idiot on this . . ."

"You can't possibly. You ask him point blank what his real name is. Even if he maintains that it's Arthur Penn—which he won't—then you just cover yourself by saying that you'd heard he'd changed it and you just wanted to make sure the record was straight. At worst it'll get you a raised eyebrow or two that will be quickly forgotten. At best," and he smiled unpleasantly, "it will get you the election in your hip pocket."

They talked for an hour more, Keating waffling over it. By the time Moe left he was only about seventy percent convinced that Keating would go along with it. Moe stood on the curbside, lighting up a cigarette and taking a deep drag. He glanced up at the moon and pulled his coat tightly around him against the stiff breeze. You could tell that winter was on its way.

He started walking, scanning the streets for a passing cab, when he suddenly felt an arm around his throat in a chokehold. Moe tried to scream for help, but his wind had been effectively and precisely cut off. His assailant dragged him into a nearby alleyway, pulling Moe as if he weighed nothing. Moe clawed at the arm around him, pounded on it in futility. Once in the alley Moe was swung around and hurled against a wall. He slammed into it with bone-jarring impact, and with a moan sank to the ground. Distantly he heard the *shikt* of a bladed weapon being drawn from its sheath, and he tried to draw air into his lungs to shout for help.

The tip of a glowing sword hovered at his chest before he could make a sound.

"I wouldn't, Modred," said Arthur quietly.

"You . . ." He swallowed. "You wouldn't kill an unarmed man."

"Perhaps," said Arthur. "Perhaps not. Are you willing to bet your life on it?"

Arthur prodded Moe gently in the ribs with Excalibur. Moe shook his head frantically.

"Now then . . . where is she?"

"Who?"

"Your mother, you traitorous little worm," Arthur snapped at him. "All of this, all the ill that has befallen me, has her stamp on it."

Moe rallied and said angrily, "You got an attitude problem, you know that? I mean, is this the way you treat the son you've seen twice in a thousand years?"

"A thousand years ago, you tried to kill me."

Modred shrugged. "So I'm not the Son of the Year. It's not my fault that I come from a broken home, is it?"

"You'll have a broken back to go with the broken

home. Where is she? Because wherever she is, it's certain that's where Merlin is. So all you have to do is tell me where I can find them, and I'll be on my way. And you'll have your skin intact, which I know in the end is what matters to you most."

"I don't know," Modred said bluntly. "That's the God's honest truth. Whenever she brought me there, she'd magically transport me. She didn't want me to know where she was, because she figured I would tell you. And that's all, and if you want to kill me, go ahead."

Arthur shook his head. "Ah, Morgan. Always the judge of character."

"She always knew you, Arthur, better than you know yourself," Modred sneered, feeling a degree of confidence that Arthur wouldn't really gut him in cold blood. "My mother is a very imaginative woman, and all you have is a really big sword . . . which, so I understand, some knights used to wield in order to make up for other less impressive attributes. Is that right?"

Never shifting his gaze from Modred, Arthur said coldly, "If she's really so imaginative . . . do tell her to imagine what I will do to her with my really big sword when I catch up with her. When next we meet, Modred . . . no mercy."

"Yeah. Swell," Modred said, looking at the unwavering sword point. "And hey, let's do this again real soon."

Arthur stepped back and loudly sheathed Excalibur. The sword and scabbard vanished from Arthur's hip, and he stood there nattily attired in a gray Brooks Brothers suit and overcoat. He backed out of the alley, a sardonic look on his face, and Moe realized that Arthur wasn't turning his back on him for a moment. He took a degree of satisfaction from that.

CHAPTRE
THE EIGHTEENTH

ARTHUR KNEW THE day was getting off to a lousy start because, the moment he walked into his campaign headquarters, Ronnie Cordoba was all over him. "Arthur, where the hell have you been? We had a strategy meeting at—"

"In a moment," Arthur said, forcing a smile. "Percival, a minute of your time."

He and Percival immediately stepped into a private room, while an annoyed Cordoba watched them go. As soon as they were alone, Arthur said, "Have you found him?" just as he had every day for the past month and a half.

"No, Mr. Penn," Percival said formally, "I have not as yet—"

"Damnit, Percival! You found the Grail in a fraction of the time, and that was a cup! Merlin, even Merlin as a child, is bigger than a damned cup!" Percival, his face neutral, did not reply. Arthur sighed. "The rest of the staff still believes that Merlin simply has elected to go off to a private boarding school?"

"Those who don't know him for who and what he is, such as Cordoba, yes. Miss Basil is most angry, however. She serves Merlin, not you or me. If he does not return soon, it is difficult to say if she will remain in service."

"We'll deal with it when and if the problem presents itself."

"And Gwen called."

That stopped Arthur in his tracks. His face darkened. "I haven't heard from her since the night of the fire. What does she want?"

"She . . . simply said she wished to hear your voice."

"I see."

There was an uncomfortable silence for a moment, and then Percival said, "Highness, it is none of my business, but Morganna is practically kin to Satan, a true princess of lies. If she was able to trick Gwen, certainly Gwen should not be faulted for—"

"You're right," Arthur informed him. "It's none of your business." And with that he walked out of the room and straight to Ronnie Cordoba, who was pointedly checking his wristwatch. "I want to discuss the debate this Friday," Arthur said bluntly. "It's important that I have all the facts at my fingertips. I'm quite concerned about the entire affair, and the more prepared I am, the better I'll feel."

He stalked through the headquarters toward his office in the back. Workers greeted him and were surprised when he did not do much more than grunt, if that. Percival shook his head. "It's nerves. That's the problem."

"Well, it wasn't a problem when Merlin was here," said Ronnie. "I never understood the relation between those two. You sure there was nothing . . . ?"

"Nothing?" Percival wasn't following the question.

"You know . . . Arthur have a thing for plucking young chickens?"

"Why would Arthur's taste for poultry . . ." And then his eyes widened and he understood. "No. No, I assure you, it was nothing like that. In many ways, Merlin is the son Arthur never had. That no one ever had."

"Oookay," said Ronnie uncertainly. "Well, the thing is, he doesn't have Merlin now, and it looks like he doesn't have Gwen. Still, he's got himself, and that should be enough."

"You would think that. Except he's probably concerned that, the last time he had only himself to depend on, everything fell apart."

"Really?" asked Ronnie. "When was that?"

Percival sighed. "Long time ago," he said. "But for Arthur, it might as well have been yesterday."

𝕿HE OWNER OF the occult supplies store down on MacDougal Street opened his doors and was surprised to find a young woman standing there, waiting for him. The owner, whose name was Drago, was a big man. His head was shaven, and he sported a large handlebar mustache. "Yes?" he rumbled. "Can I help you, Miss?"

"Yes," she said, walking past him into the cool darkness of the store. Once she would have been frightened to set foot in such a place. But that was a lifetime ago. Her eyes scanned the various accoutrements, the horoscopes, the tarot cards, the small bottles and carefully labeled ingredients for witches brews, and then she saw what she was looking for. She stepped over to a rack of ornate daggers and pulled one down from the display. It was small, in a black leather sheath. The thing that attracted her was on the pommel—a carved skull with red eyes, as large as her thumbnail.

"The lady would like a knife?"

"The lady would like this knife," she said. She slid it out of the sheath and admired the sharpness of the edge.

"Are you purchasing this knife, may I ask, for protection?" asked Drago. "Or perhaps you had a certain ritual in mind?" He smiled. "If a sacrifice is intended, that knife might not be appropriate." He pointed to a large curved dagger on the wall. "Now that, on the other hand—"

"No," she said, sliding the dagger back into its sheath. "This is just what I'll need. Small enough for easy concealment, yet large enough to effect damage."

"I would say kill, if at close quarters," said the owner. "I think I can thank my lucky stars that I am not the one the lady is after."

"Yes," said Gwen pleasantly. "You can. Plus . . . I need something else. A very special item." And she told him what it was.

He shook his head, and for a moment she was unable to hide her disappointment and looked slightly crestfallen. "That," he said, "is rather hard to come by. May I ask where you heard about it?"

"Oh, I've been studying," she said. She spoke without mirth. "I quit my job . . . or it kind of quit me . . . or I quit on myself. And since then, I've been cramming. I used to be good at that, back in college. Cramming, I mean. I've been talking to people, studying with people, finding out what I needed to do. Been busy. It's probably hopeless, because she's been doing it for centuries and me, I'm nothing . . . but you know what? I'm the good guy. And that's got to still count for something in this world, right?"

"Riiiight," Drago said cautiously. "Miss, just out of curiosity, when was the last time you slept?"

"Gave it up. Don't need it. It's like when you keep exercising a muscle, it just grows stronger and stronger," she told him, and she was sounding almost giddy about it. "So I figure, the more I exercise my brain, the stronger it's going to get. So I exercise it all the time. I sleep an hour here or there."

"That's not healthy."

Her eyes narrowed. "Maybe. But you know what's even less healthy? Blackmail. And . . . and using me against someone I love. And you know what else? Screwing with me. That can be pretty fucking unhealthy for the wrong people. For the bad guys. She's one of the bad guys, and I'm one of the good guys. Now have you got the other thing I'm looking for?"

"No."

"Do you know who might carry it?"

"No," he lied, not wanting to sic her on anyone else.

"Fine. I'll find it. How much for the knife?"

"How about," he put up his hands in a peacemaking manner, "you keep it for free . . . if you promise not to come in here again until you've had at least, I dunno . . . eighteen hours sleep."

She smiled cheerfully at that. "Deal," she told him. She turned and left the store. Drago watched her go and, only when she was nowhere in sight did he sigh in relief.

"That," he said, "is one flickin' Wiccan."

CHAPTRE
THE NINETEENTH

†

𝕿HE REEVES TELETAPE Theater had been cleared
out for the event. The television facility, situated on
Eighty-sixth Street, usually home to sitcoms and the like,
was now furnished inside with three podiums, at which
the three principal candidates would stand. There was a
center podium where the moderator would be stationed,
and on one side of this triangular arrangement, a table
where three local journalists would be seated.

Arthur surveyed the setup the same way he would have
looked over a battlefield before engaging the enemy. He
stared at the TV cameras in awe; despite all his assimi-
lation, there were certain aspects of modern-day society
that continued to boggle his mind, and instantaneous
communication was definitely one of those aspects.

He felt as if his mind was in a fog . . . so much so that,
when there was a gentle tug at his shoulder, it actually
startled him. Normally he would have been well aware of
anyone who was coming near him. He turned to see Percival smiling encouragingly at him. "Turn around, highness. Let's see you."

Arthur turned around obediently, and Percival straightened the collar of his suit jacket. He looked down and said, "Unbutton the bottom vest button."

"Why?" asked Arthur.

"It's the fashion."

"Does it matter, Percival?" he sighed. "Does any of it? Really?"

Percival moaned softly. "Highness, please, not again . . ."

Arthur sat in a nearby chair, which creaked slightly under him. He felt the despondency welling over him again, seeping out of his pores. "Do you think she'll be watching, Percival?"

"I don't know, highness. If you called her—"

"Call the woman who betrayed me?" he said, clearly trying to sound fierce, not succeeding at all. "And Merlin . . . Percival, I am here because of him. Without him . . ."

"You functioned without his help before."

"And look what happened as a result. Percival, look at this. Look at me." He plucked at the lapels of the suit. "This is not me. It is a sham, a fraud. Part of a grand scheme that I did not plan. I have no vision of it. I flounder, Percival. I sink. I . . ." He seemed too tired even to finish the thought, and finally simply shook his head and stared at the podium. Percival walked away, shaking his head, and when the floor manager came over to tell him that it was ten minutes until air time, all he did was shrug slightly in acknowledgment.

"THESE BELONG TO you?" asked the guard of Percival, chucking a thumb at Buddy and Elvis, who were standing at the stage door. They were dressed in marginally better clothing, but still put the "scruff" in "scruffiness." "They keep saying they're part of—"

"Yes, yes," Percival sighed, gesturing for them to enter. The guard watched them suspiciously as they passed through the door. "They're Mr. Penn's . . . reality consultants."

"Reality consultants?" asked the guard suspiciously.

"Most people have media consultants, but the media isn't real. It's just broadcast perceptions, edited into a semblance of reality. At least, that's Mr. Penn's view," explained Percival. "Now these two, on the other hand . . . well, they're about as real as it gets."

"Give me fiction anytime," said the guard sourly.

Buddy and Elvis followed Percival through the hallway, Buddy saying, "Thanks, man. 'Preciate it."

"Don't bother thanking me," said Percival. "The only reason I let you in is because you happened to show up at what might be a propitious time."

"Pro . . . what?"

Percival stopped and turned to face them. "Buddy," he said slowly, "his highness feels great darkness upon his brow. It happens from time to time, to all great men, but particularly to Arthur. You seem to amuse him, for reasons I cannot comprehend. You . . . are his jester, whether he realizes it or not. All kings need one. This mood has been upon him for some time now; it now threatens to hurt his performance at a time when it dare not be hurt. See if you can attend to him."

Buddy nodded once, cracked his knuckles, said, "I'm on it. Elvis, stay here. Lemme handle this one." Elvis nodded, and Buddy approached the despondent Arthur.

Arthur didn't appear to notice him. Finally he did, looking up questioningly.

"These two guys walk into a bar. You'd think one of them would have seen it," said Buddy.

Arthur continued to stare at him. "I . . . beg your pardon?"

"These two fives walk into a singles bar . . ."

Arthur shook his head and looked away.

Buddy made a repeated, faint popping sound with his lips, thoughtful for a long moment. Finally he hunkered

down, looked at Arthur eye-to-eye, and said, "Your highness, you been like this for weeks, okay? One minute
you're moping, next you're shouting at people. It's
bringin' everybody down. You're gonna lose all the mo-
mentum you built up. You think it sucks to be you? I
used to be like you, all pissy and stuff. And I wound up
like me. So if it sucks to be you, it'd suck even more if
you were like me. So believe me when I'm tellin' you, and
I say this with the utmost respect: It's time to shit or get
off the pot."

Arthur stared at him for a long moment in utter bemusement. And then, slowly, the edges of his mouth
twitched and he laughed very softly. "I believe . . . I shall
shit."

There were footsteps behind them, and Buddy turned
and joyously proclaimed, *"He's gonna shit!"* right in Bernard Keating's face.

"I'm so pleased," said Keating, slowly wiping Buddy's
spit out of his eye. There were several people in Keating's
entourage. One of them was Modred. Percival was just
behind, obviously having seen them coming, trying to get
near Arthur to warn him.

Arthur rose, waited.

"Bernie Keating," Keating said, extending a hand.
"Next mayor of New York."

"Arthur Penn. Same," Arthur replied, taking the pro-
ferred hand and giving it a brisk shake.

"I'll make it short and sweet," said Keating.

"Good."

"I'm challenging you."

"Swords or knives?"

"I mean in the debate."

"Ah. Good. That will be less messy."

"I'm challenging you to keep up with me. Think you
can do it?"

"Yes."

"We'll see."

He turned and walked off, Percival pushing through his departing entourage to get near Arthur.

"There goes a man who knows his mind," Arthur said.

"Good," said Percival. "If he ever finds it again, he'll recognize it immediately."

"Did you see that black haired, weasly guy with him?" said Buddy. "He was creepy looking. Wonder who that little bastard was?"

Arthur and Percival exchanged looks, but wisely chose not to respond.

Ronnie Cordoba jogged over to Arthur, looking rather relieved to see him. "There you are. Let's get you over to makeup."

Arthur took a step back. "Makeup?" he said cautiously.

"Yeah. Sure."

"Women wear makeup. I have put up with a great deal, but I will not look like a woman."

Ronnie stuttered, "B-but Arthur, you have to! You'll look washed out without it. I don't understand. You must have worn makeup when you did your commercials."

Arthur frowned. "Wait. They put something on my face—"

"That was it!"

"Oh. Merlin told me that was protective salve, to prevent my being severely burned by the intense lights of the cameras."

Percival nodded, amused. "That Merlin was a smart little bugger."

Arthur turned on him with unexpected fierceness. "Don't talk about Merlin that way. In the past tense, as if he's dead."

Percival stepped back involuntarily. "Arthur," he whispered harshly, glancing around to see if anyone had noticed Arthur's sudden flare of temper, "I didn't mean anything by it."

"He's all right." Arthur paused and then added fiercely, "He has to be."

* * *

FROM THE OPPOSITE corner of the studio Bernard Keating and Moe Dreskin watched Arthur, Percival, and Ronnie stride toward makeup. "He's distracted," muttered Bernie. "Distracted real bad. That's gonna cost him." He turned to Moe and waved a finger in his face. "You better be right about this fantasy of his. I don't want to come across looking like some kind of schmuck."

Moe patted him on the arm. "Trust me, Mr. Mayor."

Bernie grinned, and looked up at the monitor overhead, with the podiums for the candidates on its screen. " 'Mr. Mayor.' I like the sound of that. I could get used to that real easy."

"I knew that you could," said Moe.

IF THERE WERE the equivalent of hell on earth, then it was in New Jersey. Verona, New Jersey, to be specific—named after the town in Italy where the star-crossed lovers Romeo and Juliet had met their end. A small, unassuming jock town where, interestingly enough, creatures of evil were residing. But only in the not-so-nice sections.

It was a rundown two-story house, whose elderly owner had died ages ago, and it had sat vacant for years as courts tried to figure out who owned it. It finally reverted to distant family, who didn't even care enough to sell it themselves and so left it to a real estate agent, who went out of business a month later. Since then the house had fallen between the cracks in the attentions of all concerned. Ivy ran wild over the sides, and weeds stretching several feet high supplanted grass.

It was a dump, but Morgan called it home.

The insides had been done up superbly—exotic drapes and tapestries hung everywhere, illuminated entirely by candles. Morgan strode through the house, her long black gown swirling around her bare feet. Trailing behind her was Lance, dressed in black leather and grinning like an imbecile. "Where are we going, Morgan? What's up? I adore you, Morgan—"

"Shut up," she said tiredly.

"Yes, Morgan."

She turned and stroked his chin fondly. "I don't need you, you know."

"Yes, Morgan. I know."

"You're a pathetic creature."

"Yes." He smiled, puppy dog-like. "But I'm your pathetic creature."

"Come. We're going to watch television. There's going to be a debate starting in a few minutes. And I think it's going to be quite, quite interesting."

She walked into her inner sanctum. Pillows were scattered about for easy lounging. A television, the modern-day crystal ball, was set up on a small pedestal at one end of the room. Tonight, however, it would be used for something less arcane than spying on the movements of others. Tonight it would be used for something as pedestrian as watching a television program, broadcast live on New York 1, with the other local stations in attendance to tape highlights to be played later on their news broadcasts.

At the other end of the room was a life-size cylinder made of solid crystal. Encased inside the crystal, like a butterfly in amber, was Merlin. His eyes were open, burning with fury even after all this time. Morgan went to him and stroked the crystal lovingly. "Ah, Merlin. Your incarceration hasn't dimmed your anger, I see. But then, I suppose lengthy imprisonments are nothing new to you." She smiled, showing white, slightly pointed teeth. "You're in luck, however. Tonight I've arranged some special entertainment for you. I know you have quite an interest in politics, Merlin. We're going to watch a debate. It's going to feature someone who's a friend of yours. You remember Arthur, don't you?" Then she laughed at the

look of hope in his eyes. "You still think my fool of a half
brother will rescue you! Never! *Never*, little magician.
You're mine, do you hear? Mine, body and soul, forever."
She continued in a singsong voice as she went to turn on
the television. "Forever and ever and ever and ever . . ."

Merlin closed his eyes. Encased, helpless, immobilized
in crystal. Unable to send for help. Astral projection not
even possible. Unable to help his king cope with a world
that could be confusing and terrifying.

And worst of all, trapped in New Jersey.

T HE FLOOR DIRECTOR, earphones solidly in place,
was calling, "Five minutes, everyone!" He turned to
the audience and said, "People, please. On air in five
minutes. Please refrain from talking from this point on.
If cameras are blocking your way, feel free to watch the
proceedings in the overhead monitors. I appreciate your
cooperation. Thank you."

Arthur, stepping up to his station, looked out at the
audience, and his gaze locked with Modred's. His bastard
son gave him a sarcastic "thumbs up." Arthur wanted to
pull Excalibur and cut the little cretin in half, but now
hardly seemed the time.

"Well, well, Mr. Penn. Together again."

He turned and saw Kent Taylor standing there. He
found himself studying the Democratic nominee's
makeup. He wore it as if he had been born to. That said
something to Arthur. He glanced over toward Keating,
who was heading toward the far left podium, taking some
last-minute instructions from one of his handlers. Keating
already looked like he was melting through the makeup,
and a woman with a powder puff was applying last-
minute fixes.

"Together again, Mr. Taylor," Arthur said reasonably.

"I've been watching your campaign with great interest.
Then again, don't get too flattered—I also slow down to

watch jackknifed tractor trailers." He laughed heartily at his own joke when Arthur didn't.

The three reporters came over and introduced themselves, greeting the candidates and wishing them luck. Arthur smiled wanly and cast his gaze toward the audience once more. He was able to pick out Percival and Ronnie, who both raised clenched fists in encouragement. Arthur blinked, at first thinking they were signaling that he should punch his opponent. But their expressions didn't seem to jibe with that intent. So he chanced it and raised a clenched fist back. They seemed pleased, so Arthur presumed he had given the right response.

He did not see Gwen. He did not look for her.

There was an expectant hush as the reporters went to their side of the room and as the floor director counted down. "And five . . . four . . . three . . ." and then mouthed, "two . . . one."

An announcer intoned, "Mayoral debate, live, from the Reeves Teletape Studio." Arthur glanced up at the monitor and blinked in surprise as the words "Mayoral Debate" appeared on the screen, superimposed over the image of the candidates. He looked around, trying to figure out where the words had come from, for they certainly weren't visible to him. He shook his head. And he thought the things that Merlin did were magic.

Merlin . . .

"Good evening," said the moderator. "Thank you for tuning in. I'm your moderator, Edward Shukin. Debates are not always possible in every campaign, so I feel we should be appreciative that the three major candidates for mayor have seen fit to engage in this evening's forum. I'd like to introduce them to you now. Running as an Independent, Mr. Arthur Penn, the Republican candidate, Mr. Bernard Keating, and the Democratic candidate, Mr. Kent Taylor."

Shukin then turned to face the three journalists. "At the far left I have the first of the three journalists who will be posing questions to the candidates tonight. From the *Amsterdam News*, Mr. James Owsley—"

Owsley, African-American, raised a fist in a sarcastic black power gesture. Arthur immediately returned the gesture. Percival, still in the audience, moaned softly.

Shukin rolled merrily on, oblivious. "Next, from The *New York Times*, Ms. Sandra Schechter." Schechter, a no-nonsense redhead, allowed a quick smile. "And, from The *Daily News*, Mr. Fred Baumann." Baumann tossed a wave at the audience and smiled lopsidedly.

"The rules for this debate have been agreed upon as follows," Shukin continued. "Our panelists will pose a question to the candidates on a rotating basis. The first candidate will be given three minutes to answer. The other two candidates will then each be permitted two minutes to respond to or rebut the candidate's response. With that understood, Mr. Baumann, I believe you won the coin toss backstage."

"Damned straight. Used my coin," muttered Baumann, prompting mild laughter. "Mr. Taylor," he said, "studies indicate that voting among young people is at an all-time low. In some cases as little as six percent of eighteen-year-old registered voters have turned out to the voting booths. How would you go about addressing this trend?"

"Well," said Taylor, looking like he was warming to the subject, "I want to say that young people voting is a very important matter, very important. I also want to say thank you for having the opportunity to address you, and the voters of this city, directly. I know there's people out there who seem to think that—as a former actor—I can't speak unless I'm working off a script. Well, that's certainly not the case. I have a lot to say about all the important matters that will face this city. For example, violent crimes were up last year for the first time. Mr. Keating, as DA, apparently isn't throwing the fear of God into criminals, and I think that tells you something. If he's not being wholly effective in his current position, how effective is he going to be as mayor? Furthermore, he has gone on record as supporting the current proposed budget for next year, which includes a ten-percent cut in the budget for social services. Ten . . . percent. Not to mention cutbacks in the number of police officers in the streets. That is hardly attention being paid to the things that matter to New Yorkers. I don't think that's something that this city can truly afford. As for Mr. Penn, well, he has no record to speak of, so I don't even know how to begin addressing his rather odd tendencies. Let me tell you about myself, however. My time in *City Hall*, believe it or not, has prepared me for the real City Hall. My research into my character has been so thorough, that when I've met with mayors of cities around the country—Los Angeles, Chicago, Cleveland, Boston, to name just a few—they've all told me that I was more prepared to discuss issues than they were. Every one of them has said that if they didn't 'know better,' they'd think I was the genuine item. And I'm trusting you, the good people of New York, to realize that I am the genuine item, and can do the job for you and your interests. Thank you."

"Mr. Keating, response?" asked Shukin.

"First off, Ed, I'd also like to say thank you for having this opportunity to engage in what I'm sure will be spirited discussion with my opponents. And I also want to respond to Mr. Taylor's charges. Yes, there has been an upswing in violent crimes, and naturally that is not to be encouraged. But we are talking about an increase of precisely zero point zero two percent. And that has been attributed to the extremes of weather we had to deal with, particularly during the summer months. High heat, I'm afraid, makes people more prone to anger, and also more desperate to steal things like, say, air conditioners. The fact is that that minor jump was an aberration, compared to the last eight years of steady downward dropping of the incidence of violent crime. That is the overall record that has to be studied, and that is what has to be considered. Now in regards to the budget . . ."

"Time, I'm afraid," Shukin interrupted him, sounding a bit apologetic. "Mr. Penn?"

Arthur looked from Taylor to Keating and back again, and there was undisguised incredulity on his face. "You didn't answer the ques . . . they didn't answer the question." He looked to Baumann for confirmation, since he could clearly scarcely believe it. "Am I losing my mind? They didn't answer the bloody question. This is madness! No wonder young people don't want to vote. You're both idiots!"

"Mr. Penn!" Shukin objected, over an outroar of laughter from the audience.

Arthur paid him no mind. "Of course young people don't vote. It's a right that was handed to them, and therefore they don't appreciate it. Young people care about two things, and two things only: Those things they have to fight for, and those things they're told not to do. Going around and telling teens to vote: That's your problem right there. You're telling them *to do* something. All you have to do to engender resistance in a young person is to tell them they should do something. That it's their responsibility. That automatically means you've lumped voting in with taking out the garbage. You want to get them to vote? Here's what you do," and Arthur looked straight into camera and, wagging a finger, said, "Every young person hearing this or watching this, listen to me now and tell all your friends I said this: Don't vote! Come election day, you are absolutely *not* to vote! I forbid it! I flatly *forbid it!*"

The laughter was louder now, drowning out the sputtering Shukin, who was trying to tell Arthur he had run overtime. Arthur continued, "Do you hear me, young people? Listen to me, girls: Boys hate girls who vote. It shows they have an opinion and spunk and know their mind! Boys, girls hate boys who vote! It shows maturity and makes you attractive to them! And any adults who are listening, march straight up to your children's rooms right now and tell them in no uncertain terms: You are not to vote! If you were even *thinking* about voting, put that notion straight out of your head! Listen to your music, talk on the telephone, play your video games, and chat on computer boards, but take no, absolutely no interest at all in politics! Send the message out to every teen in the land: *Don't vote, because adults don't want you to!*" He leaned back and folded his arms, obviously satisfied. "There. That should do it."

It took a full minute to restore composure to the proceedings, and all during that time, Keating glowered more and more fiercely. When the next question, from Owsley, came to Keating, he was ready.

"Mr. Keating," Owsley said, glancing down at his notes, "incidents of police violence, particularly in the course of arrests, seem to be on the rise. These incidents occur particularly in the apprehension of African-Americans, I have noticed. Yet in the overwhelming number of instances, subsequent investigations by the police have exonerated the officers who have committed the violence. Are you satisfied with the manner in which these internal investigations are being performed, or do you intend to try and have stricter procedures implemented?"

Bernie paused a moment. His eye caught Moe in the corner, who gave him a thumbs up and a slow nod. Taking a deep breath, Bernie turned slowly to face Arthur and said, "Before we go any further, I'd like to clear up something, Mr. Penn."

Quick off the mark, Shukin jumped in and said, "Mr. Keating, you are supposed to be addressing the questioners, not the other candidates."

"Oh, this is just something very minor. Mr. Penn, who are you, really?"

There was a confused silence as the three reporters looked at each other. Taylor, obviously not wanting to be left out of the unscheduled exchange, cleared his throat loudly. "Mr. Keating, I don't understand. Are you claiming this is not Arthur Penn?"

"No, no, no," said Bernie quickly. "I am asking him to answer a simple question . . . is your name Arthur Penn?"

Arthur smiled ingratiatingly. "Don't you like my name, Mr. Keating?"

But Bernie would not be dissuaded. "No, that's not the question. Is your name really Arthur Penn?"

Percival felt a cold sweat breaking on his forehead. Buddy and Elvis were exchanging worried glances. Ronnie Cordoba was completely confused.

But Arthur did not flinch. "Is that really of interest?"

Shukin, a veteran reporter, clearly sensed that there was something brewing. "Mr. Penn," he said carefully, "you're not required to answer that. You're certainly not on any sort of trial here. But if it will," he chuckled pleasantly, "keep peace in the family . . ."

"Oh, very well. If you must uncover my deep, dark secret," said Arthur, "No. That is not my real name. It's shortened. My full name is Arthur Pendragon."

There was a mild laugh from the audience as Arthur said easily, "There, Mr. Keating. Are you quite satisfied?"

Baumann from the *Daily News* said, "Whoa! Great name! Any relation to *the* Arthur Pendragon?" When he received blank stares from all around, he said helpfully, "You know. King Arthur. Camelot. That stuff. Sue me, I majored in English lit."

Taylor said, "If we could get back to the issue at hand—"

But Bernie's voice rang out. "Why don't you answer him, sir? Why don't you tell him? You *are* King Arthur, aren't you? You believe yourself to be the original Arthur Pendragon, King of the Britons, son of Luther—"

"Uther," corrected Arthur.

"Thank you. Uther. You are him, aren't you? Aren't you?"

Shukin rapped with his knuckles on the podium and

wished that he had brought a gavel. "Mr. Keating, you can't be serious—"

But Bernie wouldn't ease up. He leaned forward, closer to the microphone, his voice lowering in intensity, and said, "He's the one who's serious. Go ahead. Look me straight in the eye and deny that you are the one, the only, the original King Arthur of Camelot. That you're over a thousand years old. That you've been in a cave all this time, and that you've returned to us because 'you're needed.' Deny it!"

There was a long silence. Arthur and Bernie stared at each other. Each trying to stare down the other. And Bernard Keating felt the full intensity of the man who *was* King Arthur Pendragon, felt the strength of his anger, the power of his spirit and grim determination. And he lowered his gaze.

And slowly Arthur looked straight into the camera, and in a tone as reasonable as if he were announcing the weather, he said, "It's true."

Percival closed his eyes. Ronnie muttered to himself, "It figures." And Buddy turned to Elvis and said, "You mean everybody doesn't know that?"

"Yes," said Arthur. "I am everything Mr. Keating says. I was trying to keep it quiet because, frankly, I didn't want to use unfair advantage." He stepped to the side of the podium, interlaced his fingers and leaned on one elbow as if he were standing next to a fireplace mantle in his study. "I mean, after all . . . a cheap politician is a cheap politician. But a king . . . good Lord! How could *anyone* possibly fight competition like that? And a legendary king to boot! No, my friends. I felt it best to keep my true identity a low profile, so as to give Messrs. Keating and Taylor a sporting chance."

The audience members looked at each other, unsure yet of exactly how they were supposed to react.

"But the word is out," said Arthur morosely. "Mr.

Keating, for whatever reason, has decided to slit his own throat at this late date by guaranteeing the election for me. Ladies and gentlemen, it is I, King Arthur who stand before you." His mood shifted and he smiled broadly. "But perhaps it's better this way, for now I do not have to make pretense of being a man from this day and age. I can speak to you as a man from the past. A man who has seen what the world was, and who has watched what the world has grown into." There was genuine wonderment in his voice. "Good Lord, when I think what life was like in the old days. Only a few piddling centuries ago, my friends! A mere droplet in the great flood that is time, and yet look how far that droplet called humanity has gone! It's incredible. Look at yourselves! By and large you're better fed than my people were. Better dressed. Healthier. Longer lived. Smarter. Taller," he said, with some regret.

"Yes. I have returned. Some of you, such as Mr. Baumann here, might be familiar with the legends. That I would return when the world needed me. But you've taken that to mean that it would be in your world's darkest hours. Well, I'm here, my friends, to tell you that is not the case. I am here to tell you that you stand on the brink of a golden age. A time of potential learning and growth that could make all your previous achievements look like mud on an anthill by comparison. And I think that perhaps you're all afraid of what you can accomplish." He paused, searching for the right words. It would have been an ideal moment for Shukin to jump in, to stop him from continuing on the totally against-the-rules monologue. Instead he seemed as spellbound as the rest of them.

"It's more than you can believe," Arthur said finally. "And so you toy with the concept of self-destruction on a global scale. But I am here to lead you away from that. You have all the answers you need, right within your grasp. And I'm here to bring a fresh perspective, and a fresh understanding, and the knowledge to help you pick and choose the right way to go. And together, my friends, together . . . we can make it work. No, I recant that. Because I've seen what was, and I've seen what is, and I tell you that it is working. We can make it work better."

The words had not been delivered in a Bible-thumping style. Instead they had been said with the quiet conviction of a man who sincerely believed every syllable of what he was saying.

Slowly, Elvis stood up and started to clap. Buddy joined him. And then someone who wasn't part of Arthur's group, and then another, and within seconds the entire studio was filled with the thunderous sound of applause. It lasted for a solid minute, and Arthur smiled through it. He didn't look at Bernie Keating or Kent Taylor or anyone at all in particular. He was looking at his mind's-eye image of Merlin and thinking, *Bloody hell, I should have done this months ago, eh, Merlin?*

ℳILES AWAY, IN New Jersey, Morgan Le Fey fumed as she stared at the TV screen. "I don't understand. It was perfect. My ploy of stealing Excalibur, that useless hunk of metal, succeeded in netting me my true goal, Merlin. Then with Merlin gone, Arthur should have become dispirited, demoralized. I even had a glorious fantasy that he would simply throw himself on his thrice-damned sword and end it all. Then the truth of his identity would be revealed on television before his precious voters, and he would be laughed out of politics as a total lunatic." She screamed at the television, "Stop your damned clapping! You're supposed to think he's crackers!"

Unsurprisingly, the TV paid no attention to Morgan.

"All right, fine," she said. "You want to build up your hopes, Arthur? Fine. I'll build them up even higher, then, and that way they'll make an even louder crash when they fall! And nothing will distract me from my purpose! Nothing!"

"Morgan?" Lance inquired, wandering in. "Will you spank me?"

She considered it. "Well, five minutes of fun wouldn't hurt . . ."

YE OLDE SOUND BITE

"One can see, Larry, from Penn's presentation that he is using the King Arthur Camelot Scenario as a metaphor for all he intends to achieve. He has locked onto this 'view from another era' to help clarify and lend a certain degree of validity to his unorthodox approach to politics and issues. And it certainly seems to be working with the electorate who are— frankly—so desperate to have their attentions and imaginations engaged by the political arena that they are eagerly embracing his man. After years of bull—pardon my French—the people of New York have been handed someone who seems both genuine and mythic, all at the same time. One can only wonder what heroic proportions he might achieve should he, in a few years, go national . . ."

CHAPTRE
THE TWENTIETH

✦

RABBI ROBERT KASMAN opened his door and saw an extremely scruffy-looking individual standing there. "Yes?" he said cautiously, keeping care to have the chain lock in place on the door.

"Hi," said Buddy. "I'm here to make sure you're registered to vote tomorrow. I'm with Arthur Penn, and—"

"Oh, the king!" said the Rabbi. "Yes, yes, I saw your fellow. Oh, not on the actual day, because they had the poor judgment to have the debate on shabbos. But it was rerun enough, you can be sure."

"I can be sure," Buddy said agreeably.

"I don't know what that crazy Keating fellow hoped to accomplish by trying to embarrass that nice man, particularly after he saved those two children. Imagine, trying to convince everyone that your man actually thought he was King Arthur. Imagine!"

"Imagine," echoed Buddy.

"Of course, just between you, me, and the hole in the wall," said the rabbi, "it wouldn't matter to me if he really did think he were King Arthur."

Buddy blinked. "You know, that's what lots of people have said to me."

"Well, I'm not surprised," said the rabbi. "I mean, we all have our own mishugas, right? New York has certainly had some genuine nuts for mayor. It would only be appropriate if we had a sincere nut for once. You know what I mean?"

"I know what you mean."

"So." The rabbi leaned against the inside of the doorframe. "What did you want to know again?"

Buddy stared at him, then scratched his head. "I can't remember."

"Oh. Well, I'm sure when you remember you'll come by again."

"You bet."

The rabbi closed his door and went on about his business. Five minutes later there was another knock at his door. He peered through the peephole, frowned, and opened the door.

"Hi," said Buddy. "I'm here to make sure you're registered to vote tomorrow . . ."

THE POLITICAL COMMENTATOR for PBS was saying, "One can only wonder what heroic proportions he might achieve should he, in a few years, go national . . ."

"This being so," the commentator was asked, "it comes down to the question of what Keating's motives could possibly have been in giving Penn such an opening? Did he really believe that Penn was actually the Arthur of legend?"

"Whatever Keating had in mind, I can only surmise that it backfired spectacularly. It's hard to say what sort of response he expected, but it could hardly have been what he got—namely, what observers are already referring to as the Camelot speech."

The commentator was on tape. It was now being viewed, for the hundredth time, by a fuming Bernie Keating. He sat in front of the VCR in his office, feeling his innards broil as he watched the tape time after frustrating time. The rest of the debate, Bernie thought, including most of his exceptional observations and responses, had been totally overshadowed by Penn's performance in the first ten minutes. A performance that he, Bernie, had helped to cue.

There was a knock at his door, and Bernie called unenthusiastically, "Come in."

Moe entered and looked around in distaste. Crumbled memos and newspapers were scattered everywhere, as were half-drunk cups of coffee and several stale doughnuts. When Bernie saw who it was, his mouth assumed the frown that came to it so naturally these days.

"So. It's the turncoat," Bernie said tonelessly. "I haven't seen you since the night of the debacle—oh, pardon me, the debate."

"Now, Bernie—"

"You can save the 'Now, Bernie' bullshit! You're outta here, Mr. Brilliance. You and your genius idea."

"You went a little far," said Moe reasonably. "When it became clear that he wasn't going to crack immediately, you should have backed off."

"Backed off? Now you're giving me backed off! I go in there with guns blazing, and you leave me with no ammo. You said he'd come out and say he was some long-dead king."

"Well, he did," said Moe reasonably.

"Yeah, but he came off smelling like a rose! Forget about this guy who says Arthur pulled a sword on him. Penn'll probably turn that to his advantage somehow." Bernie sighed and sagged back in his chair. "So where does this leave us?"

"You're asking me? I thought I was through."

"Oh, come on. How could I do that to one of the top seven PR hacks I ever knew?"

"I thought I was one of the top three."

"You're sinking fast."

"Wonderful." Moe circled the table slowly. "Well, we've still got a last-minute whirlwind crush of vote getting. It's more or less in the hands of the voters at this point. But I've been reading the polls pretty carefully, and everyone who's predicting a landslide for Penn is off base, as far as I'm concerned."

"You think so? You're not just bullshittin' now?"

"No, I'm very serious. A lot of people were suspicious of the Camelot speech. The more perceptive voters sense that Arthur really does have a screw loose. Plus there are still people who don't want to cross party lines and vote for an Independent."

"If Penn had any brains, he would have courted the Democratic nomination. He'd be as good as in."

Moe shook his head. "Men like Arthur Penn always have to carve their own way in life."

"I've never understood that sort of thinking." Bernie leaned back too far in his chair. It crashed over backward, sending him tumbling to the floor with loud curses and bruised dignity.

"No, Bernie," said Moe, "I don't suppose you would."

GWEN KNEW SHE would be there.

She had sat outside until the last of the office workers departed Arthur's campaign headquarters. There was absolutely no reason to think that she would be remaining . . . and yet somehow there was not a moment of doubt in Gwen's mind. She worked up her nerve, breathing slowly in and out, and finally she took one more deep breath, walked briskly across the street and up to the door. She pulled out her keys and was a bit surprised to find that they still worked. Apparently he hadn't changed the lock after their . . . falling out.

She opened the door, not bothering to call out, "Hello!" It seemed imbecilic, somehow. Besides, she was quite certain that the one she was seeking would seek her out in turn. *How nice. You've got a whole hunter/hunted dynamic flittering around in your head. That'll certainly put you at ease.*

She walked slowly across the office complex, looking around for some sign of life. And then she jumped two feet in the air and clutched at her chest as a calm voice said behind her, "What are you doing here?"

She spun and, sure enough . . . it was Miss Basil. The implacable stare of those frightening green eyes didn't move away from her. She was so still she could have been a statue. Those eyes of hers seemed to glow with a separate life of their own. "Well?" demanded Miss Basil.

"I . . . I . . . ." Her mouth moved, but nothing came out.

Miss Basil slowly walked toward her, although her legs didn't seem to move. "Arthur wants no part of you. Merlin isn't here. Turn. Turn now and leave. It is your only hope—"

"I need a book," Gwen said desperately.

Whether it was the nature of the pronouncement or the fact that it was said with such overwhelming urgency, Miss Basil stopped dead. She stared unblinkingly at Gwen. "Have you considered a public library?"

"It's a very special book. *The Carpathian Book of the Fey and Daemonfolk.*" She felt a little unsteady just having said it out loud. "Please. I've been looking everywhere," she said. "For ages now."

"The *Carpathian Book?* You want a copy of that, do you." Miss Basil seemed most amused. "I'm almost tempted to help you."

"If you help me, you'll help Arthur!" Gwen assured her.

But Miss Basil shrugged. "I couldn't care less about that. But if you acquire a copy of that particular reference volume, and you use it improperly . . ." She shrugged. "Well, it's said others who tried to use it were yanked into the eighth circle of hell, never to be seen again."

"I'll take that risk."

"And what makes you think it's mine to give? I didn't say I had the book, or any clue how to use it even if I did."

"I think it because . . ." She tried to steady the runaway thudding of her heart. "I think it because . . . you are not what you appear. You are a creature of myth . . . a very old one, I'd think."

"Is that what you think." There was no question in her voice, no mirth in her eyes.

Gwen managed a nod and then said, "You're the closest thing to magic I've got."

"Close? I *am* magic, little girl."

"And yet, you've done nothing to find Merlin yourself?"

"I've no reason to," Miss Basil said. "I'm in servitude to him; it doesn't mean I have to like him, or extend succor to him. His disappearance leaves my situation in limbo. I can't act against Arthur, because that would be against Merlin's wishes; but I don't have to act on Arthur's behalf either. And if Arthur were to fall, then I would be bound to nothing or no one. Nor can I take direct action against you because . . . because . . ."

Gwen waited for a reason why. Basil looked thoughtful.

"Actually, I suppose I could," she said after a time.

Gwen's blood froze, and she suddenly had a realization that death was standing three feet away and could cover that distance in no time. She also knew that to run would be to bring it down upon her. So she stood her ground, which wasn't that difficult, considering she suddenly felt numb from the waist down.

Miss Basil gave her a long, appraising look and then lowered her gaze. "Too easy. It would be like clubbing a baby seal. Besides . . ." And now she actually smiled. "You have strength in you yet. I am . . . surprised. And it takes a good deal to surprise something that has seen as much as I. Perhaps you'll provide more surprises and amusements yet."

And she told her an address.

Gwen frowned. "I know that street . . . that block. I've walked past it a hundred times. There's no bookshop there. Is this some kind of trick?"

"Why should I trick that which I could simply destroy?"

"For amusement," Gwen said dryly.

Miss Basil inclined her head slightly in acknowledgment. "Touché," she admitted. "Tell me, have you ever been looking for it?"

"No. How could I look for something that isn't there?"

"All you have to do is not look where it isn't."

Gwen blinked in confusion, then nodded and said, "I'm not sure whether to thank you or not."

"Depends whether you live or not, I suppose."

Knowing that there was no point in staying, Gwen rose and headed for the door. She heard no sound behind her, no scuffling of feet, and yet somehow she knew that when she glanced behind her—which she did—Miss Basil wouldn't be there—which she wasn't.

K ENT TAYLOR WAS dying. At least, that's how the Democratic nominee felt every time he looked at the polls.

Even as he had spent the past week running from one function to the next, pushing his charm and personality to the breaking point and beyond, he could feel the election slipping away from him. He was finding it impossible to keep up a positive front and, considering that as an actor keeping up fronts was his greatest gift, such a realization could not have been more distressing to him. He was feeling so emotionally depleted, in fact, that he had departed the Senior Citizens Action Team (SCAT) meeting early, pleading illness. In a way, that was true.

He was becoming sick of politics and, even more, sick of himself.

He drove along the lower east side, heading toward the Fifty-ninth Street bridge and an Astoria fund-raiser, glad that he had brought his own trusty Jag. He knew that someone of his status should be riding around in limos, but Kent had always been a hands-on kind of guy. He liked to drive himself, he liked to be in command of his destiny. If anything, that was the most frustrating aspect of politics: His destiny was in the hands of the sort of people who were so stupid that they still addressed him more often by the name of his character—"Henry Lee"— than they did by his own name.

And this Arthur guy! He was climbing in the polls, strong but sure, despite the totally insane performance he'd given at the debate! No . . . because of it! The capricious nature of the support people gave, the way that they were embracing him, galled Taylor no end. He had originally thought this campaign was going to be a lock. What, after all, could possibly top the exposure he'd had playing an intelligent, insightful, and popular mayor on television?

Well, he'd had that answered, hadn't he? Despite it all, what people loved the most was "reality." "Real life" television, not the types of dramas in which he starred. The turning point for Penn had come when that building caught fire. Penn had been lucky enough to be there and be the hero, and all of a sudden *he* was practically a lock. Everything else was gravy for him.

"I could have been the hero," muttered Taylor. "I played one on TV enough times." *Indeed, just think if it had been me,* he thought. *I could be the one in an unassailable position now. I could be the—*

By this point he had eased the Jag onto the Fifty-ninth Street Bridge. He thought about the legend that claimed Simon and Garfunkel had come up with "Feeling Groovy" while stuck in traffic on this particular span. Even though

there was virtually no traffic around now, he started whistling it. But then the whistle died on his lips. He'd been
driving with the top down, despite the chill of the evening
air. It gave him more of a view, which was probably why
he saw what he did. He pedaled the brake while staring
incredulously.

There was a woman on the pedestrian walkway of the
bridge. She was standing next to one of the metal tower
supports, was using the crisscross of beams to climb up
onto the railing. Her intention could not have been
clearer. She was wearing a simple white shift, and she had
long black hair that was whipping around in the chill
evening breeze.

Despite the fact that he was in the middle of the bridge,
Taylor eased his car over as if he had every right to park
there. He put on his emergency blinkers and then clam-
bered out the top of the car. Excitement pounded through
him. The thought of leaving his Jag in this precarious
situation, when he customarily only parked it in certain
garages attended twenty-four hours a day by armed
guards, was anathema to him. But the prospect of losing
the mayoral race was even more repellent, whereas the
thought of what would happen if he could slam dunk this
rescue was just too tempting.

Trying to look nonchalant, he made his way over to the
walkway, mentally pleading the whole time, "Let her be
there when I get there, let her be there when I get there."

She was. Whatever God or gods were listening to his
desperate prayers, it was obvious they were opting to cut
him a break. Because by the time he was in shouting
distance, not only had she not already jumped, but she
had instead started climbing. Slowly, steadily, she was
climbing the tower. She didn't look back at him. Instead
her full concentration was on her task. Obviously she
wanted even more elevation for her jump.

It was at that point that the enormity of what he was
trying to do settled on Kent. This wasn't scripted; he had

no idea what was going to happen here. This was someone's life he was rolling dice with. He noticed that she
was holding a bottle in her hand. *Great*, he thought. *On
top of everything, she'd probably been drinking.* He had to pro-
ceed with the utmost caution, because the major downside
of the situation suddenly presented itself to him: "MAY-
ORAL CANDIDATE CAUSES WOMAN TO JUMP."
What a headline that would make.

Very cautiously, carefully, he cleared his throat to gain
her attention. She didn't look at him. He did so again, a
little louder this time. Still nothing. A third time, louder
than before.

"If you're trying not to choke to death," her voice
floated to him, "please continue. If you're trying to get
me to notice you, you can stop. I've noticed you."

He leaned back and looked up at her, trying to remember that one-shot role as a police negotiator he'd played
nine years ago. There were things you were supposed to
do to try and gain a jumper's confidence, certain tech-
niques in dealing with potential suicides. He knew it. But
all he could think of was Mel Gibson handcuffing himself
to the jumper and then vaulting off the building in the
first *Lethal Weapon* movie. It was so unfair. He'd been up
for the role of Riggs, and goddamned Gibson had gotten
it. Kent knew he could've done that role with one hand
tied behind his—

He was getting off track.

"Hi. What's your name?" he said warily.

"You want to talk to me? Come up here."

She had to be about fifteen, maybe twenty feet above
him . . . to say nothing of the perilous plunge to the river
below. The height didn't particularly bother Taylor, nor
the challenge of the climb. He was an experienced rock
climber and had handled climbs of far greater difficulty
and danger than this. Still, he hesitated.

"Fine. Forget it. I'll just be going now," she said, her

voice deep and throaty and full of tragedy, and she made as if to release her grip.

"No! Wait!" he called out, seeing not only the hope of rescue, but the chance of resuscitating his campaign, on the verge of falling away. "I'm coming!"

He stepped up onto the rail, expertly snagged one of the diagonal crossbeams of the tower, and started up. He tried to make it look effortless, and within minutes had climbed to eye level with her. The wind whipped at him, but he held himself closer to the tower. "So . . . what's your name?" he asked again.

"What's yours?" she replied.

"Kent. Kent Taylor." He paused, waiting for some moment of recognition. "*City Hall?* Played the mayor for five years?"

"I don't watch TV."

"Oh. Well . . . as it so happens . . . I'm running for mayor of New York now."

"I see. And is that why you're here?" she said. "Hoping to get my vote? Sorry, I've got other things on my mind."

"No, no, I just . . . I saw your situation up here and I felt, well . . ."

"That you wanted to stop me from doing something stupid?"

He smiled. "Something like that."

She didn't reply immediately. He tried to remember whether that was a good sign or not. He knew it was important to keep someone like this talking . . . although maybe that was the rule for concussion victims. Every medical show he'd ever guested in was tumbling together in his head into one unrecognizable lump.

"You have a nice voice," she said abruptly.

"Thank you. So do you. Have you . . ." He hesitated, then said, "have you been drinking?"

"Oh yes."

"Then you know, it's just a little possible that maybe you're not thinking clearly. Which is why you're considering doing . . . you know . . . what you're thinking."

"You mean jumping?"

"Yes."

"Could you get closer. Your face is in shadow. I want to see if it's as nice as your voice."

He angled himself around so that he was within a couple of feet of her. He couldn't see her face terribly clearly, as the moon had gone behind a cloud, but she certainly seemed attractive enough. "Yes," she said, looking rather satisfied. "Yes, you do have a certain sort of rugged handsomeness about you."

"Thanks. Now . . . I did what you asked. How about," he took a deep breath, "how about you do what I ask, and come back down with me. That's fair, isn't it?"

"Fair?" she echoed. "Are you going to stand there and tell me life's fair? Life isn't fair, Kent."

"True. But you know, believe it or not, it beats the alternative. It really does. You know what they say about suicide? It's a permanent solution to a temporary problem."

"My problems aren't temporary, Kent. Do you want to know what my problems are?"

"Sure." *Keep her talking, keep her talking.*

"Here." With no warning, she tossed the bottle to him. He caught it reflexively and looked at her in confusion. "Take a swig," she said.

"I . . . really don't think I sh—"

She swung one arm free, closed her eyes and started to bend forward, like a bird about to lunge from its nest.

"Okay, fine." He knocked back a deep swallow. It wasn't bad, actually. A red wine, but it was pleasantly hot going down, and he felt a soft buzz in the back of his head. The last thing he needed to do now was get woozy. "S'good, actually."

"My problems," she said as if he hadn't spoken, "are . . . well, they're unique, Kent. You know what they involve?"

"Sex? Just a guess."

She blinked as she seemed to focus more on him. "That's right. That's very good. Sex. The deed. The act. The formation of the beast with two backs. That is where my problem rests, Kent."

"Lots of people have problems in that realm."

"Have you?"

He thought about the threesomes in college, and the prostitutes since then—all reliably discreet, of course. "No. But, well . . . I'm a TV star."

"Of course, of course," she said with a touch of mirth. "Know what happened to me, Kent?"

"Can't say that I do. But I'm sure it . . ."

She let out an unsteady breath. "I was sexually abused as a young girl."

"Ouch," he said.

"By my brother."

"Double ouch."

"He had his way with me," she continued, "and I, young and impressionable . . . he took advantage of me, is what he did. And then he went on to all manner of success and power, leaving me behind, the uncaring bastard. He treated me like detritus, while everyone else treated him like a king. Well, you know what? He shouldn't be allowed to get away with it."

"He absolutely shouldn't," agreed Kent.

He heard voices from the roadway and looked down. People had finally noticed them, were starting to gather and point. Cars had stopped, traffic backing up down the length of the bridge. People were getting out of their vehicles, running toward the pedestrian walkway. He heard his name mentioned as someone recognized him. Even better. With any luck someone would alert the media and they'd be able to witness his rescuing this poor, abused woman.

"So you know what I'm going to do?" asked the woman.

"You're going to jump, in hopes that he'll be sorry he drove you to it," he said. "But that would be a huge mistake."

She paused and then said, in a voice filled with quiet glee, "I have . . . an even better plan."

"And what would that be?"

"I'm going to let him think that he's on the verge of some great triumph . . . remove obstacles that might stand in his way . . . and then, at the eleventh hour, then and only then will his triumph be snatched away."

"That," he said approvingly, "sounds like an excellent plan. There's just one problem. You can't carry it off if you're dead."

"You know," she said as if this hadn't occurred to her, "you're right."

Like a bat, she swung herself over toward him while still maintaining her grip, and then she snagged his hand. "Do you know," she said, "they say that small children and people who have been drinking have the best chance of surviving falls, because they're so relaxed. I think we should find out, don't you?"

"Uh, no. No, I don't think we should do anything but get down from here."

"All right," she said agreeably, and with a sudden movement, yanked him away from the tower. Before Kent even knew what was happening, he was treading thin air. He tried to twist, lunge, get back to the tower, but there was no hope at all. From below there were screams in the crowd, which quickly blended with his own screams as he plummeted toward the river. The last thing that went through his mind, for no reason that he could possibly discern, was a sudden craving for an ice cream sandwich, and then he envisioned some sort of segment on a cable TV show where he'd seen cliff-divers easily survive falls from much higher than this, and then remembered something else about how if you didn't hold your body just right, then hitting a body of water from a height wasn't much different from hitting concrete. Then there was a hideous, broken-sack-of-bones sound as his body struck the water, and blackness enveloped him.

ORGAN LE FEY watched with grim satisfaction as people drew in close, everyone talking at once. In the distance she heard ambulances. No one was looking up at her and pointing, because no one had seen her in the first place. All they'd seen was a mayoral candidate, with election day almost upon him, getting drunk and throwing himself off a bridge in some sort of suicidal despair. As for the specially treated wine, even one sip was enough to send his blood-alcohol level through the roof . . . provided there was enough of him left to test. She took pride in the old adage that, if you want something done right, it's always best to do it yourself.

T WAS SEVERAL minutes before midnight.
Arthur sat in his dressing gown, staring at the moon out the window of his modest apartment. The moon had moved from behind the clouds and seemed quite . . . quite what? Thoughtful. Yes, that was it, if such a thing was possible. The moon looked thoughtful, pensive. Just as it reflected sunlight, it also seemed to reflect Arthur's mood.

Arthur chose a star and wished fervently on it, so fervently that he stood there for a full minute with his eyes tightly shut. When he opened them he half hoped that his wish would be granted. But Merlin had not materialized in his living room. He paced like a caged panther. It was an incredible feeling of helplessness, not even knowing where to start looking for the kidnapped seer. Was he in New York? New Jersey? The East Coast, the West Coast? Was he even in the United States? Arthur moaned and rubbed his temples. Merely contemplating the possibilities made his head hurt.

He turned and looked at the telephone. It sat there, inviting, so tempting. To talk to *her* for just a moment. That would be all he needed to patch together the relationship that had once meant so much to him. But obviously it hadn't meant anything to her, or she would not have made a mockery of it. But still . . .

He stood over the phone, a man decisive in all matters except those of the heart—a failing many men share. He resolved that, if she called him, he would talk to her. Yes, that was it. If she came to him, he would try to find it in his heart to forgive her.

"Ring," he commanded the phone.

It rang.

He took a step back, stunned, and even a little impressed with himself. Tentatively he answered it and said, "Yes?"

"Arthur, it's Ronnie here."

"Yes, of course, Ron," Arthur sighed, his shoulders sagging. "Late, isn't it?"

"Never too late for news like this. You sitting down?"

"No. Need I be?"

"For this news, you may want to," and then he continued without waiting for Arthur to seek out a chair, "Kent Taylor got hammered this evening and threw himself off the Fifty-ninth Street bridge."

"*What?*" Arthur couldn't believe it. "Taylor? The Democratic nominee? Is he dead?"

"No. But they had to pump about twenty gallons of the East River out of his lungs, and he broke half his body. He's in the hospital. He's critical."

"Of what? Is it an exceptionally bad hospital?"

Ron grew silent on the other end, clearly not understanding Arthur's reply. But then he said, "Not critical *of the hospital*. He's in critical condition."

"Threw himself off a bridge?" It didn't sound right to

Arthur somehow. It sounded almost . . . convenient.

"They said if he makes it through the next twenty-four hours, he's got a chance of pulling through."

"But . . . what happens now?" asked Arthur. "With the election, I mean."

"That's to be determined. Boy, it's certainly ironic, isn't it."

"In what way?"

"Well, the papers were all saying that Taylor took a drop in the polls. Who'd've thought he'd take it so literally?"

Chaptre
the Twenty-First

Gwen kept her face resolutely down toward the sidewalk, not even looking the campaigner in the face as he thrust a flier at her. Arthur's face smiled at her from the paper as the enthusiastic young man said, "Polls close in four hours, be sure to vote for Arthur." Gwen nodded, knowing that her concerns lay somewhere besides a voting booth.

She'd walked the block for hours, looking and looking. *Not look where it isn't.* Did that mean something, or was that simply Miss Basil being cryptic in order to confuse her. It wasn't here. She'd known it wasn't here. She'd known it all along, it was all a joke, it was . . .

She sagged onto a stoop, thinking desperately. She'd read about what happened with that candidate, Kent Taylor. She knew it was Morgan's doing; she felt it in her bones. It was all part of some great plan to take down Arthur, to build him up just before knocking the props out from under him. To make her vengeance and schemes all the more stinging when they were completed. Gwen was positive—even though she couldn't know for sure, she was positive nevertheless . . .

Positive.

Sure.

"I have to be sure," she whispered. "I have to believe it's here." Slowly she got to her feet and looked around, wondering how she could be absolutely sure of seeing something that she wasn't sure about. And then she thought about the old thing the Marines said, or maybe it was the Navy SEALS, but she remembered what it was: Failure was not an option. She had to find the book, because it was what her studies told her she needed, and she had to use it to get to Morgan, to find Merlin, to succeed. And she had to succeed because failure was not an option, and the only way to avoid failure was to find the bookstore, so it simply had to be there, that was all, it had to be there because it couldn't *not* be there. With every fiber of her being, she refused, absolutely refused, to think that it wasn't there.

She looked in front of her. It had no name, there was no bell, nothing to use to knock on the door, just simply the word BOOKS written in the window. She could practically smell the must coming off it, and she hadn't even opened the door yet. The window was so dark that she could see nothing within.

Six steps led to the door, and she took them two at a time. At the door, she placed her hand on the knob and wondered what she was going to do if she tried to turn it and it was locked. She jiggled the handle; it didn't turn. There was no sign of life from inside. Then she thought, *It has to be open. No other possibility will be allowed.* She turned the knob with authority this time, and the door opened right up. She stepped in and felt chilled, but pushed it out of her bones, and thus felt warmer.

She'd been right about the must. All the air in her lungs was immediately replaced by it. And she had never seen so many books packed into so small a place. The dust was an inch thick and the lighting so dim she couldn't make out a single title on a single spine. When she heard a creak in a floorboard nearby, it was all she could do not to jump a foot in the air. She whirled and saw an old man standing behind her. He had a pointed black beard and was peering owlishly over half-rim spectacles. He said nothing, obviously waiting for her to speak.

"I've been all over town," she said. No response. "For weeks. Looking for a book." Still no response. "I need to do something, and I need to find a particular book that can help me do it." Again, nothing. He just stared at her, even through her. "It has to do with the occult. I was told you had books on the occult here. But it doesn't say so in the window."

Finally he spoke, in a tired whisper. "When you've got the real thing, you don't advertise." He paused a moment and then said, "What do you need?"

"The Carpathian Book of the Fey and Daemonfolk."

"My," was all he said. Then he turned and disappeared behind a bookshelf. She wasn't sure if she was expected to follow him, and finally elected to. She headed around the same shelf, and blinked when she saw that the stacks seemed to extend much farther than she would have thought possible, given the confines of the store.

There was a loud *haruumph* behind her, and she whirled. He was standing there, and she had no idea how she could possibly have walked past him in the confined space, but there he was. He was holding up a book that was heavy and leathery and had a pentagram embossed on the cover. Slowly, he nodded.

There was a crack of thunder from outside, and a flash of lightning illuminated the interior of the store.

Not too melodramatic, she thought.

"How much is it?" she asked.

"What are you going to use it for?"

She took a breath, forming it into words for the first time. "To summon a demon."

He regarded her for a long moment, and then he said, "Take it."

He thrust it into her hands. She took it in surprise, impressed at its heft. "Are you sure?"

"I will not ask you for any price . . . for you, my dear, will have enough problems."

"Problems?"

"You intend to consort with demons, my dear. Even if you bind them to you, compel them to obey you . . . there is always a price to be paid. Always."

"What . . . sort of price?" she asked uneasily.

"It could be anything. The demon could ask for it immediately, or it could be karmic in nature. It might not be today, it could be tomorrow, or ten years from now, or in another incarnation. But, somehow, in some way . . . there will be a price."

"If that's the case," Gwen said grimly, "I may already be paying for it, from a previous lifetime."

𝕿HE COLONIAL ROOM at the Roosevelt Hotel, near Grand Central Station, had been made over completely in preparation for election night. The walls and ceilings had been festooned with balloons and crepe paper. Three televisions had been set up to monitor the election returns as broadcast by local news stations and network affiliates. Tables had been laid with enormous amounts of food, including chicken legs, meatballs, and countless other munchies. The room was already packed with supporters, apprehensive campaign workers, news people, and whoever else had even a semilegitimate reason for being there.

Suddenly there was a burst of applause, which quickly spread over the entirety of the room, as the workers saw Arthur enter. Elvis, Buddy, Percival, and Ronnie surrounded him, as did several other upper-echelon campaign workers. As Arthur moved through the crowd, people came in from all sides, wanting to shake his hand or even just touch his sleeve.

"Arthur," Ronnie was saying, "you're really supposed to wait upstairs until the results are tabulated. Then you make an entrance."

"My dear Ronnie," Arthur replied coolly, "you've done a marvelous job these past weeks. But this is my decision." He raised his voice so that it carried above the noise as he declared, "Whatever the results are, good or bad, yea or nay . . . we shall witness them together."

Buddy called out, "Is this some kinda king or what?"

The cheers helped to drown out, just for a moment, Arthur's wishing that Gwen were there. He wondered if she was even in the city anymore . . . if she even cared anymore, about him, or about anything.

G WEN HAD BEEN staying at the apartment of an old college friend, Sheila O'Shea ("If you're ever in trouble, just think S.O.S!" she'd always been fond of saying). Sheila, however, hadn't been home for a few days: not an unusual occurrence for someone who had a weakness for base players. This had suited Gwen just fine, particularly considering what she was about to do.

She had cleared a space in the middle of the apartment, and drawn a large pentagram on the floor. White candles were set to burn at each of the five points. Gwen made one final check to make sure that the chalk line was uninterrupted and unbroken. Then she sat on the floor outside the pentagram and opened the *Carpathian* book to a marked place.

"Two can play at this game," she said softly.

She prepared herself, took a deep breath, and started to speak words, old, ancient and—to her—incomprehensible. Outside, the thunder and lightning worsened, and she wondered whether it was just coincidence or whether she was somehow causing it.

She continued the incantation, and slowly she held up
a piece of cloth. She had no idea what impulse had
prompted her to keep it with her since she'd ripped it off
the clothing of the demon waiter who had taken Merlin.
But kept it she had. She spoke the words, being careful
not to stumble over any of them. "Take your time," the
man in the store had cautioned her. "There is no consequence for taking your time and saying them correctly;
however, if you rush and speak them incorrectly, the results can be nasty."

She held the cloth tightly, continuing to speak the
words. And now it seemed to her as if the words were
taking on a life of their own. She no longer had to avoid
stumbling over the words; they flowed through her. The
cloth began to glow, then became hotter and hotter. She
was almost through the spell, and she had to hold on to
the cloth until she had completed it, but it was getting
more difficult to hold on to with each passing moment.
She got to the last words just as she shrieked, unable to
hold the cloth anymore, and it practically flew out of her
hand.

The air within the pentagram shimmered, bent back
on itself, and the demon materialized in the heart of it. It
was brown and scaly, like a gargoyle come to life, and it
took one look at Gwen and lunged at her with a roar.
There was a sound like nails raking chalkboard, and the
demon slammed to a halt, crashing into the edges of the
pentagram, confined by the eldritch power of the mystic
shape she had drawn on the floor. As long as Gwen did
nothing to break the line, the demon could not emerge.

It glared at her with primeval fury. "Lady, you don't
know what you're screwing with."

"I've got a pretty good idea," she shot back calmly. She
was already flipping through the pages to another place
she had marked in the book. She found it and started
speaking.

The demon stiffened, recognizing it immediately.

"Stop it! That's a binding spell! You . . ." Quickly he adopted a pleading tone. "You don't want to be doing that . . . you . . ."

She didn't listen. Instead she hurried through the spell. Upon her speaking the last words, the demon sank to the floor in frustration. "Say it," she told him.

"Damn you."

"Say it," she repeated.

"I am bound, I am bound, I am bound," snarled the demon. "What wilt thou?"

"I need you to take me to Morgan."

"Ohhhh, you don't want to go to Morgan," said the demon. There was something that sounded like genuine panic in his voice.

"Oh, yes," said Gwen. "I do. I do want to go to Morgan. And you'll take me there."

"But she'll kill me! And then she'll kill you." The demon tried to strike a conversational tone. "Let's talk about this sensibly. We're caught in circumstances here. No sense both of us dying, right? So let me kill you quickly and painlessly, and at least one of us can go on living."

"And where does that leave me?" said Gwen.

"Always in my heart," he assured her.

"Nice try," said Gwen. "Take me to her. Now!"

"I can't!" He was genuinely afraid. She'd almost have felt sympathy for him if the circumstances had been otherwise. "She'll kill me, I swear!"

"You should have thought of that before you kidnapped Merlin."

"Please! Please, you . . . you're an amateur! You don't know what you're getting into! She'll . . . she'll pick you apart like an insect! And me, the things she'll do to me! When I took Merlin, that was the closure of my service to her! I was *so* looking forward to free agency! And now you come along and bind me with a piece of personal possession that you lucked into, and you're going to put me up against her, and it's not fair! It's not fair! I don't ... I ... I ..." The demon suddenly started to breathe rapidly.

Gwen looked down at it frantically. "What the hell is it now?"

"I'm—" The demon gasped repeatedly. "I'm hyperventilating."

"Yeah, right . . . this is a stupid *trick*, isn't it?"

"I swear! I swear it isn't!"

"You swear? Demons lie like humans breathe!"

Except even she had to admit that it didn't look like he was lying. He was flat on the floor, his chest continuing to rise and fall rapidly. "A-hunh! A-hunh! A-hunh!"

"Oh, Jesus Christ in the foothills. Wait here."

She went into the kitchen, grabbed a paper bag, walked back to the out-of-breath demon and extended her hand across the pentagram. It was only at that instant that she realized, in doing so, she was breaking the circle.

Instantly the demon vaulted out of the enclosure, slamming Gwen to the floor. The two of them went down in a tangle. She wanted to let out a shriek of alarm, but her throat was constricted with terror. The demon clawed at her.

No, he clawed past her, snagging the paper bag from her hand, rolled off her, and brought it up to his mouth. He breathed in and out rapidly, the bag inflating and deflating. Gwen sat up, staring at him, as he managed to get out, "Sorry" while breathing into the bag.

"Don't mention it," Gwen managed to say. She watched him until his breathing slowed to a normal level and then said, "Uhm, you want to lie down or something? I've got some Xanax in the bathroom."

"Sure, sure, thanks," he said. She went to get it and, when she returned a few moments later, she found him lying on the couch. She leaned over the demon and proffered him a Xanax and a cup of water. The demon waved off the water and simply gulped down the tranquilizers.

Then he lay back full on the bed and tried to calm down.
"I'm . . . I'm sorry—"

"Be quiet. Just get yourself together." She shook her
head. "All the demons in the world and I get one who
goes hyper in tense situations."

"Look!" said the demon. "There's demons and there's
demons." He propped himself up on one elbow. "We're
all pretty much alike to you mortals, like you're pretty
much all alike to us. Some of us just handle tension better
than others. Besides, you're not exactly Miss Tough-as-
Nails either. Look at you. Your hands are shaking. Your
eyes are glazed."

"Of course they are," snapped Gwen. "I haven't slept
for days now. I've been gathering things, working, studying, reading, running around like a lunatic, going everywhere I could to find what I was looking for. I've been
cramming for this confrontation with you . . . and with
her. I'm so loaded with uppers, I have to wear lead weights
on my belt to keep my feet on the floor."

"Oh, dear."

"You bet your ass, 'Oh dear.' "

The demon regarded her with open curiosity. Gwen
had pulled her strawberry blonde hair back in a tight bun.
She wore a tight-fitting black sweater, black slacks, and
black shoes. "You're not at all the way I remember you,
or the way Morgan described you. You were a cream puff."

"Cream puffs get stale fast." She had pulled out her
skull-headed knife from a sheathe strapped to her leg. It
made her feel a little better, waving it around. "Come on,
up. Let's go. Let's move it."

The demon nodded slowly. "My name's Morty," he
said. "I just think I should warn you . . . there's a price—"

"In dealing with demons, yeah, I know. Considering
my life up until now, it'd be hard for me to tell when
some sort of karmic backlash hits me."

"Trust me, you'll know," he said darkly.

"And you're warning me of this, why?"

"Because, you seem like a nice person. And I don't run into many of those." He glanced at the candles. "You even used white ones instead of black. It's just a nice change of pace. You, uhm . . . you sure I can't just kill you now? Save us both some—?"

She waved the dagger in the vicinity of his throat.

"No, I didn't think so," he sighed. Morty stood and weaved slightly from side to side.

"What is it now?"

"That tranquilizer—I'm feeling really woozy."

"Well, let's get moving before you get too woozy to do anything useful."

The demon walked over to her, raised his arms and said, "Hold me around the waist."

Gwen complied. Her face against the demon's back, she said, "Is this necessary for me to be transported with you?"

"Not at all," said the demon. "But I get off on it."

Before Gwen could reply, they vanished in a puff of black smoke.

𝕬LL EYES IN the ballroom were riveted on reporter Louise Simonson, standing out in the rain near a polling place, looking a bit bedraggled as she said, "With the polls closed barely an hour ago, the first returns are coming in. And it looks right from the start that the all-important mayoral race is going to be tough to call. With prevoting surveys indicating that Kent Taylor's numbers are practically nonexistent, the battle between Keating and Penn has narrowed, as we wait to find out whether swing or undecided voters will go with the feisty Republican or the genuinely original Independent."

Ronnie patted Arthur on the shoulder. "Genuinely original beats feisty any day."

"I hope you're right," Arthur said softly. All around, campaign workers were piling food on paper plates, battening down for a long night. Outside rain hammered against the windows.

"Yup, looks like it's going to be a tough race to call," continued Ronnie, and then he walked off, leaving a confused Arthur.

Arthur turned to Percival. "To call what?"

"It's a bizarre phenomenon, Sire," said Percival. "All the stations want to be the first to announce a winner. So over the years they've started predicting who the winner will be earlier and earlier in the evening. Sometimes with as little as one percent of the vote tabulated."

"Really?" asked Arthur, fascinated. "One percent? But that sounds so insane. I mean . . . isn't that the equivalent of going up to a crowd of a hundred people, picking one person, getting his opinion, and assuming that the rest of the crowd can have their opinions guessed at from this one chap?"

Percival smiled. "It's more scientific than that, highness."

"Oh." Arthur nodded. "Science. Incomprehensible. Give me magic any day."

He sat there, fidgeting with his hands. "Nervous, your highness?" asked Percival finally.

"We fought the good fight, Percival. Whatever happens, happens. I wish Merlin were here."

"What about Gwen?"

He didn't reply . . . possibly because he wasn't sure.

CHAPTRE
THE TWENTY-SECOND

GWEN LOOKED UP, saw the ominous house, and shuddered. She hugged herself tightly against the chill and wiped the pouring rain from her face. Morty was by her side.

"This is it?" she said, unimpressed.

"You sound disappointed."

"I expected a castle. Where are we?"

"New Jersey."

"New Jersey?" she said incredulously. "Christ, I used to live in New Jersey."

"Yeah, well, keep it to yourself," said Morty. "Well, let's do this. Wouldn't want to be late for our own funeral."

They headed toward the house.

MORTY WALKED QUIETLY in front of Gwen, taking several steps, pausing and listening, then gesturing for her to follow. It was nerve wracking, slow progress. Yet with this method they managed to penetrate into the hallways of Morgan's house without detection. The demon maneuvered himself and Gwen past the detection wards placed outside, and now, as they crept through hallways, dimly lit by candles along the wall, Gwen started to feel as if the corridor were closing in on her. "Oh, God," she moaned softly.

Morty turned to face her. "What?" he asked anxiously.

Her lips tight, Gwen whispered back, "I don't know. I'm starting to feel clammy. I'm sweating. My hands are trembling."

He nodded, his inhuman face etched with very human concern. "We have to get you out of here."

"No. Arthur needs Merlin. That's who I came here to get. Which way?"

The demon paused, for they had reached a corridor with a fork. He looked off to the right and to the left, then pointed left and said, "This way."

There was a horrifying crack of thunder, and suddenly lightning illuminated the hallway. To Gwen's immediate right was Morgan's face, and Gwen—nerves frayed to the breaking point—almost let out a horrific shriek. But just before she could, the demon clapped his hand over her mouth, stifling it. Her eyes widened as the thunder subsided, and she saw that it was a painting of Morgan, hanging on the wall. Feeling foolish, she brushed the demon aside and decided that some form of petty revenge had to be taken. She still had the chalk in her pocket from having drawn the pentagram. She pulled it out and, even though she was frightened, defiantly drew a mustache on the painting. Then they continued on their way.

They padded noiselessly down the hallway. At the end of the hall Gwen saw a closed door. Morty drew up short, and she bumped into him. Her hand brushed against his scaly rump. He grinned maliciously. "I didn't know you cared."

"Shut up."

"Fine." He pointed toward the door. "That's Morgan's

inner sanctum. That's where she was keeping Merlin."

She nodded, and the knife was in her hand. Its tip glittered in the dim light. She only wished that she could have wielded Excalibur. Even so, she still felt herself an enemy to reckon with.

They got to the end of the corridor, Gwen straining her ears for some indication that Morgan was in the vicinity. And she did hear something. It was a television playing somewhere, and it was tuned to the election returns. Gwen pushed past the demon now and, with boldness she desperately wished she felt, opened the door and walked into Morgan Le Fey's inner sanctum.

Morgan wasn't there. Morty came in behind Gwen and peeked over her shoulder. His sigh of relief was audible.

Unfortunately, Merlin wasn't there either. The sanctum was dark and foreboding, with a pentagram on the floor that was elaborate and decorated, unlike the amateurish one (she now felt) that Gwen had drawn on the floor of Sheila's apartment. The furniture was elaborate and gothic, books lining the walls, and a window with huge drapes adorned with bat emblems. At the far end was an altar, perfect for sacrificing small animals. Upon it were two tall candles, one white, one black, in elaborate candleholders. The white one was burned further down than the black one. Next to the black candle was a photo of Arthur. Next to the white was Keating's picture.

"What the hell—?" whispered Gwen, approaching it.

"Sympathetic Spell," the demon informed her. "She's trying to tilt the probabilities in the favor of Arthur's opponent. White candle burns out first, the other guy wins."

"That's ridiculous," Gwen retorted.

The demon shrugged and said mirthlessly, "Care to place an election bet?"

"The votes have already been cast."

"Nothing in this world is ever certain, especially where magic is involved. I know it sounds crazy. . . ."

"Actually," Gwen said thoughtfully, "knowing such things exist explains an election or two that come to mind."

Gwen then confidently bent over the candles and blew them out. She smiled briefly, and then her face fell as they both relit. "Okay, fine," she said after a moment's thought. "I'll just switch the pictures."

She reached for them and suddenly a voice from behind her said, "That won't help."

She spun. There in the shadows near the door was Morgan. "The spell is governed by my will, little queen," she said softly. "It does what I wish. This is my inner sanctum. My place of great magic. And you have no power here." With a sweep of her cloak, Morgan stepped into the sanctum, sporting a thin mustache that looked like it had been drawn on her face. It matched the one that Gwen had etched on the painting.

Gwen and Morty started to laugh. Morgan, confused, picked up a hand mirror, looked at it in annoyance, and wiped away the mustache.

"Was that funny to you?" she inquired, sounding solicitous. Suddenly she held the mirror up, and it began to gleam. The demon's reflection was visible within it.

"No! Morgan, no!" shrieked Morty, but it was too late. A bolt of light lanced out from the mirror, enveloping the demon, and Gwen could do nothing to stop it except shield her eyes. When the light subsided, Morty was gone.

No, not gone. His reflection was still in the mirror. Except it wasn't his reflection, it was *him*, and he was mouthing screams for mercy. Morgan smiled at him for a moment, and then slammed the mirror down, shattering it. Large pieces fell all over the floor.

"Seven years bad luck for you, little queen," she said softly. "It's so hard to get good help nowadays, isn't it, Lance?"

Lance, clad in leather and spikes, emerged from the shadows of the hallway nearby, snickering and glaring at

Gwen. Gwen felt ill. Part of her wanted to believe that Morgan had cast some sort of magic spell upon him, but in her heart, she knew it was just him. That he was happy this way.

She drew herself up, focused her anger on Morgan. "Where's Merlin?" she demanded.

Morgan looked amused that Gwen would take such a tone, considering the circumstances. "Oh, him." She gestured to one side of the room, and suddenly light flooded a corner of it that Gwen hadn't even realized was there before. There, as if it were a trophy, was a column of crystal with Merlin embedded inside. Her breath caught. "Oh, God," she murmured, her fingers interlacing as if in prayer. "Oh, God, I'm so sorry."

"Not half as sorry," Morgan told her, "as you're going to be."

B ERNARD KEATING, AT least, had a sense of drama. He was cloistered away in a hotel room at the Essex while his campaigners milled about downstairs. He and his people were watching the TV fixedly.

"And with two percent of the vote counted, and suicidal Democrat Kent Taylor effectively out of the running garnering less than one-tenth of the votes, we are left with Arthur Penn still running behind Republican candidate Bernard Keating. Keating has 51 percent of—"

The rest of the comments were drowned out in ragged cheers from Keating's people. Bernie, taking a drag on a cigar, looked around and shouted, "Where the hell is Moe? He should be celebrating here!"

"You fired him," said one woman. "Several times."

"Well, hell, call his place," Keating said, feeling expansive. "Tell him to get his ass over here, the stupid mother."

*   *   *

𝕴 T'S GOING TO be close," said Morgan. "Make no mistake, little queen. It will be close. But Arthur shall lose."

Gwen's eyes never left Morgan. The sorceress had not moved from the spot where Gwen had first seen her. But Lance, dressed like something out of a *Matrix* movie was already starting to creep in her direction. "You're wrong, Morgan. You're going to lose. Everything."

"My, oh my." Morgan looked down her nose at Gwen. "The little queen has become quite the bold one. I haven't forgiven you, you know, for that attack in the park." Her fingers drifted to her cheek. "I was going to seek you out after the election; let your head, sent care of a demon, be my final calling card to Arthur. But you've become quite the unpredictable enemy, haven't you, little queen. Turned the tables on me, yes you did. I'd never have credited you with the guts to search me out."

Gwen's gaze and, suddenly the point of her knife, momentarily flicked in Lance's direction. He was trying to move around the room toward her, but he froze when he saw the knife. "Don't try it, Lance. I swear I'll kill you."

"Why, Gwen," said Morgan. "You're positively a woman warrior, aren't you?"

"You don't get it, Morgan. All my life I felt like a nothing. Like everyone always stepped on me. Then along came Arthur, and he made me feel like someone. And now I've lost him. Lost him, thanks to you. Without Arthur I don't care what happens to me. I don't care if I live or die. And when you stop caring, it means you can become reckless. That, and I've been using my brains a bit. I've watched what happens. I'm figuring out the limits of your power."

"Have you now?"

Lance was creeping up on Gwen's right. Taking small, careful steps, Gwen sidled to her left, keeping a large table between herself and Lance. Still she continued to watch Morgan, Morgan the unmoving. "Yes. For example, I've figured out that when you are attacked mystically, you defend and counterattack mystically. But when you're attacked physically, the only way to ward it off is by physical means. That's why they burned witches, isn't it?"

"Hanging was also popular," said Morgan dryly.

"That's why that demon could take Merlin with his bare hands. That is why I could take you in the park. And that is why," and her voice rose suddenly, "I'm going to take you now! I'm *not* going to go back to being the way I was!"

She drew her hand back, the skull shaped dagger now held by the point, and she hurled the dagger straight at Morgan's chest. The dagger flew unerringly and plunged deep into Morgan's breast, piercing her evil heart and putting an end to her forever.

At least that's what Gwen had hoped would happen.

Actually she missed by a country mile. The dagger, weighted completely improperly for throwing, spun erratically in its flight and hit the wall behind Morgan a good three feet to her right. It thudded to the ground, way out of Gwen's reach.

"Uh-oh," muttered Gwen.

Morgan raised her hand. "Oh, little queen," she said, "you who are not afraid to die. You who are reckless. I'm going to show you that there are worse things than death. You don't want to go back to being what you were? Easily solved: We'll find something different for you to be."

A T THE ROOSEVELT Hotel Arthur was watching the set intensely now. A mask of gloom had settled over his face, which had spread to the rest of the people in the room. "I don't understand," he murmured. "Don't they know what's best for them? Look at that."

At that moment, with three percent of the voting in, Keating was at fifty-two percent, Penn at forty-eight. The newscasters were already intimating that Bernard Keating was the new mayor of New York City.

Ronnie Cordoba's cell phone rang. He answered it, then made a face and—turning to Arthur—said quietly, "It's Bernard Keating. Shall I hang up?"

Arthur shook his head and, taking the phone, put it to his ear. "Yes?" said Arthur.

"Bernie Keating here, Art!" said Keating on the other end. Noisemakers, party music, and such were audible over the phone. Keating was shouting to be heard. "Ready to concede yet?"

"Concede?"

"Yeah. You know, quit. There's no need to be a sore loser, Art."

"I wouldn't know," said Arthur evenly. "I don't make a habit of losing."

He closed the phone and handed it back to Ronnie without a word.

IT HAPPENED WITH incredible swiftness.

Gwen pivoted and leaped in Lance's direction. Lance, thinking she was trying to escape, shouted, "Don't worry, Morgan! I got her!" So saying, he grabbed for Gwen. He got a grip on her shoulders and made as if to hold her in place. It looked to all intents and purposes that he had a really solid grasp on her.

Morgan's hands were glowing. The power of the spell was already in existence, and once called into the world, the power had to be unleashed lest it backlash against the wielder. Morgan passed her hands through the air, the gestures shaping the nature of the spell, and the power was aimed right at Gwen. At the last second Gwen suddenly twisted away from Lance, breaking his grip easily, fear pumping adrenaline through her body. She dropped to the ground, shielding her eyes. Lance only had the chance to open his mouth and start to frame a question before he was bathed in the light of the spell. There was a sudden sound, like a vacuum being sucked into a bottle. One instant Lance was there, the next he wasn't.

Actually, that was not quite true. There was a large, gray rodent skittering around on the floor, squeaking angrily. Morgan looked down in dismay and said, "Rats."

Her smoldering eyes turned to Gwen, and, without saying another word, she gestured and another blast of mystic energy blew from her hand. Gwen leaped out of the way, sure-footed in her black sneakers. She felt the air sizzle around her and looked around. Where the energy bolt had struck after missing her, several large pillows and a good chunk of the floor had disappeared.

Her heart pounding like a jackhammer, Gwen moved quickly in Merlin's direction, praying that somehow the trapped magician would be able to aid her. Suddenly she stepped on something that let out an ear-piercing squeal. It was Lance. She made a quick movement with her feet as he scampered between them, and she tripped herself up. She fell heavily to the ground, slamming her elbows down and sending pain shooting up her arms. She rolled onto her back and looked up just as Morgan shouted her triumph and let fly a bolt of energy, one that would erase Gwen DeVere Queen from the face of the earth.

IN HIS APARTMENT, Moe Dreskin was busy packing and diligently ignoring the ringing phone on the nightstand. He had a feeling he knew who it was: Keating, telling him that all was forgiven, that he should c'mon over, party hardy, let's kick ass and take names.

Modred would have none of it. He said to the ringing phone, "No way. If Arthur loses, he'll kill me. If Arthur wins, mother kills me."

He picked up a pair of airline tickets, kissed them with more passion than he'd ever kissed a woman, and tossed them into his bags.

*   *   *

TIME SEEMED TO slow to a crawl. As Morgan was letting loose with the spell that she knew would rid her of Gwen, she saw the woman lunge for something to her right. But it was a desperation move, certainly, of no threat to Morgan.

The power lashed out at Gwen and, just at that second, Gwen held up a large fragment of the mirror that had been used to dispatch the demon . . . the mirror that Morgan had shattered. She was clutching it so desperately that she had already sliced her fingers, blood trickling along the edges of the glass, but that was not the important thing. No, of far greater import was that Morgan's spell struck the mirror, ricocheted, and hit the crystal column in which Merlin was trapped.

"No!" screamed Morgan, but it was too late. Like a laser cracking a diamond, the spell of disintegration pierced the crystal. A weblike pattern of lines appeared on the surface, and Merlin's small body began to glow with power. Again Morgan cried "No!" a split second before the crystal shattered into a million shards. Gwen shielded her eyes, but miraculously, or perhaps magically, not so much as a single piece cut her. Morgan, on the other hand, was unable to fend off what seemed like thousands of angry hornets stinging her. She went down, pieces of crystal embedded in her dress and skin.

Merlin stood there, his eyes smoldering with anger and power. His fists were clenched and glowing. "Morgan," he said in a dangerous voice, "you've kept bound forces with which you should not have tampered."

"You little fiend!" Morgan cried. "That's the second time you've done that. First you nearly get me cut to ribbons with my own television set, and now this. Well no more, I tell you. No more!" Her body glowed. "You're in my place now, Merlin. You cannot win!"

"Gwen! Behind me!" ordered Merlin. Gwen barely had

time to comply before Morgan's mystical attack was launched.

And on the altar, the black and white candles that had been governing the outcome of the election, had fallen together and were now melting into each other.

"$\mathfrak{I}$ N A SUDDEN reversal," the newscaster said, "returns from the upper Manhattan voting districts have tilted the balloting more toward Arthur Penn."

The roar that went up around Arthur was deafening. Over the shouting, Percival said in his ear, "Looks like we're going to be putting in a long night."

"That's certainly superior to the alternative," said Arthur.

$\mathfrak{M}$ ERLIN HAD ERECTED his mystical defenses barely in time. A sphere of pure energy surrounded him and Gwen, as Morgan's powerful spells bounced off the shields. Pillows imploded into nothingness. Walls began to melt into puddles. And Morgan's wrath grew.

Merlin, his face frozen in concentration, worked on maintaining the shields that were preserving their lives. Gwen crawled to him and demanded, "Now what?"

"You're asking me?" said Merlin desperately. "You're the one who came to the rescue. I assumed you'd figured a way out."

"I did," said Gwen. "You're it."

"Wonderful," replied Merlin.

Energy cascaded around them, dancing in little sparks. "I can't hold her back much longer," grated Merlin. "I'm too weak. I've been cooped up for too long."

"Then what are we going to do?"

"Will you stop asking me that?"

"All right," said Gwen angrily. "All right!" She started to stand. "Cover me."

Merlin looked at her, aghast. "What? What do you think this is, a Western? What do you mean, cover you?"

"I'm going to get her."

"You're insane! There are forces being unleashed here you know nothing about."

"Good," said Gwen. "If I knew about them, I'd probably be more terrified than I am right now. See you next lifetime, Merlin."

"Gwen—"

Gwen leaped out from behind the protection of Merlin's shields. She rolled across the smoldering carpet as Morgan, blind with fury, directed her attack at Gwen's quick moving form. Gwen, heart pounding with excitement, mind racing thanks to the uppers, moved with a speed that defied description. And Morgan, caught up in her anger, used her power wildly, recklessly. She did not take time to aim, or plan, or think, letting her raw fury guide her. Gwen broke right, broke left, leaped forward, then pivoted and dodged again to the right. Explosions of primal force bracketed her. A chunk of floor tilted wildly under her and she jumped off it, rolling that much closer to Morgan. A sudden instinct warned her, and she ducked to one side as a huge piece of plaster from the ceiling fell and shattered right where she'd been.

Morgan was grinning wildly. "You're going to die, Guinevere, you slut!" she shrieked. "My brother's whore! There'll be less than nothing left of you when I'm through."

Still two yards away, Gwen shot back, "All talking, bitch queen, but no action. Hiding behind your spells and your pretty lights! When it comes down to the crunch, you just don't have what it takes."

"You . . . you . . ." Raw energy flew between Morgan's palms and arced outward at Gwen. She leaped in the one direction Morgan had not anticipated—straight at her. Gwen came in low in a flying tackle, her arms wrapped around Morgan's legs, and the two of them went down in a tumble of arms and legs.

Merlin shouted from across the room, "Gwen! Don't look in her eyes! Not at such close quarters!" And Gwen, hearing his words, shut her eyes tightly, even as she and Morgan rolled, struggling hand to hand.

Then Gwen was on her back, Morgan straddling her. There was a triumphant gleam in Morgan's eyes that Gwen didn't see. "I don't need my magic to finish you, little queen." She brought her hand down, open, slapping it across Gwen's cheek. "That's just the beginning of paying you back for what you've done to me."

She snapped her fingers and suddenly the knife that Gwen had thrown at her earlier was in Morgan's hand. She was poised to bring it down squarely into Gwen's chest. The pain raced through Gwen's face even as she brought her legs up from behind and wrapped her knees around Morgan's neck. The sorceress gagged, gasping for air, as Gwen turned and slammed her down on the ground. The impact stunned Morgan momentarily, and caused her to drop the knife. Quick as lightning Gwen released her hold on Morgan and hurled herself at the knife. Her desperate fingers curled around the hilt, and before Morgan could regain her senses, Gwen had thrown herself across Morgan's prostrate form.

She held the knife over Morgan's rapidly rising breasts.

"Finish her!" shouted Merlin.

Morgan, petrified, made no move. Her gaze shifted from the knife to Gwen, but Gwen was careful not to look at her directly. Her entire concentration was on the point of the knife, poised directly over her fallen foe's heart. Gwen's hand trembled. She bit her lip.

"Damnit, woman! What are you waiting for? Kill her!" Merlin screamed.

"I—" Gwen half sobbed, exhaustion overtaking her. "I can't! I can't just kill someone. We've beaten her. Isn't that enough?"

The air crackled around them. Gwen's head flew back, her mouth open in a silent scream. And then, like a marionette, Gwen was hurled back, soaring through the air, her body twisted. She hit a wall with a sickening crunch and slid to the floor like a broken doll. A small trickle of blood ran down the side of her mouth. She did not move again.

"No," said Morgan, getting slowly to her feet. "It wasn't enough, little queen. Not nearly enough."

RTHUR WAS IN the men's room. Percival watched dismally as the latest tallies were reported. He turned to Ronnie, Elvis, and Buddy and said simply, "The gap is widening. We may lose."

ORGAN TILTED HER head back, her mouth opened wide, and she started to laugh. Then a mystic bolt hit her with full impact. Her instincts warned her barely in time to raise a most minimal shield. She fell back, terror in her eyes.

Merlin was standing there. His fists were glowing, smoke rising from them. His eyes were little more than white, pupil-less spots with energy crackling from them. Lance the Rat cowered in a corner.

"All right, Morgan." The voice of an old man rose from the throat of a young boy, and when he cracked his knuckles it sounded like thunder. "Let's see what you've got."

The air exploded.

YE OLDE SOUND BITE

†

"And with new returns coming in, we see another swing in the direction of Arthur Penn. With ten percent of the votes tallied, it now appears that the Independent candidate and Bernard Keating, the Republican candidate, are dead even. I would have to say that, at this point, it is far too early to call Arthur Penn out of the race. And as a side note, precincts are reporting record turnout among voters eighteen to twenty-four . . ."

CHAPTRE
THE TWENTY-THIRD

✠

EIGHBORS OF MORGAN'S in Verona looked out their windows, watching lights cascading from her windows. One man muttered to his wife, "I'll tell ya . . . the old bat who lives there is having one serious party."

Suddenly unleashed elemental forces erupted from the old house. The ground started to rumble, narrow crevices opened in the weed-covered grounds. Windows glowed with wild, unearthly fires. Those who were of a more imaginative bent thought that bizarre black shapes, twisted and reeking of evil, emerged from the cracks and sideboards, from the chimney and the gutters, dissipating into the rainy night—dozens of them, creatures that had been Morgan's slaves, on whose energy Morgan had fed. Poltergeists, near-formless creatures that on their own created minor mischief but that, under the control of a master necromancer, could alter probabilities on a wide scale—and even effect election returns—vanished into the night. Morgan's control of them slipped through her fingers as she used every iota of mystical energy she possessed in her battle against Merlin.

Arcane shields hovered before her, cracking and splintering. She blocked Merlin's thrusts the way a fencer would, but more and more began to slip through. She began to weaken mystically. Her energy slipped away from her.

"You cannot dampen my hatred for you!" she howled. "It continues to grow!"

"Hatred is destructive not constructive, Morgan," Merlin retorted. "And I intend to create! Create a world that you're not in!"

Merlin advanced on her, his face set. Morgan battered at his defenses, but he had had time to recuperate. The edge was his, and he was not for one moment permitting Morgan to recapture it. His lips were constantly moving, chanting, invoking the power of the gods, drawing strength from bands of mystic energy that hovered before him.

"Damn you, Merlin Hellspawn!" Morgan cried. She raised her hands above her head and abruptly dropped her defenses, pulling all her mystic reserves together. A solid black bolt of power sizzled through the air like a thing alive. And Merlin brushed it aside as if she'd tossed a feather at him. It angled upward, blasting through the roof of the old house. Sparks flew from it as it passed, caught on the shingle roof. The roof began to blaze.

Neighbors on the sidewalk pointed at the fire and hurried to call the fire department.

Morgan fell back, back further. And she started to age, deteriorating with incredible speed. Within seconds her hair was gray, then white, then falling out, her face wrinkled, her teeth brittle and breaking. The only things glowing were her eyes, in desperation. "Merlin," she croaked out, "We could rule together—"

"Go to hell," said Merlin. His hands formed the horns of Satan, and power flowed from them. Morgan hastily tried to create more shields, but Merlin's spell passed through them as if they were not there. The power surrounded Morgan, bathing her in an unearthly light, and she clenched her fists, beating at the air as she screamed her fury. "You haven't won yet! I still hate!"

Her body turned black, then pale blue. And then, with a rush of air, it exploded outward.

Merlin turned away as a wave of light and heat rushed at him carrying a foul stench that made him gag. When he looked back, in the space where Morgan had been, there was nothing.

No, not quite nothing. A black cloud was there, hovering, fuming. Merlin rushed to create a spell of containment, but before it was fully formed, the black cloud slipped away and vanished through the walls.

The ceiling overhead burst into flames. The fire had worked its way downward, and the house was going quickly. Merlin dashed over to the side of the fallen Gwen, fully expecting to find a corpse. He knelt beside her, lifted her wrist and checked her pulse. To his surprise he found one, strong and steady.

He took her face in his hands even as the room began to fill with smoke. "Gwen!" he shouted. "Get up! I don't know if I have enough power to get us both out of here! Gwen, speak to me!"

Gwen snored.

"Oh, bloody wonderful," said Merlin. A sharp cracking overhead alerted him, and he saw a flaming timber break off and fall toward them. He spoke then, spellcasting faster than he ever had in his life. From the corner of his eye, he saw a petrified rodent dashing toward them, and then the timber crashed down.

"REPEAT," SAID EDWARD Shukin to his viewing audience, "we are projecting Arthur Penn as the winner of this year's mayoral election—"

The repeat was not heard, for the cheer that had gone up when the announcement was first made totally drowned it out. In the midst of the crowd Arthur was laughing, cheering, being pounded joyfully on the back. Nubile young women hugged and kissed him, and every man wanted to shake his hand. He was alternately pushed and pulled to the podium up front, and within moments he found himself facing a mob of cheering, enthusiastic fans and workers. He smiled and put up his hands to indicate that they should quiet down, which only provoked further cheering. Laughing, he just stood there and allowed the adulation of the crowd to wash over him, wave after wave of love. It filled his soul to bursting.

Finally the crowd started to calm down enough for Arthur to begin to say, "My friends, my . . . dear friends—"

At that moment Ronnie ran up onto the stage and shouted, "Keating just conceded!" And that set off another round of cheering and applause. By the time Arthur finally got to say anything, it was past midnight.

"My friends," he said. "My dear, dear friends. It's been a long fight. It's been a difficult fight. We've had small victories along the way. We've had . . . small losses." He paused, searching for words. "The trust that this city— that you—have in me, a humble visitor from the past"— and this provoked some cheering—"has certainly been gratifying. I swear that I will uphold the trust that you have placed in me, and do the best job for New York City that any mayor has ever done."

Someone in the audience shouted, "When are you running for president?"

Arthur grinned as people applauded. "Well, let's give me a few years to get my feet wet. After all, it's a lot easier being king than being mayor or president. I have a lot to learn first." He waited for the laughter to subside. "When you're a king," he continued, "you tell people to do something, and by God they do it. When you're a mayor, they ask you why. And when you're a president they pass it over to some committee or other where a group of men

who don't give a damn what you say get together and
decide that they're not going to do it at all."

"Arthur for king!" someone shouted.

Arthur raised a clenched fist in appreciation. "Now
that's the kind of forward looking backward thinking that
I intend to make the hallmark of my career!" The applause
was thunderous.

ODRED WATCHED AS much of Arthur's speech
as he could stomach, then switched channels and
saw Keating. He was standing behind a podium, looking
ashen—looking drunk, actually—and he was saying, "I
have already contacted Mr. Penn . . . make that Mayor-
Elect Penn, I'm sorry. You don't know how sorry. No . . .
no, I shouldn't say that. He won fair and square . . . and
I would like to be among the first to congratulate the new
mayor, and pledge my support in all his future endeavors."

Taking some pleasure in a moment of destruction,
Modred kicked the TV over. The cord ripped out of the
wall, and the set made a satisfying crash as it fell to the
ground. "Arthur," Modred said tightly, "somewhere,
somehow . . . I'll find a way to kill you. And as soon as I
find a way, you'll be the first to know. Until then, rot in
hell."

He picked up his bags and started for the door, and
suddenly dropped the bags and screamed. He pitched
over, clutching at his head as if his brain were threatening
to explode out the top. He smashed into walls, at war
with his own body. And finally he collapsed out of sight
behind the bed.

He lay on the ground, gasping, thumping at his head
and then slowly, very slowly, he stopped. He waited until
his rapid breathing slowed to normal and then he got to
his feet. He felt lightheaded for a moment, but that
quickly cleared. He looked around the room as if seeing

it with new eyes, and then he caught his reflection in the mirror.

Morgan Le Fey smiled back at him.

And he laughed loud and long.

𝕵 T WAS THE early hours of the morning when Arthur finally arrived home at his modest apartment. He looked around and sighed. Merlin had advised that he keep the place, even after he moved into Gracie Mansion. He sighed again. No matter where he lived, it would seem pale in comparison to Belvedere Castle. And yet, the castle itself would seem empty now that Gwen wasn't there.

"Congratulations, Mayor Wart."

Arthur spun. There, at his bedroom door, was Merlin. His hair and eyebrows were singed. He had removed his jacket and tie, but his shirt and slacks were blackened from smoke. To Arthur he had never looked so good.

"Merlin?" He walked slowly toward him, not daring to believe it. "Merlin—is it really you?"

"Yes, Wart," he said tiredly. "It's me."

Arthur touched his shoulder gently, tentatively, and then a grin split his face. "You got away, didn't you? You little fox. I should have known." Then his voice hardened. "Where's Morgan, Merlin? Where is she hiding? Tell me, because by Excalibur there'll be a reckoning—"

Merlin raised a hand. "No need, Arthur. There's already been a reckoning. Morgan is dead."

Arthur paused in disbelief. "Dead?"

"Yes. Her body, at any rate. It's hard to destroy her utterly. At the moment all that remains of her is a little discorporated cloud of hate. And I'll get that eventually too. I'd like to put it in a bottle on my mantel. Make a nice conversation piece."

Merlin sauntered across the room and threw himself full length on Arthur's sofa. Arthur followed him, shaking his head wonderingly. "You did it. You really did it. Morgan is gone."

"Well, I had some help . . ."

"Help? How do you mean?"

Merlin told him. He told him everything—everything Gwen had said, everything that he'd done. Arthur stood there trying to take it all in. "You're saying . . . you're saying that she really saved your life."

"No," said Merlin, positioning the throw pillow under his head. "I'm not saying that. I'll be double damned if I'd ever admit that I needed anyone's help to fight my battles. However, if you say it, I won't contradict it." He stared up at the ceiling. "I was wrong about her, Arthur."

"No, Merlin." Arthur sat across from him. "You were right. You said she wasn't trustworthy, and you were right."

Merlin shook his head. "She made mistakes, true. And you have not? Everything that your precious Gwen Queen did, she did out of a sense of duty—remember she had once sworn loyalty to Lance. She was certain no lasting harm would come to you. She was betrayed by Morgan in that respect. As I recall, Morgan pulled the wool over your eyes more than one time. As a matter of fact, Modred would never have existed if—"

"I . . . gather your point, Merlin," said Arthur sheepishly.

They were silent for a time, and then Arthur said, "Merlin? How can I trust her loyalty to *me* now?"

Merlin snorted. "Good God, Arthur, that woman went through all manner of hell, on the remote chance that she'd win back your favor. Even though her motives were, in a way, honorable, she was still remorseful over what she'd done. She risked life and limb to undo the results of her handiwork."

Arthur shook his head. "I can't believe some of the things you say she was capable of."

"Neither can I," admitted Merlin. "Frankly, I suspect

she couldn't either. I never thought, Wart, that I would be trying to talk you into taking that woman back. But I owe you my honest opinion, and I will tell you this, Arthur—I would stake my immortal soul on the loyalty of Gwen Queen."

Arthur sat there, square jawed, and then said, "Can I see her?"

"Of course. She's in your bedroom."

Arthur got up and went into the bedroom. There, stretched out on the bed, was Gwen. There was an ugly bruise on her forehead, and her clothes had the same smoke discoloration as Merlin's. But she was there, and she was sound and whole. Arthur went to her side and took her hand. Her chest rose and fell steadily in sleep. "Gwen?" he said gently, shaking her shoulder.

From the doorway Merlin said, "You're wasting your time, Arthur. As near as I can tell, she was taking some sort of pills to keep herself going. You can only do that to yourself for so long before your body just says, 'Enough.' She's going to sleep for quite some time, I would say. There's not a single thing that you could say or do that would bring her around."

Arthur glanced at Merlin and then back at Gwen. Then he sat next to her on the bed, squeezed her hand and said, in a voice full of love and affection, "Gwen, would you do me the honor of becoming my wife?"

Gwen's eyes fluttered open. "Yes."

Merlin sighed and shook his head. "I give up. The entire gender makes no sense to me at all."

CHAPTRE
THE TWENTY-FOURTH

†

HE HORSES THUNDERED toward each other,
hooves kicking up clods of dirt. Astride the powerful
beasts were mounted two armored knights, lances firmly
in place, intent on each other's approach. The sun glinted
down on their shields, and the crowd roared as they met.
The lance of the knight with the blue plume in his helm
shattered against the shield of the other jouster, and a
cheer went up. The other knight, in the red plume, was
the good guy.

The horses reached the opposite ends of the field, and
the blue plumed knight was handed a new lance. He spun
his horse, shook a fist at his opponent, and the crowd
booed the unsportsmanlike gesture.

It was a beautiful day for a joust on the fields of the
Cloisters. Standing within a mile of the jousting field was
a monestary that housed tapestries and pieces of lovely
artwork. Stretched out around the Cloisters was parkland
bordered by the Henry Hudson Parkway, and 183rd
Street up to 210th Street. It was a little bit of another

century staking a claim against the encroachment of the present.

The knights were members of a performing troupe that produced medieval fairs on a regular basis around the country. But this particular medieval fair was for a very special occasion—a celebration, a party to which all of New York City had been invited. To celebrate the election of Arthur Penn to the high office of mayor of New York City.

A reviewing stand erected on the edge of the jousting field had been deliberately designed to look like something out of an ancient tournament. There was a box down front in which the royalty was supposed to sit, and Arthur had very cheerfully and willingly taken his place there, Gwen at his side. Gwen was stunning in a long white gown and a small crown with sparkling jewels on her head. Next to her sat Arthur, looking as if he'd stepped from another time. He was dressed in full chain mail. The main garment was called a hauberk, sort of a nightshirt made out of chain mail that hung to his knees, the skirt slit up the middle almost to the waist. Underneath the hauberk was a padded tunic to prevent the mail from digging into his chest. His leggings were mail tights called chaussures, tied just below his knee with a wide strip of cloth. Over the hauberk Arthur wore a white surcoat—a sleeveless white garment that had no collar or sleeves. It was split up the sides and laced up from the waist to the armpit. The long skirts fell free and were split up the middle the same as the hauberk. A roaring dragon was pictured on his chest. Around his waist was Excalibur, visible thanks to Merlin even though Arthur had not drawn it. Nor did he have any intention of drawing it.

Arthur leaned over toward Gwen. "Damn, it's amazing how hot this outfit can be."

"I can believe it. But look at them." She gestured to the excited crowds. "They love the entire concept of you as an ancient king. Occasionally you really have to give the people what they want."

He nodded. "True . . . no matter how personally uncomfortable I might be. Let's just be thankful it's the end of November rather than the middle of July. Though it is warm for this time of year."

The two knights thundered toward each other once more, and this time in a beautifully choreographed move, they knocked each other off their respective horses. The knights turned toward Arthur expectantly. An announcer clad in a jerkin who had a considerable set of lungs, shouted, "The combatants request permission from the king to continue the joust on foot." Arthur smiled and gave a thumbs up gesture. The crowd cheered, as they knew they should, as the two knights drew their swords and began hacking at each other's heavy wooden shields. Wood chips flew from the shields as they moved back and forth, up and down the field. At one point the red plumed knight went down to one knee and the blue plumed knight came in for the kill. The red plumed knight came in low, swung his sword, and caught the blue plumed knight across the middle. The air rang with the impact of the blow, and the blue plumed knight went down. The red plumed knight was up in a flash and held the blade of his sword over the fallen knight. The crowd went wild as the downed fighter put up a hand in supplication and the announcer shouted, "The blue knight yields!"

Arthur applauded the outcome along with the rest of the crowd. There was a tap on his shoulder and he turned. Percival was there, smiling. Arthur looked at him reproachfully. "Percival, you're supposed to have dressed for the occasion."

"But highness, I did."

"I hardly think that a *Final Fantasy* sweatshirt qualifies as knightly attire."

"Best I could do."

Suddenly Buddy and Elvis were on either side of Ar-

thur. They were both attired in full jesters' garb. Somehow Arthur couldn't have thought of anything more
appropriate. "May we serve you somehow, my liege?"
asked Buddy with a sweeping bow.

"Something to drink. Anything liquid, short of motor
oil. You, Gwen?" She shook her head, and Arthur said,
"Very well. More for me, then."

"You heard the man," Buddy said briskly to Elvis. "I'll
stay here in case he decides he needs anything else."

"I am . . . so blessed," Arthur deadpanned. Elvis looked
none-too-thrilled, but gamely went off to do as he was
supposed to.

"These two Jews walk into a Juice bar . . ." Buddy began.

Gwen leaned over and said softly to Arthur, "Do I get
to say 'Off with his head' at some point?"

"Not this life. Maybe the next," Arthur assured her.

COSTUMED ACTORS WANDERED about, mixed in
with the crowd. Young maidens shrunk in fear as
amused tourists snapped their photographs—the lasses
were concerned that pieces of their souls were being taken.
Knights in armor looked gallant, assassins stalked, and a
good time was being had by all.

Elvis found a booth where cider was being served, and
got a large mug of it for Arthur. He turned and bumped
into a knight clothed similarly to Arthur, except that his
surcoat was solid black. Not a spot of any other design on
it. He held a barrel helmet under his arm.

"Watch it," said Elvis, trying to get around the knight.
"Gotta bring a drink to the king."

"No, excuse me," said the black-clad knight. "That belt
buckle you're wearing is fascinating. Where is it from?"

Elvis looked down blankly at the belt buckle, and con-
sequently did not notice the small tablet that the knight
dropped into the drink he was holding. "It's from the

middle of my stomach," he said in bemusement.

"Of course it is," said the black knight, then he turned, and walked away.

G WEN WAS LOOKING oddly at him. "What's wrong, my dear?" he asked.

"You just look . . . so sad," she told him. She stroked his cheek lovingly. "I don't understand. So melancholy."

"It's difficult to explain, really," he said after a long moment. "For so long . . . from the start of this adventure, really . . . I've felt as if I was laboring under a cloud of doom."

"Worrying about Morgan will do that to you."

"Not Morgan. Fate. At a point where everything seems to be going perfectly, that has been—in the past—when the true, final horror is dropped upon me."

"That's in the past," she said firmly, giving his hand a squeeze.

"Perhaps. But I suppose that that is why you see 'melancholy' in me. There's a part of me that is almost afraid to be happy."

"Arthur," Gwen said with all seriousness, "believe me when I tell you: If anyone is the expert on being afraid to be happy, it's me. Having this sense that you're not entitled to happiness. That failure and misery are all that are due you. And I can tell you as well as anyone can just how destructive that mind-set is. If you don't believe in true happiness, you'll never have any."

"You're right. You are so right, my queen."

Percival stepped forward, looking concerned. "Is anything amiss, highness? You and the queen seem to be discussing rather intense matters."

"Nothing you need concern yourself about, good Percival. By the by, have you seen Merlin anywhere?"

"He is patrolling the area."

"Patrolling?" Gwen looked at him with puzzlement.

"Yes. He said he is . . . suspicious."

"God, now I know where you get it from," Gwen said in exasperation.

But Arthur smiled and patted her hand again. "Worry not about Merlin. He sees conspiracies everywhere."

A cup was thrust under Arthur's nose. He looked up and saw Elvis standing there, the little bells from his fool's motley jingling. "Here you go. A drink for the king."

Standing just behind Elvis, Buddy piped in, "It's good to be the king."

"As you say," said Arthur, and he took the cup in his hands and lifted it to his lips.

"Arthur," Gwen said abruptly.

Arthur lowered the cup without drinking. "Yes?"

Gwen was looking at a printed list of activities. "Arthur, that joust was the last thing. You think we can go soon? I love the gown, but I'd really like to get out of it." She smiled mischievously. "Would you care to help me?"

He laughed. "Ma'am, I'll have you know I'm betrothed."

Gwen rested her head on his shoulder, wrapping her hands around his arm. "It can't be soon enough for me, Arthur," she said.

"Nor for me," he said. "Very well then, my dear, let us say our good-byes, and we'll be off. Percival, if you would be so kind as to bring the car around. And tell Merlin we're departing, so he can relax and enjoy the rest of the afternoon, safe in the knowledge that Arthur Rex lives safely."

And then, almost as an afterthought, he downed the contents of the cup. He frowned slightly at the aftertaste. "Needs more sugar. Right, then. Shall we—?"

And suddenly a voice boomed across the field. *"Arthur! Arthur Pendragon the Coward, son of Uther the Murderer! I challenge you!"*

Arthur had half risen out of his seat, and now he sat down slowly, his gaze held by the knight in the black surcoat who stood before him. His loud words had attracted the notice of everyone within earshot. Crowds that had started to disperse began to gather once again. And Gwen, completely befuddled, paged through her program. This wasn't on the schedule. "Who the hell is that?" she asked.

Arthur didn't need to ask. Even though the other knight was helmed, Arthur recognized him. He smiled unpleasantly. "Hello, Modred," he called back. "Come to wish me success in my new career?"

"I have come to put an end to you, Pendragon. You, and your damned notions of a New Camelot."

There was no doubt in the crowd's collective mind who the bad guy was in this little scenario. Modred was roundly booed. It made no impression on him as he drew his sword and pointed it at Arthur. "Well, Pendragon? Do you dare fight me? Or will you be revealed to all here as the coward that you are?"

There were yells and catcalls as someone shouted out, "Teach him a lesson, Arthur! Clean his clock for him!" And the crowd, which thought it was watching another staged event, took up the encouragement.

Gwen looked at Arthur with rising concern. "Not . . . *the* Modred . . ."

"Only in the sense that I'm *the* Arthur. Yes, my dear, it's him, my own bastard son, come to call. It would be rude to turn him away."

Arthur started to rise and Gwen put a hand on his arm. "Arthur, please. Don't do this."

"Gwen, you said it yourself: Sometimes we have to give the people what they want."

"But they think it's an act, like the joust! Modred really wants to kill you!"

"Do you see this?" He pushed back his hair on the nape of his neck. There was a long, ugly scar angling up toward the back of his head, partly obscured by his hair. "He gave me this scar when he almost sliced my head in twain. Centuries ago."

"That doesn't matter. None of it matters."

"Highness," said Percival grimly, "let me take him. Let me champion you. You don't have to do this."

His answer was simple but elegant. "Yes. I do."

He reached down and picked up his helmet—similar to Modred's, but with a more rounded top. As he began to put it on, the crowd roared its approval.

MERLIN, ON THE other side of the field, froze in horror as he saw Arthur descend from the royal box, Excalibur already drawn from its sheath. "Oh, no," he breathed. "The great fool. We can put all of that nonsense behind us, and he still insists on playing the warrior king." He started to make his way through the crowd, urgently.

ARTHUR CARRIED A shield on his left arm, as did Modred. It was wood covered with leather, and it was formidable. Under the helmet his face was set in grim lines of determination. In his right hand he held Excalibur with such ease that you'd never expect it would take an exceptionally strong man to wield it at all with two hands, much less one.

They faced each other. The sun was overhead. Arthur circled slowly while speaking in a conversational tone of voice. "What do you say to a son who has tried to kill you?"

"How about, 'Nice try,'" Modred replied.

"Nice try."

"My next try will be nicer!" snarled Modred, and he charged. He took three steps forward and immediately staggered back, blinded by the glare of the sun. Arthur, who hadn't moved, grinned and said, "I could have killed you just then, son. First rule of battle—make certain that your opponent's eyes are in the sun, not yours."

Modred attacked again, barreling forward and swinging his sword. Arthur sidestepped the charge completely, and as Modred went past, swatted him on the rump with the flat of Excalibur's blade. The crowd roared. "Come now, Modred. Let's end this nonsense," said Arthur reasonably. "You don't have a prayer."

"No, Arthur. It's you who have no prayer. But you're too stupid to know it yet."

Modred came forward, sword swinging like a windmill. It bit deep into Arthur's shield. Arthur cut across with Excalibur, fully expecting to slice Modred's shield completely in half. Instead Excalibur glanced off the shield without even so much as making an impression.

Arthur was clearly taken aback by it. Modred enjoyed the small victory. "Found something your precious blade can't cut through? Here's something else." Modred's sword flashed and Arthur parried the blow directly, rather than taking the force of it on his shield. The two blades clanged together. Excalibur should have cut the other sword off at the hilt. It did not.

They separated and stepped back from each other. Arthur was now a bit more wary. His superiority to Modred in fighting skills was not at issue in his mind. But these weapons were on a par with his own, and that bore further investigation.

"You like my toys?" crowed Modred. "They're presents, Arthur. A legacy if you will. A gift . . . from your beloved sister."

His own armor was beginning to feel heavy on him. He grated, "Come on. Are you planning on talking me to death, or are you going to fight?" Fiercely, summoning all the power at his command, Arthur attacked.

*   *   *

ERLIN CLIMBED INTO the reviewing stand, next to Gwen, who was biting her lip. Percival was standing there, watching the proceedings as well. "Gwen," demanded Merlin, "what in hell is going on? How could you let Arthur get himself mixed up in some stupid fight?"

"How was I supposed to stop him?" asked Gwen reasonably. "You think I want him out there? He wouldn't listen to me or Percival," and Percival nodded in confirmation. She continued, "When Arthur gets an idea in his head, nothing can dissuade him."

"Tell me about it," said Merlin mournfully. "Still, I don't like this one bit." His voice trailed off, and Gwen turned to him in alarm.

"Merlin, what's wrong?"

"I smell poison."

"What? What do you mean?"

He grabbed up the cup, smelled it. "Who drank from this?"

It was Buddy who spoke up. "His highness did. Elvis brought it to him."

"It was just regular brew," Elvis protested.

"Well, it's not anymore," said Merlin.

And Gwen looked out at the field where the two men were battering at each other with swords as the full measure of what she was hearing dawned on her. "Oh, my God," she whispered.

RTHUR WAS FULLY on the offensive now. He drove down hard on Modred, Excalibur pounding on Modred's shield again and again. Huge chunks of the shield flew as Modred was not even able to mount a defense to slow Arthur for a moment. Back, back down the field Arthur sent Modred. And then he drew back Excalibur for another blow, brought down the sword, and totally misjudged the distance. Modred dodged, and Arthur swung at empty air. The miss sent him off balance, and he stumbled and almost fell. Only his warrior's reflexes saved him from tripping and hitting the ground, but by the time he recovered Modred was upon him. Modred swung hard, and Arthur took the brunt of the blow on his shield. He felt the impact far more than he should have, the blow sending vibrations of pain along his left arm. Surprised, he wheeled back, and his breath came in ragged gasps. He was sweating so heavily it was pouring into his eyes. His vision was starting to fuzz over and he felt a ringing in his ears. He couldn't understand it. Lord knew the armor was heavy, but certainly he wasn't this out of shape.

Modred attacked and they alternated now, Modred slamming at Arthur's shield, Arthur hacking at Modred's. And this time, step-by-step as they exchanged blow after blow, it was Arthur who was beginning to retreat. The crowd shouted encouragement, roared its approval for Arthur's bravery and catcalled their disapproval for Modred. They were having the time of their lives, because after all, they knew the whole thing was rigged ahead of time and that Arthur would triumph.

Arthur's right arm was starting to feel heavy. Lifting Excalibur became more and more of a burden. His legs were like two lead weights. Each blow from Modred's sword felt stronger than the one before. And then Arthur stumbled, falling back on one knee. Modred came in fast, swinging hard, and his sword sheered Arthur's shield in two. Quickly Arthur dropped the crumbling remains of his shield, gripped Excalibur with both hands, and using it as a crutch, drew himself to his feet. He swung Excalibur back and around with all the force he could muster. Modred parried the blow with his sword and it glanced off and struck Modred's shield, which shattered. Modred tossed it aside, gripping his sword with two hands as well.

They stood there facing each other, a moment frozen in time.

*   *   *

"**M**ERLIN, DO SOMETHING!" Gwen cried out. "Merlin . . . Percival . . . !"

"I can't interfere," Merlin said firmly. "Nor any of you. Arthur would never forgive us."

"It won't matter if he's dead!"

"Damn you woman, don't rob him!" Merlin warned her. "If he lives, it's his life, if he dies, it's his death. His pride may be foolish, but it's his."

"It's macho bullshit!" Gwen shot back. "When you needed help, I saved you!"

"Yes. But he's a better man than I am," Merlin told her. "But remember, I never said that."

MODRED FEINTED TO the left, then brought his sword swinging in low to the right. Arthur tried to block the blow and failed. Modred's sword bit deep into Arthur's ribs. Arthur moaned and went down to one knee, and Modred stepped back, his blade tinted red. Gasping, Arthur clutched at the wound, his face deathly white beneath his helmet.

Instead of pressing the attack, Modred stood there, admiring the damage. "How does it feel, Arthur?" he crowed. "How does it feel to take the pain instead of inflicting it for once? Want to know why you're feeling so tired? Because I poisoned you, dear brother. That's why."

Gasping for breath, Arthur looked up. His voice was a harsh whisper as he said, "Morgan?"

"My, we are the perceptive one. Modred had the spirit, but not the will. I've provided him both. Gaze on the face of the one who hates you beyond death itself." Modred lifted his visor, and it was Modred's face underneath, but the eyes, the expression, was that of Morgan Le Fey. "I've always loved you, Arthur. A sister loves her brother. And you always kill the one you love. You're going to die,

Arthur. The only question is whether it's going to be from the blade or from the blood."

Modred lowered his visor, gripped his sword firmly and swung at Arthur's head.

Arthur blocked it. Hilt to hilt, Arthur retorted in Modred's face, "You forgot to mention boredom. I might die of that, with you as an opponent." And he shoved Modred back.

Modred was visibly surprised. "I didn't think you had enough strength left in you for a last show of bravado."

"You'll find I'm full of surprises," said Arthur, a grim smile on his lips. His mouth curled back in a sneer. "You're pathetic. You couldn't even beat me fairly, you had to try and poison me. Well, it didn't work."

"I—I saw you drink the poison," stammered Modred.

"Perhaps you did," Arthur said. "And perhaps I switched the mugs." And without giving Modred a chance to think, Arthur attacked.

He did not allow himself to feel the pain. He refused to acknowledge that his arms were dead weight, that Excalibur had become unwieldy. He refused to acknowledge that he was dying. He drove Modred back, back across the vast lawn, toward an upward slope where there were rocks embedded in the side. The great sword Excalibur came faster instead of slower. The speed of Arthur's blows increased. The crowd went wild as Modred retreated farther and farther before Arthur's savage onslaught. Blood pumped furiously from Arthur's wound. The left side of Arthur's surcoat was stained red. The crowd saw it and applauded the impressive special effect.

Arthur grew stronger.

"It's impossible!" screamed Modred.

"This is all impossible!" said Arthur. "We all are! And you'll never defeat me, Morgan. Even if you kill me, you'll never defeat me."

They spun in a semicircle, and Modred squinted.

"Now what did I tell you about the sun?" said Arthur,

and brought Excalibur down with every bit of strength he had left.

He lost his grip on Excalibur. The mighty sword flew from his hands and landed on the rocky incline. Arthur stumbled, hit the ground, gasping, clutching at his wound. Under his helmet his features were twisted in pain. The poison running through his system, weighted down by his armor, his wound an agonizing pain in his side, Arthur could not rise. Instead he half staggered, half crawled toward Excalibur.

Modred stood there for a moment, unable to believe his good fortune. "You *did* drink the poison. You are dying!" He laughed Morgan's laugh and stalked the fallen king. "This is turning into a good day after all. So which kills you first, Arthur? The blade or the blood? Your choice?"

And Arthur suddenly hurled himself backward, slamming into Modred. He yanked off Modred's helmet, tossed it aside, and slammed a fist into Modred's sneering face. Then, with all his strength, he shoved Modred back. Turning, with a last, desperate effort, he lunged toward Excalibur. As he did so, he yanked off his own helmet.

Modred was coming right after him, whirling his blade so fast that it could barely be seen. It sounded like a swarm of hornets cutting through the air. Arthur barely had the strength to raise Excalibur, turned, saw Modred advancing, and as an act of desperate calculation, threw his helmet.

It bounced, rolled, and skidded right under Modred's feet. Modred tripped over it, stumbled forward . . .

. . . and fell onto Excalibur's upraised blade.

And the crowd knew. There was a moment of stunned silence as people tried to tell themselves that it was some sort of amazing special effect. That what they were seeing was all part of the show. Some actually even applauded, thinking they were witnessing a truly impressive stunt and then, with slow horror it began to sink in on them.

Then there was confused babbling, and screams, and shouts that someone should do something, do anything.

Excalibur glowed ever so briefly, as if a long hunger had been sated, and Modred and Arthur were practically nose-to-nose as Modred's body slid down the length of the mighty sword. Modred began to tremble violently, blood pouring from his mouth, and the face was Modred's but the cold, dark fury was Morgan's in his eyes as Modred whispered, "*I . . . still . . . hate . . .*"

As Modred died, the black and foul thing that passed for his mother's soul leapt from his body. It arced across the sky, a black cloud of malevolence, trying to get away, and suddenly two well-placed bolts of mystic energy nailed it. It trembled for a moment, tried to hold itself together, and then blew apart in a spectacular twinkling of light.

In the reviewing box, Merlin puffed across the top of his finger like a gunslinger blowing away the smoke from a just-fired revolver. Gwen and Percival were already out and halfway across the field. Gwen came to Arthur's side and dropped down next to him. She ripped off a piece from his surcoat and held it against the wound, and she looked up at the people standing around. "For God's sake, call an ambulance! An ambulance!"

"I already told a cop to do it the second I saw Arthur wounded!" Percival told her.

Gwen gasped at the whiteness of Arthur's skin. "Oh, God, Arthur."

He lifted a mailed hand to her cheek and stroked it, smiling sickly. "Gwen. Don't cry, my lovely Gwen. We gave them a real run for their money this time."

"Them? Who's them?"

"The fates. They have it out for me. They hate happy endings, you know." He winced. "Now don't go crying for me, Gwen. It's unseemly."

Tears streamed down her face. "I don't want to lose you, Arthur," she sobbed. "I don't think I could go through waiting for you again for another ten centuries."

"You're not going to lose me," said Arthur. "I'll always be with you."

"I don't want poetic bullshit! I want you!"

He laughed. "That's my Gwen. Never could pull anything on her."

Merlin knelt down next to them. Gwen turned and said, "Merlin! Do something!"

"I am," he said tersely, and he shoved a mushroom down Arthur's mouth.

"What the hell is that?" she demanded.

"Morgan was my pupil once; I taught her everything she knows of poisons. I ensorcelled this mushroom to handle the poison. At least, I think it will."

"You think it will?"

"She might have learned more about poisons in the meantime," was his testy response.

"What about the wound?"

But Merlin shook his head. "A curse on him, I can handle. Poison, maybe. Wounds are out of my reach. Give me Excalibur; I'll cut the armor off. Save them time in the ambulance," for in the distance they could hear the sirens fast approaching. Everyone was talking at once, shouting over one another, and yet to Arthur it seemed as if everything was slowing down to a sort of curious crawl.

"Merlin," said Arthur, and his voice sounded ghastly. "Promise you'll look after her."

"It's not fair!" shouted Gwen.

"Life isn't fair. Merlin taught me that."

Merlin was slicing the armor apart carefully. "I know. Just once I'd like to be wrong. Hold on . . . the armor's coming clear . . . he's bleeding! Damnit, someone stop the bleeding!"

Gwen was tearing apart her long gown, shoving in strips of cloth which were becoming soaked with seconds.

The ambulance was hurtling straight across the green, the crowd melting from its path.

Arthur didn't see it. The world was fading to black around him. "I love you, Gwen . . . you've got to remember that."

"Stop bleeding, Arthur!" Gwen's voice floated from very far away. "Oh, God, stop bleeding! Arthur, say something! Speak to me!" And as everything became an impenetrable haze, as the last thought of *So this is what I've been hiding from all these centuries . . . it's not so terrible . . .* fluttered across his mind, he heard Gwen shouting, *"Arthur, don't go! I love you! Arthur! Arthur . . . don't . . ."*

YE OLDE SOUND BITE

"Death came today outside the emergency ward of Columbia Presbyterian Hospital for Arthur Pendragon, Son of Uther, King of the Britons, and mayor-elect of New York City . . ."

CHAPTRE
THE TWENTY-FIFTH

✝

GWEN QUEEN SAT out on the stretch of private
beach outside the rented cottage. Getting a beach-
side cottage at this time of year in Avalon had been a
snap. Avalon, a small resort community near Atlantic
City, didn't get all that many people looking for that sort
of accommodation in the dead of winter.

Gwen pulled her heavy sweater around her and looked
out at the crashing waves. She exhaled her breath and
watched the little puff of white hover in the air in front
of her.

There was a crunch of a footfall on the sand behind her.
She turned, looked up, and smiled. "Hello, love," she said.
"Enjoy your nap?"

Arthur sat down next to her and draped an arm around
her shoulder. "Feeling quite refreshed, thank you."

They sat next to each other, basking in the warmth of
each other's presence. Finally Arthur said, "I'm glad I
came back."

"What, from your nap?"

"No, from the dead. I'd have hated to miss this sunset."

"Arthur, I wish you'd stop putting it that way." She sighed. "I keep telling you, you were only dead for under a minute."

"Is that all?" He laughed.

"Look, they bring people back from the dead all the time. Your heart stopped and they got it started again. Like they said on the news, death came for you . . . and you laughed at it and beat it back."

"Brought back from the dead. Heart restarted. Simple as that." He shook his head. "I'll never understand how so many people consider magic too unbelievable, but they accept as commonplace things that I would have once considered inconceivable."

They stared out at the ocean for a while longer. Then Gwen rested her head on his shoulder. "I like being married to you," she said.

"I'm sure we looked delightful. You in your wedding gown, I in my hospital gown with those ghastly strings down the back. Can I outlaw that as mayor?"

"I'll have it looked into. And seriously, I let you get away once. I'll be damned if I let you get away again."

She kissed him lightly. He smiled. "Let's run away," he said conspiratorially. "Right after I'm sworn in, I'll make Percival deputy mayor, and then we'll run off."

"You make it sound so tempting."

"It's meant to be."

"You can't. You know we can't. You have a destiny to fulfill."

"Oh, bugger destiny. You're starting to sound like Merlin."

"Destiny almost buggered you. Maybe you and destiny should declare a truce for a while."

"There's wisdom in what you say." He lay back on the sand. "I did so many things wrong the first time around, Gwen," said Arthur after a time. "I had so many expectations to which no one could live up. I've been given a

second chance—hell, a third chance. I desperately don't
want to make a muddle of it."

"You won't," she said confidently. "You're Arthur.
You're my husband, and you're a good man, and you'll
always do what's right. Even if it's wrong."

"Thank you." He shivered slightly. "Getting chilly.
Want to go in?"

"We could. There's an old movie on TV I always
wanted to see. A Bing Crosby film."

"I don't know the fellow, but I'm game."

"Good. It's *A Connecticut Yankee in King Arthur's Court*."
He stared at her. "Let's stay out here a while longer."

"But you said you were getting chilly."

"Then," he pulled her close to him, "we'll just have to
find some way to keep warm."

I N THE HEART of Belvedere Castle, away from pry-
ing eyes, Merlin watched Arthur and Gwen together
on the sand in New Jersey and smiled in spite of himself.
Then he turned to a small, forlorn rat scuttling about on
the floor, a rat that he had rescued at the last moment as
Morgan's house crumbled. "I suppose I was wrong about
her, wasn't I, Lance. It is nice to be wrong every once in
a while. But not too often."

Lance squeaked sadly.

Merlin ignored him and, using the magic of a remote
control, turned the channels. The image of Arthur and
Gwen on the beach vanished, to be replaced by another.
Merlin settled back with a bag of microwave popcorn to
watch Bing Crosby.